The son of a country doctor, **Harry Sinclair Lewis** (1885–1951) was born in Sauk Centre, Minnesota. His childhood and early youth were spent in the Midwest, and later he attended Yale University, where he was editor of the literary magazine. After graduating in 1907, he worked as a reporter and in editorial positions at various newspapers, magazines, and publishing houses from the East Coast to California. He was able to give this work up after a few of his stories had appeared in magazines and his first novel, *Our Mr. Wrenn* (1914), had been published. *Main Street* (1920) was his first really successful novel, and his reputation was secured by the publication of *Babbitt* (1922). Lewis was awarded a Pulitzer Prize for *Arrowsmith* (1925) but refused to accept the honor, saying the prize was meant to go to a novel that celebrated the wholesomeness of American life, something his books did not do. He did accept, however, when in 1930 he became the first American writer to receive the Nobel Prize for Literature. During the last part of his life, he spent a great deal of time in Europe and continued to write both novels and plays. In 1950, after completing his last novel, *World So Wide* (1951), he intended to take an extended tour but became ill and was forced to settle in Rome, where he spent some months working on his poems before dying.

Michael Meyer, PhD, a professor of English at the University of Connecticut, previously taught at the University of North Carolina at Charlotte and the College of William and Mary. His scholarly articles have appeared in such periodicals as *American Literature*, *Studies in the American Renaissance*, and *Virginia Quarterly Review*. An internationally recognized authority on Henry David Thoreau, he is a former president of the Thoreau Society and the coauthor of *The New Thoreau Handbook*, a standard reference. His first book, *Several More Lives to Live: Thoreau's Political Reputation in America*, was awarded the Ralph Henry Gabriel Prize by the American Studies Association. In addition to *The Bedford Introduction to Literature*, his edited volumes include *Frederick Douglass: The Narrative and Selected Writings*.

Gary Scharnhorst is Distinguished Professor Emeritus of English at the University of New Mexico, editor of *American Literary Realism*, and editor in alternating years of *American Literary Scholarship*.

SINCLAIR LEWIS

IT CAN'T HAPPEN HERE

With an Introduction by Michael Meyer and a New Afterword by Gary Scharnhorst

SIGNET CLASSICS

SIGNET CLASSICS
Published by the Penguin Group
Penguin Group (USA) LLC, 375 Hudson Street,
New York, New York 10014

USA | Canada | UK | Ireland | Australia | New Zealand | India | South Africa | China
penguin.com
A Penguin Random House Company

Published by Signet Classics, an imprint of New American Library,
a division of Penguin Group (USA) LLC

First Signet Classics Printing, October 1970
First Signet Classics Printing (Scharnhorst Afterword), January 2014

ISBN 978-0-451-46564-1

Printed in the United States of America
19 18 17 16 15

Introduction

Sinclair Lewis enjoyed a brilliant career in the 1920s portraying and satirizing what he regarded as the mediocrity, materialism, corruption, and hypocrisy of middle-class life in the United States. His five major novels of the twenties—*Main Street* (1920), *Babbitt* (1922), *Arrowsmith* (1925), *Elmer Gantry* (1927), and *Dodsworth* (1929)—were all bestsellers that served to hold a mirror up to the parochialism and provincialism of that decade. A good many Americans winced at their own reflections in those novels, but they eagerly bought Lewis's iconoclastic books, because, however much they flinched at his representations of their middle-class lives, they were finally snugly, if not smugly, comfortable in the economic security that produced their prosperous confidence.

After the stock market crash of 1929, however, there wasn't much left of the middle class of the early 1930s. Many who were previously solid, respectable breadwinners found themselves on bread lines, soup lines, and relief rolls. "Normalcy," a twenties password synonymous with security, gave way to the "jitters" as profitless corporations laid off millions of workers who drifted across the country like Oklahoma farm dust. The popular song and exuberant theme of the twenties "Ain't We Got Fun" changed its tune to "Brother Can You Spare a Dime" during the Great Depression. Although Franklin Delano Roosevelt's first inaugural address in 1933 promised a New Deal, he also let his countrymen know what the score was in grim tones:

> Values have shrunken to fantastic levels; taxes have risen; our ability to pay has fallen; government of all

> kinds is faced by serious curtailment of income; the means of exchange are frozen in the currents of trade; the withered leaves of industrial enterprise lie on every side; farmers find no markets for their produce; the savings of many years in thousands of families are gone.

Not surprisingly, the middle class was no longer interested in being discounted by bankers or by satirists. Lewis had to find new material.

Given the stormy economic and social climate of the early 1930s, Lewis had plenty of other topics to consider that were more relevant than middle-class predispositions to be foolish and venal. He found a ready-made plot in the nervous undercurrent that accompanied the volatile politics of the period. With the rise of Adolf Hitler and Benito Mussolini in Europe and the alarming popularity of a variety of demagogues from both the left and right in the United States, there was widespread concern that the country could be taken over by a fascist dictatorship. Lewis placed these fears at the center of *It Can't Happen Here.*

Published in October of 1935, the novel gave shape to the free-floating anxieties that had consumed worried citizens for several years as the country stumbled through economic turmoil desperately seeking solutions. Lewis was intimately familiar with these concerns because Dorothy Thompson, his second wife, had interviewed Hitler as a foreign correspondent in Berlin and had written a series of articles between 1931 and 1935 warning Americans about the Nazi propaganda machine that masked the vicious persecution of Jews and the growing number of concentration camps designed to annihilate them. In addition to what he heard at his breakfast table, Lewis was very much aware of the many debates swirling around him in newspapers, journals, and books. In September of 1934, for example, *The Modern Monthly* featured a symposium titled "Will Fascism Come to America?" that featured a number of leading intellectuals such as Theodore Dreiser, Norman Thomas, Charles A. Beard, and Waldo Frank debating the question, and in early 1935, the *Nation* ran a series of articles on "forerunners of American Fascism." Although Lewis is often credited with coining the phrase "it can't happen here," Herschel Brickell points out in his review of the novel in *North American Review* (December 1935) that the book actually "takes its title from the typical American remark concerning the possibility of a dictatorship in this country" (a quick search of the Internet demonstrates that the phrase continues to be used by a wide range of political perspectives to evoke the various tyrannies Lewis describes). Echoing Brickell, another contemporary reviewer, Benjamin Stolberg, aptly notes that the novel "has successfully plagiarized our social atmosphere" (*Books*, October 1935). Lewis's take, however, is that it *can* happen here.

The threat of fascism in America captured his readers' attention. *It Can't Happen Here* quickly became a national bestseller (more than 320,000 copies were sold), and it has become by now part of the same thirties' social and political fabric that Lewis wove into the novel. While Lewis's contemporaries were thirsty for the "successfully plagiarized" details about the 1930s that saturate the novel, twenty-first-century readers may sometimes feel as if they're in over their head owing to the book's deep topical nature. The novel is a kind of Sears, Roebuck catalogue of early 1930s American political figures, events, and movements both central and peripheral to the decade's issues. Scores of historical figures populate the book, such as Huey Long, Father Charles Coughlin, William Randolph Hearst, Upton Sinclair, William Allen White, Mike Gold, and for a remarkable example, thirteen actual working journalists whose names appear on page 219. Although lots of these names are perhaps unfamiliar to many readers today, Lewis's plot and characterizations are not wholly dependent upon historical knowledge for readers to understand and appreciate the novel's conflicts. The names, as well as political events and movements, certainly form the major portion of the book's highly detailed political scenery, but there's little, if any, doubt about how Lewis wants us to think about them.

Although Lewis's protagonist, Doremus Jessup, is "a mild, rather indolent and somewhat sentimental Liberal"

(p. 46) who is slow to respond to the rise of an American version of a fascist dictatorship, Lewis responded quickly and intensely to the fascist threats he saw all around him. He wrote and revised the entire novel in fewer than four months while he summered in Vermont in 1935. His preparation for the book took longer than its writing; he had been simmering with materials for several years as he recognized with increasing alarm the dangers that threatened democratic institutions. Unfortunately, his writing displays the haste in which he wrote—and so do the book's reviews. R. P. Blackmur laments that "there is hardly a literary question that it does not fail to raise and there is hardly a rule for the good conduct of novels that it does not break" (*Nation*, October 1935). Despite the many reviewers who complained about the novel's loose melodramatic plot, flat and even corny characters, weak clichéd dialogue, padded political discourse, awkward sentimentality, and heavy-handed satire and irony, many also judged the book to be a timely caveat and applauded its propagandistic value against fascism. Clifton Fadiman pronounced it to be "one of the most important books ever produced in this country" (*New Yorker*, October 1935), a book that all Americans should read to help save the country from impending political failures and potential tyrannies.

In March of 1935, two months before Sinclair Lewis began writing *It Can't Happen Here*, Walter Lippmann lamented in a popular magazine that the United States had "come to a period of discouragement. . . . Pollyanna is silenced and Cassandra is doing all the talking." There was much for Cassandra to talk about: the administration of the New Deal seemed hopelessly bogged down and the fierce strident polemics of popular leaders such as Huey Long and Father Coughlin seemed to speak more directly than the president to the poor, the dispossessed, the frustrated, and the angry. Neither the Louisiana Kingfish nor the populist radio priest freighted their remedies for the country's ills with feasible ideas or coherent programs. Immediate solutions were too important to be burdened with details and troublesome facts; it was enough for Long simply to announce the justice of a $5,000 "homestead allowance" coupled with an annual income of at least $2,000 for every American family. The Kingfish was long on proposals but short on perceiving potential problems: "Who cares," he said, "what consequences may come following the mandates of the Lord, of the Pilgrims, of Jefferson, Webster and Lincoln? He who falls in this fight falls in the radiance of the future."

The liberals who worried about the possible consequences that attended this future brave new world were particularly wary because the Old World had already produced Hitler and Mussolini. Fascism was becoming fashionable, a fact manifested by the Brown Shirts, Black Shirts, Khaki Shirts, White Shirts, and Silver Shirts—complete with matching boots—that came out of closets all over Europe and the United States. In October of 1935, the month *It Can't Happen Here* was published, William Randolph Hearst encapsuled the problem with a statement that delighted shirt makers but terrified liberals. He counseled his fellow citizens: "Whenever you hear a prominent American called a 'Fascist,' you can usually make up your mind that the man is simply a LOYAL CITIZEN WHO STANDS FOR AMERICANISM."

Lewis transforms this advice into a warning in his novel by showing how Americans elect as their president Berzelius Windrip, a folksy New England version of the dictatorial Kingfish who ushers in a fascistic regime of suppression, terror, and totalitarianism—all draped in red, white, and blue bunting. Invoking the highest patriotic principles, Windrip disguises his fascism in the historical trappings of the Republic; his Gestapo, for example, is called the Minute Men. Lewis projects a dire version of the immediate future—the story begins in 1936 and ends in 1939—by creating fictional equivalents of the trepidations liberals experienced in the mid-thirties. Although Lewis looks to the future for the actualization of what liberals feared might happen, he turns to the past for the antidote to a poisoned America. To combat Windrip's deceptive use of a past that is employed to corrupt the present, Lewis draws upon a national heritage of individualistic and democratic values in order to redeem the country from the fascism masquerading in a patriotic costume.

There is a distinct nostalgic quality to Lewis's hero, Doremus Jessup, born in 1876, an independent, liberal Vermont newspaper editor who stands up to Windrip's vicious regime. Lewis proudly presents him as a nineteenth-century individualist rather than a twentieth-century automaton. He sports a beard, which his detractors say makes him "high-brow," "different," and "artistic" instead of one of the boys. His reading confirms their suspicions about his beard; he subscribes to, among other things, the *Congressional Record*, the *New Yorker*, *Time*, the *Nation*, the *New Republic*, and the *New Masses*. Although Jessup is more articulate and more liberal than most of Lewis's protagonists, he is confronted with essentially the same kind of phenomena, even if more extreme, that chronically thwart and deny the individual in Lewis's fiction. At various opportune moments in the novel, Lewis uses Jessup as a spokesman to denounce and satirize the DAR, the KKK, Aimee McPherson, Mary Baker Eddy, Billy Sunday, Father Coughlin, William Jennings Bryan, Huey Long, Tammany graft, Chicago gangsters, Prohibition, lynchings, anti-Semitism, racism, militarism, concentration camps, torture, and political assassinations. Jessup's announced values are not fundamentally different from some of Lewis's other famous characters. Whether the vague dissatisfactions festering in George F. Babbitt, the unrealistic impulses toward reform fluttering in Carol Kennicott, or the linear, though uncertain, determination of a Martin Arrowsmith, Lewis's most interesting characters want, as Carol Kennicott puts it in *Main Street*, "a more conscious life, we're tired of seeing just a few people able to be individualists." Lewis clearly admired and identified with Jessup—so much so that he played the role of Jessup in a dramatic adaptation by the South Shore Players in Cohasset, Massachusetts, one of many of the play's productions sponsored by the Federal Theater Project throughout the country in the wake of the novel's popularity.

Jessup is a nineteenth-century styled individualist who has fallen into history; he's fallen into a world in which his allegiance to predominant American values such as self-reliance and independence mark him as a political subversive. Recalling the achievement of men such as Thaddeus Stevens and Stephen A. Douglas, he compares them to what he describes as "the wishy-washy young people today," and he wonders aloud

> if we're breeding up any paladins like those stout, grouchy old devils?—if we're producing 'em anywhere in New England?—anywhere in America?—anywhere in the world? They had guts. Independence. Did what they wanted to and thought what they liked, and everybody could go to hell. (p. 13)

Jessup subscribes to these values, and though they are implicitly subversive in a politically repressive atmosphere, Lewis describes him as understanding himself too well to consider himself a left-wing radical; instead he is a tentative liberal who basically wants to be left alone to enjoy his small-town life and newspaper work.

One of the few calm and contented moments of the novel consists of a gathering of Jessup's family and friends for a country picnic where "there was nothing modern and neurotic," writes Lewis, "nothing savoring of Freud, Adler, Marx, Bertrand Russell, or any other divinity of the 1930's" (p. 38). From the perspective of the complex, mechanized, modernized, psychologized, and homogenized thirties, Jessup longs for an era now lost. There is no going back to the past, a fact that makes it doubly attractive and no less important to Jessup—or to Lewis. Yet Jessup's sense of "social duty" (p. 104) does not permit him to ignore the present, nor does he abandon the past because finally it will be a means by which he will attempt to reshape the present.

Jessup's sense of social duty is informed by his individualism. He does not believe in collective modes of reform because he views them as absolutist and dogmatic, and he objects to any group insisting that it has the final and perfect solution for society's ills. Neither "Fascists," "Communists," "American Constitutionalists," "Monarchists," nor "preachers" have the answer, because, according to Jessup, "There is no Solution! There will never be a state of society anything like perfect!" (p. 112). He reflects Lewis's own values when he insists that "All the

Utopias—Brook Farm, Robert Owen's sanctuary of chatter, Upton Sinclair's Helicon Hall—and their regulation end in scandal, feuds, poverty, griminess, disillusion" (p. 114). And when they don't immediately end in failure such collective activities are perilous for individualists because they may turn fanatical and violent:

> Blessed be they [thinks Jessup] who are not Patriots and Idealists, and who do not feel they must dash right in and Do Something About It, something so immediately important that all doubters must be liquidated—tortured—slaughtered! Good old murder, that since the slaying of Abel by Cain has always been the new device by which all oligarchies and dictators have, for all future ages to come, removed opposition! (p. 114)

Jessup, like Lewis, shrinks from political activism and believes that a man minding his own business rather than insisting upon saving the masses is a true idealist.

Lewis's attraction to this kind of individualism is evident in a 1937 review he wrote for *Newsweek* of an edition of Henry Thoreau's *Walden*, another Yankee who minded his own business (mostly). Lewis entitled the review "One-Man Revolution," a title particularly aimed at the collectivist reforms of that decade. This is the first sentence of the piece:

> Once upon a time in America there was a scholar who conducted a one-man revolution and won it.

There is hardly anything in all of Lewis's fiction as direct and as happy as that—not in forty years of writing. For Lewis, Thoreau's success has almost a fabulous quality to it ("Once upon a time") and Lewis is grateful for the story while implicitly identifying with him. In the context of the late thirties, when America was menaced by Italy, Germany, and Japan, Lewis suggests making Thoreau the "supreme Duce" as an answer to those imposing forms of oppression. Jessup shares this supremely independent perspective but discovers that as conditions grow worse, as individuals become more frequent targets of Windrip's goons and bullies, he must take a stand.

Although Jessup's family and friends urge him to keep a low profile and not publish an editorial condemning the outrages of Windrip's regime, his mistress, Lorinda Pike, an activist, supports him. Once the editorial appears, Jessup is immediately hauled off to jail, where he reconsiders his earlier negative attitudes toward violence and wonders if his own conscientious respectability—that is, minding his own business—hasn't been one of the primary reasons why fascism has succeeded in America. It is, he thinks, the Jessups "who have let the demagogues wriggle in, without fierce enough protest" (p. 186).

Despite these reflections Jessup is extraordinarily wary of taking any extreme action. He had been brought up to revere Abolitionists such as Wendell Phillips and Harriet Beecher Stowe, but "his father had considered John Brown insane and a menace" (p. 117). Jessup's liberal roots firmly place him in a relatively passive and pacifistic political tradition. Even after his son-in-law is taken out to be shot and Jessup hears of grotesque atrocities including mass executions and concentration camp horrors, he only reluctantly agrees to light out for the territory ahead—Canada is once again the goal of a new "underground railroad" where Americans seek refuge from slavery. But his effort to escape with his family is unsuccessful and he returns enraged, muttering, "Now I know why men like John Brown became crazy killers" (p. 234). On the heels of his failure to escape, he returns home to find his son justifying book burnings and the violent suppression of dissenters. Jessup is outraged by his son's bland rationale that "you can't make an omelet without breaking eggs" (p. 238), and he promptly throws him out. After much chronic indecisiveness and resolutions undercut by irresolution—precisely the strategies Lewis uses in the plots and characterizations of *Main Street*, *Babbitt*, and *Arrowsmith*—Jessup is moved to action and works to publish the *Vermont Vigilance*, a seditious underground paper that exposes the villainy and corruption of the American Corporate State and Patriotic Party. Jessup's widowed daughter enthusiastically tucks these pamphlets inside copies of the *Reader's Digest* at the drugstore, while his younger daughter serves as a secret agent in the enemy camp and fends off lewd advances.

On July 4, 1938, with a terrible thunderstorm as the background, the Minute Men descend upon Jessup's house, wreck it, and take him away to a concentration camp, where he is nearly beaten to death. As a result of enduring the horrible conditions of the camp, Jessup feels a sense of camaraderie with the other prisoners and what Lewis describes as a "murderous hatred of their oppressors so that they, men of peace all of them, would gladly have hanged every Corpo, mild or vicious. Doremus understood John Brown much better" (p. 312). But that camaraderie does not mean that he is prepared to become a communist and abandon his individualism. "What I want," says Jessup, "is mass action by just one member, alone on a hilltop. I'm a great optimist. . . . I still hope America may some day rise to the standards of Kit Carson" (p. 311). Eventually, Jessup escapes from the camp and he works for the underground again, this time as a secret agent in Minnesota coordinating raids against the Minute Men posts. Although he is engaged in an organized response to fascism, he remains ideologically aloof, conducting what is essentially a one-man revolution. Jessup, writes Lewis, "saw now that he must remain alone, a 'Liberal,' scorned by all the noisier prophets for refusing to be a willing cat for the busy monkeys of either" fascism or communism (p. 359). He participates in the popular rebellion against the Corpo regime but the values he fights for are associated with the individual rather than with collective action: "I am convinced," he insists, "that everything that is worth while in the world has been accomplished by the free, inquiring, critical spirit, and that the preservation of this spirit is more important than any social system whatsoever" (p. 359).

To many readers in the 1930s, this essentially nineteenth-century evocation of self-reliant virtues was attractive, but it provided only the vaguest kind of political solutions to pressing political issues. Lewis's response to a potential fascist dictatorship offered no specific remedies; this was, however, not a fault but a strategy, because he was writing a satirical novel rather than a five-year plan framed by an inaugural address. Instead, he successfully aroused a generation of Americans to the dangers that swirled around them. Many of his readers recognized that though his answers to contemporary political issues might have been provisional, the questions he raised about liberty and justice remain perennial. He believed that dissent—even a cranky, erratic, eccentric, old-fashioned version of it—was not disloyalty but at the heart of an American democratic identity. Engulfed in the complexities and vulnerabilities of our post–September 11 world, Americans of nearly all political persuasions are likely to find that *It Can't Happen Here*, though firmly anchored in the politics of the 1930s, surfaces as a revealing and disturbing read.

—MICHAEL MEYER

IT CAN'T HAPPEN HERE

1

THE HANDSOME DINING ROOM of the Hotel Wessex, with its gilded plaster shields and the mural depicting the Green Mountains, had been reserved for the Ladies' Night Dinner of the Fort Beulah Rotary Club.

Here in Vermont the affair was not so picturesque as it might have been on the Western prairies. Oh, it had its points: there was a skit in which Medary Cole (grist mill & feed store) and Louis Rotenstern (custom tailoring—pressing & cleaning) announced that they were those historic Vermonters, Brigham Young and Joseph Smith, and with their jokes about imaginary plural wives they got in ever so many funny digs at the ladies present. But the occasion was essentially serious. All of America was serious now, after the seven years of depression since 1929. It was just long enough after the Great War of 1914–18 for the young people who had been born in 1917 to be ready to go to college . . . or to another war, almost any old war that might be handy.

The features of this night among the Rotarians were nothing funny, at least not obviously funny, for they were the patriotic addresses of Brigadier General Herbert Y. Edgeways, U.S.A. (ret.), who dealt angrily with the topic "Peace through Defense—Millions for Arms but Not One Cent for Tribute," and of Mrs. Adelaide Tarr Gimmitch—she who was no more renowned for her gallant anti-suffrage campaigning way back in 1919 than she was for having, during the Great War, kept the American soldiers entirely out of French cafés by the clever trick of sending them ten thousand sets of dominoes.

Nor could any social-minded patriot sneeze at her recent somewhat unappreciated effort to maintain the purity of the American Home by barring from the motion-picture industry all persons, actors or directors or cameramen, who had: (a) ever been divorced; (b) been born in any foreign country—except Great Britain, since Mrs. Gimmitch thought very highly of Queen Mary, or (c) declined to take an oath to revere the Flag, the Constitution, the Bible, and all other peculiarly American institutions.

The Annual Ladies' Dinner was a most respectable gathering—the flower of Fort Beulah. Most of the ladies and more than half of the gentlemen wore evening clothes, and it was rumored that before the feast the inner circle had had cocktails, privily served in Room 289 of the hotel. The tables, arranged on three sides of a hollow square, were bright with candles, cut-glass dishes of candy and slightly tough almonds, figurines of Mickey Mouse, brass Rotary wheels, and small silk American flags stuck in gilded hard-boiled eggs. On the wall was a banner lettered "Service Before Self," and the menu—the celery, cream of tomato soup, broiled haddock, chicken croquettes, peas, and tutti-frutti ice-cream—was up to the highest standards of the Hotel Wessex.

They were all listening, agape. General Edgeways was completing his manly yet mystical rhapsody on nationalism:

". . . for these U-nited States, a-lone among the great powers, have no desire for foreign conquest. Our highest ambition is to be darned well let alone! Our only genuine relationship to Europe is in our arduous task of having to try and educate the crass and ignorant masses that Europe has wished onto us up to something like a semblance of American culture and good manners. But, as I explained to you, we must be prepared to defend our shores against all the alien gangs of international racketeers that call themselves 'governments,' and that with such feverish envy are always eyeing our inexhaustible mines, our towering forests, our titanic and luxurious cities, our fair and far-flung fields.

"For the first time in all history, a great nation must go on arming itself more and more, not for conquest—not for jealousy—not for war—but for *peace*! Pray God it may never be necessary, but if foreign nations don't sharply heed our warning, there will, as when the proverbial dragon's teeth were sowed, spring up an armed and fearless warrior upon every square foot of these United States, so arduously cultivated and defended by our pioneer fathers, whose sword-girded images we must be . . . or we shall perish!"

The applause was cyclonic. "Professor" Emil Staubmeyer, the superintendent of schools, popped up to scream, "Three cheers for the General—hip, hip, hooray!"

All the audience made their faces to shine upon the General and Mr. Staubmeyer—all save a couple of crank pacifist women, and one Doremus Jessup, editor of the Fort Beulah *Daily Informer,* locally considered "a pretty smart fella but kind of a cynic," who whispered to his friend the Reverend Mr. Falck, "Our pioneer fathers did rather of a skimpy job in arduously cultivating some of the square feet in Arizona!"

The culminating glory of the dinner was the address of Mrs. Adelaide Tarr Gimmitch, known throughout the country as "the Unkies' Girl," because during the Great War she had advocated calling our boys in the A.E.F. "the Unkies." She hadn't merely given them dominoes; indeed her first notion had been far more imaginative. She wanted to send to every soldier at the Front a canary in a cage. Think what it would have meant to them in the way of companionship and inducing memories of home and mother! A dear little canary! And who knows—maybe you could train 'em to hunt cooties!

Seething with the notion, she got herself clear into the office of the Quartermaster General, but that stuffy machine-minded official refused her (or, really, refused the poor lads, so lonely there in the mud), muttering in a cowardly way some foolishness about lack of transport for canaries. It is said that her eyes flashed real fire, and that she faced the Jack-in-office like Joan of Arc with eyeglasses while she "gave him a piece of her mind that *he* never forgot!"

In those good days women really had a chance. They were encouraged to send their menfolks, or anybody else's menfolks, off to war. Mrs. Gimmitch addressed every soldier she met—and she saw to it that she met any of them who ventured within two blocks of her—as "My own dear boy." It is fabled that she thus saluted a colonel of marines who had come up from the ranks and who answered, "We own dear boys are certainly getting a lot of mothers these days. Personally, I'd rather have a few more mistresses." And the fable continues that she did not stop her remarks on the occasion, except to cough, for one hour and seventeen minutes, by the Colonel's wrist watch.

But her social services were not all confined to prehistoric eras. It was as recently as 1935 that she had taken up purifying the films, and before that she had first advocated and then fought Prohibition. She had also (since the vote had been forced on her) been a Republican Committeewoman in 1932, and sent to President Hoover daily a lengthy telegram of advice.

And, though herself unfortunately childless, she was esteemed as a lecturer and writer about Child Culture, and she was the author of a volume of nursery lyrics, including the immortal couplet:

All of the Roundies are resting in rows,
With roundy-roundies around their toes.

But always, 1917 or 1936, she was a raging member of the Daughters of the American Revolution.

The D.A.R. (reflected the cynic, Doremus Jessup, that evening) is a somewhat confusing organization—as confusing as Theosophy, Relativity, or the Hindu Vanishing Boy Trick, all three of which it resembles. It is composed of females who spend one half their waking hours boasting of being descended from the seditious American colonists of 1776, and the other and more ardent half in attacking all contemporaries who believe in precisely the principles for which those ancestors struggled.

The D.A.R. (reflected Doremus) has become as sacrosanct, as beyond criticism, as even the Catholic Church or the Salvation Army. And there is this to be said: it has provided hearty and innocent laughter for the judicious, since it has contrived to be just as ridiculous as the unhappily defunct Kuklux Klan, without any need of wearing, like the K.K.K., high dunces' caps and public nightshirts.

So, whether Mrs. Adelaide Tarr Gimmitch was called in to inspire military morale, or to persuade Lithuanian choral societies to begin their program with "Columbia, the Gem of the Ocean," always she was a D.A.R., and you could tell it as you listened to her with the Fort Beulah Rotarians on this happy May evening.

She was short, plump, and pert of nose. Her luxuriant gray hair (she was sixty now, just the age of the sarcastic editor, Doremus Jessup) could be seen below her youthful, floppy Leghorn hat; she wore a silk print dress with an enormous string of crystal beads, and pinned above her ripe bosom was an orchid among lilies of the valley. She was full of friendliness toward all the men present: she wriggled at them, she cuddled at them, as in a voice full of flute sounds and chocolate sauce she poured out her oration on "How You Boys Can Help Us Girls."

Women, she pointed out, had done nothing with the vote. If the United States had only listened to her back in 1919 she could have saved them all this trouble. No. Certainly not. No votes. In fact, Woman must resume her place in the Home and: "As that great author and scientist, Mr. Arthur Brisbane, has pointed out, what every woman ought to do is to have six children."

At this second there was a shocking, an appalling interruption.

One Lorinda Pike, widow of a notorious Unitarian preacher, was the manager of a country super-boarding-house that called itself "The Beulah Valley Tavern." She was a deceptively Madonna-like, youngish woman, with calm eyes, smooth chestnut hair parted in the middle, and a soft voice often colored with laughter. But on a public platform her voice became brassy, her eyes filled with embarrassing fury. She was the village scold, the village crank. She was constantly poking into things that were none of her business, and at town meetings she criticized every substantial interest in the whole country: the electric company's rates, the salaries of the schoolteachers, the Ministerial Association's high-minded censorship of books for the public library. Now, at this moment when everything should have been all Service and Sunshine, Mrs. Lorinda Pike cracked the spell by jeering:

"Three cheers for Brisbane! But what if a poor gal can't hook a man? Have her six kids out of wedlock?"

Then the good old war horse, Gimmitch, veteran of a hundred campaigns against subversive Reds, trained to ridicule out of existence the cant of Socialist hecklers and turn the laugh against them, swung into gallant action:

"My dear good woman, if a gal, as you call it, has any real charm and womanliness, she won't have to 'hook' a man––she'll find 'em lined up ten deep on her doorstep!" (Laughter and applause.)

The lady hoodlum had merely stirred Mrs. Gimmitch into noble passion. She did not cuddle at them now. She tore into it:

"I tell you, my friends, the trouble with this whole country is that so many are *selfish*! Here's a hundred and twenty million people, with 95 per cent of 'em only thinking of *self,* instead of turning to and helping the responsible business men to bring back prosperity! All these corrupt and self-seeking labor unions! Money grubbers! Thinking only of how much wages they can extort out of their unfortunate employer, with all the responsibilities he has to bear!

"What this country needs is Discipline! Peace is a great dream, but maybe sometimes it's only a pipe dream! I'm not so sure—now this will shock you, but I want you to listen to one woman who will tell you the unadulterated hard truth instead of a lot of sentimental taffy, and I'm not sure but that we need to be in a real war again, in order to learn Discipline! We don't want all this highbrow intellectuality, all this book-learning. That's good enough in its way, but isn't it, after all, just a nice toy for grownups? No, what we all of us must have, if this great land is going to go on maintaining its high position among the Congress of Nations, is Discipline—Will Power—Character!"

She turned prettily then toward General Edgeways and laughed:

"You've been telling us about how to secure peace, but come on, now, General—just among us Rotarians and Rotary Anns—'fess up! With your great experience, don't you honest, cross-your-heart, think that perhaps—just maybe—when a country has gone money-mad, like all our labor unions and workmen, with their propaganda to hoist income taxes, so that the thrifty and industrious have to pay for the shiftless ne'er-do-wells, then maybe, to save their lazy souls and get some iron into them, a war might be a good thing? Come on, now, tell your real middle name, Mong General!"

Dramatically she sat down, and the sound of clapping filled the room like a cloud of downy feathers. The crowd bellowed, "Come on, General! Stand up!" and "She's called your bluff—what you got?" or just a tolerant, "Attaboy, Gen!"

The General was short and globular, and his red face was smooth as a baby's bottom and adorned with white-gold-framed spectacles. But he had the military snort and a virile chuckle.

"Well, sir!" he guffawed, on his feet, shaking a chummy forefinger at Mrs. Gimmitch, "since you folks are bound and determined to drag the secrets out of a poor soldier, I better confess that while I do abhor war, yet there are worse things. Ah, my friends, far worse! A state of so-called peace, in which labor organizations are riddled, as by plague germs, with insane notions out of anarchistic Red Russia! A state in which college professors, newspapermen, and notorious authors are secretly promulgating these same seditious attacks on the grand old Constitution! A state in which, as a result of being fed with these mental drugs, the People are flabby, cowardly, grasping, and lacking in the fierce pride of the warrior! No, such a state is far worse than war at its most monstrous!

"I guess maybe some of the things I said in my former speech were kind of a little bit obvious and what we used to call 'old hat' when my brigade was quartered in England. About the United States only wanting peace, and freedom from all foreign entanglements. No! What I'd really like us to do would be to come out and tell the whole world: 'Now you boys never mind about the moral side of this. We have power, and power is its own excuse!'

"I don't altogether admire everything Germany and Italy have done, but you've got to hand it to 'em, they've been honest enough and realistic enough to say to the other nations, 'Just tend to your own business, will you? We've got strength and will, and for whomever has those divine qualities it's not only a right, it's a *duty*, to use 'em!' Nobody in God's world ever loved a weakling—including that weakling himself!

"And I've got good news for you! This gospel of clean and aggressive strength is spreading everywhere in this country among the finest type of youth. Why today, in 1936, there's less than 7 per cent of collegiate institutions that do not have military-training units under discipline as rigorous as the Nazis, and where once it was forced upon them by the authorities, now it is the strong young men and women who themselves demand the *right* to be trained in warlike virtues and skill—for, mark you, the girls, with their instruction in nursing and the manufacture of gas masks and the like, are becoming every whit as zealous as their brothers. And all the really *thinking* type of professors are right with 'em!

"Why, here, as recently as three years ago, a sickeningly big percentage of students were blatant pacifists, wanting to knife their own native land in the dark. But now, when the shameless fools and the advocates of Communism try to hold pacifist meetings—why, my friends, in the past five months, since January first, no less than seventy-six such exhibitionistic orgies have been raided by their fellow students, and no less than fifty-nine disloyal Red students have received their just deserts by being beaten up so severely that never again will they raise in this free country the bloodstained banner of anarchism! That, my friends, is NEWS!"

As the General sat down, amid ecstasies of applause, the village trouble maker, Mrs. Lorinda Pike, leaped up and again interrupted the love feast:

"Look here, Mr. Edgeways, if you think you can get away with this sadistic nonsense without——"

She got no farther. Francis Tasbrough, the quarry owner, the most substantial industrialist in Fort Beulah, stood grandly up, quieted Lorinda with an outstretched arm, and rumbled in his Jerusalem-the-Golden basso, "A moment please, my dear lady! All of us here locally have got used to your political principles. But as chairman, it is my unfortunate duty to remind you that General Edgeways and Mrs. Gimmitch have been invited by the club to address us, whereas you, if you will excuse my saying so, are not even related to any Rotarian but merely here as the guest of the Reverend Falck, than whom there is no one whom we more honor. So, if you will be so good—— Ah, I thank you, madame!"

Lorinda Pike had slumped into her chair with her fuse still burning. Mr. Francis Tasbrough (it rhymed with "low") did not slump; he sat like the Archbishop of Canterbury on the archiepiscopal throne.

And Doremus Jessup popped up to soothe them all, being an intimate of Lorinda, and having, since milkiest boyhood, chummed with and detested Francis Tasbrough.

This Doremus Jessup, publisher of the *Daily Informer,* for all that he was a competent business man and a writer of editorials not without wit and good New England earthiness, was yet considered the prime eccentric of Fort Beulah. He was on the school board, the library board, and he introduced people like Oswald Garrison Villard, Norman Thomas, and Admiral Byrd when they came to town lecturing.

Jessup was a littlish man, skinny, smiling, well tanned, with a small gray mustache, a small and well-trimmed gray beard—in a community where to sport a beard was to confess one's self a farmer, a Civil War veteran, or a Seventh Day Adventist. Doremus's detractors said that he maintained the beard just to be "highbrow" and "different," to try to appear "artistic." Possibly they were right. Anyway, he skipped up now and murmured:

"Well, all the birdies in their nest agree. My friend, Mrs. Pike, ought to know that freedom of speech becomes mere license when it goes so far as to criticize the Army, differ with the D.A.R., and advocate the rights of the Mob. So, Lorinda, I think you ought to apologize to the General, to whom we should be grateful for explaining to us what the ruling classes of the country really want. Come on now, my friend—jump up and make your excuses."

He was looking down on Lorinda with sternness, yet Medary Cole, president of Rotary, wondered if Doremus wasn't "kidding" them. He had been known to. Yes—no—he must be wrong, for Mrs. Lorinda Pike was (without rising) caroling, "Oh yes! I do apologize, General! Thank you for your revelatory speech!"

The General raised his plump hand (with a Masonic ring as well as a West Point ring on the sausage-shaped fingers); he bowed like Galahad or a head-waiter; he shouted with parade-ground maleness: "Not at all, not at all, madame! We old campaigners never mind a healthy scrap. Glad when anybody's enough interested in our fool ideas to go and get sore at us, huh, huh, huh!"

And everybody laughed and sweetness reigned. The program wound up with Louis Rotenstern's singing of a group of patriotic ditties: "Marching through Georgia" and "Tenting on the Old Campground" and "Dixie" and "Old Black Joe" and "I'm Only a Poor Cowboy and I Know I Done Wrong."

Louis Rotenstern was by all of Fort Beulah classed as a "good fellow," a caste just below that of "real, old-fashioned gentleman." Doremus Jessup liked to go fishing with him, and partridge-hunting; and he considered that no Fifth Avenue tailor could do anything tastier in the way of a seersucker outfit. But Louis was a jingo. He explained, and rather often, that it was not he nor his father who had been born in the ghetto in Prussian Poland, but his grandfather (whose name, Doremus suspected, had been something less stylish and Nordic than Rotenstern). Louis's pocket heroes were Calvin Coolidge, Leonard Wood, Dwight L. Moody, and Admiral Dewey (and Dewey was a born Vermonter, rejoiced Louis, who himself had been born in Flatbush, Long Island).

He was not only 100 per cent American; he exacted 40 per cent of chauvinistic interest on top of the principal. He was on every occasion heard to say, "We ought to keep all these foreigners out of the country, and what I mean, the Kikes just as much as the Wops and Hunkies and Chinks." Louis was altogether convinced that if the ignorant politicians would keep their dirty hands off banking and the stock exchange and hours of labor for salesmen in department stores, then everyone in the country would profit, as beneficiaries of increased business, and all of them (including the retail clerks) be rich as Aga Khan.

So Louis put into his melodies not only his burning voice of a Bydgoszcz cantor but all his nationalistic fervor, so that every one joined in the choruses, particularly Mrs. Adelaide Tarr Gimmitch, with her celebrated train-caller's contralto.

The dinner broke up in cataract-like sounds of happy adieux, and Doremus Jessup muttered to his goodwife Emma, a solid, kindly, worried soul, who liked knitting, solitaire, and the novels of Kathleen Norris: "Was I terrible butting in that way?"

"Oh, no, Dormouse, you did just right. I *am* fond of Lorinda Pike, but why *does* she have to show off and parade all her silly Socialist ideas?"

"You old Tory!" said Doremus. "Don't you want to invite the Siamese elephant, the Gimmitch, to drop in and have a drink?"

"I do not!" said Emma Jessup.

And in the end, as the Rotarians shuffled and dealt themselves and their innumerable motorcars, it was Frank Tasbrough who invited the choicer males, including Doremus, home for an after-party.

2

AS HE TOOK HIS WIFE home and drove up Pleasant Hill to Tasbrough's, Doremus Jessup meditated upon the epidemic patriotism of General Edgeways. But he broke it off to let himself be absorbed in the hills, as it had been his habit for the fifty-three years, out of his sixty years of life, that he had spent in Fort Beulah, Vermont.

Legally a city, Fort Beulah was a comfortable village of old red brick, old granite workshops, and houses of white clapboards or gray shingles, with a few smug little modern bungalows, yellow or seal brown. There was but little manufacturing: a small woolen mill, a sash-and-door factory, a pump works. The granite which was its chief produce came from quarries four miles away; in Fort Beulah itself were only the offices . . . all the money . . . the meager shacks of most of the quarry workers. It was a town of perhaps ten thousand souls, inhabiting about twenty thousand bodies—the proportion of soul-possession may be too high.

There was but one (comparative) skyscraper in town: the six-story Tasbrough Building, with the offices of the Tasbrough & Scarlett Granite Quarries; the offices of Doremus's son-in-law, Fowler Greenhill, M.D., and his partner, old Dr. Olmsted, of Lawyer Mungo Kitterick, of Harry Kindermann, agent for maple syrup and dairying supplies, and of thirty or forty other village samurai.

It was a downy town, a drowsy town, a town of security and tradition, which still believed in Thanksgiving, Fourth of July, Memorial Day, and to which May Day was not an occasion for labor parades but for distributing small baskets of flowers.

It was a May night—late in May of 1936—with a three-quarter moon. Doremus's house was a mile from the business-center of Fort Beulah, on Pleasant Hill, which was a spur thrust like a reaching hand out from the dark rearing mass of Mount Terror. Upland meadows, moon-glistening, he could see, among the wildernesses of spruce and maple and poplar on the ridges far above him; and below, as his car climbed, was Ethan Creek flowing through the meadows. Deep woods—rearing mountain bulwarks—the air like spring-water—serene clapboarded houses that remembered the War of 1812 and the boyhoods of those errant Vermonters, Stephen A. Douglas, the "Little Giant," and Hiram Powers and Thaddeus Stevens and Brigham Young and President Chester Alan Arthur.

"No—Powers and Arthur—they were weak sisters," pondered Doremus. "But Douglas and Thad Stevens and Brigham, the old stallion—I wonder if we're breeding up any paladins like those stout, grouchy old devils?—if we're producing 'em anywhere in New England?—anywhere in America?—anywhere in the world? They had guts. Independence. Did what they wanted to and thought what they liked, and everybody could go to hell. The youngsters today—— Oh, the aviators have plenty of nerve. The physicists, these twenty-five-year-old Ph.D.'s that violate the inviolable atom, they're pioneers. But most of the wishy-washy young people today—— Going seventy miles an hour but not going anywhere—not enough imagination to *want* to go anywhere! Getting their music by turning a dial. Getting their phrases from the comic strips instead of from Shakespeare and the Bible and Veblen and Old Bill Sumner. Pap-fed flabs! Like this smug pup Malcolm Tasbrough, hanging around Sissy! Aah!

"Wouldn't it be hell if that stuffed shirt, Edgeways, and that political Mae West, Gimmitch, were right, and we need all these military monkeyshines and maybe a fool war (to conquer some sticky-hot country we don't want on a bet!) to put some starch and git into these marionettes we call our children? Aah!

"But rats—— These hills! Castle walls. And this air. They can keep their Cotswolds and Harz Mountains and Rockies! D. Jessup—topographical patriot. And I *am* a——"

"Dormouse, would you mind driving on the right-hand side of the road—on curves, anyway?" said his wife peaceably.

An upland hollow and mist beneath the moon—a veil of mist over apple blossoms and the heavy bloom of an ancient lilac bush beside the ruin of a farmhouse burned these sixty years and more.

Mr. Francis Tasbrough was the president, general manager, and chief owner of the Tasbrough & Scarlett Granite Quarries, at West Beulah, four miles from "the Fort." He was rich, persuasive, and he had constant labor troubles. He lived in a new Georgian brick house on Pleasant Hill, a little beyond Doremus Jessup's, and in that house he maintained a private barroom luxurious as that of a motor company's advertising manager at Grosse Point. It was no more the traditional New England than was the Catholic part of Boston; and Frank himself boasted that, though his family had for six generations lived in New England, he was no tight Yankee but in his Efficiency, his Salesmanship, the complete Pan-American Business Executive.

He was a tall man, Tasbrough, with a yellow mustache and a monotonously emphatic voice. He was fifty-four, six years younger than Doremus Jessup, and when he had been four, Doremus had protected him from the results of his singularly unpopular habit of hitting the other small boys over the head with things—all kinds of things—sticks and toy wagons and lunch boxes and dry cow flops.

Assembled in his private barroom tonight, after the Rotarian Dinner, were Frank himself, Doremus Jessup, Medary Cole, the Miller, Superintendent of Schools Emil Staubmeyer, R. C. Crowley—Roscoe Conkling Crowley, the weightiest banker in Fort Beulah—and, rather surprisingly, Tasbrough's pastor, the Episcopal minister, the Rev. Mr. Falck, his old hands as delicate as porcelain, his wilderness of hair silk-soft and white, his unfleshly face betokening the Good Life. Mr. Falck came from a solid Knickerbocker family, and he had studied in Edinburgh and Oxford along with the General

Theological Seminary of New York; and in all of the Beulah Valley there was, aside from Doremus, no one who more contentedly hid away in the shelter of the hills.

The barroom had been professionally interior-decorated by a young New York gentleman with the habit of standing with the back of his right hand against his hip. It had a stainless-steel bar, framed illustrations from *La Vie Parisienne,* silvered metal tables, and chromium-plated aluminum chairs with scarlet leather cushions.

All of them except Tasbrough, Medary Cole (a social climber to whom the favors of Frank Tasbrough were as honey and fresh ripened figs), and "Professor" Emil Staubmeyer were uncomfortable in this parrot-cage elegance, but none of them, including Mr. Falck, seemed to dislike Frank's soda and excellent Scotch or the sardine sandwiches.

"And I wonder if Thad Stevens would of liked this, either?" considered Doremus. "He'd of snarled. Old cornered catamount. But probably not at the whisky!"

"Doremus," demanded Tasbrough, "why don't you take a tumble to yourself? All these years you've had a lot of fun criticizing—always being agin the government—kidding everybody—posing as such a Liberal that you'll stand for all these subversive elements. Time for you to quit playing tag with crazy ideas and come in and join the family. These are serious times—maybe twenty-eight million on relief, and beginning to get ugly—thinking they've got a vested right now to be supported.

"And the Jew Communists and Jew financiers plotting together to control the country. I can understand how, as a younger fellow, you could pump up a little sympathy for the unions and even for the Jews—though, as you know, I'll never get over being sore at you for taking the side of the strikers when those thugs were trying to ruin my whole business—burn down my polishing and cutting shops—why, you were even friendly with that alien murderer Karl Pascal, who started the whole strike—maybe I didn't enjoy firing *him* when it was all over!

"But anyway, these labor racketeers are getting together now, with Communist leaders, and determined to run the country—to tell men like *me* how to run our business!—and just like General Edgeways said, they'll refuse to serve their country if we should happen to get dragged into some war. Yessir, a mighty serious hour, and it's time for you to cut the cackle and join the really responsible citizens."

Said Doremus, "Hm. Yes, I agree it's a serious time. With all the discontent there is in the country to wash him into office, Senator Windrip has got an excellent chance to be elected President, next November, and if he is, probably his gang of buzzards will get us into some war, just to grease their insane vanity and show the world that we're the huskiest nation going. And then I, the Liberal and you, the Plutocrat, the bogus Tory, will be led out and shot at 3 A.M. Serious? Huh!"

"Rats! You're exaggerating!" said R. C. Crowley.

Doremus went on: "If Bishop Prang, our Savonarola in a Cadillac 16, swings his radio audience and his League of Forgotten Men to Buzz Windrip, Buzz will win. People will think they're electing him to create more economic security. Then watch the Terror! God knows there's been enough indication that we *can* have tyranny in America—the fix of the Southern sharecroppers, the working conditions of the miners and garment-makers, and our keeping Mooney in prison so many years. But wait till Windrip shows us how to say it with machine guns! Democracy—here and in Britain and France, it hasn't been so universal a sniveling slavery as Naziism in Germany, such an imagination-hating, pharisaic materialism as Russia—even if it has produced industrialists like you, Frank, and bankers like you, R. C., and given you altogether too much power and money. On the whole, with scandalous exceptions, Democracy's given the ordinary worker more dignity than he ever had. That may be menaced now by Windrip—all the Windrips. All right! Maybe we'll have to fight paternal dictatorship with a little sound patricide—fight machine guns with machine guns. Wait till Buzz takes charge of us. A real Fascist dictatorship!"

"Nonsense! Nonsense!" snorted Tasbrough. "That couldn't happen here in America, not possibly! We're a country of freemen."

"The answer to that," suggested Doremus Jessup, "if Mr. Falck will forgive me, is 'the hell it can't!' Why, there's no country in the world that can get more hysterical—yes, or more obsequious!—than America. Look how Huey Long became absolute monarch over Louisiana, and how the Right Honorable Mr. Senator Berzelius Windrip owns *his* State. Listen to Bishop Prang and Father Coughlin on the radio—divine oracles, to millions. Remember how casually most Americans have accepted Tammany grafting and Chicago gangs and the crookedness of so many of President Harding's appointees? Could Hitler's bunch, or Windrip's, be worse? Remember the Kuklux Klan? Remember our war hysteria, when we called sauerkraut 'Liberty cabbage' and somebody actually proposed calling German measles 'Liberty measles'? And wartime censorship of honest papers? Bad as Russia! Remember our kissing the—well, the feet of Billy Sunday, the million-dollar evangelist, and of Aimée McPherson, who swam from the Pacific Ocean clear into the Arizona desert and got away with it? Remember Voliva and Mother Eddy? . . . Remember our Red scares and our Catholic scares, when all well-informed people knew that the O.G.P.U. were hiding out in Oskaloosa, and the Republicans campaigning against Al Smith told the Carolina mountaineers that if Al won the Pope would illegitimatize their children? Remember Tom Heflin and Tom Dixon? Remember when the hick legislators in certain states, in obedience to William Jennings Bryan, who learned his biology from his pious old grandma, set up shop as scientific experts and made the whole world laugh itself sick by forbidding the teaching of evolution? . . . Remember the Kentucky night-riders? Remember how trainloads of people have gone to enjoy lynchings? Not happen here? Prohibition—shooting down people just because they *might* be transporting liquor—no, that couldn't happen in *America*! Why, where in all history has there ever been a people so ripe for a dictatorship as ours! We're ready to start on a Children's Crusade—only of adults—right now, and the Right Reverend Abbots Windrip and Prang are all ready to lead it!"

"Well, what if they are?" protested R. C. Crowley. "It might not be so bad. I don't like all these irresponsible attacks on us bankers all the time. Of course, Senator Windrip has to pretend publicly to bawl the banks out, but once he gets into power he'll give the banks their proper influence in the administration and take our expert financial advice. Yes. Why are you so afraid of the word 'Fascism,' Doremus? Just a word—just a word! And might not be so bad, with all the lazy bums we got panhandling relief nowadays, and living on my income tax and yours—not so worse to have a real Strong Man, like Hitler or Mussolini—like Napoleon or Bismarck in the good old days—and have 'em really *run* the country and make it efficient and prosperous again. 'Nother words, have a doctor who won't take any back-chat, but really boss the patient and make him get well whether he likes it or not!"

"Yes!" said Emil Staubmeyer. "Didn't Hitler save Germany from the Red Plague of Marxism? I got cousins there. I *know*!"

"Hm," said Doremus, as often Doremus did say it. "Cure the evils of Democracy by the evils of Fascism! Funny therapeutics. I've heard of their curing syphilis by giving the patient malaria, but I've never heard of their curing malaria by giving the patient syphilis!"

"Think that's nice language to use in the presence of the Reverend Falck?" raged Tasbrough.

Mr. Falck piped up, "I think it's quite nice language, and an interesting suggestion, Brother Jessup!"

"Besides," said Tasbrough, "this chewing the rag is all nonsense, anyway. As Crowley says, might be a good thing to have a strong man in the saddle, but—it just can't happen here in America."

And it seemed to Doremus that the softly moving lips of the Reverend Mr. Falck were framing, "The hell it can't!"

3

DOREMUS JESSUP, editor and proprietor of the *Daily Informer,* the Bible of the conservative Vermont farmers up and down the Beulah Valley, was born in Fort Beulah in 1876, only son of an impecunious Universalist pastor, the Reverend Loren Jessup. His mother was no less than a Bass, of Massachusetts. The Reverend Loren, a bookish man fond of flowers, merry but not noticeably witty, used to chant "Alas, alas, that a Bass of Mass should marry a minister prone to gas," and he would insist that she was all wrong ichthyologically—she should have been a cod, not a bass. There was in the parsonage little meat but plenty of books, not all theological by any means, so that before he was twelve Doremus knew the profane writings of Scott, Dickens, Thackeray, Jane Austen, Tennyson, Byron, Keats, Shelley, Tolstoy, Balzac. He graduated from Isaiah College—once a bold Unitarian venture but by 1894 an interdenominational outfit with nebulous trinitarian yearnings, a small and rustic stable of learning, in North Beulah, thirteen miles from "the Fort."

But Isaiah College has come up in the world today—excepting educationally—for in 1931 it held the Dartmouth football team down to 64 to 6.

During college, Doremus wrote a great deal of bad poetry and became an incurable book addict, but he was a fair track athlete. Naturally, he corresponded for papers in Boston and Springfield, and after graduation he was a reporter in Rutland and Worcester, with one glorious year in Boston, whose grimy beauty and shards of the past were to him what London would be to a young Yorkshireman. He was excited by concerts, art galleries, and bookshops; thrice a week he had a twenty-five-cent seat in the upper balcony of some theater; and for two months he roomed with a fellow reporter who had actually had a short story in *The Century* and who could talk about authors and technique like the very dickens. But Doremus was not particularly beefy or enduring, and the noise, the traffic, the bustle of assignments, exhausted him, and in 1901, three years after his graduation from college, when his widowed father died and left him $2980.00 and his library, Doremus went home to Fort Beulah and bought a quarter interest in the *Informer,* then a weekly.

By 1936 it was a daily, and he owned all of it . . . with a perceptible mortgage.

He was an equable and sympathetic boss; an imaginative news detective; he was, even in this ironbound Republican state, independent in politics; and in his editorials against graft and injustice, though they were not fanatically chronic, he could slash like a dog whip.

He was a third cousin of Calvin Coolidge, who had considered him sound domestically but loose politically. Doremus considered himself just the opposite.

He had married his wife, Emma, out of Fort Beulah. She was the daughter of a wagon manufacturer, a placid, prettyish, broad-shouldered girl with whom he had gone to high school.

Now, in 1936, of their three children, Philip (Dartmouth and Harvard Law School) was married and ambitiously practicing law in Worcester; Mary was the wife of Fowler Greenhill, M.D., of Fort Beulah, a gay and hustling medico, a choleric and red-headed young man, who was a wonder-worker in typhoid, acute appendicitis, obstetrics, compound fractures, and diets for anemic children. Fowler and Mary had one son, Doremus's only grandchild, the bonny David, who at eight was a timid, inventive, affectionate child with such mourning hound-dog eyes and such red-gold hair that his picture might well have been hung at a National Academy show or even been reproduced on the cover of a Women's Magazine with 2,500,000 circulation. The Greenhills' neighbors inevitably said of the boy, "My, Davy's got such an imagination, hasn't he! I guess he'll be a Writer, just like his Grampa!"

Third of Doremus's children was the gay, the pert, the dancing Cecilia, known as "Sissy," aged eighteen, where her brother Philip was thirty-two and Mary, Mrs. Greenhill, turned thirty. She rejoiced the heart of Doremus by consenting to stay home while she was finishing high school, though she talked vigorously of going off to study architecture and "simply make *millions,* my dear," by planning and erecting miraculous small homes.

Mrs. Jessup was lavishly (and quite erroneously) certain that her Philip was the spit and image of the Prince of Wales; Philip's wife, Merilla (the fair daughter of Worcester, Massachusetts), curiously like the Princess Marina; that Mary would by any stranger be taken for Katharine Hepburn; that Sissy was a dryad and David a medieval page; and that Doremus (though she knew him better than she did those changelings, her children) amazingly resembled that naval hero, Winfield Scott Schley, as he looked in 1898.

She was a loyal woman, Emma Jessup, warmly generous, a cordon bleu at making lemon-meringue pie, a parochial Tory, an orthodox Episcopalian, and completely innocent of any humor. Doremus was perpetually tickled by her kind solemnity, and it was to be chalked down to him as a singular act of grace that he refrained from pretending that he had become a working Communist and was thinking of leaving for Moscow immediately.

Doremus looked depressed, looked old, when he lifted himself, as from an invalid's chair, out of the Chrysler, in his hideous garage of cement and galvanized iron. (But it was a proud two-car garage; besides the four-year-old Chrysler, they had a new Ford convertible coupe, which Doremus hoped to drive some day when Sissy wasn't using it.)

He cursed competently as, on the cement walk from the garage to the kitchen, he barked his shins on the lawnmower, left there by his hired man, one Oscar Ledue, known always as "Shad," a large and red-faced, a sulky and surly Irish-Canuck peasant. Shad always did things like leaving lawnmowers about to snap at the shins of decent people. He was entirely incompetent and vicious. He never edged-up the flower beds, he kept his stinking old cap on his head when he brought in logs for the fireplace, he did not scythe the dandelions in the meadow till they had gone to seed, he delighted in failing to tell cook that the peas were now ripe, and he was given to shooting cats, stray dogs, chipmunks, and honey-voiced blackbirds. At least twice a day, Doremus resolved to fire him, but—— Perhaps he was telling himself the truth when he insisted that it was amusing to try to civilize this prize bull.

Doremus trotted into the kitchen, decided that he did not want some cold chicken and a glass of milk from the ice-box, nor even a wedge of the celebrated cocoanut layer cake made by their cook-general, Mrs. Candy, and mounted to his "study," on the third, the attic floor.

His house was an ample, white, clapboarded structure of the vintage of 1880, a square bulk with a mansard roof and, in front, a long porch with insignificant square white pillars. Doremus declared that the house was ugly, "but ugly in a nice way."

His study, up there, was his one perfect refuge from annoyances and bustle. It was the only room in the house that Mrs. Candy (quiet, grimly competent, thoroughly literate, once a Vermont country schoolteacher) was never allowed to clean. It was an endearing mess of novels, copies of the *Congressional Record,* of the *New Yorker, Time, Nation, New Republic, New Masses,* and *Speculum* (cloistral organ of the Medieval Society), treatises on taxation and monetary systems, road maps, volumes on exploration in Abyssinia and the Antarctic, chewed stubs of pencils, a shaky portable typewriter, fishing tackle, rumpled carbon paper, two comfortable old leather chairs, a Windsor chair at his desk, the complete works of Thomas Jefferson, his chief hero, a microscope and a collection of Vermont butterflies, Indian arrowheads, exiguous volumes of Vermont village poetry printed in local newspaper offices, the Bible, the Koran, the Book of Mormon, Science and Health, Selections from the Mahabharata, the poetry of Sandburg, Frost, Masters, Jeffers, Ogden Nash, Edgar Guest, Omar Khayyám, and Milton, a shotgun and a .22 repeating rifle, an Isaiah College banner, faded, the complete Oxford Dictionary, five fountain pens of which two would work, a vase from Crete dating from 327 B.C.—very ugly—the World Almanac for year before last, with the cover suggesting that it had been chewed by a dog, odd pairs of horn-rimmed spectacles and of rimless eyeglasses, none of which now suited his eyes, a fine, reputedly Tudor oak cabinet from Devonshire, portraits of Ethan Allen and Thaddeus Stevens, rubber wading-boots, senile red morocco slippers, a poster issued by the *Vermont Mercury* at Woodstock, on September 2, 1840, announcing a glorious Whig victory, twenty-four boxes of safety matches one by one stolen from the kitchen, assorted yellow scratch pads, seven books on Russia and Bolshevism—extraordinarily pro or extraordinarily con—a signed photograph of Theodore Roosevelt, six cigarette cartons, all half empty (according to the tradition of journalistic eccentrics, Doremus should have smoked a Good Old Pipe, but he detested the slimy ooze of nicotine-soaked spittle), a rag carpet on the floor, a withered sprig of holly with a silver Christmas ribbon, a case of seven unused genuine Sheffield razors, dictionaries in French, German, Italian, and Spanish—the first of which languages he really could read—a canary in a Bavarian gilded wicker cage, a worn linen-bound copy of *Old Hearthside Songs for Home and Picnic* whose selections he was wont to croon, holding the book on his knee, and an old cast-iron Franklin stove. Everything, indeed, that was proper for a hermit and improper for impious domestic hands.

Before switching on the light he squinted through a dormer window at the bulk of mountains cutting the welter of stars. In the center were the last lights of Fort Beulah, far below, and on the left, unseen, the soft meadows, the old farmhouses, the great dairy barns of the Ethan Mowing. It was a kind country, cool and clear as a shaft of light and, he meditated, he loved it more every quiet year of his freedom from city towers and city clamor.

One of the few times when Mrs. Candy, their housekeeper, was permitted to enter his hermit's cell was to leave there, on the long table, his mail. He picked it up and started to read briskly, standing by the table. (Time to go to bed! Too much chatter and bellyaching, this evening! Good Lord! Past midnight!) He sighed then, and sat in his Windsor chair, leaning his elbows on the table and studiously reading the first letter over again.

It was from Victor Loveland, one of the younger, more international-minded teachers in Doremus's old school, Isaiah College.

DEAR DR. JESSUP:

("Hm. 'Dr. Jessup.' Not me, m' lad. The only honorary degree I'll ever get'll be Master in Veterinary Surgery or Laureate in Embalming.")

A very dangerous situation has arisen here at Isaiah and those of us who are trying to advocate something like integrity and modernity are seriously worried—not, probably, that we need to be long, as we shall probably all get fired. Where two years ago most of our students just laughed at any idea of military drilling, they have gone warlike in a big way, with undergrads drilling with rifles, machine guns, and cute little blueprints of tanks and planes all over the place. Two of them, voluntarily, are going down to Rutland every week to take training in flying, avowedly to get ready for wartime aviation. When I cautiously ask them what the dickens war they are preparing for they just scratch and indicate they don't care much, so long as they can get a chance to show what virile proud gents they are.

Well, we've got used to that. But just this afternoon—the newspapers haven't got this yet—the Board of Trustees, including Mr. Francis Tasbrough and our president, Dr. Owen Peaseley, met and voted a resolution that—now listen to this, will you, Dr. Jessup—"Any member of the faculty or student body of Isaiah who shall in any way, publicly or privately, in print, writing, or by the spoken word, adversely criticize military training at or by Isaiah College, or in any other institution of learning in the United States, or by the state militias, federal forces, or other officially recognized military organizations in this country, shall be liable to immediate dismissal from this college, and any student who shall, with full and proper proof, bring to the attention of the President or any Trustee of the college such malign criticism by any person whatever connected in any way with the institution shall receive extra credits in his course in military training, such credits to apply to the number of credits necessary for graduation."

What can we do with such fast exploding Fascism?

VICTOR LOVELAND.

And Loveland, teacher of Greek, Latin, and Sanskrit (two lone students), had never till now meddled in any politics of more recent date than A.D. 180.

"So Frank was there at Trustees' meeting, and didn't dare tell me," Doremus sighed. "Encouraging them to become spies. Gestapo. Oh, my dear Frank, this is a serious time! You, my good bonehead, for once you said it! President Owen J. Peaseley, the bagged-faced, pious, racketeering, damned hedge-schoolmaster! But what can I do? Oh—write another editorial viewing-with-alarm, I suppose!"

He plumped into a deep chair and sat fidgeting, like a bright-eyed, apprehensive little bird.

On the door was a tearing sound, imperious, demanding.

He opened to admit Foolish, the family dog. Foolish was a reliable combination of English setter, Airedale, cocker spaniel, wistful doe, and rearing hyena. He gave one abrupt snort of welcome and nuzzled his brown satin head against Doremus's knee. His bark awakened the canary, under the absurd old blue sweater that covered its cage, and it automatically caroled that it was noon, summer noon, among the pear trees in the green Harz hills, none of which was true. But the bird's trilling, the dependable presence of Foolish, comforted Doremus, made military drill and belching politicians seem unimportant and in security he dropped asleep in the worn brown leather chair.

4

ALL THIS JUNE WEEK, Doremus was waiting for 2 P.M. on Saturday, the divinely appointed hour of the weekly prophetic broadcast by Bishop Paul Peter Prang.

Now, six weeks before the 1936 national conventions, it was probable that neither Franklin Roosevelt, Herbert Hoover, Senator Vandenberg, Ogden Mills, General Hugh Johnson, Colonel Frank Knox, nor Senator Borah would be nominated for President by either party, and that the Republican standard-bearer—meaning the one man who never has to lug a large, bothersome, and somewhat ridiculous standard—would be that loyal yet strangely honest old-line Senator, Walt Trowbridge, a man with a touch of Lincoln in him, dashes of Will Rogers and George W. Norris, a suspected trace of Jim Farley, but all the rest plain, bulky, placidly defiant Walt Trowbridge.

Few men doubted that the Democratic candidate would be that sky-rocket, Senator Berzelius Windrip—that is to say, Windrip as the mask and bellowing voice, with his satanic secretary, Lee Sarason, as the brain behind.

Senator Windrip's father was a small-town Western druggist, equally ambitious and unsuccessful, and had named him Berzelius after the Swedish chemist. Usually he was known as "Buzz." He had worked his way through a Southern Baptist college, of approximately the same academic standing as a Jersey City business college, and through a Chicago law school, and settled down to practice in his native state and to enliven local politics. He was a tireless traveler, a boisterous and humorous speaker, an inspired guesser at what political doctrines the people would like, a warm handshaker, and willing to lend money. He drank Coca-Cola with the Methodists, beer with the Lutherans, California white wine with the Jewish village merchants—and, when they were safe from observation, white-mule corn whisky with all of them.

Within twenty years he was as absolute a ruler of his state as ever a sultan was of Turkey.

He was never governor; he had shrewdly seen that his reputation for research among planters-punch recipes, varieties of poker, and the psychology of girl stenographers might cause his defeat by the church people, so he had contented himself with coaxing to the gubernatorial shearing a trained baa-lamb of a country schoolmaster whom he had gayly led on a wide blue ribbon. The state was certain that he had "given it a good administration," and they knew that it was Buzz Windrip who was responsible, not the Governor.

Windrip caused the building of impressive highroads and of consolidated country schools; he made the state buy tractors and combines and lend them to the farmers at cost. He was certain that some day America would have vast business dealings with the Russians and, though he detested all Slavs, he made the State University put in the first course in the Russian language that had been known in all that part of the West. His most original invention was quadrupling the state militia and rewarding the best soldiers in it with training in agriculture, aviation, and radio and automobile engineering.

The militiamen considered him their general and their god, and when the state attorney general announced that he was going to have Windrip indicted for having grafted $200,000 of tax money, the militia rose to Buzz Windrip's orders as though they were his private army and, occupying the legislative chambers and all the state offices, and covering the streets leading to the Capitol with machine guns, they herded Buzz's enemies out of town.

He took the United States Senatorship as though it were his manorial right, and for six years, his only rival as the most bouncing and feverish man in the Senate had been the late Huey Long of Louisiana.

He preached the comforting gospel of so redistributing wealth that every person in the country would have several thousand dollars a year (monthly Buzz changed his prediction as to how many thousand), while all the rich men were nevertheless to be allowed enough to get along, on a maximum of $500,000 a year. So everybody was happy in the prospect of Windrip's becoming president.

The Reverend Dr. Egerton Schlemil, dean of St. Agnes Cathedral, San Antonio, Texas, stated (once in a sermon, once in the slightly variant mimeographed press handout on the sermon, and seven times in interviews) that Buzz's coming into power would be "like the Heaven-blest fall of revivifying rain upon a parched and thirsty land." Dr. Schlemil did not say anything about what happened when the blest rain came and kept falling steadily for four years.

No one, even among the Washington correspondents, seemed to know precisely how much of a part in Senator Windrip's career was taken by his secretary, Lee Sarason. When Windrip had first seized power in his state, Sarason had been managing editor of the most widely circulated paper in all that part of the country. Sarason's genesis was and remained a mystery.

It was said that he had been born in Georgia, in Minnesota, on the East Side of New York, in Syria; that he was pure Yankee, Jewish, Charleston Huguenot. It was known that he had been a singularly reckless lieutenant of machine-gunners as a youngster during the Great War, and that he had stayed over, ambling about Europe, for three or four years; that he had worked on the Paris edition of the New York *Herald;* nibbled at painting and at Black Magic in Florence and Munich; had a few sociological months at the London School of Economics; associated with decidedly curious people in arty Berlin night restaurants. Returned home, Sarason had become decidedly the "hard-boiled reporter" of the shirt-sleeved tradition, who asserted that he would rather be called a prostitute than anything so sissified as "journalist." But it was suspected that nevertheless he still retained the ability to read.

He had been variously a Socialist and an anarchist. Even in 1936 there were rich people who asserted that Sarason was "too radical," but actually he had lost his trust (if any) in the masses during the hoggish nationalism after the war; and he believed now only in resolute control by a small oligarchy. In this he was a Hitler, a Mussolini.

Sarason was lanky and drooping, with thin flaxen hair, and thick lips in a bony face. His eyes were sparks at the bottoms of two dark wells. In his long hands there was bloodless strength. He used to surprise persons who were about to shake hands with him by suddenly bending their fingers back till they almost broke. Most people didn't much like it. As a newspaperman he was an expert of the highest grade. He could smell out a husband-murder, the grafting of a politician—that is to say, of a politician belonging to a gang opposed by his paper—the torture of animals or children, and this last sort of story he liked to write himself, rather than hand it to a reporter, and when he did write it, you saw the moldy cellar, heard the whip, felt the slimy blood.

Compared with Lee Sarason as a newspaperman, little Doremus Jessup of Fort Beulah was like a village parson compared with the twenty-thousand-dollar minister of a twenty-story New York institutional tabernacle with radio affiliations.

Senator Windrip had made Sarason, officially, his secretary, but he was known to be much more—bodyguard, ghost-writer, press-agent, economic adviser; and in Washington, Lee Sarason became the man most consulted and least liked by newspaper correspondents in the whole Senate Office Building.

Windrip was a young forty-eight in 1936; Sarason an aged and sagging-cheeked forty-one.

Though he probably based it on notes dictated by Windrip—himself no fool in the matter of fictional imagination—Sarason had certainly done the actual writing of Windrip's lone book, the Bible of his followers, part biography, part economic program, and part plain exhibitionistic boasting, called *Zero Hour—Over the Top.*

It was a salty book and contained more suggestions for remolding the world than the three volumes of Karl Marx and all the novels of H. G. Wells put together.

Perhaps the most familiar, most quoted paragraph of

Zero Hour, beloved by the provincial press because of its simple earthiness (as written by an initiate in Rosicrucian lore, named Sarason) was:

"When I was a little shaver back in the corn fields, we kids used to just wear one-strap suspenders on our pants, and we called them the Galluses on our Britches, but they held them up and saved our modesty just as much as if we had put on a high-toned Limey accent and talked about Braces and Trousers. That's how the whole world of what they call 'scientific economies' is like. The Marxians think that by writing of Galluses as Braces, they've got something that knocks the stuffings out of the old-fashioned ideas of Washington and Jefferson and Alexander Hamilton. Well and all, I sure believe in using every new economic discovery, like they have been worked out in the so-called Fascist countries, like Italy and Germany and Hungary and Poland—yes, by thunder, and even in Japan—we probably will have to lick those Little Yellow Men some day, to keep them from pinching our vested and rightful interests in China, but don't let that keep us from grabbing off any smart ideas that those cute little beggars have worked out!

"I want to stand up on my hind legs and not just admit but frankly holler right out that we've got to change our system a lot, maybe even change the whole Constitution (but change it legally, and not by violence) to bring it up from the horseback-and-corduroy-road epoch to the automobile-and-cement-highway period of today. The Executive has got to have a freer hand and be able to move quick in an emergency, and not be tied down by a lot of dumb shyster-lawyer congressmen taking months to shoot off their mouths in debates. BUT—and it's a But as big as Deacon Checkerboard's hay-barn back home—these new economic changes are only a means to an End, and that End is and must be, fundamentally, the same principles of Liberty, Equality, and Justice that were advocated by the Founding Fathers of this great land back in 1776!"

The most confusing thing about the whole campaign of 1936 was the relationship of the two leading parties.

Old-Guard Republicans complained that their proud party was begging for office, hat in hand; veteran Democrats that their traditional Covered Wagons were jammed with college professors, city slickers, and yachtsmen.

The rival to Senator Windrip in public reverence was a political titan who seemed to have no itch for office—the Reverend Paul Peter Prang, of Persepolis, Indiana, Bishop of the Methodist Episcopal Church, a man perhaps ten years older than Windrip. His weekly radio address, at 2 P.M. every Saturday, was to millions the very oracle of God. So supernatural was this voice from the air that for it men delayed their golf, and women even postponed their Saturday afternoon contract bridge.

It was Father Charles Coughlin, of Detroit, who had first thought out the device of freeing himself from any censorship of his political sermons on the Mount by "buying his own time on the air"—it being only in the twentieth century that mankind has been able to buy Time as it buys soap and gasoline. This invention was almost equal, in its effect on all American life and thought, to Henry Ford's early conception of selling cars cheap to millions of people, instead of selling a few as luxuries.

But to the pioneer Father Coughlin, Bishop Paul Peter Prang was as the Ford V-8 to the Model A.

Prang was more sentimental than Coughlin; he shouted more; he agonized more; he reviled more enemies by name, and rather scandalously; he told more funny stories, and ever so many more tragic stories about the repentant deathbeds of bankers, atheists, and Communists. His voice was more nasally native, and he was pure Middle West, with a New England Protestant Scotch-English ancestry, where Coughlin was always a little suspect, in the Sears-Roebuck regions, as a Roman Catholic with an agreeable Irish accent.

No man in history has ever had such an audience as Bishop Prang, nor so much apparent power. When he demanded that his auditors telegraph their congressmen to vote on a bill as he, Prang, *ex cathedra* and alone, without any college of cardinals, had been inspired to believe they ought to vote, then fifty thousand people would telephone, or drive through back-hill mud, to the nearest telegraph office and in His name give their commands to the government. Thus, by the magic of electricity, Prang made the position of any king in history look a little absurd and tinseled.

To millions of League members he sent mimeographed letters with facsimile signature, and with the salutation so craftily typed in that they rejoiced in a personal greeting from the Founder.

Doremus Jessup, up in the provincial hills, could never quite figure out just what political gospel it was that Bishop Prang thundered from his Sinai which, with its microphone and typed revelations timed to the split-second, was so much more snappy and efficient than the original Sinai. In detail, he preached nationalization of the banks, mines, waterpower, and transportation; limitation of incomes; increased wages, strengthening of the labor unions, more fluid distribution of consumer goods. But everybody was nibbling at those noble doctrines now, from Virginia Senators to Minnesota Farmer-Laborites, with no one being so credulous as to expect any of them to be carried out.

There was a theory around some place that Prang was only the humble voice of his vast organization, "The League of Forgotten Men." It was universally believed to have (though no firm of chartered accountants had yet examined its rolls) twenty-seven million members, along with proper assortments of national officers and state officers, and town officers and hordes of committees with stately names like "National Committee on the Compilation of Statistics on Unemployment and Normal Employability in the Soy-Bean Industry." Hither and yon, Bishop Prang, not as the still small voice of God but in lofty person, addressed audiences of twenty thousand persons at a time, in the larger cities all over the country, speaking in huge halls meant for prize-fighting, in cinema palaces, in armories, in baseball parks, in circus tents, while after the meetings his brisk assistants accepted membership applications and dues for the League of Forgotten Men. When his timid detractors hinted that this was all very romantic, very jolly and picturesque, but not particularly dignified, and Bishop Prang answered, "My Master delighted to speak in whatever vulgar assembly would listen to Him," no one dared answer him, "But you aren't your Master—not yet."

With all the flourish of the League and its mass meetings, there had never been a pretense that any tenet of the League, any pressure on Congress and the President to pass any particular bill, originated with anybody save Prang himself, with no collaboration from the committees or officers of the League. All that the Prang who so often crooned about the Humility and Modesty of the Saviour wanted was for one hundred and thirty million people to obey him, their Priest-King, implicitly in everything concerning their private morals, their public asseverations, how they might earn their livings, and what relationships they might have to other wage-earners.

"And that," Doremus Jessup grumbled, relishing the shocked piety of his wife Emma, "makes Brother Prang a worse tyrant than Caligula—a worse Fascist than Napoleon. Mind you, I don't *really* believe all these rumors about Prang's grafting on membership dues and the sale of pamphlets and donations to pay for the radio. It's much worse than that. I'm afraid he's an honest fanatic! That's why he's such a real Fascist menace—he's so confoundedly humanitarian, in fact so Noble, that a majority of people are willing to let him boss everything, and with a country this size, that's quite a job—quite a job, my beloved—even for a Methodist Bishop who gets enough gifts so that he can actually 'buy Time'!"

All the while, Walt Trowbridge, possible Republican candidate for President, suffering from the deficiency of being honest and disinclined to promise that he could work miracles, was insisting that we live in the United States of America and not on a golden highway to Utopia.

There was nothing exhilarating in such realism, so all this rainy week in June, with the apple blossoms and the lilacs fading, Doremus Jessup was awaiting the next encyclical of Pope Paul Peter Prang.

5

> I know the Press only too well. Almost all editors hide away in spider-dens, men without thought of Family or Public Interest or the humble delights of jaunts out-of-doors, plotting how they can put over their lies, and advance their own positions and fill their greedy pocketbooks by calumniating Statesmen who have given their all for the common good and who are vulnerable because they stand out in the fierce Light that beats around the Throne.
>
> *Zero Hour,* Berzelius Windrip.

THE JUNE MORNING shone, the last petals of the wild-cherry blossoms lay dew-covered on the grass, robins were about their brisk business on the lawn. Doremus, by nature a late-lier and pilferer of naps after he had been called at eight, was stirred to spring up and stretch his arms out fully five or six times in Swedish exercises, in front of his window, looking out across the Beulah River Valley to dark masses of pine on the mountain slopes three miles away.

Doremus and Emma had had each their own bed-room, these fifteen years, not altogether to her pleasure. He asserted that he couldn't share a bedroom with any person living, because he was a night-mutterer, and liked to make a really good, uprearing, pillow-slapping job of turning over in bed without feeling that he was dis-turbing someone.

It was Saturday, the day of the Prang revelation, but on this crystal morning, after days of rain, he did not think of Prang at all, but of the fact that Philip, his son, with wife, had popped up from Worcester for the week-end, and that the whole crew of them, along with Lorinda Pike and Buck Titus, were going to have a "real, old-fashioned, family picnic."

They had all demanded it, even the fashionable Sissy, a woman who, at eighteen, had much concern with tennis-teas, golf, and mysterious, appallingly rapid motor trips with Malcolm Tasbrough (just graduating from high school), or with the Episcopal parson's grandson, Julian Falck (freshman in Amherst). Doremus had scolded that he *couldn't* go to any blame picnic; it was his *job,* as editor, to stay home and listen to Bishop Prang's broadcast at two; but they had laughed at him and rumpled his hair and miscalled him until he had promised. . . . They didn't know it, but he had slyly borrowed a portable radio from his friend, the local R. C. priest, Father Stephen Perefixe, and he was going to hear Prang whether or no.

He was glad they were going to have Lorinda Pike—he was fond of that sardonic saint—and Buck Titus, who was perhaps his closest intimate.

James Buck Titus, who was fifty but looked thirty-eight, straight, broad-shouldered, slim-waisted, long-mustached, swarthy—Buck was the Dan'l Boone type of Old American, or, perhaps, an Indian-fighting cavalry captain, out of Charles King. He had graduated from Williams, with ten weeks in England and ten years in Montana, divided between cattle-raising, prospecting, and a horse-breeding ranch. His father, a richish railroad contractor, had left him the great farm near West Beulah, and Buck had come back home to grow apples, to breed Morgan stallions, and to read Voltaire, Anatole France, Nietzsche, and Dostoyefsky. He served in the war, as a private; detested his officers, refused a commission, and liked the Germans at Cologne. He was a useful polo player, but regarded riding to the hounds as childish. In politics, he did not so much yearn over the wrongs of Labor as feel scornful of the tight-fisted exploiters who denned in office and stinking factory. He was as near to the English country squire as one may find in America. He was a bachelor, with a big mid-Victorian house, well kept by a friendly Negro couple; a tidy place in which he sometimes entertained ladies who were not quite so tidy. He called himself an "agnostic" instead of an "atheist" only because he detested the street-bawling, tract-peddling evangelicism of the professional atheists. He was cynical, he rarely smiled, and he was unwaveringly loyal to all the Jessups. His coming to the picnic made Doremus as blithe as his grandson David.

"Perhaps, even under Fascism, the 'Church clock will stand at ten to three, and there will be honey still for tea,' " Doremus hoped, as he put on his rather dandified country tweeds.

The only stain on the preparations for the picnic was the grouchiness of the hired man, Shad Ledue. When he was asked to turn the ice-cream freezer he growled, "Why the heck don't you folks get an electric freezer?" He grumbled, most audibly, at the weight of the picnic baskets, and when he was asked to clean up the basement during their absence, he retorted only with a glare of silent fury.

"You ought to get rid of that fellow, Ledue," urged Doremus's son Philip, the lawyer.

"Oh, I don't know," considered Doremus. "Probably just shiftlessness on my part. But I tell myself I'm doing a social experiment—trying to train him to be as gracious as the average Neanderthal man. Or perhaps I'm scared of him—he's the kind of vindictive peasant that sets fire to barns. . . . Did you know that he actually reads, Phil?"

"No!"

"Yep. Mostly movie magazines, with nekked ladies and Wild Western stories, but he also reads the papers. Told me he greatly admired Buzz Windrip; says Windrip will certainly be President, and then everybody—by which, I'm afraid, Shad means only himself—will have five thousand a year. Buzz certainly has a bunch of philanthropists for followers."

"Now listen, Dad. You don't understand Senator Windrip. Oh, he's something of a demagogue—he shoots off his mouth a lot about how he'll jack up the income tax and grab the banks, but he won't—that's just molasses for the cockroaches. What he will do, and maybe only he *can* do it, is to protect us from the murdering, thieving, lying Bolsheviks that would—why, they'd like to stick all of us that are going on this picnic, all the decent clean people that are accustomed to privacy, into hall bedrooms, and make us cook our cabbage soup on a Primus stuck on a bed! Yes, or maybe 'liquidate' us entirely! No sir, Berzelius Windrip is the fellow to balk the dirty sneaking Jew spies that pose as American Liberals!"

"The face is the face of my reasonably competent son, Philip, but the voice is the voice of the Jew-baiter, Julius Streicher," sighed Doremus.

The picnic ground was among a Stonehenge of gray and lichen-painted rocks, fronting a birch grove high up on Mount Terror, on the upland farm of Doremus's cousin, Henry Veeder, a solid, reticent Vermonter of the old days. They looked through a distant mountain gap to the faint mercury of Lake Champlain and, across it, the bulwark of the Adirondacks.

Davy Greenhill and his hero, Buck Titus, wrestled in the hardy pasture grass. Philip and Dr. Fowler Greenhill, Doremus's son-in-law (Phil plump and half bald at thirty-two; Fowler belligerently red-headed and red-mustached) argued about the merits of the autogiro. Doremus lay with his head against a rock, his cap over his eyes, gazing down into the paradise of Beulah Valley—he could not have sworn to it, but he rather thought he saw an angel floating in the radiant upper air above the valley. The women, Emma and Mary Greenhill, Sissy and Philip's wife and Lorinda Pike, were setting out the picnic lunch—a pot of beans with crisp salt pork, fried chicken, potatoes warmed-over with croutons, tea biscuits, crab-apple jelly, salad, raisin pie—on a red-and-white tablecloth spread on a flat rock.

But for the parked motorcars, the scene might have been New England in 1885, and you could see the women in chip hats and tight-bodiced, high-necked frocks with bustles; the men in straw boaters with dangling ribbons and adorned with side-whiskers—Doremus's beard not clipped, but flowing like a bridal veil. When Dr. Greenhill fetched down Cousin Henry Veeder, a bulky yet shy enough pre-Ford farmer in clean, faded overalls, then was Time again unbought, secure, serene.

And the conversation had a comfortable triviality, an affectionate Victorian dullness. However Doremus might fret about "conditions," however skittishly Sissy might long for the presence of her beaux, Julian Falck and Malcolm Tasbrough, there was nothing modern and neurotic, nothing savoring of Freud, Adler, Marx, Bertrand Russell, or any other divinity of the 1930's, when Mother Emma chattered to Mary and Merilla about her rose bushes that had "winter-killed," and the new young maples that the field mice had gnawed, and the difficulty of getting Shad Ledue to bring in enough fireplace wood, and how Shad gorged pork chops and fried potatoes and pie at lunch, which he ate at the Jessups'.

And the View. The women talked about the View as honeymooners once talked at Niagara Falls.

David and Buck Titus were playing ship, now, on a rearing rock—it was the bridge, and David was Captain Popeye, with Buck his bosun; and even Dr. Greenhill, that impetuous crusader who was constantly infuriating the county board of health by reporting the slovenly state of the poor farm and the stench in the county jail, was lazy in the sun and with the greatest of concentration kept an unfortunate little ant running back and forth on a twig. His wife Mary—the golfer, the runner-up in state tennis tournaments, the giver of smart but not too bibulous cocktail parties at the country club, the wearer of smart brown tweeds with a green scarf—seemed to have dropped gracefully back into the domesticity of her mother, and to consider as a very weighty thing a recipe for celery-and-roquefort sandwiches on toasted soda crackers. She was the handsome Older Jessup Girl again, back in the white house with the mansard roof.

And Foolish, lying on his back with his four paws idiotically flopping, was the most pastorally old-fashioned of them all.

The only serious flare of conversation was when Buck Titus snarled to Doremus: "Certainly a lot of Messiahs pottin' at you from the bushes these days—Buzz Windrip and Bishop Prang and Father Coughlin and Dr. Townsend (though he seems to have gone back to Nazareth) and Upton Sinclair and Rev. Frank Buchman and Bernarr Macfadden and Willum Randolph Hearst and Governor Talmadge and Floyd Olson and—— Say, I swear the best Messiah in the whole show is this darky, Father Divine. He doesn't just promise he's going to feed the Underprivileged ten years from now—he hands out the fried drumsticks and gizzard right along with the Salvation. How about *him* for President?"

Out of nowhere appeared Julian Falck.

This young man, freshman in Amherst the past year, grandson of the Episcopal rector and living with the old man because his parents were dead, was in the eyes of Doremus the most nearly tolerable of Sissy's suitors. He was Swede-blond and wiry, with a neat, small face and canny eyes. He called Doremus "sir," and he had, unlike most of the radio-and-motor-hypnotized eighteen-year-olds in the Fort, read a book, and voluntarily—read Thomas Wolfe and William Rollins, John Strachey and Stuart Chase and Ortega. Whether Sissy preferred him to Malcolm Tasbrough, her father did not know. Malcolm was taller and thicker than Julian, and he drove his own streamline De Soto, while Julian could only borrow his grandfather's shocking old flivver.

Sissy and Julian bickered amiably about Alice Aylot's skill in backgammon, and Foolish scratched himself in the sun.

But Doremus was not being pastoral. He was being anxious and scientific. While the others jeered, "When does Dad take his audition?" and "What's he learning to be—a crooner or a hockey-announcer?" Doremus was adjusting the doubtful portable radio. Once he thought he was going to be with them in the Home Sweet Home atmosphere, for he tuned in on a program of old songs, and all of them, including Cousin Henry Veeder, who had a hidden passion for fiddlers and barn dances and parlor organs, hummed "Gaily the Troubadour" and "Maid of Athens" and "Darling Nelly Gray." But when the announcer informed them that these ditties were being sponsored by Toily Oily, the Natural Home Cathartic, and that they were being rendered by a sextette of young males horribly called "The Smoothies," Doremus abruptly shut them off.

"Why, what's the matter, Dad?" cried Sissy.

" 'Smoothies'! God! This country deserves what it's going to get!" snapped Doremus. "Maybe we need a Buzz Windrip!"

The moment, then—it should have been announced by cathedral chimes—of the weekly address of Bishop Paul Peter Prang.

Coming from an airless closet, smelling of sacerdotal woolen union suits, in Persepolis, Indiana, it leapt to the farthest stars; it circled the world at 186,000 miles a second—a million miles while you stopped to scratch. It crashed into the cabin of a whaler on a dark polar sea; into an office, paneled with linen-fold oak looted from a Nottinghamshire castle, on the sixty-seventh story of a building on Wall Street; into the foreign office in Tokio; into the rocky hollow below the shining birches upon Mount Terror, in Vermont.

Bishop Prang spoke, as he usually did, with a grave kindliness, a virile resonance, which made his self, magically coming to them on the unseen aërial pathway, at once dominating and touched with charm; and whatever his purposes might be, his words were on the side of the Angels:

"My friends of the radio audience, I shall have but six more weekly petitions to make you before the national conventions, which will decide the fate of this distraught nation, and the time has come now to act—to act! Enough of words! Let me put together certain separated phrases out of the sixth chapter of Jeremiah, which seem to have been prophetically written for this hour of desperate crisis in America:

" 'Oh ye children of Benjamin, gather yourselves together to flee out of the midst of Jerusalem. . . . Prepare ye war . . . arise and let us go up at noon. Woe unto us! for the day goeth away, for the shadows of the evening are stretched out. Arise, and let us go by night and let us destroy her palaces. . . . I am full of the fury of the Lord; I am weary with holding it in; I will pour it out upon the children abroad, and upon the assembly of young men together; for even the husband with the wife shall be taken, the aged with him that is full of days. . . . I will stretch out my hand upon the inhabitants of this land, saith the Lord. For from the least of them even unto the greatest, every one is given to covetousness; and from the prophet even unto the priest, every one dealeth falsely . . . saying Peace, Peace, when there is no Peace!'

"So spake the Book, of old. . . . But it was spoken also to America, of 1936!

"There is no Peace! For more than a year now, the League of Forgotten Men has warned the politicians, the whole government, that we are sick unto death of being the Dispossessed—and that, at last, we are more than fifty million strong; no whimpering horde, but with the will, the voices, the *votes* to enforce our sovereignty! We have in no uncertain way informed every politician that we demand—that we *demand*—certain measures, and that we will brook no delay. Again and again we have demanded that both the control of credit and the power to issue money be unqualifiedly taken away from the private banks; that the soldiers not only receive the bonus they with their blood and anguish so richly earned in '17 and '18, but that the amount agreed upon be now doubled; that all swollen incomes be severely limited and inheritances cut to such small sums as may support the heirs only in youth and in old age; that labor and farmers' unions be not merely recognized as instruments for joint bargaining but be made, like the syndicates in Italy, official parts of the government, representing the toilers; and that International Jewish Finance and, equally, International Jewish Communism and Anarchism and Atheism be, with all the stern solemnity and rigid inflexibility this great nation can show, barred from all activity. Those of you who have listened to me before will understand that I—or rather that the League of Forgotten Men—has no quarrel with individual Jews; that we are proud to have Rabbis among our directors; but those subversive international organizations which, unfortunately, are so largely Jewish, must be driven with whips and scorpions from off the face of the earth.

"These demands we have made, and how long now,

O Lord, how long, have the politicians and the smirking representatives of Big Business pretended to listen, to obey? 'Yes—yes—my masters of the League of Forgotten Men—yes, we understand—just give us time!'

"There is no more time! Their time is over and all their unholy power!

"The conservative Senators—the United States Chamber of Commerce—the giant bankers—the monarchs of steel and motors and electricity and coal—the brokers and the holding-companies—they are all of them like the Bourbon kings, of whom it was said that 'they forgot nothing and they learned nothing.'

"But they died upon the guillotine!

"Perhaps we can be more merciful to our Bourbons. Perhaps—*perhaps*—we can save them from the guillotine—the gallows—the swift firing-squad. Perhaps we shall, in our new régime, under our new Constitution, with our 'New Deal' that really *will* be a New Deal and not an arrogant experiment—perhaps we shall merely make these big bugs of finance and politics sit on hard chairs, in dingy offices, toiling unending hours with pen and typewriter as so many white-collar slaves for so many years have toiled for *them*!

"It is, as Senator Berzelius Windrip puts it, 'the zero hour,' now, this second. We have stopped bombarding the heedless ears of these false masters. We're 'going over the top.' At last, after months and months of taking counsel together, the directors of the League of Forgotten Men, and I myself, announce that in the coming Democratic national convention we shall, without one smallest reservation——"

"Listen! Listen! History being made!" Doremus cried at his heedless family.

"—use the tremendous strength of the millions of League members to secure the Democratic presidential nomination for *Senator—Berzelius—Windrip*—which means, flatly, that he will be elected—and that we of the League shall elect him—as President of these United States!

"His program and that of the League do not in all details agree. But he has implicitly pledged himself to take our advice, and, at least until election, we shall back him, absolutely—with our money, with our loyalty, with our votes . . . with our prayers. And may the Lord guide him and us across the desert of iniquitous politics and swinishly grasping finance into the golden glory of the Promised Land! God bless you!"

Mrs. Jessup said cheerily, "Why, Dormouse, that bishop isn't a Fascist at all—he's a regular Red Radical. But does this announcement of his mean anything, really?"

Oh, well, Doremus reflected, he had lived with Emma for thirty-four years, and not oftener than once or twice a year had he wanted to murder her. Blandly he said, "Why, nothing much except that in a couple of years now, on the ground of protecting us, the Buzz Windrip dictatorship will be regimenting everything, from where we may pray to what detective stories we may read."

"Sure he will! Sometimes I'm tempted to turn Communist! Funny—me with my fat-headed old Hudson-River-Valley Dutch ancestors!" marveled Julian Falck.

"Fine idea! Out of the frying pan of Windrip and Hitler into the fire of the New York *Daily Worker* and Stalin and automatics! And the Five-Year Plan—I suppose they'd tell me that it's been decided by the Commissar that each of my mares is to bear six colts a year now!" snorted Buck Titus; while Dr. Fowler Greenhill jeered:

"Aw, shoot, Dad—and you too, Julian, you young paranoiac—you're monomaniacs! Dictatorship? Better come into the office and let me examine your heads! Why, America's the only free nation on earth. Besides! Country's too big for a revolution. No, no! Couldn't happen here!"

6

I'd rather follow a wild-eyed anarchist like Em Goldman, if they'd bring more johnnycake and beans and spuds into the humble cabin of the Common Man, than a twenty-four-carat, college-graduate, ex-cabinet-member statesman that was just interested in our turning out more limousines. Call me a socialist or any blame thing you want to, as long as you grab hold of the other end of the cross-cut saw with me and help slash the big logs of Poverty and Intolerance to pieces.

Zero Hour, Berzelius Windrip.

HIS FAMILY—at least his wife and the cook, Mrs. Candy, and Sissy and Mary, Mrs. Fowler Greenhill—believed that Doremus was of fickle health; that any cold would surely turn into pneumonia; that he must wear his rubbers, and eat his porridge, and smoke fewer cigarettes, and never "overdo." He raged at them; he knew that though he did get staggeringly tired after a crisis in the office, a night's sleep made him a little dynamo again, and he could "turn out copy" faster than his spryest young reporter.

He concealed his dissipations from them like any small boy from his elders; lied unscrupulously about how many cigarettes he smoked; kept concealed a flask of Bourbon from which he regularly had one nip, only one, before he padded to bed; and when he had promised to go to sleep early, he turned off his light till he was sure that Emma was slumbering, then turned it on and happily read till two, curled under the well-loved hand-woven blankets from a loom up on Mount Terror; his legs twitching like a dreaming setter's what time the Chief

Inspector of the C.I.D., alone and unarmed, walked into the counterfeiters' hideout. And once a month or so he sneaked down to the kitchen at three in the morning and made himself coffee and washed up everything so that Emma and Mrs. Candy would never know. . . . He thought they never knew!

These small deceptions gave him the ripest satisfaction in a life otherwise devoted to public service, to trying to make Shad Ledue edge-up the flower beds, to feverishly writing editorials that would excite 3 per cent of his readers from breakfast time till noon and by 6 P.M. be eternally forgotten.

Sometimes when Emma came to loaf beside him in bed on a Sunday morning and put her comfortable arm about his thin shoulder-blades, she was sick with the realization that he was growing older and more frail. His shoulders, she thought, were pathetic as those of an anemic baby. . . . That sadness of hers Doremus never guessed.

Even just before the paper went to press, even when Shad Ledue took off two hours and charged an item of two dollars to have the lawnmower sharpened, instead of filing it himself, even when Sissy and her gang played the piano downstairs till two on nights when he did not want to lie awake, Doremus was never irritable—except, usually, between arising and the first life-saving cup of coffee.

The wise Emma was happy when he was snappish before breakfast. It meant that he was energetic and popping with satisfactory ideas.

After Bishop Prang had presented the crown to Senator Windrip, as the summer hobbled nervously toward the national political conventions, Emma was disturbed. For Doremus was silent before breakfast, and he had rheumy eyes, as though he was worried, as though he had slept badly. Never was he cranky. She missed hearing him croaking, "Isn't that confounded idiot, Mrs. Candy, *ever* going to bring in the coffee? I suppose she's sitting there reading her Testament! And will you be so kind as to tell me, my good woman, why Sissy *never* gets up for breakfast, even after the rare nights when she goes to bed at 1 A.M.? And—and will you look out at that walk! Covered with dead blossoms. That swine Shad hasn't swept it for a week. I swear, I *am* going to fire him, and right away, this morning!"

Emma would have been happy to hear these familiar animal sounds, and to cluck in answer, "Oh, why, that's terrible! I'll go tell Mrs. Candy to hustle in the coffee right away!"

But he sat unspeaking, pale, opening his *Daily Informer* as though he were afraid to see what news had come in since he had left the office at ten.

When Doremus, back in the 1920's, had advocated the recognition of Russia, Fort Beulah had fretted that he was turning out-and-out Communist.

He, who understood himself abnormally well, knew that far from being a left-wing radical, he was at most a mild, rather indolent and somewhat sentimental Liberal, who disliked pomposity, the heavy humor of public men, and the itch for notoriety which made popular preachers and eloquent educators and amateur play-producers and rich lady reformers and rich lady sportswomen and almost every brand of rich lady come preeningly in to see newspaper editors, with photographs under their arms, and on their faces the simper of fake humility. But for all cruelty and intolerance, and for the contempt of the fortunate for the unfortunate, he had not mere dislike but testy hatred.

He had alarmed all his fellow editors in northern New England by asserting the innocence of Tom Mooney, questioning the guilt of Sacco and Vanzetti, condemning our intrusion in Haiti and Nicaragua, advocating an increased income tax, writing, in the 1932 campaign, a friendly account of the Socialist candidate, Norman Thomas (and afterwards, to tell the truth, voting for Franklin Roosevelt), and stirring up a little local and ineffective hell regarding the serfdom of the Southern sharecroppers and the California fruit-pickers. He even suggested editorially that when Russia had her factories and railroads and giant farms really going—say, in 1945—she might conceivably be the pleasantest country in the world for the (mythical!) Average Man. When he wrote that editorial, after a lunch at which he had been irritated by the smug croaking of Frank Tasbrough and R. C. Crowley, he really did get into trouble. He got named Bolshevik, and in two days his paper lost a hundred and fifty out of its five thousand circulation.

Yet he was as little of a Bolshevik as Herbert Hoover.

He was, and he knew it, a small-town bourgeois Intellectual. Russia forbade everything that made his toil worth enduring: privacy, the right to think and to criticize as he freakishly pleased. To have his mind policed by peasants in uniform—rather than that he would live in an Alaska cabin, with beans and a hundred books and a new pair of pants every three years.

Once, on a motor trip with Emma, he stopped in at a summer camp of Communists. Most of them were City College Jews or neat Bronx dentists, spectacled, and smooth-shaven except for foppish small mustaches. They were hot to welcome these New England peasants and to explain the Marxian gospel (on which, however, they furiously differed). Over macaroni and cheese in an unpainted dining shack, they longed for the black bread of Moscow. Later, Doremus chuckled to find how much they resembled the Y.M.C.A. campers twenty miles down the highway—equally Puritanical, hortatory, and futile, and equally given to silly games with rubber balls.

Once only had he been dangerously active. He had supported the strike for union recognition against the quarry company of Francis Tasbrough. Men whom Doremus had known for years, solid cits like Superintendent of Schools Emil Staubmeyer, and Charley Betts of the furniture store, had muttered about "riding him out of town on a rail." Tasbrough reviled him—even now, eight years later. After all this, the strike had been lost, and the strike-leader, an avowed Communist named Karl Pascal, had gone to prison for "inciting to violence." When Pascal, best of mechanics, came out, he went to work in a littered little Fort Beulah garage owned by a friendly, loquacious, belligerent Polish Socialist named John Pollikop.

All day long Pascal and Pollikop yelpingly raided each other's trenches in the battle between Social Democracy and Communism, and Doremus often dropped in to stir them up. That was hard for Tasbrough, Staubmeyer, Banker Crowley, and Lawyer Kitterick to bear.

If Doremus had not come from three generations of debt-paying Vermonters, he would by now have been a penniless wandering printer . . . and possibly less detached about the Sorrows of the Dispossessed.

The conservative Emma complained: "How you can tease people this way, pretending you really *like* greasy mechanics like this Pascal (and I suspect you even have a sneaking fondness for Shad Ledue!) when you could just associate with decent, prosperous people like Frank—it's beyond me! What they must *think* of you, sometimes! They don't understand that you're really not a Socialist one bit, but really a nice, kind-hearted, responsible man. Oh, I ought to smack you, Dormouse!"

Not that he liked being called "Dormouse."

But then, no one did so except Emma and, in rare slips of the tongue, Buck Titus. So it was endurable.

7

When I am protestingly dragged from my study and the family hearthside into the public meetings that I so much detest, I try to make my speech as simple and direct as those of the Child Jesus talking to the Doctors in the Temple.

Zero Hour, Berzelius Windrip.

THUNDER IN THE MOUNTAINS, clouds marching down the Beulah Valley, unnatural darkness covering the world like black fog, and lightning that picked out ugly scarps of the hills as though they were rocks thrown up in an explosion.

To such fury of the enraged heavens, Doremus awakened on that morning of late July.

As abruptly as one who, in the death cell, startles out of sleep to the realization, "Today they'll hang me!" he sat up, bewildered, as he reflected that today Senator Berzelius Windrip would probably be nominated for President.

The Republican convention was over, with Walt Trowbridge as presidential candidate. The Democratic convention, meeting in Cleveland, with a good deal of gin, strawberry soda, and sweat, had finished the committee reports, the kind words said for the Flag, the assurances to the ghost of Jefferson that he would be delighted by what, if Chairman Jim Farley consented, would be done here this week. They had come to the nominations—Senator Windrip had been nominated by Colonel Dewey Haik, Congressman, and power in the American Legion. Gratifying applause and hasty elimination had greeted such Favorite Sons of the several states as Al Smith,

Carter Glass, William McAdoo, and Cordell Hull. Now, on the twelfth ballot, there were four contestants left, and they, in order of votes, were Senator Windrip, President Franklin D. Roosevelt, Senator Robinson of Arkansas, and Secretary of Labor Frances Perkins.

Great and dramatic shenanigans had happened, and Doremus Jessup's imagination had seen them all clearly as they were reported by the hysterical radio and by bulletins from the A.P. that fell redhot and smoking upon his desk at the *Informer* office.

In honor of Senator Robinson, the University of Arkansas brass band marched in behind a leader riding in an old horse-drawn buggy which was plastered with great placards proclaiming "Save the Constitution" and "Robinson for Sanity." The name of Miss Perkins had been cheered for two hours, while the delegates marched with their state banners, and President Roosevelt's name had been cheered for three—cheered affectionately and quite homicidally, since every delegate knew that Mr. Roosevelt and Miss Perkins were far too lacking in circus tinsel and general clownishness to succeed at this critical hour of the nation's hysteria, when the electorate wanted a ringmaster-revolutionist like Senator Windrip.

Windrip's own demonstration, scientifically worked up beforehand by his secretary-press-agent-private-philosopher, Lee Sarason, yielded nothing to others'. For Sarason had read his Chesterton well enough to know that there is only one thing bigger than a very big thing, and that is a thing so very small that it can be seen and understood.

When Colonel Dewey Haik put Buzz's name in nomination, the Colonel wound up by shouting, "One thing more! Listen! It is the special request of Senator Windrip that you do *not* waste the time of this history-making assembly by any cheering of his name—any cheering whatever. We of the League of Forgotten Men (yes—and Women!) don't want empty acclaim, but a solemn consideration of the desperate and immediate needs of 60 per cent of the population of the United States. No cheers—but may Providence guide us in the most solemn thinking we have ever done!"

As he finished, down the center aisle came a private procession. But this was no parade of thousands. There were only thirty-one persons in it, and the only banners were three flags and two large placards.

Leading it, in old blue uniforms, were two G.A.R. veterans, and between, arm-in-arm with them, a Confederate in gray. They were such very little old men, all over ninety, leaning one on another and glancing timidly about in the hope that no one would laugh at them.

The Confederate carried a Virginia regimental banner, torn as by shrapnel; and one of the Union veterans lifted high a slashed flag of the First Minnesota.

The dutiful applause which the convention had given to the demonstrations of other candidates had been but rain-patter compared with the tempest which greeted the three shaky, shuffling old men. On the platform the band played, inaudibly, "Dixie," then "When Johnny Comes Marching Home Again," and, standing on his chair midway of the auditorium, as a plain member of his state delegation, Buzz Windrip bowed—bowed—bowed and tried to smile, while tears started from his eyes and he sobbed helplessly, and the audience began to sob with him.

Following the old men were twelve Legionnaires, wounded in 1918—stumbling on wooden legs, dragging themselves between crutches; one in a wheel chair, yet so young-looking and gay; and one with a black mask before what should have been a face. Of these, one carried an enormous flag, and another a placard demanding: "Our Starving Families Must Have the Bonus—We Want Only Justice—We Want Buzz for President."

And leading them, not wounded, but upright and strong and resolute, was Major General Hermann Meinecke, United States Army. Not in all the memory of the older reporters had a soldier on active service ever appeared as a public political agitator. The press whispered one to another, "That general'll get canned, unless Buzz is elected—then he'd probably be made Duke of Hoboken."

Following the soldiers were ten men and women, their toes through their shoes, and wearing rags that were the more pitiful because they had been washed and rewashed till they had lost all color. With them tottered four pallid children, their teeth rotted out, between them just managing to hold up a placard declaring, "We Are on Relief. We Want to Become Human Beings Again. We Want Buzz!"

Twenty feet behind came one lone tall man. The delegates had been craning around to see what would follow the relief victims. When they did see, they rose, they bellowed, they clapped. For the lone man—— Few of the crowd had seen him in the flesh; all of them had seen him a hundred times in press pictures, photographed among litters of books in his study—photographed in conference with President Roosevelt and Secretary Ickes—photographed shaking hands with Senator Windrip—photographed before a microphone, his shrieking mouth a dark open trap and his lean right arm thrown up in hysterical emphasis; all of them had heard his voice on the radio till they knew it as they knew the voices of their own brothers; all of them recognized, coming through the wide main entrance, at the end of the Windrip parade, the apostle of the Forgotten Men, Bishop Paul Peter Prang.

Then the convention cheered Buzz Windrip for four unbroken hours.

In the detailed descriptions of the convention which the news bureaus sent following the feverish first bulletins, one energetic Birmingham reporter pretty well proved that the Southern battle flag carried by the Confederate veteran had been lent by the museum in Richmond and the Northern flag by a distinguished meat-packer of Chicago who was the grandson of a Civil War general.

Lee Sarason never told anyone save Buzz Windrip that both flags had been manufactured on Hester Street, New York, in 1929, for the patriotic drama, *Morgan's Riding*, and that both came from a theatrical warehouse.

Before the cheering, as the Windrip parade neared the platform, they were greeted by Mrs. Adelaide Tarr Gimmitch, the celebrated author, lecturer, and composer, who—suddenly conjured onto the platform as if whisked out of the air—sang to the tune of "Yankee Doodle" words which she herself had written:

Berzelius Windrip went to Wash.,
A riding on a hobby—
To throw Big Business out, by Gosh,
And be the People's Lobby!

Chorus:

Buzz and buzz and keep it up,
Our cares and needs he's toting,
You are a most ungrateful pup,
Unless for Buzz you're voting!

The League of the Forgotten Men
Don't like to be forgotten,
They went to Washington and then
They sang, "There's something rotten!"

That joyous battle song was sung on the radio by nineteen different prima donnas before midnight, by some sixteen million less vocal Americans within forty-eight hours, and by at least ninety million friends and scoffers in the struggle that was to come. All through the campaign, Buzz Windrip was able to get lots of jolly humor out of puns on going to Wash., and to wash. Walt Trowbridge, he jeered, wasn't going to either of them!

Yet Lee Sarason knew that in addition to this comic masterpiece, the cause of Windrip required an anthem more elevated in thought and spirit, befitting the seriousness of crusading Americans.

Long after the convention's cheering for Windrip had ended and the delegates were again at their proper business of saving the nation and cutting one another's throats, Sarason had Mrs. Gimmitch sing a more inspirational hymn, with words by Sarason himself, in collaboration with a quite remarkable surgeon, one Dr. Hector Macgoblin.

This Dr. Macgoblin, soon to become a national monument, was as accomplished in syndicated medical journalism, in the reviewing of books about education and psychoanalysis, in preparing glosses upon the philosophies of Hegel, Professor Guenther, Houston Stewart Chamberlain, and Lothrop Stoddard, in the rendition of

Mozart on the violin, in semi-professional boxing, and in the composition of epic poetry, as he was in the practice of medicine.

Dr. Macgoblin! What a man!

The Sarason-Macgoblin ode, entitled "Bring Out the Old-time Musket," became to Buzz Windrip's band of liberators what "Giovanezza" was to the Italians, "The Horst Wessel Song" to the Nazis, "The International" to all Marxians. Along with the convention, the radio millions heard Mrs. Adelaide Tarr Gimmitch's contralto, rich as peat, chanting:

BRING OUT THE OLD-TIME MUSKET

Dear Lord, we have sinned, we have slumbered,
And our flag lies stained in the dust,
And the souls of the Past are calling, calling,
"Arise from your sloth—you must!"
Lead us, O soul of Lincoln,
Inspire us, spirit of Lee,
To rule all the world for righteousness,
To fight for the right,
To awe with our might,
As we did in 'sixty-three.

Chorus:

See, youth with desire hot glowing,
See, maiden, with fearless eye,
Leading our ranks
Thunder the tanks,
Aëroplanes cloud the sky.

Bring out the old-time musket,
Rouse up the old-time fire!
See, all the world is crumbling,
Dreadful and dark and dire.
America! Rise and conquer
The world to our heart's desire!

"Great showmanship. P. T. Barnum or Flo Ziegfeld never put on a better," mused Doremus, as he studied the A.P. flimsies, as he listened to the radio he had had temporarily installed in his office. And, much later: "When Buzz gets in, he won't be having any parade of wounded soldiers. That'll be bad Fascist psychology. All those poor devils he'll hide away in institutions, and just bring out the lively young human slaughter cattle in uniforms. Hm."

The thunderstorm, which had mercifully lulled, burst again in wrathful menace.

All afternoon the convention balloted, over and over, with no change in the order of votes for the presidential candidate. Toward six, Miss Perkins's manager threw her votes to Roosevelt, who gained then on Senator Windrip. They seemed to have settled down to an all-night struggle, and at ten in the evening Doremus wearily left the office. He did not, tonight, want the sympathetic and extremely feminized atmosphere of his home, and he dropped in at the rectory of his friend Father Perefixe. There he found a satisfyingly unfeminized, untalcumized group. The Reverend Mr. Falck was there. Swart, sturdy young Perefixe and silvery old Falck often worked together, were fond of each other, and agreed upon the advantages of clerical celibacy and almost every other doctrine except the supremacy of the Bishop of Rome. With them were Buck Titus, Louis Rotenstern, Dr. Fowler Greenhill, and Banker Crowley, a financier who liked to cultivate an appearance of free intellectual discussion, though only after the hours devoted to refusing credit to desperate farmers and storekeepers.

And not to be forgotten was Foolish the dog, who that thunderous morning had suspected his master's worry, followed him to the office, and all day long had growled at Haik and Sarason and Mrs. Gimmitch on the radio and showed an earnest conviction that he ought to chew up all flimsies reporting the convention.

Better than his own glacial white-paneled drawing room with its portraits of dead Vermont worthies, Doremus liked Father Perefixe's little study, and its combination of churchliness, of freedom from Commerce (at least ordinary Commerce), as displayed in a crucifix and a plaster statuette of the Virgin and a shrieking red-and-green Italian picture of the Pope, with practical affairs, as shown in the oak roll-top desk and steel filing-cabinet and well-worn portable typewriter. It was a pious hermit's cave with the advantages of leather chairs and excellent rye highballs.

The night passed as the eight of them (for Foolish too had his tipple of milk) all sipped and listened; the night passed as the convention balloted, furiously, unavailingly . . . that congress six hundred miles away, six hundred miles of befogged night, yet with every speech, every derisive yelp, coming into the priest's cabinet in the same second in which they were heard in the hall at Cleveland.

Father Perefixe's housekeeper (who was sixty-five years old to his thirty-nine, to the disappointment of all the scandal-loving local Protestants) came in with scrambled eggs, cold beer.

"When my dear wife was still among us, she used to send me to bed at midnight," sighed Dr. Falck.

"My wife does now!" said Doremus.

"So would mine, I betcha—if I had one," said Louis Rotenstern derisively.

"Father Steve, here, and I are the only guys with a sensible way of living," crowed Buck Titus. "Celibates. We can go to bed with our pants on, or not go to bed at all," and Father Perefixe murmured, "But it's curious, Buck, what people find to boast of—you that you're free of God's tyranny and also that you can go to bed in your pants—Mr. Falck and Dr. Greenhill and I that God is so lenient with us that some nights He lets us off from sick-calls and we can go to bed with 'em off! And Louis because—— Listen! Listen! Sounds like business!"

Colonel Dewey Haik, Buzz's proposer, was announcing that Senator Windrip felt it would be only modest of him to go to his hotel now, but he had left a letter which he, Haik, would read. And he did read it, inexorably.

Windrip stated that, just in case anyone did not completely understand his platform, he wanted to make it all ringingly clear.

Summarized, the letter explained that he was all against the banks but all for the bankers—except the Jewish bankers, who were to be driven out of finance entirely; that he had thoroughly tested (but unspecified) plans to make all wages very high and the prices of everything produced by these same highly paid workers very low; that he was 100 per cent for Labor, but 100 per cent against all strikes; and that he was in favor of the United States so arming itself, so preparing to produce its own coffee, sugar, perfumes, tweeds, and nickel instead of importing them, that it could defy the World . . . and maybe, if that World was so impertinent as to defy America in turn, Buzz hinted, he might have to take it over and run it properly.

Each moment the brassy importunities of the radio seemed to Doremus the more offensive, while the hillside slept in the heavy summer night, and he thought about the mazurka of the fireflies, the rhythm of crickets like the rhythm of the revolving earth itself, the voluptuous breezes that bore away the stink of cigars and sweat and whisky breaths and mint chewing-gum that seemed to come to them from the convention over the sound waves, along with the oratory.

It was after dawn, and Father Perefixe (unclerically stripped to shirt-sleeves and slippers) had just brought them in a grateful tray of onion soup, with a gob of Hamburg steak for Foolish, when the opposition to Buzz collapsed and hastily, on the next ballot, Senator Berzelius Windrip was nominated as Democratic Candidate for President of the United States.

Doremus, Buck Titus, Perefixe, and Falck were for a time too gloomy for speech—so possibly was the dog Foolish, as well, for at the turning off of the radio he tail-thumped in only the most tentative way.

R. C. Crowley gloated, "Well, all my life I've voted Republican, but here's a man that—— Well, I'm going to vote for Windrip!"

Father Perefixe said tartly, "And I've voted Democratic ever since I came from Canada and got naturalized, but this time I'm going to vote Republican. What about you fellows?"

Rotenstern was silent. He did not like Windrip's reference to Jews. The ones he knew best—no, they were Americans! Lincoln was his tribal god too, he vowed.

"Me? I'll vote for Walt Trowbridge, of course," growled Buck.

"So will I," said Doremus. "No! I won't either! Trowbridge won't have a chance. I think I'll indulge in the luxury of being independent, for once, and vote Prohibition or the Battle-Creek bran-and-spinach ticket, or anything that makes some sense!"

It was after seven that morning when Doremus came home, and, remarkably enough, Shad Ledue, who was supposed to go to work at seven, was at work at seven. Normally he never left his bachelor shack in Lower Town till ten to eight, but this morning he was on the job, chopping kindling. (Oh yes, reflected Doremus—that probably explained it. Kindling-chopping, if practised early enough, would wake up everyone in the house.)

Shad was tall and hulking; his shirt was sweat-stained; and as usual he needed a shave. Foolish growled at him. Doremus suspected that at some time he had been kicking Foolish. He wanted to honor Shad for the sweaty shirt, the honest toil, and all the rugged virtues, but even as a Liberal American Humanitarian, Doremus found it hard always to keep up the Longfellow's-Village-Blacksmith-cum-Marx attitude consistently and not sometimes backslide into a belief that there must be *some* crooks and swine among the toilers as, notoriously, there were so shockingly many among persons with more than $3500 a year.

"Well—been sitting up listening to the radio," purred Doremus. "Did you know the Democrats have nominated Senator Windrip?"

"That so?" Shad growled.

"Yes. Just now. How you planning to vote?"

"Well now, I'll tell you, Mr. Jessup." Shad struck an attitude, leaning on his ax. Sometimes he could be quite pleasant and condescending, even to this little man who was so ignorant about coon-hunting and the games of craps and poker.

"I'm going to vote for Buzz Windrip. He's going to fix it so everybody will get four thousand bucks, immediate, and I'm going to start a chicken farm. I can make a bunch of money out of chickens! I'll show some of these guys that think they're so rich!"

"But, Shad, you didn't have so much luck with chickens when you tried to raise 'em in the shed back there. You, uh, I'm afraid you sort of let their water freeze up on 'em in winter, and they all died, you remember."

"Oh, them? So what! Heck! There was too few of 'em. I'm not going to waste *my* time foolin' with just a couple dozen chickens! When I get five-six thousand of 'em to make it worth my while, *then* I'll show you! You bet." And, most patronizingly: "Buzz Windrip is O.K."

"I'm glad he has your *imprimatur.*"

"Huh?" said Shad, and scowled.

But as Doremus plodded up on the back porch he heard from Shad a faint derisive:

"O.K., Chief!"

8

I don't pretend to be a very educated man, except maybe educated in the heart, and in being able to feel for the sorrows and fears of every ornery fellow human being. Still and all, I've read the Bible through, from kiver to kiver, like my wife's folks say down in Arkansas, some eleven times; I've read all the law books they've printed; and as to contemporaries, I don't guess I've missed much of all the grand literature produced by Bruce Barton, Edgar Guest, Arthur Brisbane, Elizabeth Dilling, Walter Pitkin, and William Dudley Pelley.

This last gentleman I honor not only for his rattling good yarns, and his serious work in investigating life beyond the grave and absolutely proving that only a blind fool could fail to believe in Personal Immortality, but, finally, for his public-spirited and self-sacrificing work in founding the Silver Shirts. These true knights, even if they did not attain quite all the success they deserved, were one of our most noble and Galahad-like attempts to combat the sneaking, snaky, sinister, surreptitious, seditious plots of the Red Radicals and other sour brands of Bolsheviks that incessantly threaten the American standards of Liberty, High Wages, and Universal Security.

These fellows have Messages, and we haven't got time for anything in literature except a straight, hard-hitting, heart-throbbing Message!

Zero Hour, Berzelius Windrip.

DURING THE VERY first week of his campaign, Senator Windrip clarified his philosophy by issuing his distinguished proclamation: "The Fifteen Points of Victory for the Forgotten Men." The fifteen planks, in his own words (or maybe in Lee Sarason's words, or Dewey Haik's words), were these:

(1) All finance in the country, including banking, insurance, stocks and bonds and mortgages, shall be under the absolute control of a Federal Central Bank, owned by the government and conducted by a Board appointed by the President, which Board shall, without need of recourse to Congress for legislative authorization, be empowered to make all regulations governing finance. Thereafter, as soon as may be practicable, this said Board shall consider the nationalization and government-ownership, for the Profit of the Whole People, of all mines, oilfields, water power, public utilities, transportation, and communication.

(2) The President shall appoint a commission, equally divided between manual workers, employers, and representatives of the Public, to determine which Labor Unions are qualified to represent the Workers; and report to the Executive, for legal action, all pretended labor organizations, whether "Company Unions," or "Red Unions," controlled by Communists and the so-called "Third International." The duly recognized Unions shall be constituted Bureaus of the Government, with power of decision in all labor disputes. Later, the same investigation and official recognition shall be extended to farm organizations. In this elevation of the position of the Worker, it shall be emphasized that the League of Forgotten Men is the chief bulwark against the menace of destructive and un-American Radicalism.

(3) In contradistinction to the doctrines of Red Radicals, with their felonious expropriation of the arduously acquired possessions which insure to aged persons their security, this League and Party will guarantee Private Initiative and the Right to Private Property for all time.

(4) Believing that only under God Almighty, to Whom we render all homage, do we Americans hold our vast Power, we shall guarantee to all persons absolute freedom of religious worship, provided, however, that no atheist, agnostic, believer in Black Magic, nor any Jew who shall refuse to swear allegiance to the New Testa-

ment, nor any person of any faith who refuses to take the Pledge to the Flag, shall be permitted to hold any public office or to practice as a teacher, professor, lawyer, judge, or as a physician, except in the category of Obstetrics.

(5) Annual net income per person shall be limited to $500,000. No accumulated fortune may at any one time exceed $3,000,000 per person. No one person shall, during his entire lifetime, be permitted to retain an inheritance or various inheritances in total exceeding $2,000,000. All incomes or estates in excess of the sums named shall be seized by the Federal Government for use in Relief and in Administrative expenses.

(6) Profit shall be taken out of War by seizing all dividends over and above 6 per cent that shall be received from the manufacture, distribution, or sale, during Wartime, of all arms, munitions, aircraft, ships, tanks, and all other things directly applicable to warfare, as well as from food, textiles, and all other supplies furnished to the American or to any allied army.

(7) Our armaments and the size of our military and naval establishments shall be consistently enlarged until they shall equal, but—since this country has no desire for foreign conquest of any kind—not surpass, in every branch of the forces of defense, the martial strength of any other single country or empire in the world. Upon inauguration, this League and Party shall make this its first obligation, together with the issuance of a firm proclamation to all nations of the world that our armed forces are to be maintained solely for the purpose of insuring world peace and amity.

(8) Congress shall have the sole right to issue money and immediately upon our inauguration it shall at least double the present supply of money, in order to facilitate the fluidity of credit.

(9) We cannot too strongly condemn the un-Christian attitude of certain otherwise progressive nations in their discriminations against the Jews, who have been among the strongest supporters of the League, and who will continue to prosper and to be recognized as fully Americanized, though only so long as they continue to support our ideals.

(10) All Negroes shall be prohibited from voting, holding public office, practicing law, medicine, or teaching in any class above the grade of grammar school, and they shall be taxed 100 per cent of all sums in excess of $10,000 per family per year which they may earn or in any other manner receive. In order, however, to give the most sympathetic aid possible to all Negroes who comprehend their proper and valuable place in society, all such colored persons, male or female, as can prove that they have devoted not less than forty-five years to such suitable tasks as domestic service, agricultural labor, and common labor in industries, shall at the age of sixty-five be permitted to appear before a special Board, composed entirely of white persons, and upon proof that while employed they have never been idle except through sickness, they shall be recommended for pensions not to exceed the sum of $500.00 per person per year, nor to exceed $700.00 per family. Negroes shall, by definition, be persons with at least one sixteenth colored blood.

(11) Far from opposing such high-minded and economically sound methods of the relief of poverty, unemployment, and old age as the EPIC plan of the Hon. Upton Sinclair, the "Share the Wealth" and "Every Man a King" proposals of the late Hon. Huey Long to assure every family $5000 a year, the Townsend plan, the Utopian plan, Technocracy, and all competent schemes of unemployment insurance, a Commission shall immediately be appointed by the New Administration to study, reconcile, and recommend for immediate adoption the best features in these several plans for Social Security, and the Hon. Messrs. Sinclair, Townsend, Eugene Reed, and Howard Scott are herewith invited to in every way advise and collaborate with that Commission.

(12) All women now employed shall, as rapidly as possible, except in such peculiarly feminine spheres of activity as nursing and beauty parlors, be assisted to return to their incomparably sacred duties as home-makers and as mothers of strong, honorable future Citizens of the Commonwealth.

(13) Any person advocating Communism, Socialism, or Anarchism, advocating refusal to enlist in case of war,

or advocating alliance with Russia in any war whatsoever, shall be subject to trial for high treason, with a minimum penalty of twenty years at hard labor in prison, and a maximum of death on the gallows, or other form of execution which the judges may find convenient.

(14) All bonuses promised to former soldiers of any war in which America has ever engaged shall be immediately paid in full, in cash, and in all cases of veterans with incomes of less than $5,000.00 a year, the formerly promised sums shall be doubled.

(15) Congress shall, immediately upon our inauguration, initiate amendments to the Constitution providing (a), that the President shall have the authority to institute and execute all necessary measures for the conduct of the government during this critical epoch; (b), that Congress shall serve only in an advisory capacity, calling to the attention of the President and his aides and Cabinet any needed legislation, but not acting upon same until authorized by the President so to act; and (c), that the Supreme Court shall immediately have removed from its jurisdiction the power to negate, by ruling them to be unconstitutional or by any other judicial action, any or all acts of the President, his duly appointed aides, or Congress.

Addendum: It shall be strictly understood that, as the League of Forgotten Men and the Democratic Party, as now constituted, have no purpose nor desire to carry out any measure that shall not unqualifiedly meet with the desire of the majority of voters in these United States, the League and Party regard none of the above fifteen points as obligatory and unmodifiable except No. 15, and upon the others they will act or refrain from acting in accordance with the general desire of the Public, who shall under the new régime be again granted an individual freedom of which they have been deprived by the harsh and restrictive economic measures of former administrations, both Republican and Democratic.

"But what does it mean?" marveled Mrs. Jessup, when her husband had read the platform to her. "It's so inconsistent. Sounds like a combination of Norman Thomas and Calvin Coolidge. I don't seem to understand it. I wonder if Mr. Windrip understands it himself?"

"Sure. You bet he does. It mustn't be supposed that because Windrip gets that intellectual dressmaker Sarason to prettify his ideas up for him he doesn't recognize 'em and clasp 'em to his bosom when they're dolled up in two-dollar words. I'll tell you just what it all means: Articles One and Five mean that if the financiers and transportation kings and so on don't come through heavily with support for Buzz they may be threatened with bigger income taxes and some control of their businesses. But they are coming through, I hear, handsomely—they're paying for Buzz's radio and his parades. Two, that by controlling their unions directly, Buzz's gang can kidnap all Labor into slavery. Three backs up the security for Big Capital and Four brings the preachers into line as scared and unpaid press-agents for Buzz.

"Six doesn't mean anything at all—munition firms with vertical trusts will be able to wangle one 6 per cent on manufacture, one on transportation, and one on sales—at least. Seven means we'll get ready to follow all the European nations in trying to hog the whole world. Eight means that by inflation, big industrial companies will be able to buy their outstanding bonds back at a cent on the dollar, and Nine that all Jews who don't cough up plenty of money for the robber baron will be punished, even including the Jews who haven't much to cough up. Ten, that all well-paying jobs and businesses held by Negroes will be grabbed by the Poor White Trash among Buzz's worshipers—and that instead of being denounced they'll be universally praised as patriotic protectors of Racial Purity. Eleven, that Buzz'll be able to pass the buck for not creating any real relief for poverty. Twelve, that women will later lose the vote and the right to higher education and be foxed out of all decent jobs and urged to rear soldiers to be killed in foreign wars. Thirteen, that anybody who opposes Buzz in any way at all can be called a Communist and scragged for it. Why, under this clause, Hoover and Al Smith and Ogden Mills—yes, and you and me—will all be Communists.

"Fourteen, that Buzz thinks enough of the support of the veterans' vote to be willing to pay high for it—in other people's money. And Fifteen—well, that's the one lone clause that really does mean something; and it means that Windrip and Lee Sarason and Bishop Prang and I guess maybe this Colonel Dewey Haik and this Dr. Hector Macgoblin—you know, this doctor that helps write the high-minded hymns for Buzz—they've realized that this country has gone so flabby that any gang daring enough and unscrupulous enough, and smart enough not to *seem* illegal, can grab hold of the entire government and have all the power and applause and salutes, all the money and palaces and willin' women they want.

"They're only a handful, but just think how small Lenin's gang was at first, and Mussolini's and Hitler's and Kemal Pasha's, and Napoleon's! You'll see all the liberal preachers and modernist educators and discontented newspapermen and farm agitators—maybe they'll worry at first, but they'll get caught up in the web of propaganda, like we all were in the Great War, and they'll all be convinced that, even if our Buzzy maybe *has* got a few faults, he's on the side of the plain people, and against all the tight old political machines, and they'll rouse the country for him as the Great Liberator (and meanwhile Big Business will just wink and sit tight!), and then, by God, this crook—oh, I don't know whether he's more of a crook or an hysterical religious fanatic—along with Sarason and Haik and Prang and Macgoblin—these five men will be able to set up a régime that'll remind you of Henry Morgan the pirate capturing a merchant ship."

"But will Americans stand for it long?" whimpered Emma. "Oh, no, not people like us—the descendants of the pioneers!"

"Dunno. I'm going to try help see that they don't. . . . Of course you understand that you and I and Sissy and Fowler and Mary will probably be shot if I do try to do anything. . . . Hm! I sound brave enough now, but probably I'll be scared to death when I hear Buzz's private troops go marching by!"

"Oh, you will be careful, won't you?" begged Emma.

"Oh. Before I forget it. How many times must I tell you, Dormouse, not to give Foolish chicken bones—they'll stick in his poor throat and choke him to death. And you just *never* remember to take the keys out of the car when you put it in the garage at night! I'm perfectly *sure* Shad Ledue or somebody will steal it one of these nights!"

Father Stephen Perefixe, when he read the Fifteen Points, was considerably angrier than Doremus.

He snorted, "What? Negroes, Jews, women—they all banned and they leave us Catholics out, this time? Hitler didn't neglect us. *He's* persecuted us. Must be that Charley Coughlin. He's made us too respectable!"

Sissy, who was eager to go to a school of architecture and become a creator of new styles in houses of glass and steel; Lorinda Pike, who had plans for a Carlsbad-Vichy-Saratoga in Vermont; Mrs. Candy, who aspired to a home bakery of her own when she should be too old for domestic labor—they were all of them angrier than either Doremus or Father Perefixe.

Sissy sounded not like a flirtatious girl but like a battling woman as she snarled, "So the League of Forgotten Men is going to make us a League of Forgotten Women! Send us back to washing diapers and leaching out ashes for soap! Let us read Louisa May Alcott and Barrie—except on the Sabbath, of course! Let us sleep in humble gratitude with men——"

"Sissy!" wailed her mother.

"—like Shad Ledue! Well, Dad, you can sit right down and write Busy Berselius for me that I'm going to England on the next boat!"

Mrs. Candy stopped drying the water glasses (with the soft dishtowels which she scrupulously washed out daily) long enough to croak, "What nasty men! I do hope they get shot soon," which for Mrs. Candy was a startlingly long and humanitarian statement.

"Yes. Nasty enough. But what I've got to keep remembering is that Windrip is only the lightest cork on the whirlpool. He didn't plot all this thing. With all the justified discontent there is against the smart politicians and the Plush Horses of Plutocracy—oh, if it hadn't been one Windrip, it'd been another. . . . We had it coming, we Respectables. . . . But that isn't going to make us like it!" thought Doremus.

9

> Those who have never been on the inside in the Councils of State can never realize that with really high-class Statesmen, their chief quality is not political canniness, but a big, rich, overflowing Love for all sorts and conditions of people and for the whole land. That Love and that Patriotism have been my sole guiding principles in Politics. My one ambition is to get all Americans to realize that they are, and must continue to be, the greatest Race on the face of this old Earth, and second, to realize that whatever apparent Differences there may be among us, in wealth, knowledge, skill, ancestry or strength—though, of course, all this does not apply to people who are *racially* different from us—we are all brothers, bound together in the great and wonderful bond of National Unity, for which we should all be very glad. And I think we ought to for this be willing to sacrifice any individual gains at all.
>
> *Zero Hour,* Berzelius Windrip.

BERZELIUS WINDRIP, of whom in late summer and early autumn of 1936 there were so many published photographs—showing him popping into cars and out of aëroplanes, dedicating bridges, eating corn pone and side-meat with Southerners and clam chowder and bran with Northerners, addressing the American Legion, the Liberty League, the Y.M.H.A., the Young People's Socialist League, the Elks, the Bartenders' and Waiters' Union, the Anti-Saloon League, the Society for the Propagation of the Gospel in Afghanistan—showing him kissing lady centenarians and shaking hands with ladies called Madame, but never the opposite—showing him in Savile Row riding-clothes on Long Island and in overalls and a khaki shirt in the Ozarks—this Buzz Windrip was almost a dwarf, yet with an enormous head, a bloodhound head, of huge ears, pendulous cheeks, mournful eyes. He had a luminous, ungrudging smile which (declared the Washington correspondents) he turned on and off deliberately, like an electric light, but which could make his ugliness more attractive than the simpers of any pretty man.

His hair was so coarse and black and straight, and worn so long in the back, that it hinted of Indian blood. In the Senate he preferred clothes that suggested the competent insurance salesman, but when farmer constituents were in Washington he appeared in an historic ten-gallon hat with a mussy gray "cutaway" which somehow you erroneously remembered as a black "Prince Albert."

In that costume, he looked like a sawed-off museum model of a medicine-show "doctor," and indeed it was rumored that during one law-school vacation Buzz Windrip had played the banjo and done card tricks and handed down medicine bottles and managed the shell game for no less scientific an expedition than Old Dr. Alagash's Traveling Laboratory, which specialized in the Choctaw Cancer Cure, the Chinook Consumption Soother, and the Oriental Remedy for Piles and Rheumatism Prepared from a World-old Secret Formula by the Gipsy Princess, Queen Peshawara. The company, ardently assisted by Buzz, killed off quite a number of persons who, but for their confidence in Dr. Alagash's bottles of water, coloring matter, tobacco juice, and raw corn whisky, might have gone early enough to doctors. But since then, Windrip had redeemed himself, no doubt, by ascending from the vulgar fraud of selling bogus medicine, standing in front of a megaphone, to the dignity of selling bogus economics, standing on an indoor platform under mercury-vapor lights in front of a microphone.

He was in stature but a small man, yet remember that so were Napoleon, Lord Beaverbrook, Stephen A. Douglas, Frederick the Great, and the Dr. Goebbels who is privily known throughout Germany as "Wotan's Mickey Mouse."

Doremus Jessup, so inconspicuous an observer, watching Senator Windrip from so humble a Bœotia, could not explain his power of bewitching large audiences. The Senator was vulgar, almost illiterate, a public liar easily detected, and in his "ideas" almost idiotic, while his celebrated piety was that of a traveling salesman for church furniture, and his yet more celebrated humor the sly cynicism of a country store.

Certainly there was nothing exhilarating in the actual words of his speeches, nor anything convincing in his philosophy. His political platforms were only wings of a windmill. Seven years before his present credo—derived from Lee Sarason, Hitler, Gottfried Feder, Rocco, and probably the revue *Of Thee I Sing*—little Buzz, back home, had advocated nothing more revolutionary than better beef stew in the county poor-farms, and plenty of graft for loyal machine politicians, with jobs for their brothers-in-law, nephews, law partners, and creditors.

Doremus had never heard Windrip during one of his orgasms of oratory, but he had been told by political reporters that under the spell you thought Windrip was Plato, but that on the way home you could not remember anything he had said.

There were two things, they told Doremus, that distinguished this prairie Demosthenes. He was an actor of genius. There was no more overwhelming actor on the stage, in the motion pictures, nor even in the pulpit. He would whirl arms, bang tables, glare from mad eyes, vomit Biblical wrath from a gaping mouth; but he would also coo like a nursing mother, beseech like an aching lover, and in between tricks would coldly and almost contemptuously jab his crowds with figures and facts—figures and facts that were inescapable even when, as often happened, they were entirely incorrect.

But below this surface stagecraft was his uncommon natural ability to be authentically excited by and with his audience, and they by and with him. He could dramatize his assertion that he was neither a Nazi nor a Fascist but a Democrat—a homespun Jeffersonian-Lincolnian-

Clevelandian-Wilsonian Democrat—and (sans scenery and costume) make you see him veritably defending the Capitol against barbarian hordes, the while he innocently presented as his own warm-hearted Democratic inventions, every anti-libertarian, anti-Semitic madness of Europe.

Aside from his dramatic glory, Buzz Windrip was a Professional Common Man.

Oh, he was common enough. He had every prejudice and aspiration of every American Common Man. He believed in the desirability and therefore the sanctity of thick buckwheat cakes with adulterated maple syrup, in rubber trays for the ice cubes in his electric refrigerator, in the especial nobility of dogs, all dogs, in the oracles of S. Parkes Cadman, in being chummy with all waitresses at all junction lunch rooms, and in Henry Ford (when he became President, he exulted, maybe he could get Mr. Ford to come to supper at the White House), and the superiority of anyone who possessed a million dollars. He regarded spats, walking sticks, caviar, titles, tea-drinking, poetry not daily syndicated in newspapers, and all foreigners, possibly excepting the British, as degenerate.

But he was the Common Man twenty-times-magnified by his oratory, so that while the other Commoners could understand his every purpose, which was exactly the same as their own, they saw him towering among them, and they raised hands to him in worship.

In the greatest of all native American arts (next to the talkies, and those Spirituals in which Negroes express their desire to go to heaven, to St. Louis, or almost any place distant from the romantic old plantations), namely, in the art of Publicity, Lee Sarason was in no way inferior even to such acknowledged masters as Edward Bernays, the late Theodore Roosevelt, Jack Dempsey, and Upton Sinclair.

Sarason had, as it was scientifically called, been "building up" Senator Windrip for seven years before his nomination as President. Where other Senators were encouraged by their secretaries and wives (no potential dictator ought ever to have a visible wife, and none ever has had, except Napoleon) to expand from village back-slapping to noble, rotund, Ciceronian gestures, Sarason had encouraged Windrip to keep up in the Great World all of the clownishness which (along with considerable legal shrewdness and the endurance to make ten speeches a day) had endeared him to his simple-hearted constituents in his native state.

Windrip danced a hornpipe before an alarmed academic audience when he got his first honorary degree; he kissed Miss Flandreau at the South Dakota beauty contest; he entertained the Senate, or at least the Senate galleries, with detailed accounts of how to catch catfish—from the bait-digging to the ultimate effects of the jug of corn whisky; he challenged the venerable Chief Justice of the Supreme Court to a duel with sling-shots.

Though she was not visible, Windrip did have a wife—Sarason had none, nor was likely to; and Walt Trowbridge was a widower. Buzz's lady stayed back home, raising spinach and chickens and telling the neighbors that she expected to go to Washington *next* year, the while Windrip was informing the press that his "Frau" was so edifyingly devoted to their two small children and to Bible study that she simply could not be coaxed to come East.

But when it came to assembling a political machine, Windrip had no need of counsel from Lee Sarason.

Where Buzz was, there were the vultures also. His hotel suite, in the capital city of his home state, in Washington, in New York, or in Kansas City, was like—well, Frank Sullivan once suggested that it resembled the office of a tabloid newspaper upon the impossible occasion of Bishop Cannon's setting fire to St. Patrick's Cathedral, kidnaping the Dionne quintuplets, and eloping with Greta Garbo in a stolen tank.

In the "parlor" of any of these suites, Buzz Windrip sat in the middle of the room, a telephone on the floor beside him, and for hours he shrieked at the instrument, "Hello—yuh—speaking," or at the door, "Come in—come in!" and "Sit down 'n' take a load off your feet!" All day, all night till dawn, he would be bellowing, "Tell him he can take his bill and go climb a tree," or "Why certainly, old man—tickled to death to support it—utility corporations cer'nly been getting a raw deal," and "You tell the Governor I want Kippy elected sheriff and I want the indictment against him quashed and I want it damn quick!" Usually, squatted there cross-legged, he would be wearing a smart belted camel's-hair coat with an atrocious checked cap.

In a fury, as he was at least every quarter hour, he would leap up, peel off the overcoat (showing either a white boiled shirt and clerical black bow, or a canary-yellow silk shirt with a scarlet tie), fling it on the floor, and put it on again with slow dignity, while he bellowed his anger like Jeremiah cursing Jerusalem, or like a sick cow mourning its kidnaped young.

There came to him stockbrokers, labor leaders, distillers, anti-vivisectionists, vegetarians, disbarred shyster lawyers, missionaries to China, lobbyists for oil and electricity, advocates of war and of war against war. "Gaw! Every guy in the country with a bad case of the gimmes comes to see me!" he growled to Sarason. He promised to further their causes, to get an appointment to West Point for the nephew who had just lost his job in the creamery. He promised fellow politicians to support their bills if they would support his. He gave interviews upon subsistance farming, backless bathing suits, and the secret strategy of the Ethiopian army. He grinned and knee-patted and back-slapped; and few of his visitors, once they had talked with him, failed to look upon him as their Little Father and to support him forever. . . . The few who did fail, most of them newspapermen, disliked the smell of him more than before they had met him. . . . Even they, by the unusual spiritedness and color of their attacks upon him, kept his name alive in every column. . . . By the time he had been a Senator for one year, his machine was as complete and smooth-running—and as hidden away from ordinary passengers—as the engines of a liner.

On the beds in any of his suites there would, at the same time, repose three top-hats, two clerical hats, a green object with a feather, a brown derby, a taxi-driver's cap, and nine ordinary, Christian brown felts.

Once, within twenty-seven minutes, he talked on the telephone from Chicago to Palo Alto, Washington, Buenos Aires, Wilmette, and Oklahoma City. Once, in half a day, he received sixteen calls from clergymen asking him to condemn the dirty burlesque show, and seven from theatrical promoters and real-estate owners asking him to praise it. He called the clergymen "Doctor" or "Brother" or both; he called the promoters "Buddy" and "Pal"; he gave equally ringing promises to both; and for both he loyally did nothing whatever.

Normally, he would not have thought of cultivating foreign alliances, though he never doubted that some day, as President, he would be leader of the world orchestra, Lee Sarason insisted that Buzz look into a few international fundamentals, such as the relationship of sterling to the lira, the proper way in which to address a baronet, the chances of the Archduke Otto, the London oyster bars and the brothels near the Boulevard de Sebastopol best to recommend to junketing Representatives.

But the actual cultivation of foreign diplomats resident in Washington he left to Sarason, who entertained them on terrapin and canvasback duck with black-currant jelly, in his apartment that was considerably more tapestried than Buzz's own ostentatiously simple Washington quarters. . . . However, in Sarason's place, a room with a large silk-hung Empire double bed was reserved for Buzz.

It was Sarason who had persuaded Windrip to let him write *Zero Hour,* based on Windrip's own dictated notes, and who had beguiled millions into reading—and even thousands into buying—that Bible of Economic Justice; Sarason who had perceived there was now such a spate of private political weeklies and monthlies that it was a distinction not to publish one; Sarason who had the inspiration for Buzz's emergency radio address at 3 A.M. upon the occasion of the Supreme Court's throttling the N.R.A., in May, 1935. . . . Though not many adherents, including Buzz himself, were quite certain as to whether he was pleased or disappointed; though not many actually heard the broadcast itself, everyone in the country except sheep-herders and Professor Albert Einstein heard about it and was impressed.

Yet it was Buzz who all by himself thought of first

offending the Duke of York by refusing to appear at the Embassy dinner for him in December, 1935, thus gaining, in all farm kitchens and parsonages and barrooms, a splendid reputation for Homespun Democracy; and of later mollifying His Highness by calling on him with a touching little home bouquet of geraniums (from the hothouse of the Japanese ambassador), which endeared him, if not necessarily to Royalty yet certainly to the D.A.R., the English-Speaking Union, and all motherly hearts who thought the pudgy little bunch of geraniums too sweet for anything.

By the newspapermen Buzz was credited with having insisted on the nomination of Perley Beecroft for vice-president at the Democratic convention, after Doremus Jessup had frenetically ceased listening. Beecroft was a Southern tobacco-planter and storekeeper, an ex-Governor of his state, married to an ex-schoolteacher from Maine who was sufficiently scented with salt spray and potato blossoms to win any Yankee. But it was not his geographical superiority which made Mr. Beecroft the perfect running mate for Buzz Windrip but that he was malaria-yellowed and laxly mustached, where Buzz's horsey face was ruddy and smooth; while Beecroft's oratory had a vacuity, a profundity of slowly enunciated nonsense, which beguiled such solemn deacons as were irritated by Buzz's cataract of slang.

Nor could Sarason ever have convinced the wealthy that the more Buzz denounced them and promised to distribute their millions to the poor, the more they could trust his "common sense" and finance his campaign. But with a hint, a grin, a wink, a handshake, Buzz could convince them, and their contributions came in by the hundred thousand, often disguised as assessments on imaginary business partnerships.

It had been the peculiar genius of Berzelius Windrip not to wait until he should be nominated for this office or that to begin shanghaiing his band of buccaneers. He had been coaxing in supporters ever since the day when, at the age of four, he had captivated a neighborhood comrade by giving him an ammonia pistol which later he thriftily stole back from the comrade's pocket. Buzz might not have learned, perhaps could not have learned, much from sociologists Charles Beard and John Dewey, but they could have learned a great deal from Buzz.

And it was Buzz's, not Sarason's, master stroke that, as warmly as he advocated everyone's getting rich by just voting to be rich, he denounced all "Fascism" and "Naziism," so that most of the Republicans who were afraid of Democratic Fascism, and all the Democrats who were afraid of Republican Fascism, were ready to vote for him.

10

> While I hate befogging my pages with scientific technicalities and even neologies, I feel constrained to say here that the most elementary perusal of the Economy of Abundance would convince any intelligent student that the Cassandras who miscall the much-needed increase in the fluidity of our currential circulation "Inflation," erroneously basing their parallel upon the inflationary misfortunes of certain European nations in the era 1919–1923, fallaciously and perhaps inexcusably fail to comprehend the different monetary status in America inherent in our vastly greater reservoir of Natural Resources.
>
> *Zero Hour,* Berzelius Windrip.

MOST OF THE mortgaged farmers.

Most of the white-collar workers who had been unemployed these three years and four and five.

Most of the people on relief rolls who wanted more relief.

Most of the suburbanites who could not meet the installment payments on the electric washing machine.

Such large sections of the American Legion as believed that only Senator Windrip would secure for them, and perhaps increase, the bonus.

Such popular Myrtle Boulevard or Elm Avenue preachers as, spurred by the examples of Bishop Prang and Father Coughlin, believed they could get useful publicity out of supporting a slightly queer program that promised prosperity without anyone's having to work for it.

The remnants of the Kuklux Klan, and such leaders

of the American Federation of Labor as felt they had been inadequately courted and bepromised by the old-line politicians, and the non-unionized common laborers who felt they had been inadequately courted by the same A.F. of L.

Back-street and over-the-garage lawyers who had never yet wangled governmental jobs.

The Lost Legion of the Anti-Saloon League—since it was known that, though he drank a lot, Senator Windrip also praised teetotalism a lot, while his rival, Walt Trowbridge, though he drank but little, said nothing at all in support of the Messiahs of Prohibition. These messiahs had not found professional morality profitable of late, with the Rockefellers and Wanamakers no longer praying with them nor paying.

Besides these necessitous petitioners, a goodish number of burghers who, while they were millionaires, yet maintained that their prosperity had been sorely checked by the fiendishness of the bankers in limiting their credit.

These were the supporters who looked to Berzelius Windrip to play the divine raven and feed them handsomely when he should become President, and from such came most of the fervid elocutionists who campaigned for him through September and October.

Pushing in among this mob of camp followers who identified political virtue with money for their rent came a flying squad who suffered not from hunger but from congested idealism: Intellectuals and Reformers and even Rugged Individualists, who saw in Windrip, for all his clownish swindlerism, a free vigor which promised a rejuvenation of the crippled and senile capitalistic system.

Upton Sinclair wrote about Buzz and spoke for him just as in 1917, unyielding pacifist though he was, Mr. Sinclair had advocated America's whole-hearted prosecution of the Great War, forseeing that it would unquestionably exterminate German militarism and thus forever end all wars. Most of the Morgan partners, though they may have shuddered a little at association with Upton Sinclair, saw that, however much income they themselves might have to sacrifice, only Windrip could start the Business Recovery; while Bishop Manning of New York City pointed out that Windrip always spoke reverently of the church and its shepherds, whereas Walt Trowbridge went horseback-riding every Sabbath morning and had never been known to telegraph any female relative on Mother's Day.

On the other hand, the *Saturday Evening Post* enraged the small shopkeepers by calling Windrip a demagogue, and the New York *Times,* once Independent Democrat, was anti-Windrip. But most of the religious periodicals announced that with a saint like Bishop Prang for backer, Windrip must have been called of God.

Even Europe joined in.

With the most modest friendliness, explaining that they wished not to intrude on American domestic politics but only to express personal admiration for that great Western advocate of peace and prosperity, Berzelius Windrip, there came representatives of certain foreign powers, lecturing throughout the land: General Balbo, so popular here because of his leadership of the flight from Italy to Chicago in 1933; a scholar who, though he now lived in Germany and was an inspiration to all patriotic leaders of German Recovery, yet had graduated from Harvard University and had been the most popular piano-player in his class—namely, Dr. Ernst (Putzi) Hanfstängl; and Great Britain's lion of diplomacy, the Gladstone of the 1930's, the handsome and gracious Lord Lossiemouth who, as Prime Minister, had been known as the Rt. Hon. Ramsay MacDonald, P.C.

All three of them were expensively entertained by the wives of manufacturers, and they persuaded many millionaires who, in the refinement of wealth, had considered Buzz vulgar, that actually he was the world's one hope of efficient international commerce.

Father Coughlin took one look at all the candidates and indignantly retired to his cell.

Mrs. Adelaide Tarr Gimmitch, who would surely have written to the friends she had made at the Rotary Club Dinner in Fort Beulah if she could only have remembered the name of the town, was a considerable figure in the campaign. She explained to women voters how kind it was of Senator Windrip to let them go on voting, so far; and she sang "Berzelius Windrip's gone to Wash." an average of eleven times a day.

Buzz himself, Bishop Prang, Senator Porkwood (the fearless Liberal and friend of labor and the farmers), and Colonel Osceola Luthorne, the editor, though their prime task was reaching millions by radio, also, in a forty-day train trip, traveled over 27,000 miles, through every state in the Union, on the scarlet-and-silver, ebony-paneled, silk-upholstered, streamlined, Diesel-engined, rubber-padded, air-conditioned, aluminum Forgotten Men Special.

It had a private bar that was forgotten by none save the Bishop.

The train fares were the generous gift of the combined railways.

Over six hundred speeches were discharged, ranging from eight-minute hallos delivered to the crowds gathered at stations, to two-hour fulminations in auditoriums and fairgrounds. Buzz was present at every speech, usually starring, but sometimes so hoarse that he could only wave his hand and croak, "Howdy, folks!" while he was spelled by Prang, Porkwood, Colonel Luthorne, or such volunteers from his regiment of secretaries, doctoral consulting specialists in history and economics, cooks, bartenders, and barbers, as could be lured away from playing craps with the accompanying reporters, photographers, sound-recorders, and broadcasters. Tieffer of the United Press has estimated that Buzz thus appeared personally before more than two million persons.

Meanwhile, almost daily hurtling by aëroplane between Washington and Buzz's home, Lee Sarason supervised dozens of telephone girls and scores of girl stenographers, who answered thousands of daily telephone calls and letters and telegrams and cables—and boxes containing poisoned candy. . . . Buzz himself had made the rule that all these girls must be pretty, reasonable, thoroughly skilled, and related to people with political influence.

For Sarason it must be said that in this bedlam of "public relations" he never once used *contact* as a transitive verb.

The Hon. Perley Beecroft, vice-presidential candidate, specialized on the conventions of fraternal orders, religious denominations, insurance agents, and traveling men.

Colonel Dewey Haik, who had nominated Buzz at Cleveland, had an assignment unique in campaigning—one of Sarason's slickest inventions. Haik spoke for Windrip not in the most frequented, most obvious places, but at places so unusual that his appearance there made news—and Sarason and Haik saw to it that there were nimble chroniclers present to get that news. Flying in his own plane, covering a thousand miles a day, he spoke to nine astonished miners whom he caught in a copper mine a mile below the surface—while thirty-nine photographers snapped the nine; he spoke from a motorboat to a stilled fishing fleet during a fog in Gloucester harbor; he spoke from the steps of the Sub-Treasury at noon on Wall Street; he spoke to the aviators and ground crew at Shushan Airport, New Orleans—and even the flyers were ribald only for the first five minutes, till he had described Buzz Windrip's gallant but ludicrous efforts to learn to fly; he spoke to state policemen, to stamp-collectors, players of chess in secret clubs, and steeplejacks at work; he spoke in breweries, hospitals, magazine offices, cathedrals, crossroad churches forty-by-thirty, prisons, lunatic asylums, night clubs—till the art editors began to send photographers the memo: "For Pete's sake, no more fotos Kunnel Haik spieling in sporting houses and hoosegow."

Yet went on using the pictures.

For Colonel Dewey Haik was a figure as sharp-lighted, almost, as Buzz Windrip himself. Son of a decayed Tennessee family, with one Confederate general grandfather and one a Dewey of Vermont, he had picked cotton, become a youthful telegraph operator, worked his way through the University of Arkansas and the University of Missouri law school, settled as a lawyer in a Wyoming village and then in Oregon, and during the war (he was in 1936 but forty-four years old) served in France as captain of infantry, with credit. Returned to America, he had been elected to Congress, and became a colonel in the militia. He studied military history; he learned to fly, to box, to fence; he was a ramrod-like figure yet had a fairly amiable smile; he was liked equally by disciplinary army officers of high rank, and by such roughnecks as Mr. Shad Ledue, the Caliban of Doremus Jessup.

Haik brought to Buzz's fold the very picaroons who had most snickered at Bishop Prang's solemnity.

All this while, Hector Macgoblin, the cultured doctor and burly boxing fan, co-author with Sarason of the campaign anthem, "Bring Out the Old-time Musket," was specializing in the inspiration of college professors, associations of high-school teachers, professional baseball teams, training-camps of pugilists, medical meetings, summer schools in which well-known authors taught the art of writing to earnest aspirants who could never learn to write, golf tournaments, and all such cultural congresses.

But the pugilistic Dr. Macgoblin came nearer to danger than any other campaigner. During a meeting in Alabama, where he had satisfactorily proved that no Negro with less than 25 per cent "white blood" can ever rise to the cultural level of a patent-medicine salesman, the meeting was raided, the costly residence section of the whites was raided, by a band of colored people headed by a Negro who had been a corporal on the Western Front in 1918. Macgoblin and the town were saved by the eloquence of a colored clergyman.

Truly, as Bishop Prang said, the apostles of Senator Windrip were now preaching his Message unto all manner of men, even unto the Heathen.

But what Doremus Jessup said, to Buck Titus and Father Perefixe, was:

"This is revolution in terms of Rotary."

11

> When I was a kid, one time I had an old-maid teacher that used to tell me, "Buzz, you're the thickest-headed dunce in school." But I noticed that she told me this a whole lot oftener than she used to tell the other kids how smart they were, and I came to be the most talked-about scholar in the whole township. The United States Senate isn't so different, and I want to thank a lot of stuffed shirts for their remarks about Yours Truly.
>
> *Zero Hour,* Berzelius Windrip.

BUT THERE WERE certain of the Heathen who did not heed those heralds Prang and Windrip and Haik and Dr. Macgoblin.

Walt Trowbridge conducted his campaign as placidly as though he were certain to win. He did not spare himself, but he did not moan over the Forgotten Men (he'd been one himself, as a youngster, and didn't think it was so bad!) nor become hysterical at a private bar in a scarlet-and-silver special train. Quietly, steadfastly, speaking on the radio and in a few great halls, he explained that he did advocate an enormously improved distribution of wealth, but that it must be achieved by steady digging and not by dynamite that would destroy more than it excavated. He wasn't particularly thrilling. Economics rarely are, except when they have been dramatized by a Bishop, staged and lighted by a Sarason, and passionately played by a Buzz Windrip with rapier and blue satin tights.

For the campaign the Communists had brightly brought out their sacrificial candidates—in fact, all seven of the current Communist parties had. Since, if they all stuck together, they might entice 900,000 votes, they had avoided such bourgeois grossness by enthusiastic schisms, and their creeds now included: *The* Party, the Majority Party, the Leftist Party, the Trotzky Party, the Christian Communist Party, the Workers' Party, and, less baldly named, something called the American Nationalist Patriotic Coöperative Fabian Post-Marxian Communist Party—it sounded like the names of royalty but was otherwise dissimilar.

But these radical excursions were not very significant compared with the new Jeffersonian Party, suddenly fathered by Franklin D. Roosevelt.

Forty-eight hours after the nomination of Windrip at Cleveland, President Roosevelt had issued his defiance.

Senator Windrip, he asserted, had been chosen "not by the brains and hearts of genuine Democrats but by their temporarily crazed emotions." He would no more support Windrip because he claimed to be a Democrat than he would support Jimmy Walker.

Yet, he said, he could not vote for the Republican Party, the "party of intrenched special privilege," however much, in the past three years, he had appreciated the loyalty, the honesty, the intelligence of Senator Walt Trowbridge.

Roosevelt made it clear that his Jeffersonian or True Democratic faction was not a "third party" in the sense that it was to be permanent. It was to vanish as soon as honest and coolly thinking men got control again of the old organization. Buzz Windrip aroused mirth by dubbing it the "Bull Mouse Party," but President Roosevelt was joined by almost all the liberal members of Congress, Democratic or Republican, who had not followed Walt Trowbridge; by Norman Thomas and the Socialists who had not turned Communist; by Governors Floyd Olson and Olin Johnston; and by Mayor La Guardia.

The conspicuous fault of the Jeffersonian Party, like the personal fault of Senator Trowbridge, was that it represented integrity and reason, in a year when the electorate hungered for frisky emotions, for the peppery sensations associated, usually, not with monetary systems and taxation rates but with baptism by immersion in the creek, young love under the elms, straight whisky, angelic orchestras heard soaring down from the full moon, fear of death when an automobile teeters above a canyon, thirst in a desert and quenching it with spring water—all the primitive sensations which they thought they found in the screaming of Buzz Windrip.

Far from the hot-lighted ballrooms where all these crimson-tuniced bandmasters shrillsquabbled as to which should lead for the moment the tremendous spiritual jazz, far off in the cool hills a little man named Doremus Jessup, who wasn't even a bass drummer but only a citizen editor, wondered in confusion what he should do to be saved.

He wanted to follow Roosevelt and the Jeffersonian Party—partly for admiration of the man; partly for the pleasure of shocking the ingrown Republicanism of Vermont. But he could not believe that the Jeffersonians would have a chance; he did believe that, for all the mothball odor of many of his associates, Walt Trowbridge was a valiant and competent man; and night and day Doremus bounced up and down Beulah Valley campaigning for Trowbridge.

Out of his very confusion there came into his writing a desperate sureness which surprised accustomed readers of the *Informer.* For once he was not amused and tolerant. Though he never said anything worse of the Jeffersonian Party than that it was ahead of its times, in both editorials and news stories he went after Buzz Windrip and his gang with whips, turpentine, and scandal.

In person, he was into and out of shops and houses all morning long, arguing with voters, getting miniature interviews.

He had expected that traditionally Republican Vermont would give him too drearily easy a task in preaching Trowbridge. What he found was a dismaying preference for the theoretically Democratic Buzz Windrip. And that preference, Doremus perceived, wasn't even a pathetic trust in Windrip's promises of Utopian bliss for everyone in general. It was a trust in increased cash for the voter himself, and for his family, very much in particular.

Most of them had, among all the factors in the campaign, noticed only what they regarded as Windrip's humor, and three planks in his platform: Five, which promised to increase taxes on the rich; Ten, which condemned the Negroes—since nothing so elevates a dispossessed farmer or a factory worker on relief as to have some race, any race, on which he can look down; and, especially, Eleven, which announced, or seemed to announce, that the average toiler would immediately receive $5000 a year. (And ever-so-many railway-station debaters explained that it would really be $10,000. Why, they were going to have every cent offered by Dr. Townsend, plus everything planned by the late Huey Long, Upton Sinclair, and the Utopians, all put together!)

So beatifically did hundreds of old people in Beulah Valley believe this that they smilingly trotted into Raymond Pridewell's hardware store, to order new kitchen stoves and aluminum sauce pans and complete bathroom furnishings, to be paid for on the day after inauguration. Mr. Pridewell, a cobwebbed old Henry Cabot Lodge Republican, lost half his trade by chasing out these happy heirs to fabulous estates, but they went on dreaming, and Doremus, nagging at them, discovered that mere figures are defenseless against a dream . . . even a dream of new Plymouths and unlimited cans of sausages and motion-picture cameras and the prospect of never having to arise till 7:30 A.M.

Thus answered Alfred Tizra, "Snake" Tizra, friend to Doremus's handyman, Shad Ledue. Snake was a steel-tough truck-driver and taxi-owner who had served sentences for assault and for transporting bootleg liquor. He had once made a living catching rattlesnakes and copperheads in southern New England. Under President Windrip, Snake jeeringly assured Doremus, he would have enough money to start a chain of roadhouses in all the dry communities in Vermont.

Ed Howland, one of the lesser Fort Beulah grocers, and Charley Betts, furniture and undertaking, while they were dead against anyone getting groceries, furniture, or even undertaking on Windrip credit, were all for the population's having credit on other wares.

Aras Dilley, a squatter dairy farmer living with a toothless wife and seven slattern children in a tilted and unscrubbed cabin way up on Mount Terror, snarled at Doremus—who had often taken food baskets and boxes of shotgun shells and masses of cigarettes to Aras—"Well, want to tell you, when Mr. Windrip gets in, we farmers are going to fix our own prices on our crops, and not you smart city fellows!"

Doremus could not blame him. While Buck Titus, at fifty, looked thirty-odd, Aras, at thirty-four, looked fifty.

Lorinda Pike's singularly unpleasant partner in the Beulah Valley Tavern, one Mr. Nipper, whom she hoped soon to lose, combined boasting how rich he was with gloating how much more he was going to get under Windrip. "Professor" Staubmeyer quoted nice things Windrip had said about higher pay for teachers. Louis Rotenstern, to prove that his heart, at least, was not Jewish, became more lyric than any of them. And even Frank Tasbrough of the quarries, Medary Cole of the grist mill and real-estate holdings, R. C. Crowley of the bank, who presumably were not tickled by projects of higher income taxes, smiled pussy-cattishly and hinted that Windrip was a "lot sounder fellow" than people knew.

But no one in Fort Beulah was a more active crusader for Buzz Windrip than Shad Ledue.

Doremus had known that Shad possessed talent for argument and for display; that he had once persuaded old Mr. Pridewell to trust him for a .22 rifle, value twenty-three dollars; that, removed from the sphere of coal bins and grass-stained overalls, he had once sung "Rollicky Bill the Sailor" at a smoker of the Ancient and Independent Order of Rams; and that he had enough memory to be able to quote, as his own profound opinions, the editorials in the Hearst newspapers. Yet even knowing all this equipment for a political career, an equipment not much short of Buzz Windrip's, Doremus was surprised to find Shad soapboxing for Windrip among the quarry-workers, then actually as chairman of a rally in Oddfellows' Hall. Shad spoke little, but with brutal taunting of the believers in Trowbridge and Roosevelt.

At meetings where he did not speak, Shad was an incomparable bouncer, and in that valued capacity he was summoned to Windrip rallies as far away as Burlington. It was he who, in a militia uniform, handsomely riding a large white plow-horse, led the final Windrip parade in Rutland . . . and substantial men of affairs, even dry-goods jobbers, fondly called him "Shad."

Doremus was amazed, felt a little apologetic over his failure to have appreciated this new-found paragon, as he sat in American Legion Hall and heard Shad bellowing: "I don't pretend to be anything but a plain working-stiff, but there's forty million workers like me, and we know that Senator Windrip is the first statesman in years that thinks of what guys like us need before he thinks one doggone thing about politics. Come on, you bozos! The swell folks tell you to not be selfish! Walt Trowbridge tells you to not be selfish! Well, *be* selfish, and vote for the one man that's willing to *give* you something—give *you* something!—and not just grab off every cent and every hour of work that he can get!"

Doremus groaned inwardly, "Oh, my Shad! And you're doing most of this on my time!"

Sissy Jessup sat on the running board of her coupé (hers by squatter's right), with Julian Falck, up from Amherst for the week-end, and Malcolm Tasbrough wedged in on either side of her.

"Oh nuts, let's quit talking politics. Windrip's going to be elected, so why waste time yodeling when we could drive down to the river and have a swim," complained Malcolm.

"He's not going to win without our putting up a tough scrap against him. I'm going to talk to the high-school alumni this evening—about how they got to tell their parents to vote for either Trowbridge or Roosevelt," snapped Julian Falck.

"Haa, haa, haa! And of course the parents will be tickled to death to do whatever you tell 'em, Yulian! You college men certainly are the goods! Besides—— Want to be serious about this fool business?" Malcolm had the insolent self-assurance of beef, slick black hair, and a large car of his own; he was the perfect leader of Black Shirts, and he looked contemptuously on Julian who, though a year older, was pale and thinnish. "Matter of fact, it'll be a good thing to have Buzz. He'll put a damn quick stop to all this radicalism—all this free speech and libel of our most fundamental institutions——"

"Boston *American;* last Tuesday; page eight," murmured Sissy.

"—and no wonder you're scared of him, Yulian! He sure will drag some of your favorite Amherst anarchist profs off to the hoosegow, and maybe you too, Comrade!"

The two young men looked at each other with slow fury. Sissy quieted them by raging, "Freavensake! Will you two heels quit scrapping? . . . Oh, my dears, this beastly election! Beastly! Seems as if it's breaking up every town, every home. . . . My poor Dad! Doremus is just about all in!"

12

> I shall not be content till this country can produce every single thing we need, even coffee, cocoa, and rubber, and so keep all our dollars at home. If we can do this and at the same time work up tourist traffic so that foreigners will come from every part of the world to see such remarkable wonders as the Grand Canyon, Glacier and Yellowstone etc. parks, the fine hotels of Chicago, & etc., thus leaving their money here, we shall have such a balance of trade as will go far to carry out my often-criticized yet completely sound idea of from $3000 to $5000 per year for every single family—that is, I mean every real American family. Such an aspiring Vision is what we want, and not all this nonsense of wasting our time at Geneva and talky-talk at Lugano, wherever that is.
>
> *Zero Hour,* Berzelius Windrip.

ELECTION DAY would fall on Tuesday, November third, and on Sunday evening of the first, Senator Windrip played the finale of his campaign at a mass meeting in Madison Square Garden, in New York. The Garden would hold, with seats and standing room, about 19,000, and a week before the meeting every ticket had been sold—at from fifty cents to five dollars, and then by speculators resold and resold, at from one dollar to twenty.

Doremus had been able to get one single ticket from an acquaintance on one of the Hearst dailies—which, alone among the New York papers, were supporting Windrip—and on the afternoon of November first he traveled the three hundred miles to New York for his first visit in three years.

It had been cold in Vermont, with early snow, but the white drifts lay to the earth so quietly, in unstained air, that the world seemed a silver-painted carnival, left to silence. Even on a moonless night, a pale radiance came from the snow, from the earth itself, and the stars were drops of quicksilver.

But, following the redcap carrying his shabby Gladstone bag, Doremus came out of the Grand Central, at six o'clock, into a gray trickle of cold dishwater from heaven's kitchen sink. The renowned towers which he expected to see on Forty-second Street were dead in their mummy cloths of ragged fog. And as to the mob that, with cruel disinterest, galloped past him, a new and heedless smear of faces every second, the man from Fort Beulah could think only that New York must be holding its county fair in this clammy drizzle, or else that there was a big fire somewhere.

He had sensibly planned to save money by using the subway—the substantial village burgher is so poor in the city of the Babylonian gardens!—and he even remembered that there were still to be found in Manhattan five-cent trolley cars, in which a rustic might divert himself by looking at sailors and poets and shawled women from the steppes of Kazakstan. To the redcap he had piped with what he conceived to be traveled urbanity, "Guess'll take a trolley—jus' few blocks." But deafened and dizzied and elbow-jabbed by the crowd, soaked and depressed, he took refuge in a taxi, then wished he hadn't, as he saw the slippery rubber-colored pavement, and as his taxi got wedged among other cars stinking of carbon-monoxide and frenziedly tooting for release from the jam—a huddle of robot sheep bleating their terror with mechanical lungs of a hundred horsepower.

He painfully hesitated before going out again from his small hotel in the West Forties, and when he did, when he muddily crept among the shrill shopgirls, the weary chorus girls, the hard cigar-clamping gamblers, and the pretty young men on Broadway, he felt himself, with the rubbers and umbrella which Emma had forced upon him, a very Caspar Milquetoast.

He most noticed a number of stray imitation soldiers, without side-arms or rifles, but in a uniform like that of an American cavalryman in 1870: slant-topped blue forage caps, dark blue tunics, light blue trousers, with yellow stripes at the seam, tucked into leggings of black rubberoid for what appeared to be the privates, and boots of sleek black leather for officers. Each of them had on the right side of his collar the letters "M.M." and on the left, a five-pointed star. There were so many of them; they swaggered so brazenly, shouldering civilians out of the way; and upon insignificances like Doremus they looked with frigid insolence.

He suddenly understood.

These young condottieri were the "Minute Men": the private troops of Berzelius Windrip, about which Doremus had been publishing uneasy news reports. He was thrilled and a little dismayed to see them now—the printed words made brutal flesh.

Three weeks ago Windrip had announced that Colonel Dewey Haik had founded, just for the campaign, a nationwide league of Windrip marching-clubs, to be called the Minute Men. It was probable that they had been in formation for months, since already they had three or four hundred thousand members. Doremus was afraid the M.M.'s might become a permanent organization, more menacing than the Kuklux Klan.

Their uniform suggested the pioneer America of Cold Harbor and of the Indian fighters under Miles and Custer. Their emblem, their swastika (here Doremus saw the cunning and mysticism of Lee Sarason), was a five-pointed star, because the star on the American flag was five-pointed, whereas the stars of both the Soviet banner and the Jews—the shield of David—were six-pointed.

The fact that the Soviet star, actually, was also five-pointed, no one noticed, during these excited days of regeneration. Anyway, it was a nice idea to have this star simultaneously challenge the Jews and the Bolsheviks—the M.M.'s had good intentions, even if their symbolism did slip a little.

Yet the craftiest thing about the M.M.'s was that they wore no colored shirts, but only plain white when on parade, and light khaki when on outpost duty, so that Buzz Windrip could thunder, and frequently, "Black shirts? Brown shirts? Red shirts? Yes, and maybe cow-brindle shirts! All these degenerate European uniforms of tyranny! No sir! The Minute Men are not Fascist or Communist or anything at all but plain Democratic—the knight-champions of the rights of the Forgotten Men—the shock troops of Freedom!"

Doremus dined on Chinese food, his invariable self-indulgence when he was in a large city without Emma, who stated that chow mein was nothing but fried excelsior with flour-taste gravy. He forgot the leering M.M. troopers a little; he was happy in glancing at the gilded wood-carvings, at the octagonal lanterns painted with doll-like Chinese peasants crossing arched bridges, at a quartette of guests, two male and two female, who looked like Public Enemies and who all through dinner quarreled with restrained viciousness.

When he headed toward Madison Square Garden and the culminating Windrip rally, he was plunged into a maelstrom. A whole nation seemed querulously to be headed the same way. He could not get a taxicab, and walking through the dreary storm some fourteen blocks to Madison Square Garden he was aware of the murderous temper of the crowd.

Eighth Avenue, lined with cheapjack shops, was packed with drab, discouraged people who yet, tonight, were tipsy with the hashish of hope. They filled the sidewalks, nearly filled the pavement, while irritable motors squeezed tediously through them, and angry policemen were pushed and whirled about and, if they tried to be haughty, got jeered at by lively shopgirls.

Through the welter, before Doremus's eyes, jabbed a flying wedge of Minute Men, led by what he was later to recognize as a cornet of M.M.'s. They were not on duty, and they were not belligerent; they were cheering, and singing "Berzelius Windrip went to Wash.," reminding Doremus of a slightly drunken knot of students from an inferior college after a football victory. He was to remember them so afterward, months afterward, when the enemies of the M.M.'s all through the country derisively called them "Mickey Mouses" and "Minnies."

An old man, shabbily neat, stood blocking them and yelled, "To hell with Buzz! Three cheers for F.D.R.!"

The M.M.'s burst into hoodlum wrath. The cornet in command, a bruiser uglier even than Shad Ledue, hit the old man on the jaw, and he sloped down, sickeningly. Then, from nowhere, facing the cornet, there was a chief petty officer of the navy, big, smiling, reckless. The C.P.O. bellowed, in a voice tuned to hurricanes, "Swell bunch o' tin soldiers! Nine o' yuh to one grandpappy! Just about even——"

The cornet socked him; he laid out the cornet with one foul to the belly; instantly the other eight M.M.'s were on the C.P.O., like sparrows after a hawk, and he crashed, his face, suddenly veal-white, laced with rivulets of blood. The eight kicked him in the head with their thick marching-shoes. They were still kicking him when Doremus wriggled away, very sick, altogether helpless.

He had not turned away quickly enough to avoid seeing an M.M. trooper, girlish-faced, crimson-lipped, fawn-eyed, throw himself on the fallen cornet and, whimpering, stroke that roustabout's roast-beef cheeks with shy gardenia-petal fingers.

There were many arguments, a few private fist fights, and one more battle, before Doremus reached the auditorium.

A block from it some thirty M.M.'s, headed by a battalion-leader—something between a captain and a major—started raiding a street meeting of Communists. A Jewish girl in khaki, her bare head soaked with rain, was beseeching from the elevation of a wheelbarrow, "Fellow travelers! Don't just chew the rag and 'sympathize'! Join us! Now! It's life and death!" Twenty feet from the Communists, a middle-aged man who looked like a social worker was explaining the Jeffersonian Party, recalling the record of President Roosevelt, and reviling the Communists next door as word-drunk un-American cranks. Half his audience were people who might be competent voters; half of them—like half of any group on this evening of tragic fiesta—were cigarette-sniping boys in hand-me-downs.

The thirty M.M.'s cheerfully smashed into the Communists. The battalion leader reached up, slapped the girl speaker, dragged her down from the wheelbarrow. His followers casually waded in with fists and blackjacks.

Doremus, more nauseated, feeling more helpless than ever, heard the smack of a blackjack on the temple of a scrawny Jewish intellectual.

Amazingly, then, the voice of the rival Jeffersonian leader spiraled up into a scream: "Come on, *you*! Going to let those hellhounds attack our Communist friends—friends *now,* by God!" With which the mild bookworm leaped into the air, came down squarely upon a fat Mickey Mouse, capsized him, seized his blackjack, took time to kick another M.M.'s shins before arising from the wreck, sprang up, and waded into the raiders as, Doremus guessed, he would have waded into a table of statistics on the proportion of butter fat in loose milk in 97.7 per cent of shops on Avenue B.

Till then, only half-a-dozen Communist Party members had been facing the M.M.'s, their backs to a garage wall. Fifty of their own, fifty Jeffersonians besides, now joined them, and with bricks and umbrellas and deadly volumes of sociology they drove off the enraged M.M.'s—partisans of Bela Kun side by side with the partisans of Professor John Dewey—until a riot squad of policemen battered their way in to protect the M.M.'s by arresting the girl Communist speaker and the Jeffersonian.

Doremus had often "headed up" sports stories about "Madison Square Garden Prize Fights," but he did know that the place had nothing to do with Madison Square, from which it was a day's journey by bus, that it was decidedly not a garden, that the fighters there did not fight for "prizes" but for fixed partnership shares in the business, and that a good many of them did not fight at all.

The mammoth building, as in exhaustion Doremus crawled up to it, was entirely ringed with M.M.'s, elbow to elbow, all carrying heavy canes, and at every entrance, along every aisle, the M.M.'s were rigidly in line, with their officers galloping about, whispering orders, and bearing uneasy rumors like scared calves in a dipping-pen.

These past weeks hungry miners, dispossessed farmers, Carolina mill hands had greeted Senator Windrip with a flutter of worn hands beneath gasoline torches. Now he was to face, not the unemployed, for they could not afford fifty-cent tickets, but the small, scared side-street traders of New York, who considered themselves altogether superior to clodhoppers and mine-creepers, yet were as desperate as they. The swelling mass that Doremus saw, proud in seats or standing chin-to-nape in the aisles, in a reek of dampened clothes, was not romantic; they were people concerned with the tailor's goose, the tray of potato salad, the card of hooks-and-eyes, the leech-like mortgage on the owner-driven taxi, with, at home, the baby's diapers, the dull safety-razor blade, the awful rise in the cost of rump steak and kosher chicken. And a few, and very proud, civil-service clerks and letter carriers and superintendents of small apartment houses, curiously fashionable in seventeen-dollar ready-made suits and feebly stitched foulard ties, who boasted, "I don't know why all these bums go on relief. I may not be such a wiz, but let me tell you, even since 1929, I've never made less than *two thousand dollars a year*!"

Manhattan peasants. Kind people, industrious people, generous to their aged, eager to find any desperate cure for the sickness of worry over losing the job.

Most facile material for any rabble-rouser.

The historic rally opened with extreme dullness. A regimental band played the *Tales from Hoffman* barcarole with no apparent significance and not much more liveliness. The Reverend Dr. Hendrik Van Lollop of St. Apologue's Lutheran Church offered prayer, but one felt that probably it had not been accepted. Senator Porkwood provided a dissertation on Senator Windrip which was composed in equal parts of apostolic adoration of Buzz and of the uh-uh-uh's with which Hon. Porkwood always interspersed his words.

And Windrip wasn't yet even in sight.

Colonel Dewey Haik, nominator of Buzz at the Cleveland convention, was considerably better. He told three jokes, and an anecdote about a faithful carrier pigeon in the Great War which had seemed to understand, really better than many of the human soldiers, just why it was that the Americans were over there fighting for France against Germany. The connection of this ornithological hero with the virtues of Senator Windrip did not seem evident, but, after having sat under Senator Porkwood, the audience enjoyed the note of military gallantry.

Doremus felt that Colonel Haik was not merely rambling but pounding on toward something definite. His voice became more insistent. He began to talk about Windrip: "my friend—the one man who dares beard the monetary lion—the man who in his great and simple heart cherishes the woe of every common man as once did the brooding tenderness of Abraham Lincoln." Then, wildly waving toward a side entrance, he shrieked, "And here he comes! My friends—Buzz Windrip!"

The band hammered out "The Campbells Are Coming." A squadron of Minute Men, smart as Horse Guards, carrying long lances with starred pennants, clicked into the gigantic bowl of the auditorium, and after them, shabby in an old blue-serge suit, nervously twisting a sweat-stained slouch hat, stooped and tired, limped Berzelius Windrip. The audience leaped up, thrusting one another aside to have a look at the deliverer, cheering like artillery at dawn.

Windrip started prosaically enough. You felt rather sorry for him, so awkwardly did he lumber up the steps to the platform, across to the center of the stage. He stopped; stared owlishly. Then he quacked monotonously:

"The first time I ever came to New York I was a greenhorn—no, don't laugh, mebbe I still am! But I had already been elected a United States Senator, and back home, the way they'd serenaded me, I thought I was some punkins. I thought my name was just about as familiar to everybody as Al Capone's or Camel Cigarettes or Castoria—Babies Cry For It. But I come to New York on my way to Washington, and say, I sat in my hotel lobby here for three days, and the only fellow ever spoke to me was the hotel detective! And when he did come up and address me, I was tickled to death—I thought he was going to tell me the whole burg was pleased by my condescending to visit 'em. But all he wanted to know was, was I a guest of the hotel and did I have any right to be holding down a lobby chair permanently that way! And tonight, friends, I'm pretty near as scared of Old Gotham as I was then!"

The laughter, the hand-clapping, were fair enough, but the proud electors were disappointed by his drawl, his weary humility.

Doremus quivered hopefully, "Maybe he isn't going to get elected!"

Windrip outlined his too-familiar platform—Doremus was interested only in observing that Windrip misquoted his own figures regarding the limitation of fortunes, in Point Five.

He slid into a rhapsody of general ideas—a mishmash of polite regards to Justice, Freedom, Equality, Order, Prosperity, Patriotism, and any number of other noble but slippery abstractions.

Doremus thought he was being bored, until he discovered that, at some moment which he had not noticed, he had become absorbed and excited.

Something in the intensity with which Windrip looked at his audience, looked at all of them, his glance slowly taking them in from the highest-perched seat to the nearest, convinced them that he was talking to each individual, directly and solely; that he wanted to take each of them into his heart; that he was telling them the truths, the imperious and dangerous facts, that had been hidden from them.

"They say I want money—power! Say, I've turned down offers from law firms right here in New York of three times the money I'll get as President! And power—why, the President is the servant of every citizen in the country, and not just of the considerate folks, but also of every crank that comes pestering him by telegram and phone and letter. And yet, it's true, it's absolutely true I do want power, great, big, imperial power—but not for myself—no—for *you*!—the power of your permission to smash the Jew financiers who've enslaved you, who're working you to death to pay the interest on their bonds; the grasping bankers—and not all of 'em Jews by a darn sight!—the crooked labor-leaders just as much as the crooked bosses, and, most of all, the sneaking spies of Moscow that want you to lick the boots of their self-appointed tyrants that rule not by love and loyalty, like I want to, but by the horrible power of the whip, the dark cell, the automatic pistol!"

He pictured, then, a Paradise of democracy in which, with the old political machines destroyed, every humblest worker would be king and ruler, dominating representatives elected from among his own kind of people, and these representatives not growing indifferent, as hitherto they had done, once they were far off in Washington, but kept alert to the public interest by the supervision of a strengthened Executive.

It sounded almost reasonable, for a while.

The supreme actor, Buzz Windrip, was passionate yet never grotesquely wild. He did not gesture too extravagantly; only, like Gene Debs of old, he reached out a bony forefinger which seemed to jab into each of them and hook out each heart. It was his mad eyes, big staring tragic eyes, that startled them, and his voice, now thundering, now humbly pleading, that soothed them.

He was so obviously an honest and merciful leader; a man of sorrows and acquaint with woe.

Doremus marveled, "I'll be hanged! Why, he's a darn good sort when you come to meet him! And warm-hearted. He makes me feel as if I'd been having a good evening with Buck and Steve Perefixe. What if Buzz is right? What if—in spite of all the demagogic pap that, I suppose, he has got to feed out to the boobs—he's right in claiming that it's only he, and not Trowbridge or Roosevelt, that can break the hold of the absentee owners? And these Minute Men, his followers—oh, they were pretty nasty, what I saw out on the street, but still, most of 'em are mighty nice, clean-cut young fellows. Seeing Buzz and then listening to what he actually says does kind of surprise you—kind of make you think!"

But what Mr. Windrip actually *had* said, Doremus could not remember an hour later, when he had come out of the trance.

He was so convinced then that Windrip would win that, on Tuesday evening, he did not remain at the *Informer* office until the returns were all in. But if he did not stay for the evidences of the election, they came to him.

Past his house, after midnight, through muddy snow tramped a triumphant and reasonably drunken parade, carrying torches and bellowing to the air of "Yankee Doodle" new words revealed just that week by Mrs. Adelaide Tarr Gimmitch:

The snakes disloyal to our Buzz
We're riding on a rail,
They'll wish to God they never was,
When we get them in jail!

Chorus:

Buzz and buzz and keep it up
To victory he's floated.
You were a most ungrateful pup,
Unless for Buzz you voted.

Every M.M. gets a whip
To use upon some traitor,
And every Antibuzz we skip
Today, we'll tend to later.

"Antibuzz," a word credited to Mrs. Gimmitch but more probably invented by Dr. Hector Macgoblin, was to be extensively used by lady patriots as a term expressing such vicious disloyalty to the State as might call for the firing squad. Yet, like Mrs. Gimmitch's splendid synthesis "Unkies," for soldiers of the A.E.F., it never really caught on.

Among the winter-coated paraders Doremus and Sissy thought they could make out Shad Ledue, Aras Dilley, that philoprogenitive squatter from Mount Terror, Charley Betts, the furniture dealer, and Tony Mogliani, the fruit-seller, most ardent expounder of Italian Fascism in central Vermont.

And, though he could not be sure of it in the dimness behind the torches, Doremus rather thought that the lone large motorcar following the procession was that of his neighbor, Francis Tasbrough.

Next morning, at the *Informer* office, Doremus did not learn of so very much damage wrought by the triumphant Nordics—they had merely upset a couple of privies, torn down and burned the tailor-shop sign of Louis Rotenstern, and somewhat badly beaten Clifford Little, the jeweler, a slight, curly-headed young man whom Shad Ledue despised because he organized theatricals and played the organ in Mr. Falck's church.

That night Doremus found, on his front porch, a notice in red chalk upon butcher's paper:

> *You will get yrs Dorey sweethart unles you get rite down on yr belly and crawl in front of the MM and the League and the Chief and I*
>
> *A friend*

It was the first time that Doremus had heard of "the Chief," a sound American variant of "the Leader" or "the Head of the Government," as a popular title for Mr. Windrip. It was soon to be made official.

Doremus burned the red warning without telling his family. But he often woke to remember it, not very laughingly.

13

> And when I get ready to retire I'm going to build me an up-to-date bungalow in some lovely resort, not in Como or any other of the proverbial Grecian isles you may be sure, but in somewheres like Florida, California, Santa Fe, & etc., and devote myself just to reading the classics, like Longfellow, James Whitcomb Riley, Lord Macaulay, Henry Van Dyke, Elbert Hubbard, Plato, Hiawatha, & etc. Some of my friends laugh at me for it, but I have always cultivated a taste for the finest in literature. I got it from my Mother as I did everything that some people have been so good as to admire in me.
>
> *Zero Hour,* Berzelius Windrip.

CERTAIN THOUGH DOREMUS had been of Windrip's election, the event was like the long-dreaded passing of a friend.

"All right. Hell with this country, if it's like that. All these years I've worked—and I never did want to be on all these committees and boards and charity drives!—and don't *they* look silly now! What I always wanted to do was to sneak off to an ivory tower—or anyway, celluloid, imitation ivory—and read everything I've been too busy to read."

Thus Doremus, in late November.

And he did actually attempt it, and for a few days reveled in it, avoiding everyone save his family and Lorinda, Buck Titus, and Father Perefixe. Mostly, though, he found that he did not relish the "classics" he had so far missed, but those familiar to his youth: *Ivanhoe*, *Huckleberry Finn*, *Midsummer Night's Dream*,

The Tempest, *L'Allegro*, *The Way of All Flesh* (not quite so youthful, there), *Moby-Dick*, the *Earthly Paradise*, *St. Agnes' Eve*, *The Idylls of the King*, most of Swinburne, *Pride and Prejudice*, *Religio Medici*, *Vanity Fair*.

Probably he was not so very different from President-Elect Windrip in his rather uncritical reverence toward any book he had heard of before he was thirty. . . . No American whose fathers have lived in the country for over two generations is so utterly different from any other American.

In one thing, Doremus's literary escapism failed him thoroughly. He tried to relearn Latin, but he could not now, uncajoled by a master, believe that "Mensa, mensae, mensae, mensam, mensa"—all that idiotic A table, of a table, to a table, toward a table, at in by or on a table—could bear him again as once it had to the honey-sweet tranquillity of Vergil and the Sabine Farm.

Then he saw that in everything his quest failed him.

The reading was good enough, toothsome, satisfying, except that he felt guilty at having sneaked away to an Ivory Tower at all. Too many years he had made a habit of social duty. He wanted to be "in" things, and he was daily more irritable as Windrip began, even before his inauguration, to dictate to the country.

Buzz's party, with the desertions to the Jeffersonians, had less than a majority in Congress. "Inside dope" came to Doremus from Washington that Windrip was trying to buy, to flatter, to blackmail opposing Congressmen. A President-Elect has unhallowed power, if he so wishes, and Windrip—no doubt with promises of abnormal favors in the way of patronage—won over a few. Five Jeffersonian Congressmen had their elections challenged. One sensationally disappeared, and smoking after his galloping heels there was a devilish fume of embezzlements. And with each such triumph of Windrip, all the well-meaning, cloistered Doremuses of the country were the more anxious.

All through the "Depression," ever since 1929, Doremus had felt the insecurity, the confusion, the sense of futility in trying to do anything more permanent than shaving or eating breakfast, that was general to the country. He could no longer plan, for himself or for his dependants, as the citizens of this once unsettled country had planned since 1620.

Why, their whole lives had been predicated on the privilege of planning. Depressions had been only cyclic storms, certain to end in sunshine; Capitalism and parliamentary government were eternal, and eternally being improved by the honest votes of Good Citizens.

Doremus's grandfather, Calvin, Civil War veteran and ill-paid, illiberal Congregational minister, had yet planned, "My son, Loren, shall have a theological education, and I think we shall be able to build a fine new house in fifteen or twenty years." That had given him a reason for working, and a goal.

His father, Loren, had vowed, "Even if I have to economize on books a little, and perhaps give up this extravagance of eating meat four times a week—very bad for the digestion, anyway—my son, Doremus, shall have a college education, and when, as he desires, he becomes a publicist, I think perhaps I shall be able to help him for a year or two. And then I hope—oh, in a mere five or six years more—to buy that complete Dickens with all the illustrations—oh, an extravagance, but a thing to leave to my grandchildren to treasure forever!"

But Doremus Jessup could not plan, "I'll have Sissy go to Smith before she studies architecture," or "If Julian Falck and Sissy get married and stick here in the Fort, I'll give 'em the southwest lot and some day, maybe fifteen years from now, the whole place will be filled with nice kids again!" No. Fifteen years from now, he sighed, Sissy might be hustling hash for the sort of workers who called the waiter's art "hustling hash"; and Julian might be in a concentration camp—Fascist *or* Communist!

The Horatio Alger tradition, from rags to Rockefellers, was clean gone out of the America it had dominated.

It seemed faintly silly to hope, to try to prophesy, to give up sleep on a good mattress for toil on a typewriter, and as for saving money—idiotic!

And for a newspaper editor—for one who must know, at least as well as the Encyclopaedia, everything about local and foreign history, geography, economics, politics, literature, and methods of playing football—it was maddening that it seemed impossible now to know anything surely.

"He don't know what it's all about" had in a year or two changed from a colloquial sneer to a sound general statement regarding almost any economist. Once, modestly enough, Doremus had assumed that he had a decent knowledge of finance, taxation, the gold standard, agricultural exports, and he had smilingly pontificated everywhere that Liberal Capitalism would pastorally lead into State Socialism, with governmental ownership of mines and railroads and water-power so settling all inequalities of income that every lion of a structural steel worker would be willing to lie down with any lamb of a contractor, and all the jails and tuberculosis sanatoria would be clean empty.

Now he knew that he knew nothing fundamental and, like a lone monk stricken with a conviction of sin, he mourned, "If I only knew more! . . . Yes, and if I could only remember statistics!"

The coming and the going of the N.R.A., the F.E.R.A., the P.W.A., and all the rest, had convinced Doremus that there were four sets of people who did not clearly understand anything whatever about how the government must be conducted: all the authorities in Washington; all of the citizenry who talked or wrote profusely about politics; the bewildered untouchables who said nothing; and Doremus Jessup.

"But," said he, "now, after Buzz's inauguration, everything is going to be completely simple and comprehensible again—the country is going to be run as his private domain!"

Julian Falck, now sophomore in Amherst, had come home for Christmas vacation, and he dropped in at the *Informer* office to beg from Doremus a ride home before dinner.

He called Doremus "sir" and did not seem to think he was a comic fossil. Doremus liked it.

On the way they stopped for gasoline at the garage of John Pollikop, the seething Social Democrat, and were waited upon by Karl Pascal—sometime donkey-engine-man at Tasbrough's quarry, sometime strike leader, sometime political prisoner in the county jail on a thin charge of inciting to riot, and ever since then, a model of Communistic piety.

Pascal was a thin man, but sinewy; his gaunt and humorous face of a good mechanic was so grease-darkened that the skin above and below his eyes seemed white as a fish-belly, and, in turn, that pallid rim made his eyes, alert dark gipsy eyes, seem the larger. . . . A panther chained to a coal cart.

"Well, what you going to do after this election?" said Doremus. "Oh! That's a fool question! I guess none of us chronic kickers want to say much about what we plan to do after January, when Buzz gets his hands on us. Lie low, eh?"

"I'm going to lie the lowest lie that I ever did. You bet! But maybe there'll be a few Communist cells around here now, when Fascism begins to get into people's hair. Never did have much success with my propaganda before, but now, you watch!" exulted Pascal.

"You don't seem so depressed by the election," marveled Doremus, while Julian offered, "No—you seem quite cheerful about it!"

"Depressed! Why good Lord, Mr. Jessup, I thought you knew your revolutionary tactics better than that, way you supported us in the quarry strike—even if you *are* the perfect type of small capitalist bourgeois! Depressed? Why, can't you see, if the Communists had paid for it they couldn't have had anything more elegant for our purposes than the election of a pro-plutocrat, itching militarist dictator like Buzz Windrip! Look! He'll get everybody plenty dissatisfied. But they can't do anything, barehanded against the armed troops. Then he'll whoop it up for a war, and so millions of people will have arms and food rations in their hands—all ready for the revolution! Hurray for Buzz and John Prang the Baptist!"

"Karl, it's funny about you. I honestly believe you believe in Communism!" marveled young Julian. "Don't you?"

"Why don't you go and ask your friend Father Perefixe if he believes in the Virgin?"

"But you seem to like America, and you don't seem so fanatical, Karl. I remember when I was a kid of about ten and you—I suppose you were about twenty-five or -six then—you used to slide with us and whoop like hell, and you made me a ski-stick."

"Sure I like America. Came here when I was two years old—I was born in Germany—my folks weren't Heinies, though—my dad was French and my mother a Hunkie from Serbia. (Guess that makes me a hundred per cent American, all right!) I think we've got the Old Country beat, lots of ways. Why, say, Julian, over there I'd have to call you 'Mein Herr' or 'Your Excellency,' or some fool thing, and you'd call me, 'I say-uh, Pascal!' and Mr. Jessup here, my Lord, he'd be 'Commendatore' or 'Herr Doktor'! No, I like it here. There's symptoms of possible future democracy. But—but—what burns me up—it isn't that old soap-boxer's chestnut about how one tenth of 1 per cent of the population at the top have an aggregate income equal to 42 per cent at the bottom. Figures like that are too astronomical. Don't mean a thing in the world to a fellow with his eyes—and nose—down in a transmission box—fellow that doesn't see the stars except after 9 P.M. on odd Wednesdays. But what burns me up is the fact that even before this Depression, in what you folks called prosperous times, 7 per cent of all the families in the country earned $500 a year or less—remember, those weren't the unemployed, on relief; those were the guys that had the honor of still doing honest labor.

"Five hundred dollars a year is ten dollars a week—and that means one dirty little room for a family of four people! It means $5.00 a week for all their food—eighteen cents per day per person for food!—and even the lousiest prisons allow more than that. And the magnificent remainder of $2.50 a week, that means nine cents per day per person for clothes, insurance, carfares, doctors' bills, dentists' bills, and for God's sake, amusements—amusements!—and all the rest of the nine cents a day they can fritter away on their Fords and autogiros and, when they feel fagged, skipping across the pond on the *Normandie*! Seven per cent of all the fortunate American families where the old man *has* got a job!"

Julian was silent; then whispered, "You know—fellow gets discussing economics in college—theoretically sympathetic—but to see your own kids living on eighteen cents a day for grub—I guess that would make a man pretty extremist!"

Doremus fretted, "But what percentage of forced labor in your Russian lumber camps and Siberian prison mines are getting more than that?"

"Haaa! That's all baloney! That's the old standard comeback at every Communist—just like once, twenty years ago, the muttonheads used to think they'd crushed any Socialist when they snickered 'If all the money was divided up, inside five years the hustlers would have all of it again.' Prob'ly there's some standard *coup de grace* like that in Russia, to crush anybody that defends America. Besides!" Karl Pascal glowed with nationalistic fervor. "We Americans aren't like those dumb Russki peasants! We'll do a whole lot better when *we* get Communism!"

And on that, his employer, the expansive John Pollikop, a woolly Scotch terrier of a man, returned to the garage. John was an excellent friend of Doremus; had, indeed, been his bootlegger all through Prohibition, personally running in his whisky from Canada. He had been known, even in that singularly scrupulous profession, as one of its most trustworthy practitioners. Now he flowered into mid-European dialectics:

"Evenin', Mist' Jessup, evenin', Julian! Karl fill up y' tank for you? You want t' watch that guy—he's likely to hold out a gallon on you. He's one of these crazy dogs of Communists—they all believe in Violence instead of Evolution and Legality. Them—why say, if they hadn't been so crooked, if they'd joined me and Norman Thomas and the other *intelligent* Socialists in a United Front with Roosevelt and the Jeffersonians, why say, we'd of licked the pants off Buzzard Windrip! Windrip and his plans!"

("Buzzard" Windrip. That was good, Doremus reflected. He'd be able to use it in the *Informer!*)

Pascal protested, "Not that Buzzard's personal plans and ambitions have got much to do with it. Altogether too easy to explain everything just blaming it on Windrip. Why don't you *read* your Marx, John, instead of always gassing about him? Why, Windrip's just something nasty that's been vomited up. Plenty others still left fermenting in the stomach—quack economists with every sort of economic ptomaine! No, Buzz isn't important—it's the sickness that made us throw him up that we've got to attend to—the sickness of more than 30 per cent permanently unemployed, and growing larger. Got to cure it!"

"Can you crazy Tovarishes cure it?" snapped Pollikop, and, "Do you think Communism will cure it?" skeptically wondered Doremus, and, more politely, "Do you really think Karl Marx had the dope?" worried Julian, all three at once.

"You bet your life we can!" said Pascal vaingloriously.

As Doremus, driving away, looked back at them, Pascal and Pollikop were removing a flat tire together and quarreling bitterly, quite happily.

Doremus's attic study had been to him a refuge from the tender solicitudes of Emma and Mrs. Candy and his daughters, and all the impulsive hand-shaking strangers who wanted the local editor to start off their campaigns for the sale of life insurance or gas-saving carburetors, for the Salvation Army or the Red Cross or the Orphans' Home or the Anti-cancer Crusade, or the assorted magazines which would enable to go through college young men who at all cost should be kept out of college.

It was a refuge now from the considerably less tender solicitudes of supporters of the President-Elect. On the pretense of work, Doremus took to sneaking up there in mid-evening; and he sat not in an easy chair but stiffly, at his desk, making crosses and five-pointed stars and six-pointed stars and fancy delete signs on sheets of yellow copy paper, while he sorely meditated.

Thus, this evening, after the demands of Karl Pascal and John Pollikop:

" 'The Revolt against Civilization!'

"But there's the worst trouble of this whole cursed business of analysis. When I get to defending Democracy against Communism and Fascism and what-not, I sound just like the Lothrop Stoddards—why, I sound almost like a Hearst editorial on how some college has got to kick out a Dangerous Red instructor in order to preserve our Democracy for the ideals of Jefferson and Washington! Yet somehow, singing the same words, I have a notion my tune is entirely different from Hearst's. I *don't* think we've done very well with all the plowland and forest and minerals and husky human stock we've had. What makes me sick about Hearst and the D.A.R. is that if *they* are against Communism, I have to be for it, and I don't want to be!

"Wastage of resources, so they're about gone—that's been the American share in the revolt against Civilization.

"We *can* go back to the Dark Ages! The crust of learning and good manners and tolerance is so thin! It would just take a few thousand big shells and gas bombs to wipe out all the eager young men, and all the libraries and historical archives and patent offices, all the laboratories and art galleries, all the castles and Periclean temples and Gothic cathedrals, all the cooperative stores and motor factories—every storehouse of learning. No inherent reason why Sissy's grandchildren—if anybody's grandchildren will survive at all—shouldn't be living in caves and heaving rocks at catamounts.

"And what's the solution of preventing this debacle? Plenty of 'em! The Communists have a patent Solution they know will work. So have the Fascists, and the rigid American Constitutionalists—who *call* themselves advocates of Democracy, without any notion what the word ought to mean; and the Monarchists—who are certain that if we could just resurrect the Kaiser and the Czar and King Alfonso, everybody would be loyal and happy again, and the banks would simply force credit on small business men at 2 per cent. And all the preachers—they tell you that they alone have the inspired Solution.

"Well, gentlemen, I have listened to all your Solutions, and I now inform you that I, and I alone, except perhaps for Walt Trowbridge and the ghost of Pareto, have the perfect, the inevitable, the only Solution, and that is: There is no Solution! There will never be a state of society anything like perfect!

"There never will be a time when there won't be a large proportion of people who feel poor no matter how much they have, and envy their neighbors who know how to wear cheap clothes showily, and envy neighbors who can dance or make love or digest better."

Doremus suspected that, with the most scientific state, it would be impossible for iron deposits always to find themselves at exactly the rate decided upon two years before by the National Technocratic Minerals Commission, no matter how elevated and fraternal and Utopian the principles of the commissioners.

His Solution, Doremus pointed out, was the only one that did not flee before the thought that a thousand years from now human beings would probably continue to die of cancer and earthquake and such clownish mishaps as slipping in bathtubs. It presumed that mankind would continue to be burdened with eyes that grow weak, feet that grow tired, noses that itch, intestines vulnerable to bacilli, and generative organs that are nervous until the age of virtue and senility. It seemed to him unidealistically probable, for all the "contemporary furniture" of the 1930's, that most people would continue, at least for a few hundred years, to sit in chairs, eat from dishes upon tables, read books—no matter how many cunning phonographic substitutes might be invented, wear shoes or sandals, sleep in beds, write with some sort of pens, and in general spend twenty or twenty-two hours a day much as they had spent them in 1930, in 1630. He suspected that tornadoes, floods, droughts, lightning, and mosquitoes would remain, along with the homicidal tendency known in the best of citizens when their sweethearts go dancing off with other men.

And, most fatally and abysmally, his Solution guessed that men of superior cunning, of slyer foxiness, whether they might be called Comrades, Brethren, Commissars, Kings, Patriots, Little Brothers of the Poor, or any other rosy name, would continue to have more influence than slower-witted men, however worthy.

* * *

All the warring Solutions—except his, Doremus chuckled—were ferociously propagated by the Fanatics, the "Nuts."

He recalled an article in which Neil Carothers asserted that the "rabble-rousers" of America in the mid-'thirties had a long and dishonorable ancestry of prophets who had felt called upon to stir up the masses to save the world, and save it in the prophets' own way, and do it right now, and most violently: Peter the Hermit, the ragged, mad, and stinking monk who, to rescue the (unidentified) tomb of the Savior from undefined "outrages by the pagans," led out on the Crusades some hundreds of thousands of European peasants, to die on the way of starvation, after burning, raping, and murdering fellow peasants in foreign villages all along the road.

There was John Ball who "in 1381 was a share-the-wealth advocate; he preached equality of wealth, the abolition of class distinctions, and what would now be called communism," and whose follower, Wat Tyler, looted London, with the final gratifying result that afterward Labor was by the frightened government more oppressed than ever. And nearly three hundred years later, Cromwell's methods of expounding the sweet winsomeness of Purity and Liberty were shooting, slashing, clubbing, starving, and burning people, and after him the workers paid for the spree of bloody righteousness with blood.

Brooding about it, fishing in the muddy slew of recollection which most Americans have in place of a clear pool of history, Doremus was able to add other names of well-meaning rabble-rousers:

Marat and Danton and Robespierre, who helped shift the control of France from the moldy aristocrats to the stuffy, centime-pinching shopkeepers. Lenin and Trotzky who gave to the illiterate Russian peasants the privileges of punching a time clock and of being as learned, gay, and dignified as the factory hands in Detroit; and Lenin's man, Borodin, who extended this boon to China. And that William Randolph Hearst who in 1898 was the Lenin of Cuba and switched the mastery of the golden isle from the cruel Spaniards to the peaceful, unarmed, brotherly-loving Cuban politicians of today.

The American Moses, Dowie, and his theocracy at

Zion City, Illinois, where the only results of the direct leadership of God—as directed and encouraged by Mr. Dowie and by his even more spirited successor, Mr. Voliva—were that the holy denizens were deprived of oysters and cigarettes and cursing, and died without the aid of doctors instead of with it, and that the stretch of road through Zion City incessantly caused the breakage of springs on the cars of citizens from Evanston, Wilmette, and Winnetka, which may or not have been a desirable Good Deed.

Cecil Rhodes, his vision of making South Africa a British paradise, and the actuality of making it a graveyard for British soldiers.

All the Utopias—Brook Farm, Robert Owen's sanctuary of chatter, Upton Sinclair's Helicon Hall—and their regulation end in scandal, feuds, poverty, griminess, disillusion.

All the leaders of Prohibition, so certain that their cause was world-regenerating that for it they were willing to shoot down violators.

It seemed to Doremus that the only rabble-rouser to build permanently had been Brigham Young, with his bearded Mormon captains, who not only turned the Utah desert into an Eden but made it pay and kept it up.

Pondered Doremus: Blessed be they who are not Patriots and Idealists, and who do not feel they must dash right in and Do Something About It, something so immediately important that all doubters must be liquidated—tortured—slaughtered! Good old murder, that since the slaying of Abel by Cain has always been the new device by which all oligarchies and dictators have, for all future ages to come, removed opposition!

In this acid mood Doremus doubted the efficacy of all revolutions; dared even a little to doubt our two American revolutions—against England in 1776, and the Civil War.

For a New England editor to contemplate even the smallest criticism of these wars was what it would have been for a Southern Baptist fundamentalist preacher to question Immortality, the Inspiration of the Bible, and the ethical value of shouting Hallelujah. Yet had it, Doremus queried nervously, been necessary to have four years of inconceivably murderous Civil War, followed by twenty years of commercial oppression of the South, in order to preserve the Union, free the slaves, and establish the equality of Industry with Agriculture? Had it been just to the Negroes themselves to throw them so suddenly, with so little preparation, into full citizenship, that the Southern states, in what they considered self-defense, disqualified them at the polls and lynched them and lashed them? Could they not, as Lincoln at first desired and planned, have been freed without the vote, then gradually and competently educated, under federal guardianship, so that by 1890 they might, without too much enmity, have been able to enter fully into all the activities of the land?

A generation and a half (Doremus meditated) of the sturdiest and most gallant killed or crippled in the Civil War or, perhaps worst of all, becoming garrulous professional heroes and satellites of the politicians who in return for their solid vote made all lazy jobs safe for the G.A.R. The most valorous, it was they who suffered the most, for while the John D. Rockefellers, the J. P. Morgans, the Vanderbilts, Astors, Goulds, and all their nimble financial comrades of the South, did not enlist, but stayed in the warm, dry counting-house, drawing the fortune of the country into their webs, it was Jeb Stuart, Stonewall Jackson, Nathaniel Lyon, Pat Cleburne, and the knightly James B. McPherson who were killed . . . and with them Abraham Lincoln.

So, with the hundreds of thousands who should have been the progenitors of new American generations drained away, we could show the world, which from 1780 to 1860 had so admired men like Franklin, Jefferson, Washington, Hamilton, the Adamses, Webster, only such salvages as McKinley, Benjamin Harrison, William Jennings Bryan, Harding . . . and Senator Berzelius Windrip and his rivals.

Slavery had been a cancer, and in that day was known no remedy save bloody cutting. There had been no X-rays of wisdom and tolerance. Yet to sentimentalize this cutting, to justify and rejoice in it, was an altogether evil thing, a national superstition that was later to lead to other Unavoidable Wars—wars to free Cubans, to free Filipinos who didn't want our brand of freedom, to End All Wars.

Let us, thought Doremus, not throb again to the bugles of the Civil War, nor find diverting the gallantry of Sherman's dashing Yankee boys in burning the houses of lone women, nor particularly admire the calmness of General Lee as he watched thousands writhe in the mud.

He even wondered if, necessarily, it had been such a desirable thing for the Thirteen Colonies to have cut themselves off from Great Britain. Had the United States remained in the British Empire, possibly there would have evolved a confederation that could have enforced World Peace, instead of talking about it. Boys and girls from Western ranches and Southern plantations and Northern maple groves might have added Oxford and York Minster and Devonshire villages to their own domain. Englishmen, and even virtuous Englishwomen, might have learned that persons who lack the accent of a Kentish rectory or of a Yorkshire textile village may yet in many ways be literate; and that astonishing numbers of persons in the world cannot be persuaded that their chief aim in life ought to be to increase British exports on behalf of the stockholdings of the Better Classes.

It is commonly asserted, Doremus remembered, that without complete political independence the United States could not have developed its own peculiar virtues. Yet it was not apparent to him that America was any more individual than Canada or Australia; that Pittsburgh and Kansas City were to be preferred before Montreal and Melbourne, Sydney and Vancouver.

No questioning of the eventual wisdom of the "radicals" who had first advocated these two American revolutions, Doremus warned himself, should be allowed to give any comfort to that eternal enemy: the conservative manipulators of privilege who damn as "dangerous agitators" any man who menaces their fortunes; who jump in their chairs at the sting of a gnat like Debs, and blandly swallow a camel like Windrip.

Between the rabble-rousers—chiefly to be detected by desire for their own personal power and notoriety—and the un-self-seeking fighters against tryanny, between William Walker or Danton, and John Howard or William Lloyd Garrison, Doremus saw, there was the difference between a noisy gang of thieves and an honest man noisily defending himself against thieves. He had been brought up to revere the Abolitionists: Lovejoy, Garrison, Wendell Phillips, Harriet Beecher Stowe—though his father had considered John Brown insane and a menace, and had thrown sly mud at the marble statues of Henry Ward Beecher, the apostle in the fancy vest. And Doremus could not do otherwise than revere the Abolitionists now, though he wondered a little if Stephen Douglas and Thaddeus Stephens and Lincoln, more cautious and less romantic men, might not have done the job better.

"Is it just possible," he sighed, "that the most vigorous and boldest idealists have been the worst enemies of human progress instead of its greatest creators? Possible that plain men with the humble trait of minding their own business will rank higher in the heavenly hierarchy than all the plumed souls who have shoved their way in among the masses and insisted on saving them?"

14

I joined the Christian, or as some call it, the Campbellite Church as a mere boy, not yet dry behind the ears. But I wished then and I wish now that it were possible for me to belong to the whole glorious brotherhood; to be one in Communion at the same time with the brave Presbyterians that fight the pusillanimous, mendacious, destructive, tom-fool Higher Critics, so-called; and with the Methodists who so strongly oppose war yet in war-time can always be counted upon for Patriotism to the limit; and with the splendidly tolerant Baptists, the earnest Seventh-Day Adventists, and I guess I could even say a kind word for the Unitarians, as that great executive William Howard Taft belonged to them, also his wife.

Zero Hour, Berzelius Windrip.

OFFICIALLY, Doremus belonged to the Universalist Church, his wife and children to the Episcopal—a natural American transition. He had been reared to admire Hosea Ballou, the Universalist St. Augustine who, from his tiny parsonage in Barnard, Vermont, had proclaimed his faith that even the wickedest would have, after earthly death, another chance of salvation. But now, Doremus could scarce enter the Fort Beulah Universalist Church. It had too many memories of his father, the pastor, and it was depressing to see how the old-time congregations, in which two hundred thick beards would wag in the grained pine benches every Sunday morning, and their womenfolks and children line up beside the patriarchs, had dwindled to aged widows and farmers and a few schoolteachers.

But in this time of seeking, Doremus did venture there. The church was a squat and gloomy building of granite, not particularly enlivened by the arches of colored slate above the windows, yet as a boy Doremus had thought it and its sawed-off tower the superior of Chartres. He had loved it as in Isaiah College he had loved the Library which, for all its appearance of being a crouching redbrick toad, had meant to him freedom for spiritual discovery—still cavern of a reading room where for hours one could forget the world and never be nagged away to supper.

He found, on his one attendance at the Universalist Church, a scattering of thirty disciples, being addressed by a "supply," a theological student from Boston, monotonously shouting his well-meant, frightened, and slightly plagiaristic eloquence in regard to the sickness of Abijah, the son of Jeroboam. Doremus looked at the church walls, painted a hard and glistening green, unornamented, to avoid all the sinful trappings of papistry, while he listened to the preacher's hesitant droning:

"Now, uh, now what so many of us fail to realize is how, uh, how sin, how any sin that we, uh, we ourselves may commit, any sin reflects not on ourselves but on those that we, uh, that we hold near and dear——"

He would have given anything, Doremus yearned, for a sermon which, however irrational, would passionately lift him to renewed courage, which would bathe him in consolation these beleagured months. But with a shock of anger he saw that that was exactly what he had been condemning just a few days ago: the irrational dramatic power of the crusading leader, clerical or political.

Very well then—sadly. He'd just have to get along without the spiritual consolation of the church that he had known in college days.

No, first he'd try the ritual of his friend Mr. Falck—the Padre, Buck Titus sometimes called him.

In the cozy Anglicanism of St. Crispin's P. E. Church, with its imitation English memorial brasses and imitation Celtic font and brass-eagle reading desk and dusty-smelling maroon carpet, Doremus listened to Mr. Falck: "Almighty God, the Father of our Lord Jesus Christ, who desireth not the death of a sinner, but rather that he may turn from his wickedness, and live; and hath given power and commandment to his Ministers, to declare and pronounce to his people, being penitent, the Absolution and Remission of their sins——"

Doremus glanced at the placidly pious façade of his wife, Emma. The lovely, familiar old ritual seemed meaningless to him now, with no more pertinence to a life menaced by Buzz Windrip and his Minute Men, no more comfort for having lost his old deep pride in being an American, than a stage revival of an equally lovely and familiar Elizabethan play. He looked about nervously. However exalted Mr. Falck himself might be, most of the congregation were Yorkshire pudding. The Anglican Church was, to them, not the aspiring humility of Newman nor the humanity of Bishop Brown (both of whom left it!) but the sign and proof of prosperity—an ecclesiastical version of owning a twelve-cylinder Cadillac—or even more, of knowing that one's grandfather owned his own surrey and a respectable old family horse.

The whole place smelled to Doremus of stale muffins. Mrs. R. C. Crowley was wearing white gloves and on her bust—for a Mrs. Crowley, even in 1936, did not yet have breasts—was a tight bouquet of tuberoses. Francis Tasbrough had a morning coat and striped trousers and on the lilac-colored pew cushion beside him was (unique in Fort Beulah) a silk top-hat. And even the wife of Doremus's bosom, or at least of his breakfast coffee, the good Emma, had a pedantic expression of superior goodness which irritated him.

"Whole outfit stifles me!" he snapped. "Rather be at a yelling, jumping Holy Roller orgy—no—that's Buzz Windrip's kind of jungle hysterics. I want a church, if there can possibly be one, that's advanced beyond the jungle and beyond the chaplains of King Henry the Eighth. I know why, even though she's painfully conscientious, Lorinda never goes to church."

Lorinda Pike, on that sleety December afternoon, was darning a tea cloth in the lounge of her Beulah Valley Tavern, five miles up the river from the Fort. It wasn't, of course, a tavern: it was a super-boarding-house as regards its twelve guest bedrooms, and a slightly too arty tearoom in its dining facilities. Despite his long affection for Lorinda, Doremus was always annoyed by the Singhalese brass finger bowls, the North Carolina table mats, and the Italian ash trays displayed for sale on wabbly card tables in the dining room. But he had to admit that the tea was excellent, the scones light, the Stilton sound, Lorinda's private rum punches admirable, and that Lorinda herself was intelligent yet adorable—particularly when, as on this gray afternoon, she was bothered neither by other guests nor by the presence of that worm, her partner, Mr. Nipper, whose pleasing notion it was that because he had invested a few thousand in the Tavern he should have none of the work or responsibility and half the profits.

Doremus thrust his way in, patting off the snow, puffing to recover from the shakiness caused by skidding all the way from Fort Beulah. Lorinda nodded carelessly, dropped another stick on the fireplace, and went back to her darning with nothing more intimate than "Hullo. Nasty out."

"Yuh—fierce."

But as they sat on either side the hearth their eyes had no need of smiling for a bridge between them.

Lorinda reflected, "Well, my darling, it's going to be pretty bad. I guess Windrip & Co. will put the woman's struggle right back in the sixteen-hundreds, with Anne Hutchinson and the Antinomians."

"Sure. Back to the kitchen."

"Even if you haven't got one!"

"Any worse than us men? Notice that Windrip never *mentioned* free speech and the freedom of the press in his articles of faith? Oh, he'd 've come out for 'em strong and hearty if he'd even thought of 'em!"

"That's so. Tea, darling?"

"No. Linda, damn it, I feel like taking the family and sneaking off to Canada *before* I get nabbed—right after Buzz's inauguration."

"No. You mustn't. We've got to keep all the newspapermen that'll go on fighting him, and not go sniffling up to the garbage pail. Besides! What would I do without you?" For the first time Lorinda sounded importunate.

"You'll be a lot less suspect if I'm not around. But I guess you're right. I can't go till they put the skids under me. Then I'll have to vanish. I'm too old to stand jail."

"Not too old to make love, I hope! That *would* be hard on a girl!"

"Nobody ever is, except the kind that used to be too young to make love! Anyway, I'll stay—for a while."

He had, suddenly, from Lorinda, the resoluteness he had sought in church. He would go on trying to sweep back the ocean, just for his own satisfaction. It meant, however, that his hermitage in the Ivory Tower was closed with slightly ludicrous speed. But he felt strong again, and happy. His brooding was interrupted by Lorinda's curt:

"How's Emma taking the political situation?"

"Doesn't know there is one! Hears me croaking, and she heard Walt Trowbridge's warning on the radio, last evening—did you listen in?—and she says, 'Oh my, how dreadful!' and then forgets all about it and worries about the saucepan that got burnt! She's lucky! Oh well, she probably calms me down and keeps me from becoming a *complete* neurote! Probably that's why I'm so darned everlastingly fond of her. And yet I'm chump enough to wish you and I were together—uh—recognizedly together, all the time—and could fight together to keep some little light burning in this coming new glacial epoch. I do. All the time. I think that, at this moment, all things considered, I should like to kiss you."

"Is that so unusual a celebration?"

"Yes. Always. Always it's the first time again! Look, Linda, do you ever stop to think how curious it is, that with—everything between us—like that night in the hotel at Montreal—we neither one of us seem to feel any guilt, any embarrassment—can sit and gossip like this?"

"No, dear. . . . Darling! . . . It doesn't seem a bit curious. It was all so natural. So good!"

"And yet we're reasonably responsible people——"

"Of course. That's why nobody suspects us, not even

Emma. Thank God she doesn't, Doremus! I wouldn't hurt her for anything, not even for your kind-hearted favors!"

"Beast!"

"Oh, you might be suspected, all by yourself. It's known that you sometimes drink likker and play poker and tell 'hot ones.' But who'd ever suspect that the local female crank, the suffragist, the pacifist, the anti-censorshipist, the friend of Jane Addams and Mother Bloor, could be a libertine! Highbrows! Bloodless reformers! Oh, and I've known so many women agitators, all dressed in Carrie Nation hatchets and modest sheets of statistics, that have been ten times as passionate, intolerably passionate, as any cream-faced plump little Kept Wife in chiffon stepins!"

For a moment their embracing eyes were not merely friendly and accustomed and careless.

He fretted, "Oh I think of you all the time and want you and yet I think of Emma too—and I don't even have the fine novelistic egotism of feeling guilty and intolerably caught in complexities. Yes, it does all seem so natural. Dear Linda!"

He stalked restlessly to the casement window, looking back at her every second step. It was dusk now, and the roads smoking. He stared out inattentively—then very attentively indeed.

"That's curious. Curiouser and curiouser. Standing back behind that big bush, lilac bush I guess it is, across the road, there's a fellow watching this place. I can see him in the headlights when ever a car comes along. And I think it's my hired man, Oscar Ledue—Shad." He started to draw the cheerful red-and-white curtains.

"No! No! Don't draw them! He'll get suspicious."

"That's right. Funny, his watching there—if it *is* him. He's supposed to be at my house right now, looking at the furnace—winters, he only works for me couple of hours a day, works in the sash factory, rest of the time, but he ought to—— A little light blackmail, I suppose. Well, he can publish everything he saw today, wherever he wants to!"

"Only what he saw today?"

"Anything! Any day! I'm awfully proud—old dish rag like me, twenty years older than you!—to be your lover!"

And he was proud, yet all the while he was remembering the warning in red chalk that he had found on his front porch after the election. Before he had time to become very complicated about it, the door vociferously banged open, and his daughter, Sissy, sailed in.

"Wot-oh, wot-oh, wot-oh! Toodle-oo! Good-morning, Jeeves! Mawnin', Miss Lindy. How's all de folks on de ole plantation everywhere I roam? Hello, Dad. No, it isn't cocktails—least, just one very small cocktail—it's youthful spirits! My God, but it's cold! Tea, Linda, my good woman—tea!"

They had tea. A thoroughly domestic circle.

"Race you home, Dad," said Sissy, when they were ready to go.

"Yes—no—wait a second! Lorinda: lend me a flashlight."

As he marched out of the door, marched belligerently across the road, in Doremus seethed all the agitated anger he had been concealing from Sissy. And part hidden behind bushes, leaning on his motorcycle, he did find Shad Ledue.

Shad was startled; for once he looked less contemptuously masterful than a Fifth Avenue traffic policeman, as Doremus snapped, "What you doing there?" and he stumbled in answering: "Oh I just—something happened to my motor-bike."

"So! You ought to be home tending the furnace, Shad."

"Well, I guess I got my machine fixed now. I'll hike along."

"No. My daughter is to drive me home, so you can put your motorcycle in the back of my car and drive it back." (Somehow, he had to talk privately to Sissy, though he was not in the least certain what it was he had to say.)

"Her? Rats! Sissy can't drive for sour apples! Crazy's a loon!"

"Ledue! Miss Sissy is a highly competent driver. At least she satisfies me, and if you really feel she doesn't quite satisfy *your* standard——"

"Her driving don't make a damn bit of difference to me one way or th' other! G'-night!"

Recrossing the road, Doremus rebuked himself, "That was childish of me. Trying to talk to him like a gent! But how I would enjoy murdering him!"

He informed Sissy, at the door, "Shad happened to come along—motorcycle in bad shape—let him take my Chrysler—I'll drive with you."

"Fine! Only six boys have had their hair turn gray, driving with me, this week."

"And I—I meant to say, I think I'd better do the driving. It's pretty slippery tonight."

"Wouldn't that destroy you! Why, my dear idiot parent, I'm the best driver in——"

"You can't drive for sour apples! Crazy, that's all! Get in! I'm driving, d'you hear? Night, Lorinda."

"All right, dearest Father," said Sissy with an impishness which reduced his knees to feebleness.

He assured himself, though, that this flip manner of Sissy, characteristic of even the provincial boys and girls who had been nursed on gasoline, was only an imitation of the nicer New York harlots and would not last more than another year or two. Perhaps this rattle-tongued generation needed a Buzz Windrip Revolution and all its pain.

"Beautiful, I know it's swell to drive carefully, but do you have to emulate the prudent snail?" said Sissy.

"Snails don't skid."

"No, they get run over. Rather skid!"

"So your father's a fossil!"

"Oh, I wouldn't——"

"Well, maybe he is, at that. There's advantages. Anyway: I wonder if there isn't a lot of bunk about Age being so cautious and conservative, and Youth always being so adventurous and bold and original? Look at the young Nazis and how they enjoy beating up the Communists. Look at almost any college class—the students disapproving of the instructor because he's iconoclastic and ridicules the sacred home-town ideas. Just this afternoon, I was thinking, driving out here——"

"Listen, Dad, do you go to Lindy's often?"

"Why—why, not especially. Why?"

"Why don't you—— What are you two so scared of? You two wild-haired reformers—you and Lindy belong together. Why don't you—you know—kind of be lovers?"

"Good God Almighty! Cecilia! I've never heard a *decent* girl talk that way in all my life!"

"Tst! Tst! Haven't you? Dear, dear! So sorry!"

"Well, my Lord—— At least you've got to admit that it's slightly unusual for an apparently loyal daughter to suggest her father's deceiving her mother! Especially a fine lovely mother like yours!"

"Is it? Well, maybe. Unusual to suggest it—aloud. But I wonder if lots of young females don't sometimes kind of *think* it, just the same, when they see the Venerable Parent going stale!"

"Sissy——"

"Hey, watch that telephone pole!"

"Hang it, I didn't go anywheres near it! Now you look here, Sissy: you simply must not be so froward—or forward, whichever it is; I always get those two words balled up. This is serious business. I've never heard of such a preposterous suggestion as Linda—Lorinda and I being lovers. My dear child, you simply *can't* be flip about such final things as that!"

"Oh, *can't* I! Oh, sorry, Dad. I just mean—— About Mother Emma. Course I wouldn't have anybody hurt her, not even Lindy and you. But, why, bless you, Venerable, she'd never even dream of such a thing. You could have your nice pie and she'd never miss one single slice. Mother's mental grooves aren't, uh, well, they aren't so very sex-conditioned, if that's how you say it—more sort of along the new-vacuum-cleaner complex, if you know what I mean—page Freud! Oh, she's swell, but not so analytical and——"

"Are those your ethics, then?"

"Huh? Well for cat's sake, why not? Have a swell time that'll get you full of beans again and yet not hurt anybody's feelings? Why, say, that's the entire second chapter in my book on ethics!"

"Sissy! Have you, by any chance, any vaguest notion of what you're talking about, or think you're talking about? Of course—and perhaps we ought to be ashamed of our cowardly negligence—but I, and I don't suppose your mother, have taught you so very much about 'sex' and——"

"Thank heaven! You spared me the dear little flower and its simply shocking affair with that tough tomcat of a tiger lily in the next bed—excuse me—I mean in the next plot. I'm so glad you did. Pete's sake! I'd certainly hate to blush every time I looked at a garden!"

"Sissy! Child! Please! You mustn't be so beastly *cute*! These are all weighty things——"

Penitently: "I know, Dad. I'm sorry. It's just—if you only knew how wretched I feel when I see you so wretched and so quiet and everything. This horrible Windrip, League of Forgodsakers business has got you down, hasn't it! If you're going to fight 'em, you've got to get some pep back into you—you've got to take off the lace mitts and put on the brass knuckles—and I got kind of a hunch Lorinda might do that for you, and only her. Heh! Her pretending to be so high-minded! (Remember that old wheeze Buck Titus used to love so—'If you're saving the fallen women, save me one'? Oh, not so good. I guess we'll take that line right out of the sketch!) But anyway, our Lindy has a pretty moist and hungry eye——"

"Impossible! Impossible! By the way, Sissy! What do you know about all of this? Are you a virgin?"

"Dad! Is that your idea of a question to—— Oh, I guess I was asking for it. And the answer is: Yes. So far. But not promising one single thing about the future. Let me tell you right now, if conditions in this country do get as bad as you've been claiming they will, and Julian Falck is threatened with having to go to war or go to prison or some rotten thing like that, I'm most certainly not going to let any maidenly modesty interfere between me and him, and you might just as well be prepared for that!"

"It *is* Julian then, not Malcolm?"

"Oh, I think so. Malcolm gives me a pain in the neck. He's getting all ready to take his proper place as a colonel or something with Windrip's wooden soldiers. And I am so fond of Julian! Even if he is the doggonedest, most impractical soul—like his grandfather—or you!

He's a sweet thing. We sat up purring pretty nothings till about two, last night, I guess."

"Sissy! But you haven't—— Oh, my little girl! Julian is probably decent enough—not a bad sort—but you—— You haven't let Julian take any familiarities with you?"

"Dear quaint old word! As if anything could be so awfully much more familiar than a good, capable, 10,000 h.p. kiss! But darling, just so you won't worry—no. The few times, late nights, in our sitting room, when I've slept with Julian—well, we've *slept*!"

"I'm glad, but—— Your apparent—probably only apparent—information on a variety of delicate subjects slightly embarrasses me."

"Now you listen to me! And this is something you ought to be telling me, not me you, Mr. Jessup! Looks as if this country, and most of the world—I *am* being serious, now, Dad; plenty serious, God help us all!—it looks as if we're headed right back into barbarism. It's war! There's not going to be much time for coyness and modesty, any more than there is for a base-hospital nurse when they bring in the wounded. Nice young ladies—they're *out*! It's Lorinda and me that you men are going to want to have around, isn't it—isn't it—now isn't it?"

"Maybe—perhaps," Doremus sighed, depressed at seeing a little more of his familiar world slide from under his feet as the flood rose.

They were coming into the Jessup driveway. Shad Ledue was just leaving the garage.

"Skip in the house, quick, will you!" said Doremus to his girl.

"Sure. But do be careful, hon!" She no longer sounded like his little daughter, to be protected, adorned with pale blue ribbons, slyly laughed at when she tried to show off in grown-up ways. She was suddenly a dependable comrade, like Lorinda.

Doremus slipped resolutely out of his car and said calmly:

"Shad!"

"Yuh?"

"D'you take the car keys into the kitchen?"

"Huh? No. I guess I left 'em in the car."

"I've told you a hundred times they belong inside."

"Yuh? Well, how'd you like *Miss Cecilia's* driving? Have a good visit with old Mrs. Pike?"

He was derisive now, beyond concealment.

"Ledue, I rather think you're fired—right now!"

"Well! Just feature that! O.K., Chief! I was just going to tell you that we're forming a second chapter of the League of Forgotten Men in the Fort, and I'm to be the secretary. They don't pay much—only about twice what you pay me—pretty tight-fisted—but it'll mean something in politics. Good-night!"

Afterward, Doremus was sorry to remember that, for all his longshoreman clumsiness, Shad had learned a precise script in his red Vermont schoolhouse, and enough mastery of figures so that probably he would be able to keep this rather bogus secretaryship. Too bad!

When, as League secretary, a fortnight later, Shad wrote to him demanding a donation of two hundred dollars to the League, and Doremus refused, the *Informer* began to lose circulation within twenty-four hours.

15

Usually I'm pretty mild, in fact many of my friends are kind enough to call it "Folksy," when I'm writing or speechifying. My ambition is to "live by the side of the road and be a friend to man." But I hope that none of the gentlemen who have honored me with their enmity think for one single moment that when I run into a gross enough public evil or a persistent enough detractor, I can't get up on my hind legs and make a sound like a two-tailed grizzly in April. So right at the start of this account of my ten-year fight with them, as private citizen, State Senator, and U. S. Senator, let me say that the Sangfrey River Light, Power, and Fuel Corporation are—and I invite a suit for libel—the meanest, lowest, cowardliest gang of yellow-livered, back-slapping, hypocritical gun-toters, bomb-throwers, ballot-stealers, ledger-fakers, givers of bribes, suborners of perjury, scab-hirers, and general lowdown crooks, liars, and swindlers that ever tried to do an honest servant of the People out of an election—not but what I have always succeeded in licking them, so that my indignation at these homicidal kleptomaniacs is not personal but entirely on behalf of the general public.

Zero Hour, Berzelius Windrip.

ON WEDNESDAY, January 6, 1937, just a fortnight before his inauguration, President-Elect Windrip announced his appointments of cabinet members and of diplomats.

Secretary of State: his former secretary and press-agent, Lee Sarason, who also took the position of High Marshal, or Commander-in-Chief, of the Minute Men, which organization was to be established permanently, as an innocent marching club.

Secretary of the Treasury: one Webster R. Skittle, president of the prosperous Fur & Hide National Bank of St. Louis—Mr. Skittle had once been indicted on a charge of defrauding the government on his income tax, but he had been acquitted, more or less, and during the campaign, he was said to have taken a convincing way of showing his faith in Buzz Windrip as the Savior of the Forgotten Men.

Secretary of War: Colonel Osceola Luthorne, formerly editor of the Topeka (Kans.) *Argus*, and the *Fancy Goods and Novelties Gazette;* more recently high in real estate. His title came from his position on the honorary staff of the Governor of Tennessee. He had long been a friend and fellow campaigner of Windrip.

It was a universal regret that Bishop Paul Peter Prang should have refused the appointment as Secretary of War, with a letter in which he called Windrip "My dear Friend and Collaborator" and asserted that he had actually meant it when he had said he desired no office. Later, it was a similar regret when Father Coughlin refused the Ambassadorship to Mexico, with no letter at all but only a telegram cryptically stating, "Just six months too late."

A new cabinet position, that of Secretary of Education and Public Relations, was created. Not for months would Congress investigate the legality of such a creation, but meantime the new post was brilliantly held by Hector Macgoblin, M.D., Ph.D., Hon. Litt.D.

Senator Porkwood graced the position of Attorney General, and all the other offices were acceptably filled by men who, though they had roundly supported Windrip's almost socialistic projects for the distribution of excessive fortunes, were yet known to be thoroughly sensible men, and no fanatics.

It was said, though Doremus Jessup could never prove it, that Windrip learned from Lee Sarason the Spanish custom of getting rid of embarrassing friends and enemies by appointing them to posts abroad, preferably quite far abroad. Anyway, as Ambassador to Brazil, Windrip appointed Herbert Hoover, who not very enthusiastically accepted; as Ambassador to Germany, Senator Borah; as Governor of the Philippines, Senator Robert La Follette, who refused; and as Ambassadors to the Court of St. James's, France, and Russia, none other than Upton Sinclair, Milo Reno, and Senator Bilbo of Mississippi.

These three had a fine time. Mr. Sinclair pleased the British by taking so friendly an interest in their politics that he openly campaigned for the Independent Labor Party and issued a lively brochure called "I, Upton Sinclair, Prove That Prime-Minister Walter Elliot, Foreign Secretary Anthony Eden, and First Lord of the Admiralty Nancy Astor Are All Liars and Have Refused to Accept My Freely Offered Advice." Mr. Sinclair also aroused considerable interest in British domestic circles by advocating an act of Parliament forbidding the wearing of evening clothes and all hunting of foxes except with shotguns; and on the occasion of his official reception at Buckingham Palace, he warmly invited King George and Queen Mary to come and live in California.

Mr. Milo Reno, insurance salesman and former president of the National Farm Holiday Association, whom all the French royalists compared to his great predecessor, Benjamin Franklin, for forthrightness, became the greatest social favorite in the international circles of Paris, the Basses-Pyrénées, and the Riviera, and was once photographed playing tennis at Antibes with the Duc de Tropez, Lord Rothermere, and Dr. Rudolph Hess.

Senator Bilbo had, possibly, the best time of all.

Stalin asked his advice, as based on his ripe experience in the *Gleichshaltung* of Mississippi, about the cultural organization of the somewhat backward natives of Tadjikistan, and so valuable did it prove that Excellency Bilbo was invited to review the Moscow military celebration, the following November seventh, in the same stand with the very highest class of representatives of the classless state. It was a triumph for His Excellency. Generalissimo Voroshilov fainted after 200,000 Soviet troops, 7000 tanks, and 9000 aëroplanes had passed by; Stalin had to be carried home after reviewing 317,000; but Ambassador Bilbo was there in the stand when the very last of the 626,000 soldiers had gone by, all of them saluting him under the quite erroneous impression that he was the Chinese Ambassador; and he was still tirelessly returning their salutes, fourteen to the minute, and softly singing with them the "International."

He was less of a hit later, however, when to the unsmiling Anglo-American Association of Exiles to Soviet Russia from Imperialism, he sang to the tune of the "International" what he regarded as amusing private words of his own:

Arise, ye prisoners of starvation,
From Russia make your getaway.
They are all rich in Bilbo's nation.
God bless the U. S. A.!

Mrs. Adelaide Tarr Gimmitch, after her spirited campaign for Mr. Windrip, was publicly angry that she was offered no position higher than a post in the customs office in Nome, Alaska, though this was offered to her very urgently indeed. She had demanded that there be created, especially for her, the cabinet position of Secretaryess of Domestic Science, Child Welfare, and Anti-Vice. She threatened to turn Jeffersonian, Republican, or Communistic, but in April she was heard of in Hollywood, writing the scenario for a giant picture to be called, *They Did It in Greece.*

As an insult and boy-from-home joke, the President-Elect appointed Franklin D. Roosevelt minister to Liberia. Mr. Roosevelt's opponents laughed very much, and opposition newspapers did cartoons of him sitting unhappily in a grass hut with a sign on which "N.R.A." had been crossed out and "U.S.A." substituted. But Mr. Roosevelt declined with so amiable a smile that the joke seemed rather to have slipped.

The followers of President Windrip trumpeted that it was significant that he should be the first president inaugurated not on March fourth, but on January twentieth according to the provision of the new Twentieth Amendment to the Constitution. It was a sign straight from Heaven (though, actually, Heaven had not been the author of the amendment, but Senator George W. Norris of Nebraska), and proved that Windrip was starting a new paradise on earth.

The inauguration was turbulent. President Roosevelt declined to be present—he politely suggested that he was about half ill unto death, but that same noon he was seen in a New York shop, buying books on gardening and looking abnormally cheerful.

More than a thousand reporters, photographers, and radio men covered the inauguration. Twenty-seven constituents of Senator Porkwood, of all sexes, had to sleep on the floor of the Senator's office, and a hall-bedroom in the suburb of Bladensburg rented for thirty dollars for two nights. The presidents of Brazil, the Argentine, and Chile flew to the inauguration in a Pan-American aëroplane, and Japan sent seven hundred students on a special train from Seattle.

A motor company in Detroit had presented to Windrip a limousine with armor plate, bulletproof glass, a hidden nickel-steel safe for papers, a concealed private bar, and upholstery made from the Troissant tapestries of 1670. But Buzz chose to drive from his home to the Capitol in his old Hupmobile sedan, and his driver was a youngster from his home town whose notion of a uniform for state occasions was a blue-serge suit, red tie, and derby hat. Windrip himself did wear a topper, but he saw to it that Lee Sarason saw to it that the one hundred and thirty million plain citizens learned, by radio, even while the inaugural parade was going on, that he had borrowed the topper for this one sole occasion from a New York Republican Representative who had ancestors.

But following Windrip was an un-Jacksonian escort of soldiers: the American Legion and, immensely grander than the others, the Minute Men, wearing trench helmets of polished silver and led by Colonel Dewey Haik in scarlet tunic and yellow riding-breeches and helmet with golden plumes.

Solemnly, for once looking a little awed, a little like a small-town boy on Broadway, Windrip took the oath, administered by the Chief Justice (who disliked him very much indeed) and, edging even closer to the microphone, squawked, "My fellow citizens, as the President of the United States of America, I want to inform you that the *real* New Deal has started right this minute, and we're all going to enjoy the manifold liberties to which our history entitles us—and have a whale of a good time doing it! I thank you!"

That was his first act as President. His second was to take up residence in the White House, where he sat down in the East Room in his stocking feet and shouted at Lee Sarason, "This is what I've been planning to do now for six years! I bet this is what Lincoln used to do! Now let 'em assassinate me!"

His third, in his rôle as Commander-in-Chief of the Army, was to order that the Minute Men be recognized as an unpaid but official auxiliary of the Regular Army, subject only to their own officers, to Buzz, and to High Marshal Sarason; and that rifles, bayonets, automatic pistols, and machine guns be instantly issued to them by government arsenals. That was at 4 P.M. Since 3 P.M., all over the country, bands of M.M.'s had been sitting gloating over pistols and guns, twitching with desire to seize them.

Fourth coup was a special message, next morning, to Congress (in session since January fourth, the third having been a Sunday), demanding the instant passage of a bill embodying Point Fifteen of his election platform—that he should have complete control of legislation and execution, and the Supreme Court be rendered incapable of blocking anything that it might amuse him to do.

By Joint Resolution, with less than half an hour of debate, both houses of Congress rejected that demand before 3 P.M., on January twenty-first. Before six, the President had proclaimed that a state of martial law existed during the "present crisis," and more than a hundred Congressmen had been arrested by Minute Men, on direct orders from the President. The Congressmen who were hot-headed enough to resist were cynically charged with "inciting to riot"; they who went quietly were not charged at all. It was blandly explained to the agitated press by Lee Sarason that these latter quiet lads had been so threatened by "irresponsible and seditious elements" that they were merely being safeguarded. Sarason did not use the phrase "protective arrest," which might have suggested things.

To the veteran reporters it was strange to see the titular Secretary of State, theoretically a person of such dignity and consequence that he could deal with the representatives of foreign powers, acting as press-agent and yes-man for even the President.

There were riots, instantly, all over Washington, all over America.

The recalcitrant Congressmen had been penned in the district jail. Toward it, in the winter evening, marched a mob that was noisily mutinous toward the Windrip for whom so many of them had voted. Among the mob buzzed hundreds of Negroes, armed with knives and old pistols, for one of the kidnaped Congressmen was a Negro from Georgia, the first colored Georgian to hold high office since carpetbagger days.

Surrounding the jail, behind machine guns, the rebels found a few Regulars, many police, and a horde of Minute Men, but at these last they jeered, calling them "Minnie Mouses" and "tin soldiers" and "mama's boys." The M.M.'s looked nervously at their officers and at the Regulars who were making so professional a pretense of not being scared. The mob heaved bottles and dead fish. Half-a-dozen policemen with guns and night sticks, trying to push back the van of the mob, were buried under a human surf and came up grotesquely battered and ununiformed—those who ever did come up again. There were two shots; and one Minute Man slumped to the jail steps, another stood ludicrously holding a wrist that spurted blood.

The Minute Men—why, they said to themselves, they'd never meant to be soldiers anyway—just wanted to have some fun marching! They began to sneak into the edges of the mob, hiding their uniform caps. That instant, from a powerful loudspeaker in a lower window of the jail brayed the voice of President Berzelius Windrip:

"I am addressing my own boys, the Minute Men, everywhere in America! To you and you only I look for help to make America a proud, rich land again. You have been scorned. They thought you were the 'lower classes.' They wouldn't give you jobs. They told you to sneak off like bums and get relief. They ordered you into lousy C.C.C. camps. They said you were no good, because you were poor. *I* tell you that you are, ever since yesterday noon, the highest lords of the land—the aristocracy—the makers of the new America of freedom and justice. Boys! I need you! Help me—help me to help you! Stand fast! Anybody tries to block you—give the swine the point of your bayonet!"

A machine-gunner M.M., who had listened reverently, let loose. The mob began to drop, and into the backs of the wounded as they went staggering away the M.M. infantry, running, poked their bayonets. Such a juicy squash it made, and the fugitives looked so amazed, so funny, as they tumbled in grotesque heaps!

The M.M.'s hadn't, in dreary hours of bayonet drill, known this would be such sport. They'd have more of it now—and hadn't the President of the United States himself told each of them, personally, that he needed their aid?

When the remnants of Congress ventured to the Capitol, they found it seeded with M.M.'s, while a regiment of Regulars, under Major General Meinecke, paraded the grounds.

The Speaker of the House, and the Hon. Mr. Perley Beecroft, Vice-President of the United States and Presiding Officer of the Senate, had the power to declare that quorums were present. (If a lot of members chose to dally in the district jail, enjoying themselves instead of attending Congress, whose fault was that?) Both houses passed a resolution declaring Point Fifteen temporarily in effect, during the "crisis"—the legality of the passage was doubtful, but just who was to contest it, even though the members of the Supreme Court had not been placed under protective arrest . . . merely confined each to his own house by a squad of Minute Men!

Bishop Paul Peter Prang had (his friends said afterward) been dismayed by Windrip's stroke of state. Surely, he complained, Mr. Windrip hadn't quite remembered to include Christian Amity in the program he had taken from the League of Forgotten Men. Though Mr. Prang had contentedly given up broadcasting ever since the victory of Justice and Fraternity in the person of Berzelius Windrip, he wanted to caution the public again, but when he telephoned to his familiar station, WLFM in Chicago, the manager informed him that "just temporarily, all access to the air was forbidden," except as it was especially licensed by the offices of Lee Sarason. (Oh, that was only one of sixteen jobs that Lee and his six hundred new assistants had taken on in the past week.)

Rather timorously, Bishop Prang motored from his home in Persepolis, Indiana, to the Indianapolis airport and took a night plane for Washington, to reprove, perhaps even playfully to spank, his naughty disciple, Buzz.

He had little trouble in being admitted to see the President. In fact, he was, the press feverishly reported, at the White House for six hours, though whether he was with the President all that time they could not discover. At three in the afternoon Prang was seen to leave by a private entrance to the executive offices and take a taxi. They noted that he was pale and staggering.

In front of his hotel he was elbowed by a mob who in curiously unmenacing and mechanical tones yelped, "Lynch um—downutha enemies Windrip!" A dozen M.M.'s pierced the crowd and surrounded the Bishop. The Ensign commanding them bellowed to the crowd, so that all might hear, "You cowards leave the Bishop alone! Bishop, come with us, and we'll see you're safe!"

Millions heard on their radios that evening the official announcement that, to ward off mysterious plotters, probably Bolsheviks, Bishop Prang had been safely shielded in the district jail. And with it a personal statement from President Windrip that he was filled with joy at having been able to "rescue from the foul agitators my friend and mentor, Bishop P. P. Prang, than whom there is no man living who I so admire and respect."

There was, as yet, no absolute censorship of the press; only a confused imprisonment of journalists who offended the government or local officers of the M.M.'s; and the papers chronically opposed to Windrip carried by no means flattering hints that Bishop Prang had rebuked the President and been plain jailed, with no nonsense about a "rescue." These mutters reached Persepolis.

Not all the Persepolitans ached with love for the Bishop or considered him a modern St. Francis gathering up the little fowls of the fields in his handsome LaSalle car. There were neighbors who hinted that he was a window-peeping snooper after bootleggers and obliging grass widows. But proud of him, their best advertisement, they certainly were, and the Persepolis Chamber of Commerce had caused to be erected at the Eastern gateway to Main Street the sign: "Home of Bishop Prang, Radio's Greatest Star."

So as one man Persepolis telegraphed to Washington, demanding Prang's release, but a messenger in the Executive Offices who was a Persepolis boy (he was, it is true, a colored man, but suddenly he became a favorite son, lovingly remembered by old schoolmates) tipped off the Mayor that the telegrams were among the hundredweight of messages that were daily hauled away from the White House unanswered.

Then a quarter of the citizenry of Persepolis mounted a special train to "march" on Washington. It was one of those small incidents which the opposition press could use as a bomb under Windrip, and the train was accompanied by a score of high-ranking reporters from Chicago and, later, from Pittsburgh, Baltimore, and New York.

While the train was on its way—and it was curious what delays and sidetrackings it encountered—a company of Minute Men at Logansport, Indiana, rebelled against having to arrest a group of Catholic nuns who were accused of having taught treasonably. High Marshal Sarason felt that there must be a Lesson, early and impressive. A battalion of M.M.'s, sent from Chicago in fast trucks, arrested the mutinous company, and shot every third man.

When the Persepolitans reached Washington, they were tearfully informed, by a brigadier of M.M.'s who met them at the Union Station, that poor Bishop Prang had been so shocked by the treason of his fellow Indianans that he had gone melancholy mad and they had tragically been compelled to shut him up in St. Elizabeth's government insane asylum.

No one willing to carry news about him ever saw Bishop Prang again.

The Brigadier brought greetings to the Persepolitans from the President himself, and an invitation to stay at the Willard, at government expense. Only a dozen accepted; the rest took the first train back, not amiably; and from then on there was one town in America in which no M.M. ever dared to appear in his ducky forage cap and dark-blue tunic.

The Chief of Staff of the Regular Army had been deposed; in his place was Major General Emmanuel Coon. Doremus and his like were disappointed by General Coon's acceptance, for they had always been informed, even by the *Nation,* that Emmanuel Coon, though a professional army officer who did enjoy a fight, preferred that that fight be on the side of the Lord; that he was generous, literate, just, and a man of honor—and honor was the one quality that Buzz Windrip wasn't even expected to understand. Rumor said that Coon (as "Nordic" a Kentuckian as ever existed, a descendant of men who had fought beside Kit Carson and Commodore Perry) was particularly impatient with the puerility of anti-Semitism, and that nothing so pleased him as, when he heard new acquaintances being superior about the Jews, to snarl, "Did you by any chance happen to notice that my name is Emmanuel Coon and that Coon might be a corruption of some name rather familiar on the East Side of New York?"

"Oh well, I suppose even General Coon feels, 'Orders are Orders,' " sighed Doremus.

President Windrip's first extended proclamation to the country was a pretty piece of literature and of tenderness. He explained that powerful and secret enemies of American principles—one rather gathered that they were a combination of Wall Street and Soviet Russia—upon discovering, to their fury, that he, Berzelius, was going to be President, had planned their last charge. Everything would be tranquil in a few months, but meantime there was a Crisis, during which the country must "bear with him."

He recalled the military dictatorship of Lincoln and Stanton during the Civil War, when civilian suspects were arrested without warrant. He hinted how delightful everything was going to be—right away now—just a moment—just a moment's patience—when he had things in hand; and he wound up with a comparison of the Crisis to the urgency of a fireman rescuing a pretty girl from a "conflagration," and carrying her down a ladder, for her own sake, whether she liked it or not, and no matter how appealingly she might kick her pretty ankles.

The whole country laughed.

"Great card, that Buzz, but mighty competent guy," said the electorate.

"I should worry whether Bish Prang or any other nut is in the boobyhatch, long as I get my five thousand bucks a year, like Windrip promised," said Shad Ledue to Charley Betts, the furniture man.

It had all happened within the eight days following Windrip's inauguration.

16

I have no desire to be President. I would much rather do my humble best as a supporter of Bishop Prang, Ted Bilbo, Gene Talmadge or any other broad-gauged but peppy Liberal. My only longing is to Serve.

Zero Hour, Berzelius Windrip.

LIKE MANY BACHELORS given to vigorous hunting and riding, Buck Titus was a fastidious housekeeper, and his mid-Victorian farmhouse fussily neat. It was also pleasantly bare: the living room a monastic hall of heavy oak chairs, tables free of dainty covers, numerous and rather solemn books of history and exploration, with the conventional "sets," and a tremendous fireplace of rough stone. And the ash trays were solid pottery and pewter, able to cope with a whole evening of cigarette-smoking. The whisky stood honestly on the oak buffet, with siphons, and with cracked ice always ready in a thermos jug.

It would, however, have been too much to expect Buck Titus not to have red-and-black imitation English hunting-prints.

This hermitage, always grateful to Doremus, was sanctuary now, and only with Buck could he adequately damn Windrip & Co. and people like Francis Tasbrough, who in February was still saying, "Yes, things do look kind of hectic down there in Washington, but that's just because there's so many of these bullheaded politicians that still think they can buck Windrip. Besides, anyway, things like that couldn't ever happen here in New England."

And, indeed, as Doremus went on his lawful occasions

past the red-brick Georgian houses, the slender spires of old white churches facing the Green, as he heard the lazy irony of familiar greetings from his acquaintances, men as enduring as their Vermont hills, it seemed to him that the madness in the capital was alien and distant and unimportant as an earthquake in Tibet.

Constantly, in the *Informer,* he criticized the government but not too acidly.

The hysteria can't last; be patient, and wait and see, he counseled his readers.

It was not that he was afraid of the authorities. He simply did not believe that this comic tyranny could endure. *It can't happen here,* said even Doremus—even now.

The one thing that most perplexed him was that there could be a dictator seemingly so different from the fervent Hitlers and gesticulating Fascists and the Cæsars with laurels round bald domes; a dictator with something of the earthy American sense of humor of a Mark Twain, a George Ade, a Will Rogers, an Artemus Ward. Windrip could be ever so funny about solemn jaw-drooping opponents, and about the best method of training what he called "a Siamese flea hound." Did that, puzzled Doremus, make him less or more dangerous?

Then he remembered the most cruel-mad of all pirates, Sir Henry Morgan, who had thought it ever so funny to sew a victim up in wet rawhide and watch it shrink in the sun.

From the perseverance with which they bickered, you could tell that Buck Titus and Lorinda were much fonder of each other than they would admit. Being a person who read little and therefore took what he did read seriously, Buck was distressed by the normally studious Lorinda's vacation liking for novels about distressed princesses, and when she airily insisted that they were better guides to conduct than Anthony Trollope or Thomas Hardy, Buck roared at her and in the feebleness of baited strength, nervously filled pipes and knocked them out against the stone mantel. But he approved of the relationship between Doremus and Lorinda, which only he (and Shad Ledue!) had guessed, and over Doremus, ten years his senior, this shaggy-headed woodsman fussed like a thwarted spinster.

To both Doremus and Lorinda, Buck's overgrown shack became their refuge. And they needed it, late in February, five weeks or thereabouts after Windrip's election.

Despite strikes and riots all over the country, bloodily put down by the Minute Men, Windrip's power in Washington was maintained. The most liberal four members of the Supreme Court resigned and were replaced by surprisingly unknown lawyers who called President Windrip by his first name. A number of Congressmen were still being "protected" in the District of Columbia jail; others had seen the blinding light forever shed by the goddess Reason and happily returned to the Capitol. The Minute Men were increasingly loyal—they were still unpaid volunteers, but provided with "expense accounts" considerably larger than the pay of the regular troops. Never in American history had the adherents of a President been so well satisfied; they were not only appointed to whatever political jobs there were but to ever so many that really were not; and with such annoyances as Congressional Investigations hushed, the official awarders of contracts were on the merriest of terms with all contractors. . . . One veteran lobbyist for steel corporations complained that there was no more sport in his hunting—you were not only allowed but expected to shoot all government purchasing-agents sitting.

None of the changes was so publicized as the Presidential mandate abruptly ending the separate existence of the different states, and dividing the whole country into eight "provinces"—thus, asserted Windrip, economizing by reducing the number of governors and all other state officers and, asserted Windrip's enemies, better enabling him to concentrate his private army and hold the country.

The new "Northeastern Province" included all of New York State north of a line through Ossining, and all of New England except a strip of Connecticut shore as far east as New Haven. This was, Doremus admitted, a natural and homogeneous division, and even more natural seemed the urban and industrial "Metropolitan Province," which included Greater New York, Westchester County up to Ossining, Long Island, the strip of Connecticut dependent on New York City, New Jersey, northern Delaware, and Pennsylvania as far as Reading and Scranton.

Each province was divided into numbered districts, each district into lettered counties, each county into townships and cities, and only in these last did the old names, with their traditional appeal, remain to endanger President Windrip by memories of honorable local history. And it was gossiped that, next, the government would change even the town names—that they were already thinking fondly of calling New York "Berzelian" and San Francisco "San Sarason." Probably that gossip was false.

The Northeastern Province's six districts were: 1, Upper New York State west of and including Syracuse; 2, New York east of it; 3, Vermont and New Hampshire; 4, Maine; 5, Massachusetts; 6, Rhode Island and the unraped portion of Connecticut.

District 3, Doremus Jessup's district, was divided into the four "counties" of southern and northern Vermont, and southern and northern New Hampshire, with Hanover for capital—the District Commissioner merely chased the Dartmouth students out and took over the college buildings for his offices, to the considerable approval of Amherst, Williams, and Yale.

So Doremus was living, now, in Northeastern Province, District 3, County B, township of Beulah, and over him for his admiration and rejoicing were a provincial commissioner, a district commissioner, a county commissioner, an assistant county commissioner in charge of Beulah Township, and all their appertaining M.M. guards and emergency military judges.

Citizens who had lived in any one state for more than ten years seemed to resent more hotly the loss of that state's identity than they did the castration of the Congress and Supreme Court of the United States—indeed, they resented it almost as much as the fact that, while late January, February, and most of March went by, they still were not receiving their governmental gifts of $5000 (or perhaps it would beautifully be $10,000) apiece; had indeed received nothing more than cheery bulletins from Washington to the effect that the "Capital Levy Board," or C.L.B. was holding sessions.

Virginians whose grandfathers had fought beside Lee shouted that they'd be damned if they'd give up the hallowed state name and form just one arbitrary section of an administrative unit containing eleven Southern states; San Franciscans who had considered Los Angelinos even worse than denizens of Miami now wailed with agony when California was sundered and the northern portion lumped in with Oregon, Nevada, and others as the "Mountain and Pacific Province," while southern California was, without her permission, assigned to the Southwestern Province, along with Arizona, New Mexico, Texas, Oklahoma, and Hawaii. As some hint of Buzz Windrip's vision for the future, it was interesting to read that this Southwestern Province was also to be permitted to claim "all portions of Mexico which the United States may from time to time find it necessary to take over, as a protection against the notorious treachery of Mexico and the Jewish plots there hatched."

"Lee Sarason is even more generous than Hitler and Alfred Rosenberg in protecting the future of other countries," sighed Doremus.

As Provincial Commissioner of the Northeastern Province, comprising Upper New York State and New England, was appointed Colonel Dewey Haik, that soldier-lawyer-politician-aviator who was the chilliest-blooded and most arrogant of all the satellites of Windrip yet had so captivated miners and fishermen during the campaign. He was a strong-flying eagle who liked his meat bloody. As District Commissioner of District 3—Vermont and New Hampshire—appeared, to Doremus's mingled derision and fury, none other than John Sullivan Reek, that stuffiest of stuffed-shirts, that most gaseous gas bag, that most amenable machine politician of Northern New England; a Republican ex-governor who had, in the alembic of Windrip's patriotism, rosily turned Leaguer.

No one had ever troubled to be obsequious to the Hon. J. S. Reek, even when he had been Governor. The weediest back-country Representative had called him "Johnny," in the gubernatorial mansion (twelve rooms and a leaky roof); and the youngest reporter had bawled, "Well, what bull you handing out today, Ex?"

It was this Commissioner Reek who summoned all the editors in his district to meet him at his new viceregal lodge in Dartmouth Library and receive the precious privileged information as to how much President Windrip and his subordinate commissioners admired the gentlemen of the press.

Before he left for the press conference in Hanover, Doremus received from Sissy a "poem"—at least she called it that—which Buck Titus, Lorinda Pike, Julian Falck, and she had painfully composed, late at night, in Buck's fortified manor house:

Be meek with Reek,
Go fake with Haik.
One rhymes with sneak,
And t' other with snake.
Haik, with his beak,
Is on the make,
But Sullivan Reek—
Oh God!

"Well, anyway, Windrip's put everybody to work. And he's driven all these unsightly billboards off the highways—much better for the tourist trade," said all the old editors, even those who wondered if the President wasn't perhaps the least bit arbitrary.

As he drove to Hanover, Doremus saw hundreds of huge billboards by the road. But they bore only Windrip propaganda and underneath, "with the compliments of a loyal firm" and—very large—"Montgomery Cigarettes" or "Jonquil Foot Soap." On the short walk from a parking-space to the former Dartmouth campus, three several men muttered to him, "Give us a nickel for a cuppa coffee, Boss—a Minnie Mouse has got my job and the Mouses won't take me—they say I'm too old." But that may have been propaganda from Moscow.

On the long porch of the Hanover Inn, officers of the Minute Men were reclining in deck chairs, their spurred boots (in all the M.M. organization there was no cavalry) up on the railing.

Doremus passed a science building in front of which was a pile of broken laboratory glassware, and in one stripped laboratory he could see a small squad of M.M.'s drilling.

District Commissioner John Sullivan Reek affectionately received the editors in a classroom. . . . Old men, used to being revered as prophets, sitting anxiously in trifling chairs, facing a fat man in the uniform of an M.M. commander, who smoked an unmilitary cigar as his pulpy hand waved greeting.

Reek took not more than an hour to relate what would have taken the most intelligent man five or six hours—that is, five minutes of speech and the rest of the five hours to recover from the nausea caused by having to utter such shameless rot. . . . President Windrip, Secretary of State Sarason, Provincial Commissioner Haik, and himself, John Sullivan Reek, they were all being misrepresented by the Republicans, the Jeffersonians, the Communists, England, the Nazis, and probably the jute and herring industries; and what the government wanted was for any reporter to call on any member of this Administration, and especially on Commissioner Reek, at any time—except perhaps between 3 and 7 A.M.—and "get the real low-down."

Excellency Reek announced, then: "And now, gentlemen, I am giving myself the privilege of introducing you to all four of the County Commissioners, who were just chosen yesterday. Probably each of you will know personally the commissioner from your own county, but I want you to intimately and cooperatively know all four, because, whomever they may be, they join with me in my unquenchable admiration of the press."

The four County Commissioners, as one by one they shambled into the room and were introduced, seemed to Doremus an oddish lot: A moth-eaten lawyer known more for his quotations from Shakespeare and Robert W. Service than for his shrewdness before a jury. He was luminously bald except for a prickle of faded rusty hair, but you felt that, if he had his rights, he would have the floating locks of a tragedian of 1890.

A battling clergyman famed for raiding roadhouses.

A rather shy workman, an authentic proletarian, who seemed surprised to find himself there. (He was replaced, a month later, by a popular osteopath with an interest in politics and vegetarianism.)

The fourth dignitary to come in and affectionately bow to the editors, a bulky man, formidable-looking in his uniform as a battalion leader of Minute Men, introduced as the Commissioner for northern Vermont, Doremus Jessup's county, was Mr. Oscar Ledue, formerly known as "Shad."

Mr. Reek called him "Captain" Ledue. Doremus remembered that Shad's only military service, prior to Windrip's election, had been as an A.E.F. private who had never got beyond a training-camp in America and whose fiercest experience in battle had been licking a corporal when in liquor.

"Mr. Jessup," bubbled the Hon. Mr. Reek, "I imagine you must have met Captain Ledue—comes from your charming city."

"Uh-uh-ur," said Doremus.

"Sure," said Captain Ledue. "I've met old Jessup, all right, all right! He don't know what it's all about. He don't know the first thing about the economics of our social Revolution. He's a Cho-vinis. But he isn't such a bad old coot, and I'll let him ride as long as he behaves himself!"

"Splendid!" said the Hon. Mr. Reek.

17

Like beefstake and potatoes stick to your ribs even if you're working your head off, so the words of the Good Book stick by you in perplexity and tribulation. If I ever held a high position over my people, I hope that my ministers would be quoting, from II Kings, 18; 31 & 32: "Come out to me, and then eat ye every man of his own vine, and every one of his fig tree, and drink ye every one the waters of his cistern, until I come and take you away to a land of corn and wine, a land of bread and vineyards, a land of olive oil and honey, that ye may live and not die."

Zero Hour, Berzelius Windrip.

DESPITE THE CLAIMS of Montpelier, the former capital of Vermont, and of Burlington, largest town in the state, Captain Shad Ledue fixed on Fort Beulah as executive center of County B, which was made out of nine former counties of northern Vermont. Doremus never decided whether this was, as Lorinda Pike asserted, because Shad was in partnership with Banker R. C. Crowley in the profits derived from the purchase of quite useless old dwellings as part of his headquarters, or for the even sounder purpose of showing himself off, in battalion leader's uniform with the letters "C.C." beneath the five-pointed star on his collar, to the pals with whom he had once played pool and drunk applejack, and to the "snobs" whose lawns he once had mowed.

Besides the condemned dwellings, Shad took over all of the former Scotland County courthouse and established his private office in the judge's chambers, merely chucking out the law books and replacing them with piles of magazines devoted to the movies and the detection of crime, hanging up portraits of Windrip, Sarason, Haik, and Reek, installing two deep chairs upholstered in poison-green plush (ordered from the store of the loyal Charley Betts but, to Betts's fury, charged to the government, to be paid for if and when) and doubling the number of judicial cuspidors.

In the top center drawer of his desk Shad kept a photograph from a nudist camp, a flask of Benedictine, a .44 revolver, and a dog whip.

County commissioners were allowed from one to a dozen assistant commissioners, depending on the population. Doremus Jessup was alarmed when he discovered that Shad had had the shrewdness to choose as assistants men of some education and pretense to manners, with "Professor" Emil Staubmeyer as Assistant County Commissioner in charge of the Township of Beulah, which included the villages of Fort Beulah, West and North Beulah, Beulah Center, Trianon, Hosea, and Keezmet.

As Shad had, without benefit of bayonets, become a captain, so Mr. Staubmeyer (author of *Hitler and Other Poems of Passion*—unpublished) automatically became a doctor.

Perhaps, thought Doremus, he would understand Windrip & Co. better through seeing them faintly reflected in Shad and Staubmeyer than he would have in the confusing glare of Washington; and understand thus that a Buzz Windrip—a Bismarck—a Cæsar—a Pericles was like all the rest of itching, indigesting, aspiring humanity except that each of these heroes had a higher degree of ambition and more willingness to kill.

By June, the enrollment of the Minute Men had increased to 562,000, and the force was now able to accept as new members only such trusty patriots and pugilists as it preferred. The War Department was frankly allowing them not just "expense money" but payment ranging from ten dollars a week for "inspectors" with a few hours of weekly duty in drilling, to $9700 a year for "brigadiers" on full time, and $16,000 for the High Marshal, Lee Sarason . . . fortunately without interfering with the salaries from his other onerous duties.

The M.M. ranks were: inspector, more or less corresponding to private; squad leader, or corporal; cornet, or sergeant; ensign, or lieutenant; battalion leader, a combination of captain, major, and lieutenant colonel; commander, or colonel; brigadier, or general; high marshal, or commanding general. Cynics suggested that these honorable titles derived more from the Salvation Army than the fighting forces, but be that cheap sneer justified or no, the fact remains that an M.M. helot had ever so much more pride in being called an "inspector," an awing designation in all police circles, than in being a "private."

Since all members of the National Guard were not only allowed but encouraged to become members of the Minute Men also, since all veterans of the Great War were given special privileges, and since "Colonel" Osceola Luthorne, the Secretary of War, was generous about lending regular army officers to Secretary of State Sarason for use as drill masters in the M.M.'s, there was a surprising proportion of trained men for so newly born an army.

Lee Sarason had proven to President Windrip by statistics from the Great War that college education, and even the study of the horrors of other conflicts, did not weaken the masculinity of the students, but actually made them more patriotic, flag-waving, and skillful in the direction of slaughter than the average youth, and nearly every college in the country was to have, this coming autumn, its own battalion of M.M.'s, with drill counting as credit toward graduation. The collegians were to be schooled as officers. Another splendid source of M.M. officers were the gymnasiums and the classes in Business Administration of the Y.M.C.A.

Most of the rank and file, however, were young farmers delighted by the chance to go to town and to drive automobiles as fast as they wanted to; young factory employees who preferred uniforms and the authority to kick elderly citizens above overalls and stooping over machines; and rather a large number of former criminals, ex-bootleggers, ex-burglars, ex-labor racketeers, who, for their skill with guns and leather life-preservers, and for their assurances that the majesty of the Five-Pointed

Star had completely reformed them, were forgiven their earlier blunders in ethics and were warmly accepted in the M.M. Storm Troops.

It was said that one of the least of these erring children was the first patriot to name President Windrip "the Chief," meaning Führer, or Imperial Wizard of the K.K.K., or Il Duce, or Imperial Potentate of the Mystic Shrine, or Commodore, or University Coach, or anything else supremely noble and good-hearted. So, on the glorious anniversary of July 4, 1937, more than five hundred thousand young uniformed vigilantes, scattered in towns from Guam to Bar Harbor, from Point Barrow to Key West, stood at parade rest and sang, like the choiring seraphim:

Buzz and buzz and hail the Chief,
And his five-pointed sta-ar,
The U.S. ne'er can come to grief
With us prepared for wa-ar.

Certain critical spirits felt that this version of the chorus of "Buzz and Buzz," now the official M.M. anthem, showed, in a certain roughness, the lack of Adelaide Tarr Gimmitch's fastidious hand. But nothing could be done about it. She was said to be in China, organizing chain letters. And even while that uneasiness was over the M.M., upon the very next day came the blow.

Someone on High Marshal Sarason's staff noticed that the U.S.S.R.'s emblem was not a six-pointed star, but a five-pointed one, even like America's, so that we were not insulting the Soviets at all.

Consternation was universal. From Sarason's office came sulphurous rebuke to the unknown idiot who had first made the mistake (generally he was believed to be Lee Sarason) and the command that a new emblem be suggested by every member of the M.M. Day and night for three days, M.M. barracks were hectic with telegrams, telephone calls, letters, placards, and thousands of young men sat with pencils and rulers earnestly drawing tens of thousands of substitutes for the five-pointed star: circles in triangles, triangles in circles, pentagons, hexagons, alphas and omegas, eagles, aëroplanes, arrows, bombs bursting in air, bombs bursting in bushes, billy-goats, rhinoceri, and the Yosemite Valley. It was circulated that a young ensign on High Marshal Sarason's staff had, in agony over the error, committed suicide. Everybody thought that this hara-kiri was a fine idea and showed sensibility on the part of the better M.M.'s; and they went on thinking so even after it proved that the Ensign had merely got drunk at the Buzz Backgammon Club and talked about suicide.

In the end, despite his uncounted competitors, it was the great mystic, Lee Sarason himself, who found the perfect new emblem—a ship's steering wheel.

It symbolized, he pointed out, not only the Ship of State but also the wheels of American industry, the wheels and the steering wheel of motorcars, the wheel diagram which Father Coughlin had suggested two years before as symbolizing the program of the National Union for Social Justice, and, particularly, the wheel emblem of the Rotary Club.

Sarason's proclamation also pointed out that it would not be too far-fetched to declare that, with a little drafting treatment, the arms of the Swastika could be seen as unquestionably related to the circle, and how about the K.K.K. of the Kuklux Klan? Three K's made a triangle, didn't they? and everybody knew that a triangle was related to a circle.

So it was that in September, at the demonstrations on Loyalty Day (which replaced Labor Day), the same wide-flung seraphim sang:

> *Buzz and buzz and hail the Chief,*
> *And th' mystic steering whee-el,*
> *The U.S. ne'er can come to grief*
> *While we defend its we-al.*

In mid-August, President Windrip announced that, since all its aims were being accomplished, the League of Forgotten Men (founded by one Rev. Mr. Prang, who was mentioned in the proclamation only as a person in past history) was now terminated. So were all the older parties, Democratic, Republican, Farmer-Labor, or what not. There was to be only one: The American Corporate

State and Patriotic Party—no! added the President, with something of his former good-humor: "there are two parties, the Corporate and those who don't belong to any party at all, and so, to use a common phrase, are just out of luck!"

The idea of the Corporate or Corporative State, Secretary Sarason had more or less taken from Italy. All occupations were divided into six classes: agriculture, industry, commerce, transportation and communication, banking and insurance and investment, and a grab-bag class including the arts, sciences, and teaching. The American Federation of Labor, the Railway Brotherhoods, and all other labor organizations, along with the Federal Department of Labor, were supplanted by local Syndicates composed of individual workers, above which were Provincial Confederations, all under governmental guidance. Parallel to them in each occupation were Syndicates and Confederations of employers. Finally, the six Confederations of workers and the six Confederations of employers were combined in six joint federal Corporations, which elected the twenty-four members of the National Council of Corporations, which initiated or supervised all legislation relating to labor or business.

There was a permanent chairman of this National Council, with a deciding vote and the power of regulating all debate as he saw fit, but he was not elected—he was appointed by the President; and the first to hold the office (without interfering with his other duties) was Secretary of State Lee Sarason. Just to safeguard the liberties of Labor, this chairman had the right to dismiss any unreasonable member of the National Council.

All strikes and lockouts were forbidden under federal penalties, so that workmen listened to reasonable government representatives and not to unscrupulous agitators.

Windrip's partisans called themselves the Corporatists or, familiarly, the "Corpos," which nickname was generally used.

By ill-natured people the Corpos were called "the Corpses." But they were not at all corpse-like. That description would more correctly, and increasingly, have applied to their enemies.

* * *

Though the Corpos continued to promise a gift of at least $5000 to every family, "as soon as funding of the required bond issue shall be completed," the actual management of the poor, particularly of the more surly and dissatisfied poor, was undertaken by the Minute Men.

It could now be published to the world, and decidedly it was published, that unemployment had, under the benign reign of President Berzelius Windrip, almost disappeared. Almost all workless men were assembled in enormous labor camps, under M.M. officers. Their wives and children accompanied them and took care of the cooking, cleaning, and repair of clothes. The men did not merely work on state projects; they were also hired out at the reasonable rate of one dollar a day to private employers. Of course, so selfish is human nature even in Utopia, this did cause most employers to discharge the men to whom they had been paying more than a dollar a day, but that took care of itself, because these overpaid malcontents in their turn were forced into the labor camps.

Out of their dollar a day, the workers in the camps had to pay from seventy to ninety cents a day for board and lodging.

There was a certain discontentment among people who had once owned motorcars and bathrooms and eaten meat twice daily, at having to walk ten or twenty miles a day, bathe once a week, along with fifty others, in a long trough, get meat only twice a week—when they got it—and sleep in bunks, a hundred in a room. Yet there was less rebellion than a mere rationalist like Walt Trowbridge, Windrip's ludicrously defeated rival, would have expected, for every evening the loudspeaker brought to the workers the precious voices of Windrip and Sarason, Vice-President Beecroft, Secretary of War Luthorne, Secretary of Education and Propaganda Macgoblin, General Coon, or some other genius, and these Olympians, talking to the dirtiest and tiredest mudsills as warm friend to friend, told them that they were the honored foundation stones of a New Civilization, the advance guards of the conquest of the whole world.

They took it, too, like Napoleon's soldiers. And they

had the Jews and the Negroes to look down on, more and more. The M.M.'s saw to that. Every man is a king so long as he has someone to look down on.

Each week the government said less about the findings of the board of inquiry which was to decide how the $5000 per person could be wangled. It became easier to answer malcontents with a cuff from a Minute Man than by repetitious statements from Washington.

But most of the planks in Windrip's platform really were carried out—according to a sane interpretation of them. For example, inflation.

In America of this period, inflation did not even compare with the German inflation of the 1920's, but it was sufficient. The wage in the labor camps had to be raised from a dollar a day to three, with which the workers were receiving an equivalent of sixty cents a day in 1914 values. Everybody delightfully profited, except the very poor, the common workmen, the skilled workmen, the small business men, the professional men, and old couples living on annuities or their savings—these last did really suffer a little, as their incomes were cut in three. The workers, with apparently tripled wages, saw the cost of everything in the shops much more than triple.

Agriculture, which was most of all to have profited from inflation, on the theory that the mercurial crop-prices would rise faster than anything else, actually suffered the most of all, because, after a first flurry of foreign buying, importers of American products found it impossible to deal in so skittish a market, and American food exports—such of them as were left—ceased completely.

It was Big Business, that ancient dragon which Bishop Prang and Senator Windrip had gone forth to slay, that had the interesting time.

With the value of the dollar changing daily, the elaborate systems of cost-marking and credit of Big Business were so confused that presidents and sales-managers sat in their offices after midnight, with wet towels. But they got some comfort, because with the depreciated dollar they were able to recall all bonded indebtedness and, paying it off at the old face values, get rid of it at thirty cents on the hundred. With this, and the currency so wavering that employees did not know just what they ought to get in wages, and labor unions eliminated, the larger industrialists came through the inflation with perhaps double the wealth, in real values, that they had had in 1936.

And two other planks in Windrip's encyclical vigorously respected were those eliminating the Negroes and patronizing the Jews.

The former race took it the less agreeably. There were horrible instances in which whole Southern counties with a majority of Negro population were overrun by the blacks and all property seized. True, their leaders alleged that this followed massacres of Negroes by Minute Men. But as Dr. Macgoblin, Secretary of Culture, so well said, this whole subject was unpleasant and therefore not helpful to discuss.

All over the country, the true spirit of Windrip's Plank Nine, regarding the Jews, was faithfully carried out. It was understood that the Jews were no longer to be barred from fashionable hotels, as in the hideous earlier day of race prejudice, but merely to be charged double rates. It was understood that Jews were never to be discouraged from trading but were merely to pay higher graft to commissioners and inspectors and to accept without debate all regulations, wage rates, and price lists decided upon by the stainless Anglo-Saxons of the various merchants' associations. And that all Jews of all conditions were frequently to sound their ecstasy in having found in America a sanctuary, after their deplorable experiences among the prejudices of Europe.

In Fort Beulah, Louis Rotenstern, since he had always been the first to stand up for the older official national anthems, "The Star-Spangled Banner" or "Dixie" and now for "Buzz and Buzz," since he had of old been considered almost an authentic friend by Francis Tasbrough and R. C. Crowley, and since he had often good-naturedly pressed the unrecognized Shad Ledue's Sunday pants without charge, was permitted to retain his tailor shop, though it was understood that he was to charge members of the M.M. prices that were only nominal, or quarter nominal.

But one Harry Kindermann, a Jew who had profiteered enough as agent for maple-sugar and dairy machinery so that in 1936 he had been paying the last installment on his new bungalow and on his Buick, had always been what Shad Ledue called "a fresh Kike." He had laughed at the flag, the Church, and even Rotary. Now he found the manufacturers canceling his agencies, without explanation.

By the middle of 1937 he was selling frankfurters by the road, and his wife, who had been so proud of the piano and the old American pine cupboard in their bungalow, was dead, from pneumonia caught in the one-room tar-paper shack into which they had moved.

At the time of Windrip's election, there had been more than 80,000 relief administrators employed by the federal and local governments in America. With the labor camps absorbing most people on relief, this army of social workers, both amateurs and long-trained professional uplifters, was stranded.

The Minute Men controlling the labor camps were generous: they offered the charitarians the same dollar a day that the proletarians received, with special low rates for board and lodging. But the cleverer social workers received a much better offer: to help list every family and every unmarried person in the country, with his or her finances, professional ability, military training and, most important and most tactfully to be ascertained, his or her secret opinion of the M.M.'s and of the Corpos in general.

A good many of the social workers indignantly said that this was asking them to be spies, stool pigeons for the American Oh Gay Pay Oo. These were, on various unimportant charges, sent to jail or, later, to concentration camps—which were also jails, but the private jails of the M.M.'s, unshackled by any old-fashioned, nonsensical prison regulations.

In the confusion of the summer and early autumn of 1937, local M.M. officers had a splendid time making their own laws, and such congenital traitors and bellyachers as Jewish doctors, Jewish musicians, Negro journalists, socialistic college professors, young men who preferred reading or chemical research to manly service with the M.M.'s, women who complained when their men had been taken away by the M.M.'s and had disappeared, were increasingly beaten in the streets, or arrested on charges that would not have been very familiar to pre-Corpo jurists.

And, increasingly, the bourgeois counter revolutionists began to escape to Canada; just as once, by the "underground railroad" the Negro slaves had escaped into that free Northern air.

In Canada, as well as in Mexico, Bermuda, Jamaica, Cuba, and Europe, these lying Red propagandists began to publish the vilest little magazines, accusing the Corpos of murderous terrorism—allegations that a band of six M.M.'s had beaten an aged rabbi and robbed him; that the editor of a small labor paper in Paterson had been tied to his printing press and left there while the M.M.'s burned the plant; that the pretty daughter of an ex-Farmer-Labor politician in Iowa had been raped by giggling young men in masks.

To end this cowardly flight of the lying counter revolutionists (many of whom, once accepted as reputable preachers and lawyers and doctors and writers and ex-congressmen and ex-army officers, were able to give a wickedly false impression of Corpoism and the M.M.'s to the world outside America) the government quadrupled the guards who were halting suspects at every harbor and at even the minutest trails crossing the border; and in one quick raid, it poured M.M. storm troopers into all airports, private or public, and all aëroplane factories, and thus, they hoped, closed the air lanes to skulking traitors.

As one of the most poisonous counter revolutionists in the country, Ex-Senator Walt Trowbridge, Windrip's rival in the election of 1936, was watched night and day by a rotation of twelve M.M. guards. But there seemed to be small danger that this opponent, who, after all, was a crank but not an intransigent maniac, would make himself ridiculous by fighting against the great Power which (per Bishop Prang) Heaven had been pleased to send for the healing of distressed America.

Trowbridge remained prosaically on a ranch he owned in South Dakota, and the government agent commanding the M.M.'s (a skilled man, trained in breaking strikes) reported that on his tapped telephone wire and in his steamed-open letters, Trowbridge communicated nothing more seditious than reports on growing alfalfa. He had with him no one but ranch hands and, in the house, an innocent aged couple.

Washington hoped that Trowbridge was beginning to see the light. Maybe they would make him Ambassador to Britain, vice Sinclair.

On the Fourth of July, when the M.M.'s gave their glorious but unfortunate tribute to the Chief and the Five-pointed Star, Trowbridge gratified his cow-punchers by holding an unusually pyrotechnic celebration. All evening skyrockets flared up, and round the home pasture glowed pots of Roman fire. Far from cold-shouldering the M.M. guards, Trowbridge warmly invited them to help set off rockets and join the gang in beer and sausages. The lonely soldier boys off there on the prairie—they were so happy shooting rockets!

An aëroplane with a Canadian license, a large plane, flying without lights, sped toward the rocket-lighted area and, with engine shut off, so that the guards could not tell whether it had flown on, circled the pasture outlined by the Roman fire and swiftly landed.

The guards had felt sleepy after the last bottle of beer. Three of them were napping on the short, rough grass.

They were rather disconcertingly surrounded by men in masking flying-helmets, men carrying automatic pistols, who handcuffed the guards that were still awake, picked up the others, and stored all twelve of them in the barred baggage compartment of the plane.

The raiders' leader, a military-looking man, said to Walt Trowbridge, "Ready, sir?"

"Yep. Just take those four boxes, will you, please, Colonel?"

The boxes contained photostats of letters and documents.

Unregally clad in overalls and a huge straw hat, Senator Trowbridge entered the pilots' compartment. High and swift and alone, the plane flew toward the premature Northern Lights.

Next morning, still in overalls, Trowbridge breakfasted at the Fort Garry Hotel with the Mayor of Winnipeg.

A fortnight later, in Toronto, he began the republication of his weekly, *A Lance for Democracy,* and on the cover of the first number were reproductions of four letters indicating that before he became President, Berzelius Windrip had profited through personal gifts from financiers to an amount of over $1,000,000. To Doremus Jessup, to some thousands of Doremus Jessups, were smuggled copies of the *Lance,* though possession of it was punishable (perhaps not legally, but certainly effectively) by death.

But it was not till the winter, so carefully did his secret agents have to work in America, that Trowbridge had in full operation the organization called by its operatives the "New Underground," the "N.U.," which aided thousands of counter revolutionists to escape into Canada.

18

> In the little towns, ah, there is the abiding peace that I love, and that can never be disturbed by even the noisiest Smart Alecks from these haughty megalopolises like Washington, New York, & etc.
>
> *Zero Hour,* Berzelius Windrip.

DOREMUS'S POLICY of "wait and see," like most Fabian policies, had grown shaky. It seemed particularly shaky in June, 1937, when he drove to North Beulah for the fortieth graduation anniversary of his class in Isaiah College.

As the custom was, the returned alumni wore comic costumes. His class had sailor suits, but they walked about, bald-headed and lugubrious, in these well-meant garments of joy, and there was a look of instability even in the eyes of the three members who were ardent Corpos (being local Corpo commissioners).

After the first hour Doremus saw little of his classmates. He had looked up his familiar correspondent, Victor Loveland, teacher in the classical department who, a year ago, had informed him of President Owen J. Peaseley's ban on criticism of military training.

At its best, Loveland's jerry-built imitation of an Anne Hathaway cottage had been no palace—Isaiah assistant professors did not customarily rent palaces. Now, with the pretentiously smart living room heaped with burlap-covered chairs and rolled rugs and boxes of books, it looked like a junkshop. Amid the wreckage sat Loveland, his wife, his three children, and one Dr. Arnold King, experimenter in chemistry.

"What's all this?" said Doremus.

"I've been fired. As too 'radical,' " growled Loveland.

"Yes! And his most vicious attack has been on Glicknow's treatment of the use of the aorist in Hesiod!" wailed his wife.

"Well, I deserve it—for not having been vicious about anything since A.D. 300! Only thing I'm ashamed of is that they're not firing me for having taught my students that the Corpos have taken most of their ideas from Tiberius, or maybe for having decently tried to assassinate District Commissioner Reek!" said Loveland.

"Where you going?" inquired Doremus.

"That's just it! We don't know! Oh, first to my dad's house—which is a six-room packing-box in Burlington—Dad's got diabetes. But teaching—— President Peaseley kept putting off signing my new contract and just informed me ten days ago that I'm through—much too late to get a job for next year. Myself, I don't care a damn! Really I don't! I'm glad to have been made to admit that as a college prof I haven't been, as I so liked to convince myself, any Erasmus Junior, inspiring noble young souls to dream of chaste classic beauty—save the mark!—but just a plain hired man, another counter-jumper in the Marked-down Classics Goods Department, with students for bored customers, and as subject to being hired and fired as any janitor. Do you remember that in Imperial Rome, the teachers, even the tutors of the nobility, were slaves—allowed a lot of leeway, I suppose, in their theories about the anthropology of Crete, but just as likely to be strangled as the other slaves! I'm not kicking——"

Dr. King, the chemist, interrupted with a whoop: "Sure you're kicking! Why the hell not? With three kids? Why not kick! Now me, I'm lucky! I'm half Jew—one of these sneaking, cunning Jews that Buzz Windrip and his boyfriend Hitler tell you about; so cunning I suspected what was going on months ago and so—I've also just been fired, Mr. Jessup—I arranged for a job with the Universal Electric Corporation. . . . They don't mind Jews there, as long as they sing at their work and find boondoggles worth a million a year to the company—at thirty-five hundred a year salary! A fond farewell to all my grubby studies! Though—" and Doremus thought he was, at heart, sadder than Loveland "—I do kind of hate to give up my research. Oh, hell with 'em!"

The version of Owen J. Peaseley, M.A. (Oberlin), LL.D. (Conn. State), president of Isaiah College, was quite different.

"Why no, Mr. Jessup! We believe absolutely in freedom of speech and thought, here at old Isaiah. The fact is that we are letting Loveland go only because the Classics Department is overstaffed—so little demand for Greek and Sanskrit and so on, you know, with all this modern interest in quantitative bio-physics and aëroplane-repairing and so on. But as to Dr. King—um—I'm afraid we did a little feel that he was riding for a fall, boasting about being a Jew and all, you know, and—— But can't we talk of pleasanter subjects? You have probably learned that Secretary of Culture Macgoblin has now completed his plan for the appointment of a director of education in each province and district?—and that Professor Almeric Trout of Aumbry University is slated for Director in our Northeastern Province? Well, I have something very gratifying to add. Dr. Trout—and what a profound scholar, what an eloquent orator he is!—did you know that in Teutonic 'Almeric' means 'noble prince'?—and he's been so kind as to designate me as Director of Education for the Vermont-New Hampshire District! Isn't that thrilling! I wanted you to be one of the first to hear it, Mr. Jessup, because of course one of the chief jobs of the Director will be to work with and through the newspaper editors in the great task of spreading correct Corporate ideals and combating false theories—yes, oh yes."

It seemed as though a large number of people were zealous to work with and through the editors these days, thought Doremus.

He noticed that President Peaseley resembled a dummy made of faded gray flannel of a quality intended for petticoats in an orphan asylum.

The Minute Men's organization was less favored in the staid villages than in the industrial centers, but all through the summer it was known that a company of M.M.'s had been formed in Fort Beulah and were drilling in the Armory under National Guard officers and County Commissioner Ledue, who was seen sitting up nights in his luxurious new room in Mrs. Ingot's boarding-house, reading a manual of arms. But Doremus declined to go look at them, and when his rustic but ambitious reporter, "Doc" (otherwise Otis) Itchitt, came in throbbing about the M.M.'s and wanted to run an illustrated account in the Saturday *Informer,* Doremus sniffed.

It was not till their first public parade, in August, that Doremus saw them, and not gladly.

The whole countryside had turned out; he could hear them laughing and shuffling beneath his office window; but he stubbornly stuck to editing an article on fertilizers for cherry orchards. (And he loved parades, childishly!) Not even the sound of a band pounding out "Boola, Boola" drew him to the window. Then he was plucked up by Dan Wilgus, the veteran job compositor and head of the *Informer* chapel, a man tall as a house and possessed of such a sweetning black mustache as had not otherwise been seen since the passing of the old-time bartender. "You got to take a look, Boss; great show!" implored Dan.

Through the Chester-Arthur, red-brick prissiness of President Street, Doremus saw marching a surprisingly well-drilled company of young men in the uniforms of Civil War cavalrymen, and just as they were opposite the *Informer* office, the town band rollicked into "Marching through Georgia." The young men smiled, they stepped more quickly, and held up their banner with the steering wheel and M.M. upon it.

When he was ten, Doremus had seen in this self-same street a Memorial Day parade of the G.A.R. The veterans were an average of under fifty then, and some of them only thirty-five; they had swung ahead lightly and gayly—and to the tune of "Marching through Georgia." So now in 1937 he was looking down again on the veterans of Gettysburg and Missionary Ridge. Oh—he could see them all—Uncle Tom Veeder, who had made him the willow whistles; old Mr. Crowley with his cornflower eyes; Jack Greenhill who played leapfrog with the kids and who was to die in Ethan Creek—— They found him with thick hair dripping. Doremus thrilled to the M.M. flags, the music, the valiant young men, even while he hated all they marched for, and hated the Shad Ledue whom he incredulously recognized in the brawny horseman at the head of the procession.

He understood now why the young men marched to war. But "Oh yeh—you *think* so!" he could hear Shad sneering through the music.

The unwieldy humor characteristic of American politicians persisted even through the eruption. Doremus read about and sardonically "played up" in the *Informer* a minstrel show given at the National Convention of Boosters' Clubs at Atlantic City, late in August. As endmen and interlocutor appeared no less distinguished persons than Secretary of the Treasury Webster R. Skittle, Secretary of War Luthorne, and Secretary of Education and Public Relations, Dr. Macgoblin. It was good, old-time Elks Club humor, uncorroded by any of the notions of dignity and of international obligations which, despite his great services, that queer stick Lee Sarason was suspected of trying to introduce. Why (marveled the Boosters) the Big Boys were so democratic that they even kidded themselves and the Corpos, that's how unassuming they were!

"Who was this lady I seen you going down the street with?" demanded the plump Mr. Secretary Skittle (disguised as a colored wench in polka-dotted cotton) of Mr. Secretary Luthorne (in black-face and large red gloves).

"That wasn't no lady, that was Walt Trowbridge's paper."

"Ah don't think Ah cognosticates youse, Mist' Bones."

"Why—you know—'A Nance for Plutocracy.' "

Clean fun, not too confusingly subtle, drawing the people (several millions listened on the radio to the Boosters' Club show) closer to their great-hearted masters.

But the high point of the show was Dr. Macgoblin's daring to tease his own faction by singing:

Buzz and booze and biz, what fun!
This job gets drearier and drearier,
When I get out of Washington,
I'm going to Siberia!

It seemed to Doremus that he was hearing a great deal about the Secretary of Education. Then, in late September, he heard something not quite pleasant about Dr. Macgoblin. The story, as he got it, ran thus:

Hector Macgoblin, that great surgeon-boxer-poet-sailor, had always contrived to have plenty of enemies, but after the beginning of his investigation of schools, to purge them of any teachers he did not happen to like, he made so unusually many that he was accompanied by bodyguards. At this time in September, he was in New York, finding quantities of "subversive elements" in Columbia University—against the protests of President Nicholas Murray Butler, who insisted that he had already cleaned out all willful and dangerous thinkers, especially the pacifists in the medical school—and Macgoblin's bodyguards were two former instructors in philosophy who in their respective universities had been admired even by their deans for everything except the fact that they would get drunk and quarrelsome. One of them, in that state, always took off one shoe and hit people over the head with the heel, if they argued in defense of Jung.

With these two in uniforms as M.M. battalion leaders—his own was that of a brigadier—after a day usefully spent in kicking out of Columbia all teachers who had voted for Trowbridge, Dr. Macgoblin started off with his brace of bodyguards to try out a wager that he could take a drink at every bar on Fifty-second Street and still not pass out.

He had done well when, at ten-thirty, being then affectionate and philanthropic, he decided that it would be a splendid idea to telephone his revered former teacher in Leland Stanford, the biologist Dr. Willy Schmidt, once of Vienna, now in Rockefeller Institute. Macgoblin was indignant when someone at Dr. Schmidt's apartment informed him that the doctor was out. Furiously: "Out? Out? What d'you mean he's out? Old goat like that got no right to be out! At midnight! Where is he? This is the Police Department speaking! Where is he?"

Dr. Schmidt was spending the evening with that gentle scholar, Rabbi Dr. Vincent de Verez.

Macgoblin and his learned gorillas went to call on De Verez. On the way nothing of note happened except that when Macgoblin discussed the fare with the taxi-driver, he felt impelled to knock him out. The three, and they were in the happiest, most boyish of spirits, burst joyfully into Dr. de Verez's primeval house in the Sixties. The entrance hall was shabby enough, with a humble show of the good rabbi's unbrellas and storm rubbers, and had the invaders seen the bedrooms they would have found them Trappist cells. But the long living room, front- and back-parlor thrown together, was half museum, half lounge. Just because he himself liked such things and resented a stranger's possessing them, Macgoblin looked sniffily at a Beluchi prayer rug, a Jacobean court cupboard, a small case of incunabula and of Arabic manuscripts in silver upon scarlet parchment.

"Swell joint! Hello, Doc! How's the Dutchman? How's the antibody research going? These are Doc Nemo and Doc, uh, Doc Whoozis, the famous glue lifters. Great frenzh mine. Introduce us to your Jew friend."

Now it is more than possible that Rabbi de Verez had never heard of Secretary of Education Macgoblin.

The houseman who had let in the intruders and who nervously hovered at the living-room door—he is the sole authority for most of the story—said that Macgoblin staggered, slid on a rug, almost fell, then giggled foolishly as he sat down, waving his plug-ugly friends to chairs and demanding, "Hey, Rabbi, how about some whisky? Lil Scotch and soda. I know you Geōnim never lap up anything but snow-cooled nectar handed out by a maiden with a dulcimer, singing of Mount Abora, or maybe just a little shot of Christian children's sacrificial blood—ha, ha, just a joke, Rabbi; I know these 'Protocols of the Elders of Zion' are all the bunk, but awful handy in propaganda, just the same and—— But I mean, for plain Goyim like us, a little real hootch! *Hear me?*"

Dr. Schmidt started to protest. The Rabbi, who had been carding his white beard, silenced him and, with a wave of his fragile old hand, signaled the waiting houseman, who reluctantly brought in whisky and siphons.

The three coördinators of culture almost filled their glasses before they poured in the soda.

"Look here, de Verez, why don't you kikes take a tumble to yourselves and get out, beat it, exeunt bearing corpses, and start a real Zion, say in South America?"

The Rabbi looked bewildered at the attack. Dr. Schmidt snorted, "Dr. Macgoblin—once a promising pupil of mine—is Secretary of Education and a lot of t'ings—I don't know vot!—at Washington. Corpo!"

"Oh!" The Rabbi sighed. "I have heard of that cult, but my people have learned to ignore persecution. We have been so impudent as to adopt the tactics of your Early Christian Martyrs! Even if we were invited to your Corporate feast—which, I understand, we most warmly are not!—I am afraid we should not be able to attend. You see, we believe in only one Dictator, God, and I am afraid we cannot see Mr. Windrip as a rival to Jehovah!"

"Aah, that's all baloney!" murmured one of the learned gunmen, and Macgoblin shouted, "Oh, can the two-dollar words! There's just one thing where we agree with the dirty, Kike-loving Communists—that's in chucking the whole bunch of divinities, Jehovah and all the rest of 'em, that've been on relief so long!"

The Rabbi was unable even to answer, but little Dr. Schmidt (he had a doughnut mustache, a beer belly, and black button boots with soles half-an-inch thick) said, "Macgoblin, I suppose I may talk frank wit' an old student, there not being any reporters or loutspeakers arount. Do you know why you are drinking like a pig? Because you are ashamt! Ashamt that you, once a promising researcher, should have solt out to freebooters with brains like decayed liver and——"

"That'll do from you, Prof!"

"Say, we oughtta tie those seditious sons of hounds up and beat the daylight out of 'em!" whimpered one of the watchdogs.

Macgoblin shrieked, "You highbrows—you stinking intellectuals! You, you Kike, with your lush-luzurious library, while Common People been starving—would be now if the Chief hadn't saved 'em! Your c'lection books—stolen from the pennies of your poor, dumb, foot-kissing congregation of pushcart peddlers!"

The Rabbi sat bespelled, fingering his beard, but Dr. Schmidt leaped up, crying, "You three scoundrels were not invited here! You pushed your way in! Get out! Go! Get out!"

One of the accompanying dogs demanded of Macgoblin, "Going to stand for these two Yiddles insulting us—insulting the whole by God Corpo state and the M.M. uniform? Kill 'em!"

Now, to his already abundant priming, Macgoblin had added two huge whiskies since he had come. He yanked out his automatic pistol, fired twice. Dr. Schmidt toppled. Rabbi de Verez slid down in his chair, his temple throbbing out blood. The houseman trembled at the door, and one of the guards shot at him, then chased him down the street, firing, and whooping with the humor of the joke. This learned guard was killed instantly, at a street crossing, by a traffic policeman.

Macgoblin and the other guard were arrested and brought before the Commissioner of the Metropolitan District, the great Corpo viceroy, whose power was that of three or four state governors put together.

Dr. de Verez, though he was not yet dead, was too sunken to testify. But the Commissioner thought that in a case so closely touching the federal government, it would not be seemly to postpone the trial.

Against the terrified evidence of the Rabbi's Russian-Polish houseman were the earnest (and by now sober) accounts of the federal Secretary of Education, and of his surviving aide, formerly Assistant Professor of Philosophy in Pelouse University. It was proven that not only de Verez but also Dr. Schmidt was a Jew—which, incidentally, he 100 per cent was not. It was almost proven that this sinister pair had been coaxing innocent Corpos into De Verez's house and performing upon them what a scared little Jewish stool pigeon called "ritual murders."

Macgoblin and friend were acquitted on grounds of self-defense and handsomely complimented by the Commissioner—and later in telegrams from President

Windrip and Secretary of State Sarason—for having defended the Commonwealth against human vampires and one of the most horrifying plots known in history.

The policeman who had shot the other guard wasn't, so scrupulous was Corpo justice, heavily punished—merely sent out to a dreary beat in the Bronx. So everybody was happy.

But Doremus Jessup, on receiving a letter from a New York reporter who had talked privately with the surviving guard, was not so happy. He was not in a very gracious temper, anyway. County Commissioner Shad Ledue, on grounds of humanitarianism, had made him discharge his delivery boys and employ M.M.'s to distribute (or cheerfully chuck into the river) the *Informer*. "Last straw—plenty last," he raged.

He had read about Rabbi de Verez and seen pictures of him. He had once heard Dr. Willy Schmidt speak, when the State Medical Association had met at Fort Beulah, and afterward had sat near him at dinner. If they were murderous Jews, then he was a murderous Jew too, he swore, and it was time to do something for his Own People.

That evening—it was late in September, 1937—he did not go home to dinner at all but, with a paper container of coffee and a slab of pie untouched before him, he stooped at his desk in the *Informer* office, writing an editorial which, when he had finished it, he marked: "Must. 12-pt bold face—box top front p."

The beginning of the editorial, to appear the following morning, was:

> Believing that the inefficiency and crimes of the Corpo administration were due to the difficulties attending a new form of government, we have waited patiently for their end. We apologize to our readers for that patience.
>
> It is easy to see now, in the revolting crime of a drunken cabinet member against two innocent and valuable old men like Dr. Schmidt and the Rev. Dr. de Verez, that we may expect nothing but murderous

extirpation of all honest opponents of the tyranny of Windrip and his Corpo gang.

Not that all of them are as vicious as Macgoblin. Some are merely incompetent—like our friends Ledue, Reek, and Haik. But their ludicrous incapability permits the homicidal cruelty of their chieftains to go on without check.

Buzzard Windrip, the "Chief," and his pirate gang——

A smallish, neat, gray-bearded man, furiously rattling an aged typewriter, typing with his two forefingers.

Dan Wilgus, head of the composing room, looked and barked like an old sergeant and, like an old sergeant, was only theoretically meek to his superior officer. He was shaking when he brought in this copy and, almost rubbing Doremus's nose in it, protested, "Say, boss, you don't honest t' God think we're going to set this up, do you?"

"I certainly do!"

"Well, I don't! Rattlesnake poison! It's all right *your* getting thrown in the hoosegow and probably shot at dawn, if you like that kind of sport, but we've held a meeting of the chapel, and we all say, damned if we'll risk our necks too!"

"All right, you yellow pup! All right, Dan, I'll set it myself!"

"Aw, don't! Gosh, I don't want to have to go to your funeral after the M.M.'s get through with you, and say, 'Don't he look unnatural!' "

"After working for me for twenty years, Dan! Traitor!"

"Look here! I'm no Enoch Arden or—oh, what the hell was his name?—Ethan Frome or Benedict Arnold or whatever it was!—and more 'n once I've licked some galoot that was standing around a saloon telling the world you were the lousiest highbrow editor in Vermont, and at that, I guess maybe he was telling the truth, but same time——" Dan's effort to be humorous and coaxing broke, and he wailed, "God, boss, please don't!"

"I know, Dan. Prob'ly our friend Shad Ledue will be

annoyed. But I can't go on standing things like slaughtering old de Verez any more and—— Here! Gimme that copy!"

While compositors, pressmen, and the young devil stood alternately fretting and snickering at his clumsiness, Doremus ranged up before a type case, in his left hand the first composing-stick he had held in ten years, and looked doubtfully at the case. It was like a labyrinth to him. "Forgot how it's arranged. Can't find anything except the e-box!" he complained.

"Hell! I'll do it! All you pussyfooters get the hell out of this! You don't know one doggone thing about who set this up!" Dan Wilgus roared, and the other printers vanished!—as far as the toilet door.

In the editorial office, Doremus showed proofs of his indiscretion to Doc Itchitt, that enterprising though awkward reporter, and to Julian Falck, who was off now to Amherst but who had been working for the *Informer* all summer, combining unprintable articles on Adam Smith with extremely printable accounts of golf and dances at the country club.

"Gee, I hope you will have the nerve to go on and print it—and same time, I hope you don't! They'll get you!" worried Julian.

"Naw! Gwan and print it! They won't dare to do a thing! They may get funny in New York and Washington, but you're too strong in the Beulah Valley for Ledue and Staubmeyer to dare lift a hand!" brayed Doc Itchitt, while Doremus considered, "I wonder if this smart young journalistic Judas wouldn't like to see me in trouble and get hold of the *Informer* and turn it Corpo?"

He did not stay at the office till the paper with his editorial had gone to press. He went home early, and showed the proof to Emma and Sissy. While they were reading it, with yelps of disapproval, Julian Falck slipped in.

Emma protested, "Oh, you can't—you mustn't do it! What will become of us all? Honestly, Dormouse, I'm not scared for myself, but what would I do if they beat you or put in prison or something? It would just break my heart to think of you in a cell! And without any clean underclothes! It isn't too late to stop it, is it?"

"No. As a matter of fact the paper doesn't go to bed till eleven. . . . Sissy, what do you think?"

"I don't know what to think! Oh damn!"

"Why Sis-sy," from Emma, quite mechanically.

"It used to be, you did what was right and got a nice stick of candy for it," said Sissy. "Now, it seems as if whatever's right is wrong. Julian—funny-face—what do you think of Pop's kicking Shad in his sweet hairy ears?"

"Why, Sis——"

Julian blurted, "I think it'd be fierce if somebody didn't try to stop these fellows. I wish I could do it. But how could I?"

"You've probably answered the whole business," said Doremus. "If a man is going to assume the right to tell several thousand readers what's what—most agreeable, hitherto—he's got a kind of what you might say priestly obligation to tell the truth. 'O cursed spite.' Well! I think I'll drop into the office again. Home about midnight. Don't sit up, anybody—and Sissy, and you, Julian, that particularly goes for you two night prowlers! As for me and my house, we will serve the Lord—and in Vermont, that means going to bed."

"And alone!" murmured Sissy.

"Why—Cecilia—Jes-sup!"

As Doremus trotted out, Foolish, who had sat adoring him, jumped up, hoping for a run.

Somehow, more than all of Emma's imploring, the dog's familiar devotion made Doremus feel what it might be to go to prison.

He had lied. He did not return to the office. He drove up the valley to the Tavern and to Lorinda Pike.

But on the way he stopped in at the home of his son-in-law, bustling young Dr. Fowler Greenhill; not to show him the proof but to have—perhaps in prison? another memory of the domestic life in which he had been rich. He stepped quietly into the front hall of the Greenhill house—a jaunty imitation of Mount Vernon; very prosperous and secure, gay with the brass-knobbed walnut furniture and painted Russian boxes which Mary Greenhill affected. Doremus could hear David (but surely it was past his bedtime?—what time *did* nine-year-old kids go to bed these degenerate days?) excitedly chattering with his father, and his father's partner, old Dr. Marcus Olmsted, who was almost retired but who kept up the obstetrics and eye-and-ear work for the firm.

Doremus peeped into the living room, with its bright curtains of yellow linen. David's mother was writing letters, a crisp, fashionable figure at a maple desk complete with yellow quill pen, engraved notepaper, and silver-backed blotter. Fowler and David were lounging on the two wide arms of Dr. Olmsted's chair.

"So you don't think you'll be a doctor, like your dad and me?" Dr. Olmsted was quizzing.

David's soft hair fluttered as he bobbed his head in the agitation of being taken seriously by grown-ups.

"Oh—oh—oh yes, I would like to. Oh, I think it'd be slick to be a doctor. But I want to be a newspaper, like Granddad. That'd be a wow! You said it!"

("Da-vid! Where you ever pick up such language!")

"You see, Uncle-Doctor, a doctor, oh gee, he has to stay up all night, but an editor, he just sits in his office and takes it easy and never has to worry about nothing!"

That moment, Fowler Greenhill saw his father-in-law making monkey faces at him from the door and admonished David, "Now, not always! Editors have to work pretty hard sometimes—just think of when there's train wrecks and floods and everything! I'll tell you. Did you know I have magic power?"

"What's 'magic power,' Daddy?"

"I'll show you. I'll summon your granddad here from misty deeps——"

("But will he come?" grunted Dr. Olmsted.)

"—and have him tell you all the troubles an editor has. Just make him come flying through the air!"

"Aw, gee, you couldn't do *that,* Dad!"

"Oh, can't I!" Fowler stood solemnly, the overhead lights making soft his harsh red hair, and he windmilled his arms, hooting, "Presto—vesto—adsit—Granddad Jessup—voilà!"

And there, coming through the doorway, sure enough *was* Granddad Jessup!

* * *

Doremus remained only ten minutes, saying to himself, "Anyway, nothing bad can happen, here, in this solid household." When Fowler saw him to the door, Doremus sighed to him, "Wish Davy were right—just had to sit in the office and not worry. But I suppose some day I'll have a run-in with the Corpos."

"I hope not. Nasty bunch. What do you think, Dad? That swine Shad Ledue told me yesterday they wanted me to join the M.M.'s as medical officer. Fat chance! I told him so."

"Watch out for Shad, Fowler. He's vindictive. Made us rewire our whole building."

"I'm not scared of Captain General Ledue or fifty like him! Hope he calls me in for a bellyache some day! I'll give him a good sedative—potassium of cyanide. Maybe I'll some day have the pleasure of seeing that gent in his coffin. That's the advantage the doctor has, you know! G'-night, Dad! Sleep tight!"

A good many tourists were still coming up from New York to view the colored autumn of Vermont, and when Doremus arrived at the Beulah Valley Tavern he had irritably to wait while Lorinda dug out extra towels and looked up train schedules and was polite to old ladies who complained that there was too much—or not enough—sound from the Beulah River Falls at night. He could not talk to her apart until after ten. There was, meanwhile, a curious exalted luxury in watching each lost minute threaten him with the approach of the final press time, as he sat in the tea room, imperturbably scratching through the leaves of the latest *Fortune.*

Lorinda led him, at ten-fifteen, into her little office—just a roll-top desk, a desk chair, one straight chair, and a table piled with heaps of defunct hotel-magazines. It was spinsterishly neat yet smelled still of the cigar smoke and old letter files of proprietors long since gone.

"Let's hurry, Dor. I'm having a little dust-up with that snipe Nipper." She plumped down at the desk.

"Linda, read this proof. For tomorrow's paper. . . . No. Wait. Stand up."

"Eh?"

He himself took the desk chair and pulled her down on his knees. "Oh, *you*!" she snorted, but she nuzzled her cheek against his shoulder and murmured contentedly.

"Read this, Linda. For tomorrow's paper. I think I'm going to publish it, all right—got to decide finally before eleven—but ought I to? I was sure when I left the office, but Emma was scared——"

"Oh, *Emma*! Sit still. Let me see it." She read quickly. She always did. At the end she said emotionlessly, "Yes. You must run it. Doremus! They've actually come to us here—the Corpos—it's like reading about typhus in China and suddenly finding it in your own house!"

She rubbed his shoulder with her cheek again, and raged, "Think of it! That Shad Ledue—and I taught him for a year in district school, though I was only two years older than he was—and what a nasty bully he was, too! He came to me a few days ago, and he had the nerve to propose that if I would give lower rates to the M.M.'s—he sort of hinted it would be nice of me to serve M.M. officers free—they would close their eyes to my selling liquor here, without a license or anything! Why, he had the inconceivable nerve to tell me, and *condescendingly*! my dear—that he and his fine friends would be willing to hang out here a lot! Even Staubmeyer—oh, our 'professor' is blossoming out as quite a sporting character! And when I chased Ledue out, with a flea in his ear—— Well, just this morning I got a notice that I have to appear in the county court tomorrow—some complaint from my endearing partner, Mr. Nipper—seems he isn't satisfied with the division of our work here—and honestly, my darling, he never does one blame thing but sit around and bore my best customers to death by telling what a swell hotel he used to have in Florida. And Nipper has taken his things out of here and moved into town. I'm afraid I'll have an unpleasant time, trying to keep from telling him what I think of him, in court."

"Good Lord! Look, sweet, have you got a lawyer for it?"

"Lawyer? Heavens no! Just a misunderstanding—on little Nipper's part."

"You'd better. The Corpos are using the courts for all

sorts of graft and for accusations of sedition. Get Mungo Kitterick, my lawyer."

"He's dumb. Ice water in his veins."

"I know, but he's a tidier-up, like so many lawyers. Likes to see everything all neat in pigeonholes. He may not care a damn for justice, but he'll be awfully pained by any irregularities. Please get him, Lindy, because they've got Effingham Swan presiding at court tomorrow."

"Who?"

"Swan—the Military Judge for District Three—that's a new Corpo office. Kind of circuit judge with court-martial powers. This Effingham Swan—I had Doc Itchitt interview him today, when he arrived—he's the perfect gentleman-Fascist—Oswald Mosley style. Good family—whatever that means. Harvard graduate. Columbia Law School, year at Oxford. But went into finance in Boston. Investment banker. Major or something during the war. Plays polo and sailed in a yacht race to Bermuda. Itchitt says he's a big brute, with manners smoother than a butterscotch sundae and more language than a bishop."

"But I'll be glad to have a *gentleman* to explain things to, instead of Shad."

"A gentleman's blackjack hurts just as much as a mucker's!"

"Oh, *you*!" with irritated tenderness, running her forefinger along the line of his jaw.

Outside, a footstep.

She sprang up, sat down primly in the straight chair. The footsteps went by. She mused:

"All this trouble and the Corpos—— They're going to do something to you and me. We'll become so roused up that—either we'll be desperate and really cling to each other and everybody else in the world can go to the devil or, what I'm afraid is more likely, we'll get so deep into rebellion against Windrip, we'll feel so terribly that we're standing for something, that we'll want to give up everything else for it, even give up you and me. So that no one can ever find out and criticize. We'll have to be beyond criticism."

"No! I won't listen. We will fight, but how can we ever get so involved—detached people like us——"

"You *are* going to publish that editorial tomorrow?"

"Yes."

"It's not too late to kill it?"

He looked at the clock over her desk—so ludicrously like a grade-school clock that it ought to have been flanked with portraits of George and Martha. "Well, yes, it is too late—almost eleven. Couldn't get to the office till 'way past."

"You're sure you won't worry about it when you go to bed tonight? Dear, I so don't want you to worry! You're sure you don't want to telephone and kill the editorial?"

"Sure. Absolute!"

"I'm glad! Me, I'd rather be shot than go sneaking around, crippled with fear. Bless you!"

She kissed him and hurried off to another hour or two of work, while he drove home whistling vaingloriously.

But he did not sleep well, in his big black-walnut bed. He startled to the night noises of an old frame house—the easing walls, the step of bodiless assassins creeping across the wooden floors all night long.

19

An honest propagandist for any Cause, that is, one who honestly studies and figures out the most effective way of putting over his Message, will learn fairly early that it is not fair to ordinary folks—it just confuses them—to try to make them swallow all the true facts that would be suitable to a higher class of people. And one seemingly small but almighty important point he learns, if he does much speechifying, is that you can win over folks to your point of view much better in the evening, when they are tired out from work and not so likely to resist you, than at any other time of day.

Zero Hour, Berzelius Windrip.

THE FORT BEULAH *Informer* had its own three-story-and-basement building, on President Street between Elm and Maple, opposite the side entrance of the Hotel Wessex. On the top story was the composing room; on the second, the editorial and photographic departments and the bookkeeper; in the basement, the presses; and on the first or street floor, the circulation and advertising departments, and the front office, open to the pavement, where the public came to pay subscriptions and insert want-ads. The private room of the editor, Doremus Jessup, looked out on President Street through one not too dirty window. It was larger but little more showy than Lorinda Pike's office at the Tavern, but on the wall it did have historic treasures in the way of a water-stained surveyor's-map of Fort Beulah Township in 1891, a contemporary oleograph portrait of President McKinley complete with eagles, flags, cannon, and the Ohio state flower, the scarlet carnation, a group photograph of the New England Editorial Association (in which Doremus was the third blur in a derby hat in the fourth row), and an entirely bogus copy of a newspaper announcing Lincoln's death. It was reasonably tidy—in the patent letter file, otherwise empty, there were only 2½ pairs of winter mittens, and an 18-gauge shotgun shell.

Doremus was, by habit, extremely fond of his office. It was the only place aside from his study at home that was thoroughly his own. He would have hated to leave it or to share it with anyone—possibly excepting Buck and Lorinda—and every morning he came to it expectantly, from the ground floor, up the wide brown stairs, through the good smell of printer's ink.

He stood at the window of this room before eight, the morning when his editorial appeared, looking down at the people going to work in shops and warehouses. A few of them were in Minute Men uniforms. More and more even the part-time M.M.'s wore their uniforms when on civilian duties. There was a bustle among them. He saw them unfold copies of the *Informer*; he saw them look up, point up, at his window. Heads close, they irritably discussed the front page of the paper. R. C. Crowley went by, early as ever on his way to open the bank, and stopped to speak to a clerk from Ed Howland's grocery, both of them shaking their heads. Old Dr. Olmsted, Fowler's partner, and Louis Rotenstern halted on a corner. Doremus knew they were both friends of his, but they were dubious, perhaps frightened as they looked at an *Informer.*

The passing of people became a gathering, the gathering a crowd, the crowd a mob, glaring up at his office, beginning to clamor. There were dozens of people there unknown to him: respectable farmers in town for shopping, unrespectables in town for a drink, laborers from the nearest work camp and all of them eddying around M.M. uniforms. Probably many of them cared nothing about insults to the Corpo state, but had only the unprejudiced, impersonal pleasure in violence natural to most people.

Their mutter became louder, less human, more like

the snap of burning rafters. Their glances joined in one. He was, frankly, scared.

He was half conscious of big Dan Wilgus, the head compositor, beside him, hand on his shoulder, but saying nothing, and of Doc Itchitt cackling, "My—my precious—hope they don't—God, I hope they don't come up here!"

The mob acted then, swift and together, on no more of an incitement than an unknown M.M.'s shout: "Ought to burn the place, lynch the whole bunch of traitors!" They were running across the street, into the front office. He could hear a sound of smashing, and his fright was gone in protective fury. He galloped down the wide stairs, and from five steps above the front office looked on the mob, equipped with axes and brush hooks grabbed from in front of Pridewell's near-by hardware store, slashing at the counter facing the front door, breaking the glass case of souvenir postcards and stationery samples, and with obscene hands reaching across the counter to rip the blouse of the girl clerk.

Doremus cried, "Get out of this, all you bums!"

They were coming toward him, claws hideously opening and closing, but he did not await that coming. He clumped down the stairs, step by step, trembling not from fear but from insane anger. One large burgher seized his arm, began to bend it. The pain was atrocious. At that moment (Doremus almost smiled, so grotesquely was it like the nick-of-time rescue by the landing party of Marines) into the front office Commissioner Shad Ledue marched, at the head of twenty M.M.'s with unsheathed bayonets, and, lumpishly climbing up on the shattered counter, bellowed:

"That'll do from you guys! Lam out of this, the whole damn bunch of you!"

Doremus's assailant had dropped his arm. Was he actually, wondered Doremus, to be warmly indebted to Commissioner Ledue, to Shad Ledue? Such a powerful, dependable fellow—the dirty swine!

Shad roared on: "We're not going to bust up this place. Jessup sure deserves lynching, but we got orders from Hanover—the Corpos are going to take over this plant and use it. Beat it, you!"

A wild woman from the mountains—in another existence she had knitted at the guillotine—had thrust through to the counter and was howling up at Shad, "They're traitors! Hang 'em! We'll hang *you,* if you stop us! I want my five thousand dollars!"

Shad casually stooped down from the counter and slapped her. Doremus felt his muscles tense with the effort to get at Shad, to revenge the good lady who, after all, had as much right as Shad to slaughter him, but he relaxed, impatiently gave up all desire for mock heroism. The bayonets of the M.M.'s who were clearing out the crowd were reality, not to be attacked by hysteria.

Shad, from the counter, was blatting in a voice like a sawmill, "Snap into it, Jessup! Take him along, men."

And Doremus, with no volition whatever, was marching through President Street, up Elm Street, and toward the courthouse and county jail, surrounded by four armed Minute Men. The strangest thing about it, he reflected, was that a man could go off thus, on an uncharted journey which might take years, without fussing over plans and tickets, without baggage, without even an extra clean handkerchief, without letting Emma know where he was going, without letting Lorinda—oh, Lorinda could take care of herself. But Emma would worry.

He realized that the guard beside him, with the chevrons of a squad leader, or corporal, was Aras Dilley, the slatternly farmer from up on Mount Terror whom he had often helped . . . or thought he had helped.

"Ah, Aras!" said he.

"Huh!" said Aras.

"Come on! Shut up and keep moving!" said the M.M. behind Doremus, and prodded him with the bayonet.

It did not, actually, hurt much, but Doremus spat with fury. So long now he had unconsciously assumed that his dignity, his body, were sacred. Ribald Death might touch him, but no more vulgar stranger.

Not till they had almost reached the courthouse could he realize that people were looking at him—at Doremus Jessup!—as a prisoner being taken to jail. He tried to be proud of being a political prisoner. He couldn't. Jail was jail.

* * *

The county lockup was at the back of the courthouse, now the center of Ledue's headquarters. Doremus had never been in that or any other jail except as a reporter, pityingly interviewing the curious, inferior sort of people who did mysteriously get themselves arrested.

To go into that shameful back door—he who had always stalked into the front entrance of the courthouse, the editor, saluted by clerk and sheriff and judge!

Shad was not in sight. Silently Doremus's four guards conducted him through a steel door, down a corridor, to a small cell reeking of chloride of lime and, still unspeaking, they left him there. The cell had a cot with a damp straw mattress and damper straw pillow, a stool, a wash basin with one tap for cold water, a pot, two hooks for clothes, a small barred window, and nothing else whatever except a jaunty sign ornamented with embossed forget-me-nots and a text from Deuteronomy, "He shall be free at home one year."

"I hope so!" said Doremus, not very cordially.

It was before nine in the morning. He remained in that cell, without speech, without food, with only tap water caught in his doubled palm and with one cigarette an hour, until after midnight, and in the unaccustomed stillness he saw how in prison men could eventually go mad.

"Don't whine, though. You here a few hours, and plenty of poor devils in solitary for years and years, put there by tyrants worse than Windrip . . . yes, and sometimes put there by nice, good, social-minded judges that I've played bridge with!"

But the reasonableness of the thought didn't particularly cheer him.

He could hear a distant babble from the bull pen, where the drunks and vagrants, and the petty offenders among the M.M.'s, were crowded in enviable comradeship, but the sound was only a background for the corroding stillness.

He sank into a twitching numbness. He felt that he was choking, and gasped desperately. Only now and then did he think clearly—then only of the shame of imprisonment or, even more emphatically, of how hard the wooden stool was on his ill-upholstered rump, and how much pleasanter it was, even so, than the cot, whose mattress had the quality of crushed worms.

Once he felt that he saw the way clearly:

"The tyranny of this dictatorship isn't primarily the fault of Big Business, nor of the demagogues who do their dirty work. It's the fault of Doremus Jessup! Of all the conscientious, respectable, lazy-minded Doremus Jessups who have let the demagogues wriggle in, without fierce enough protest.

"A few months ago I thought the slaughter of the Civil War, and the agitation of the violent Abolitionists who helped bring it on, were evil. But possibly they *had* to be violent, because easy-going citizens like me couldn't be stirred up otherwise. If our grandfathers had had the alertness and courage to see the evils of slavery and of a government conducted by gentlemen for gentlemen only, there wouldn't have been any need of agitators and war and blood.

"It's my sort, the Responsible Citizens who've felt ourselves superior because we've been well-to-do and what we thought was 'educated,' who brought on the Civil War, the French Revolution, and now the Fascist Dictatorship. It's I who murdered Rabbi de Verez. It's I who persecuted the Jews and the Negroes. I can blame no Aras Dilley, no Shad Ledue, no Buzz Windrip, but only my own timid soul and drowsy mind. Forgive, O Lord!

"Is it too late?"

Once again, as darkness was coming into his cell like the inescapable ooze of a flood, he thought furiously:

"And about Lorinda. Now that I've been kicked into reality—got to be one thing or the other: Emma (who's my bread) or Lorinda (my wine) but I can't have both.

"Oh, damn! What twaddle! Why can't a man have both bread and wine and not prefer one before the other?

"Unless, maybe, we're all coming into a day of battles when the fighting will be too hot to let a man stop for anything save bread . . . and maybe, even, too hot to let him stop for that!"

The waiting—the waiting in the smothering cell—the relentless waiting while the filthy window glass turned from afternoon to a bleak darkness.

What was happening out there? What had happened to Emma, to Lorinda, to the *Informer* office, to Dan Wilgus, to Buck and Sissy and Mary and David?

Why, it was today that Lorinda was to answer the action against her by Nipper! Today! (Surely all that must have been done with a year ago!) What had happened? Had Military Judge Effingham Swan treated her as she deserved?

But Doremus slipped again from this living agitation into the trance of waiting—waiting; and, catnapping on the hideously uncomfortable little stool, he was dazed when at some unholily late hour (it was just after midnight) he was aroused by the presence of armed M.M.'s outside his barred cell door, and by the hill-billy drawl of Squad Leader Aras Dilley:

"Well, guess y' better git up now, better git up! Jedge wants to see you—jedge says he wants to see you. Heh! Guess y' didn't ever think I'd be a squad leader, *did* yuh, Mist' Jessup!"

Doremus was escorted through angling corridors to the familiar side entrance of the courtroom—the entrance where once he had seen Thad Dilley, Aras's degenerate cousin, shamble in to receive sentence for clubbing his wife to death. . . . He could not keep from feeling that Thad and he were kin, now.

He was kept waiting—waiting!—for a quarter hour outside the closed courtroom door. He had time to consider the three guards commanded by Squad Leader Aras. He happened to know that one of them had served a sentence at Windsor for robbery with assault; and one, a surly young farmer, had been rather doubtfully acquitted on a charge of barn-burning in revenge against a neighbor.

He leaned against the slightly dirty gray plaster wall of the corridor.

"Stand straight there, you! What the hell do you think

this is? And keeping us up late like this!" said the rejuvenated, the redeemed Aras, waggling his bayonet and shining with desire to use it on the bourjui.

Doremus stood staight.

He stood very straight, he stood rigid, beneath a portrait of Horace Greeley.

Till now, Doremus had liked to think of that most famous of radical editors, who had been a printer in Vermont from 1825 to 1828, as his colleague and comrade. Now he felt colleague only to the revolutionary Karl Pascals.

His legs, not too young, were trembling; his calves ached. Was he going to faint? What was happening in there, in the courtroom?

To save himself from the disgrace of collapsing, he studied Aras Dilley. Though his uniform was fairly new, Aras had managed to deal with it as his family and he had dealt with their house on Mount Terror—once a sturdy Vermont Cottage with shining white clapboards, now mud-smeared and rotting. His cap was crushed in, his breeches spotted, his leggings gaping, and one tunic button hung by a thread.

"I wouldn't particularly want to be dictator over an Aras, but I most particularly do not want him and his like to be dictators over me, whether they call them Fascists or Corpos or Communists or Monarchists or Free Democratic Electors or anything else! If that makes me a reactionary kulak, all right! I don't believe I ever really liked the shiftless brethren, for all my lying handshaking. Do you think the Lord calls on us to love the cowbirds as much as the swallows? I don't! Oh, I know; Aras has had a hard time: mortgage and seven kids. But Cousin Henry Veeder and Dan Wilgus—yes, and Pete Vutong, the Canuck, that lives right across the road from Aras and has just exactly the same kind of land—they were all born poor, and they've lived decently enough. They can wash their ears and their door sills, at least. I'm cursed if I'm going to give up the American-Wesleyan doctrine of Free Will and of Will to Accomplishment entirely, even if it does get me read out of the Liberal Communion!"

Aras had peeped into the courtroom, and he stood giggling.

Then Lorinda came out—after midnight!

Her partner, the wart Nipper, was following her, looking sheepishly triumphant.

"Linda! Linda!" called Doremus, his hands out, ignoring the snickers of the curious guards, trying to move toward her. Aras pushed him back and at Lorinda sneered, "Go on—move on, there!" and she moved. She seemed twisted and rusty as Doremus would have thought her bright steeliness could never have been.

Aras cackled, "Haa, haa, haa! Your friend, Sister Pike——"

"My wife's friend!"

"All right, boss. Have it your way! Your wife's friend, Sister Pike, got hers for trying to be fresh with Judge Swan! She's been kicked out of her partnership with Mr. Nipper—he's going to manage that Tavern of theirn, and Sister Pike goes back to pot-walloping in the kitchen, like she'd ought to!—like maybe some of your womenfolks, that think they're so almighty stylish and independent, will be having to, pretty soon!"

Again Doremus had sense enough to regard the bayonets; and a mighty voice from inside the courtroom trumpeted: "Next case! D. Jessup!"

On the judges' bench were Shad Ledue in uniform as an M.M. battalion leader, ex-superintendent Emil Staubmeyer presenting the rôle of ensign, and a third man, tall, rather handsome, rather too face-massaged, with the letters "M.J." on the collar of his uniform as commander, or pseudo-colonel. He was perhaps fifteen years younger than Doremus.

This, Doremus knew, must be Military Judge Effingham Swan, sometime of Boston.

The Minute Men marched him in front of the bench and retired, with only two of them, a milky-faced farm boy and a former gas-station attendant, remaining on guard inside the double doors of the side entrance . . . the entrance for criminals.

Commander Swan loafed to his feet and, as though

he were greeting his oldest friend, cooed at Doremus, "My dear fellow, so sorry to have to trouble you. Just a routine query, you know. Do sit down. Gentlemen, in the case of Mr. Doremus, surely we need not go through the farce of formal inquiry. Let's all sit about that damn big silly table down there—place where they always stick the innocent defendants and the guilty attorneys, y' know—get down from this high altar—little too mystical for the taste of a vulgar bucket-shop gambler like myself. After you, Professor; after you, my dear Captain." And, to the guards, "Just wait outside in the hall, will you? Close the doors."

Staubmeyer and Shad looking, despite Effingham Swan's frivolity, as portentous as their uniforms could make them, clumped down to the table. Swan followed them airily, and to Doremus, still standing, he gave his tortoise-shell cigarette case, caroling, "Do have a smoke, Mr. Doremus. Must we all be so painfully formal?"

Doremus reluctantly took a cigarette, reluctantly sat down as Swan waved him to a chair—with something not quite so airy and affable in the sharpness of the gesture.

"My name is Jessup, Commander. Doremus is my first name."

"Ah, I see. It could be. Quite so. Very New England. Doremus." Swan was leaning back in his wooden armchair, powerful trim hands behind his neck. "I'll tell you, my dear fellow. One's memory is so wretched, you know. I'll just call you 'Doremus,' *sans* Mister. Then, d' you see, it might apply to either the first (or Christian, as I believe one's wretched people in Back Bay insist on calling it)—either the Christian or the surname. Then we shall feel all friendly and secure. Now, Doremus, my dear fellow, I begged my friends in the M.M.—I do trust they were not too importunate, as these parochial units sometimes do seem to be—but I ordered them to invite you here, really, just to get your advice as a journalist. Does it seem to you that most of the peasants here are coming to their senses and ready to accept the Corpo *fait accompli*?"

Doremus grumbled, "But I understood I was dragged here—and if you want to know, your squad was all of what you call 'importunate'!—because of an editorial I wrote about President Windrip."

"Oh, was that you, Doremus? You see?—I was right—one does have such a wretched memory! I do seem now to remember some minor incident of the sort—you know—mentioned in the agenda. Do have another cigarette, my dear fellow."

"Swan! I don't care much for this cat-and-mouse game—at least, not while I'm the mouse. What are your charges against me?"

"Charges? Oh, my only aunt! Just trifling things—criminal libel and conveying secret information to alien forces and high treason and homicidal incitement to violence—you know, the usual boresome line. And all so easily got rid of, my Doremus, if you'd just be persuaded—you see how quite pitifully eager I am to be friendly with you, and to have the inestimable aid of your experience here—if you'd just decide that it might be the part of discretion—so suitable, y' know, to your venerable years——"

"Damn it, I'm not venerable, nor anything like it. Only sixty. Sixty-one, I should say."

"Matter of ratio, my dear fellow. I'm forty-seven m'self, and I have no doubt the young pups already call *me* venerable! But as I was saying, Doremus——"

(Why was it he winced with fury every time Swan called him that?)

"—with your position as one of the Council of Elders, and with your responsibilities to your family—it would be *too* sick-making if anything happened to *them,* y' know!—you just can't afford to be too brash! And all we desire is for you to play along with us in your paper—I would adore the chance of explaining some of the Corpos' and the Chief's still unrevealed plans to you. You'd see such a new light!"

Shad grunted, "Him? Jessup couldn't see a new light if it was on the end of his nose!"

"A moment, my dear Captain. . . . And also, Doremus, of course we shall urge you to help us by giving us a complete list of every person in this vicinity that you know of who is secretly opposed to the Administration."

"Spying? Me?"

"Quite!"

"If I'm accused of—— I insist on having my lawyer,

Mungo Kitterick, and on being tried, not all this bear-baiting——"

"Quaint name. Mungo Kitterick! Oh, my only aunt! Why does it give me so absurd a picture of an explorer with a Greek grammar in his hand? You don't quite understand, my Doremus. *Habeas corpus*—due processes of law—too, too bad!—all those ancient sanctities, dating, no doubt, from Magna Charta, been suspended—oh, but just temporarily, y' know—state of crisis—unfortunate necessity martial law——"

"Damn it, Swan——"

"Commander, my dear fellow—ridiculous matter of military discipline, y' know—*such* rot!"

"You know mighty well and good it isn't temporary! It's permanent—that is, as long as the Corpos last."

"It could be!"

"Swan—Commander—you get that 'it could be' and 'my aunt' from the Reggie Fortune stories, don't you?"

"Now there *is* a fellow detective-story fanatic! But how too bogus!"

"And that's Evelyn Waugh! You're quite a literary man for so famous a yachtsman and horseman, Commander."

"Horsemun, yachtsmun, lit-er-ary man! Am I, Doremus, even in my *sanctum sanctorum,* having, as the lesser breeds would say, the pants kidded off me? Oh, my Doremus, that couldn't be! And just when one is so feeble, after having been so, shall I say excoriated, by your so amiable friend, Mrs. Lorinda Pike? No, no! How too unbefitting the majesty of the law!"

Shad interrupted again, "Yeh, we had a swell time with your girl-friend, Jessup. But I already had the dope about you and her before."

Doremus sprang up, his chair crashing backward on the floor. He was reaching for Shad's throat across the table. Effingham Swan was on him, pushing him back into another chair. Doremus hiccuped with fury. Shad had not even troubled to rise, and he was going on contemptuously:

"Yuh, you two have quite some trouble if you try to pull any spy stuff on the Corpos. My, my, Doremus, ain't we had fun, Lindy and you, playing footie-footie these last couple years! Didn't nobody know about it, did they! But what *you* didn't know was Lindy—and don't it beat hell a long-nosed, skinny old maid like her can have so much pep!—and she's been cheating on you right along, sleeping with every doggone man boarder she's had at the Tavern, and of course with her little squirt of a partner, Nipper!"

Swan's great hand—hand of an ape with a manicure—held Doremus in his chair. Shad snickered. Emil Staubmeyer, who had been sitting with fingertips together, laughed amiably. Swan patted Doremus's back.

He was less sunken by the insult to Lorinda than by the feeling of helpless loneliness. It was so late; the night so quiet. He would have been glad if even the M.M. guards had come in from the hall. Their rustic innocence, however barnyardishly brutal, would have been comforting after the easy viciousness of the three judges.

Swan was placidly resuming: "But I suppose we really must get down to business—however agreeable, my dear clever literary detective, it would be to discuss Agatha Christie and Dorothy Sayers and Norman Klein. Perhaps we can some day, when the Chief puts us both in the same prison! There's really, my dear Doremus, no need of your troubling your legal gentleman, Mr. Monkey Kitteridge. I am quite authorized to conduct this trial—for quaintly enough, Doremus, it *is* a trial, despite the delightful St. Botolph's atmosphere! And as to testimony, I already have all I need, both in the good Miss Lorinda's inadvertent admissions, in the actual text of your editorial criticizing the Chief, and in the quite thorough reports of Captain Ledue and Dr. Staubmeyer. One really ought to take you out and shoot you—and one is quite empowered to do so, oh quite!—but one has one's faults—one is really too merciful. And perhaps we can find a better use for you than as fertilizer—you are, you know, rather too much on the skinny side to make adequate fertilizer.

"You are to be released on parole, to assist and coach Dr. Staubmeyer who, by orders from Commissioner Reek, at Hanover, has just been made editor of the *Informer*, but who doubtless lacks certain points of technical training. You will help him—oh, gladly, I am sure!—until he learns.

Then we'll see what we'll do with you! . . . You will write editorials, with all your accustomed brilliance—oh, I assure you, people constantly stop on Boston Common to discuss your masterpieces; have done for years! But you'll write only as Dr. Staubmeyer tells you. *Understand?* Oh. Today—since 'tis already past the witching hour—you will write an abject apology for your diatribe—oh yes, very much on the abject side! You know—you veteran journalists do these things so neatly—just admit you were a cockeyed liar and that sort of thing—bright and bantering—*you* know! And next Monday you will, like most of the other ditchwater-dull papers, begin the serial publication of the Chief's *Zero Hour.* You'll enjoy that!"

Clatter and shouts at the door. Protests from the unseen guards. Dr. Fowler Greenhill pounding in, stopping with arms akimbo, shouting as he strode down to the table, "What do you three comic judges think you're doing?"

"And who may our impetuous friend be? He annoys me, rather," Swan asked of Shad.

"Doc Fowler—Jessup's son-in-law. And a bad actor. Why, couple days ago I offered him charge of medical inspection for all the M.M.'s in the county, and he said—this red-headed smart aleck here!—he said you and me and Commissioner Reek and Doc Staubmeyer and all of us were a bunch of hoboes that'd be digging ditches in a labor camp if we hadn't stole some officers' uniforms!"

"Ah, did he indeed?" purred Swan.

Fowler protested: "He's a liar. I never mentioned you. I don't even know who you are."

"My name, good sir, is Commander Effingham Swan, M.J.!"

"Well, M. J., that still doesn't enlighten me. Never heard of you!"

Shad interrupted, "How the hell did you get past the guards, Fowler?" (He who had never dared call that long-reaching, swift-moving redhead anything more familiar than "Doc.")

"Oh, all your Minnie Mouses know me. I've treated most of your brightest gunmen for unmentionable diseases. I just told them at the door that I was wanted in here professionally."

Swan was at his silkiest: "Oh, and how we *did* want you, my dear fellow—though we didn't know it until this moment. So you are one of these brave rustic Æsculapiuses?"

"I am! And if you were in the war—which I should doubt, from your pansy way of talking—you may be interested to know that I am also a member of the American Legion—quit Harvard and joined up in 1918 and went back afterwards to finish. And I want to warn you three half-baked Hitlers——"

"Ah! But my dear friend! A mil-i-tary man! How too *too*! Then we shall have to treat you as a responsible person—responsible for your idiocies—not just as the uncouth clodhopper that you appear!"

Fowler was leaning both fists on the table. "Now I've had enough! I'm going to push in your booful face——"

Shad had his fists up, was rounding the table, but Swan snapped, "No! Let him finish! He may enjoy digging his own grave. You know—people do have such quaint variant notions about sports. Some laddies actually like to go fishing—all those slimy scales and the shocking odor! By the way, Doctor, before it's too late, I would like to leave with you the thought for the day that I was also in the war to end wars—a major. But go on. I do so want to listen to you yet a little."

"Cut the cackle, will you, M. J.? I've just come here to tell you that I've had enough—everybody's had enough—of your kidnaping Mr. Jessup—the most honest and useful man in the whole Beulah Valley! Typical low-down sneaking kidnapers! If you think your phony Rhodes-Scholar accent keeps you from being just another cowardly, murdering Public Enemy, in your toy-soldier uniform——"

Swan held up his hand in his most genteel Back Bay manner. "A moment, Doctor, if you will be so good?" And to Shad: "I should think we'd heard enough from the Comrade, wouldn't you, Commissioner? Just take the bastard out and shoot him."

"O. K.! Swell!" Shad chuckled; and, to the guards at

the half-open door, "Get the corporal of the guard and a squad—six men—loaded rifles—make it snappy, see?"

The guards were not far down the corridor, and their rifles were already loaded. It was in less than a minute that Aras Dilley was saluting from the door, and Shad was shouting, "Come here! Grab this dirty crook!" He pointed at Fowler. "Take him along outside."

They did, for all of Fowler's struggling. Aras Dilley jabbed Fowler's right wrist with a bayonet. It spilled blood down on his hand, so scrubbed for surgery, and like blood his red hair tumbled over his forehead.

Shad marched out with them, pulling his automatic pistol from its holster and looking at it happily.

Doremus was held, his mouth was clapped shut, by two guards as he tried to reach Fowler. Emil Staubmeyer seemed a little scared, but Effingham Swan, suave and amused, leaned his elbows on the table and tapped his teeth with a pencil.

From the courtyard, the sound of a rifle volley, a terrifying wail, one single emphatic shot, and nothing after.

20

> The real trouble with the Jews is that they are cruel. Anybody with a knowledge of history knows how they tortured poor debtors in secret catacombs, all through the Middle Ages. Whereas the Nordic is distinguished by his gentleness and his kind-heartedness to friends, children, dogs, and people of inferior races.
>
> *Zero Hour,* Berzelius Windrip.

THE REVIEW in Dewey Haik's provincial court of Judge Swan's sentence on Greenhill was influenced by County Commissioner Ledue's testimony that after the execution he found in Greenhill's house a cache of the most seditious documents: copies of Trowbridge's *Lance for Democracy,* books by Marx and Trotzky, Communistic pamphlets urging citizens to assassinate the Chief.

Mary, Mrs. Greenhill, insisted that her husband had never read such things; that, if anything, he had been too indifferent to politics. Naturally, her word could not be taken against that of Commissioner Ledue, Assistant Commissioner Staubmeyer (known everywhere as a scholar and man of probity), and Military Judge Effingham Swan. It was necessary to punish Mrs. Greenhill—or, rather, to give a strong warning to other Mrs. Greenhills—by seizing all the property and money Greenhill had left her.

Anyway, Mary did not fight very vigorously. Perhaps she realized her guilt. In two days she turned from the crispest, smartest, most swift-spoken woman in Fort Beulah into a silent hag, dragging about in shabby and unkempt black. Her son and she went to live with her father, Doremus Jessup.

Some said that Jessup should have fought for her and her property. But he was not legally permitted to do so. He was on parole, subject, at the will of the properly constituted authorities, to a penitentiary sentence.

So Mary returned to the house and the overfurnished bedroom she had left as a bride. She could not, she said, endure its memories. She took the attic room that had never been quite "finished off." She sat up there all day, all evening, and her parents never heard a sound. But within a week her David was playing about the yard most joyfully . . . playing that he was an M.M. officer.

The whole house seemed dead, and all that were in it seemed frightened, nervous, forever waiting for something unknown—all save David and, perhaps, Mrs. Candy, bustling in her kitchen.

Meals had been notoriously cheerful at the Jessups'; Doremus chattered to an audience of Mrs. Candy and Sissy, flustering Emma with the most outrageous assertions—that he was planning to go to Greenland; that President Windrip had taken to riding down Pennsylvania Avenue on an elephant; and Mrs. Candy was as unscrupulous as all good cooks in trying to render them speechlessly drowsy after dinner and to encourage the stealthy expansion of Doremus's already rotund little belly, with her mince pie, her apple pie with enough shortening to make the eyes pop out in sweet anguish, the fat corn fritters and candied potatoes with the broiled chicken, the clam chowder made with cream.

Now, there was little talk among the adults at table and, though Mary was not showily "brave," but colorless as a glass of water, they were nervously watching her. Everything they spoke of seemed to point toward the murder and the Corpos; if you said, "It's quite a warm fall," you felt that the table was thinking, "So the M.M.'s can go on marching for a long time yet before snow flies," and then you choked and asked sharply for the gravy. Always Mary was there, a stone statue chilling the warm and commonplace people packed in beside her.

So it came about that David dominated the table talk, for the first delightful time in his nine years of experiment with life, and David liked that very much indeed, and his grandfather liked it not nearly so well.

He chattered, like an entire palmful of monkeys, about Foolish, about his new playmates (children of Medary Cole, the miller), about the apparent fact that crocodiles are rarely found in the Beulah River, and the more moving fact that the Rotenstern young had driven with their father clear to Albany.

Now Doremus was fond of children; approved of them; felt with an earnestness uncommon to parents and grandparents that they were human beings and as likely as the next one to become editors. But he hadn't enough sap of the Christmas holly in his veins to enjoy listening without cessation to the bright prattle of children. Few males have, outside of Louisa May Alcott. He thought (though he wasn't very dogmatic about it) that the talk of a Washington correspondent about politics was likely to be more interesting than Davy's remarks on cornflakes and garter snakes, so he went on loving the boy and wishing he would shut up. And escaped as soon as possible from Mary's gloom and Emma's suffocating thoughtfulness, wherein you felt, every time Emma begged, "Oh, you *must* take just a *little* more of the nice chestnut dressing, Mary dearie," that you really ought to burst into tears.

Doremus suspected that Emma was, essentially, more appalled by his having gone to jail than by the murder of her son-in-law. Jessups simply didn't go to jail. People who went to jail were *bad,* just as barn-burners and men accused of that fascinatingly obscure amusement, a "statutory offense," were bad; and as for bad people, you might try to be forgiving and tender, but you didn't sit down to meals with them. It was all so irregular, and most upsetting to the household routine!

So Emma loved him and worried about him till he wanted to go fishing and actually did go so far as to get out his flies.

But Lorinda had said to him, with eyes brilliant and unworried, "And I thought you were just a cud-chewing Liberal that didn't mind being milked! I am so proud of you! You've encouraged me to fight against—— Listen, the minute I heard about your imprisonment I chased Nipper out of my kitchen with a bread knife! . . . Well, anyway, I thought about doing it!"

The office was deader than his home. The worst of it was that it wasn't so very bad—that, he saw, he could slip into serving the Corpo state with, eventually, no more sense of shame than was felt by old colleagues of his who in pre-Corpo days had written advertisements for fraudulent mouth washes or tasteless cigarettes, or written for supposedly reputable magazines mechanical stories about young love. In a waking nightmare after his imprisonment, Doremus had pictured Staubmeyer and Ledue in the *Informer* office standing over him with whips, demanding that he turn out sickening praise for the Corpos, yelling at him until he rose and killed and was killed. Actually, Shad stayed away from the office, and Doremus's master, Staubmeyer, was ever so friendly and modest and rather nauseatingly full of praise for his craftsmanship. Staubmeyer seemed satisfied when, instead of the "apology" demanded by Swan, Doremus stated that "Henceforth this paper will cease all criticisms of the present government."

Doremus received from District Commissioner Reed a jolly telegram thanking him for "gallantly deciding turn your great talent service people and correcting errors doubtless made by us in effort set up new more realistic state." Ur! said Doremus and did not chuck the message at the clothes-basket waste-basket, but carefully walked over and rammed it down amid the trash.

He was able, by remaining with the *Informer* in her prostitute days, to keep Staubmeyer from discharging Dan Wilgus, who was sniffy to the new boss and unnaturally respectful now to Doremus. And he invented what he called the "Yow-yow editorial." This was a dirty device of stating as strongly as he could an indictment of Corpoism, then answering it as feebly as he could, as with a whining "Yow-yow-yow—that's what *you* say!" Neither Staubmeyer nor Shad caught him at it, but Doremus hoped fearfully that the shrewd Effingham Swan would never see the Yow-yows.

So week on week he got along not too badly—and there was not one minute when he did not hate this filthy slavery, when he did not have to force himself to stay there, when he did not snarl at himself, "Then why *do* you stay?"

His answers to that challenge came glibly and conventionally enough: "He was too old to start in life again. And he had a wife and family to support"—Emma, Sissy, and now Mary and David.

All these years he had heard responsible men who weren't being quite honest—radio announcers who soft-soaped speakers who were fools and wares that were trash, and who canaryishly chirped "Thank you, Major Blister" when they would rather have kicked Major Blister, preachers who did not believe the decayed doctrines they dealt out, doctors who did not dare tell lady invalids that they were sex-hungry exhibitionists, merchants who peddled brass for gold—heard all of them complacently excuse themselves by explaining that they were too old to change and that they had "a wife and family to support."

Why not let the wife and family die of starvation or get out and hustle for themselves, if by no other means the world could have the chance of being freed from the most boresome, most dull, and foulest disease of having always to be a little dishonest?

So he raged—and went on grinding out a paper dull and a little dishonest—but not forever. Otherwise the history of Doremus Jessup would be too drearily common to be worth recording.

Again and again, figuring it out on rough sheets of copy paper (adorned also with concentric circles, squares, whorls, and the most improbable fish), he estimated that even without selling the *Informer* or his house, as under Corpo espionage he certainly could not if he fled to Canada, he could cash in about $20,000. Say enough to give him an income of a thousand a year—twenty dollars a week, provided he could smuggle the money out of the country, which the Corpos were daily making more difficult.

Well, Emma and Sissy and Mary and he *could* live on that, in a four-room cottage, and perhaps Sissy and Mary could find work.

But as for himself——

It was all very well to talk about men like Thomas Mann and Lion Feuchtwanger and Romain Rolland, who in exile remained writers whose every word was in demand, about Professors Einstein or Salvemini, or, under Corpoism, about the recently exiled or self-exiled Americans, Walt Trowbridge, Mike Gold, William Allen White, John Dos Passos, H. L. Mencken, Rexford Tugwell, Oswald Villard. Nowhere in the world, except possibly in Greenland or Germany, would such stars be unable to find work and soothing respect. But what was an ordinary newspaper hack, especially if he was over forty-five, to do in a strange land—and more especially if he had a wife named Emma (or Carolina or Nancy or Griselda or anything else) who didn't at all fancy going and living in a sod hut on behalf of honesty and freedom?

So debated Doremus, like some hundreds of thousands of other craftsmen, teachers, lawyers, what-not, in some dozens of countries under a dictatorship, who were aware enough to resent the tyranny, conscientious enough not to take its bribes cynically, yet not so abnormally courageous as to go willingly to exile or dungeon or chopping-block—particularly when they "had wives and families to support."

Doremus hinted once to Emil Staubmeyer that Emil was "getting onto the ropes so well" that he thought of getting out, of quitting newspaper work for good.

The hitherto friendly Mr. Staubmeyer said sharply, "What'd you do? Sneak off to Canada and join the propagandists against the Chief? Nothing doing! You'll stay right here and help me—help us!" And that afternoon Commissioner Shad Ledue shouldered in and grumbled, "Dr. Staubmeyer tells me you're doing pretty fairly good work, Jessup, but I want to warn you to keep it up. Remember that Judge Swan only let you out on parole . . . to me! You can do fine if you just set your mind to it!"

"If you just set your mind to it!" The one time when the boy Doremus had hated his father had been when he used that condescending phrase.

He saw that, for all the apparent prosaic calm of day after day on the paper, he was equally in danger of slipping into acceptance of his serfdom and of whips and bars if he didn't slip. And he continued to be just as sick each time he wrote: "The crowd of fifty thousand people who greeted President Windrip in the university stadium at Iowa City was an impressive sign of the constantly growing interest of all Americans in political affairs," and Staubmeyer changed it to: "The vast and enthusiastic crowd of seventy thousand loyal admirers who wildly applauded and listened to the stirring address of the Chief in the handsome university stadium in beautiful Iowa City, Iowa, is an impressive yet quite typical sign of the growing devotion of all true Americans to political study under the inspiration of the Corpo government."

Perhaps his worst irritations were that Staubmeyer had pushed a desk and his sleek, sweaty person into Doremus's private office, once sacred to his solitary grouches, and that Doc Itchitt, hitherto his worshiping disciple, seemed always to be secretly laughing at him.

Under a tyranny, most friends are a liability. One quarter of them turn "reasonable" and become your enemies, one quarter are afraid to stop and speak, and one quarter are killed and you die with them. But the blessed final quarter keep you alive.

When he was with Lorinda, gone was all the pleasant toying and sympathetic talk with which they had relieved boredom. She was fierce now, and vibrant. She drew him close enough to her, but instantly she would be thinking of him only as a comrade in plots to kill off the Corpos. (And it was pretty much a real killing-off that she meant; there wasn't left to view any great amount of her plausible pacifism.)

She was busy with good and perilous works. Partner Nipper had not been able to keep her in the Tavern kitchen; she had so systematized the work that she had many days and evenings free, and she had started a cooking-class for farm girls and young farm wives who, caught between the provincial and the industrial generations, had learned neither good rural cooking with a wood fire, nor yet how to deal with canned goods and electric grills—and who most certainly had not learned how to combine so as to compel the tight-fisted little locally owned power-and-light companies to furnish electricity at tolerable rates.

"Heavensake, keep this quiet, but I'm getting acquainted with these country gals—getting ready for the day when we begin to organize against the Corpos. I depend on them, not the well-to-do women that used to want suffrage but that can't endure the thought of revolution," Lorinda whispered to him. "We've got to *do* something."

"All right, Lorinda B. Anthony," he sighed.

And Karl Pascal stuck.

At Pollikop's garage, when he first saw Doremus after the jailing, he said, "God, I was sorry to hear about their pinching you, Mr. Jessup! But say, aren't you ready to join us Communists now?" (He looked about anxiously as he said it.)

"I thought there weren't any more Bolos."

"Oh, we're supposed to be wiped out. But I guess you'll notice a few mysterious strikes starting now and then, even though there *can't* be any more strikes! Why aren't you joining us? There's where you belong, c-comrade!"

"Look here, Karl: you've always said the difference between the Socialists and the Communists was that you believed in complete ownership of all means of production, not just utilities; and that you admitted the violent class war and the Socialists didn't. That's poppycock! The real difference is that you Communists serve Russia. It's your Holy Land. Well—Russia has all my prayers, right after the prayers for my family and for the Chief, but what I'm interested in civilizing and protecting against its enemies isn't Russia but America. Is that so banal to say? Well, it wouldn't be banal for a Russian comrade to observe that he was for Russia! And America needs our propaganda more every day. Another thing: I'm a middle-class intellectual. I'd never call myself any such a damn silly thing, but since you Reds coined it, I'll have to accept it. That's my class, and that's what I'm interested in. The proletarians are probably noble fellows, but I certainly do not think that the interests of the middle-class intellectuals and the proletarians are the same. They want bread. We want—well, all right, say it, we want cake! And when you get a proletarian ambitious enough to want cake, too—why, in America, he becomes a middle-class intellectual just as fast as he can—*if* he can!"

"Look here, when you think of 3 per cent of the people owning 90 percent of the wealth——"

"I don't think of it! It does *not* follow that because a good many of the intellectuals belong to the 97 per cent of the broke—that plenty of actors and teachers and nurses and musicians don't get any better paid than stage hands or electricians, therefore their interests are the same. It isn't what you earn but how you spend it that fixes your class—whether you prefer bigger funeral services or more books. I'm tired of apologizing for not having a dirty neck!"

"Honestly, Mr. Jessup, that's damn nonsense, and you know it!"

"Is it? Well, it's my American covered-wagon damn nonsense, and not the propaganda-aëroplane damn nonsense of Marx and Moscow!"

"Oh, you'll join us yet."

"Listen, Comrade Karl, Windrip and Hitler will join Stalin long before the descendants of Dan'l Webster. You see, we don't like murder as a way of argument—that's what really marks the Liberal!"

About *his* future Father Perefixe was brief: "I'm going back to Canada where I belong—away to the freedom of the King. Hate to give up, Doremus, but I'm no Thomas à Becket, but just a plain, scared, fat little clark!"

The surprise among old acquaintances was Medary Cole, the miller.

A little younger than Francis Tasbrough and R. C. Crowley, less intensely aristocratic than those noblemen, since only one generation separated him from a chin-whiskered Yankee farmer and not two, as with them, he had been their satellite at the Country Club and, as to solid virtue, been president of the Rotary Club. He had always considered Doremus a man who, without such excuse as being a Jew or a Hunky or poor, was yet flippant about the sanctities of Main Street and Wall Street. They were neighbors, as Cole's "Cape Cod cottage" was just below Pleasant Hill, but they had not by habit been droppers-in.

Now, when Cole came bringing David home, or calling for his daughter Angela, David's new mate, toward supper time of a chilly fall evening, he stopped gratefully for a hot rum punch, and asked Doremus whether he really thought inflation was "such a good thing."

He burst out, one evening, "Jessup, there isn't another person in this town I'd dare say this to, not even my wife, but I'm getting awful sick of having these Minnie Mouses dictate where I have to buy my gunnysacks and what I can pay my men. I won't pretend I ever cared much for labor unions. But in those days, at least the union members did get some of the swag. Now it goes to support the M.M.'s. We pay them and pay them big to bully us. It don't look so reasonable as it did in 1936. But, golly, don't tell anybody I said that!"

And Cole went off shaking his head, bewildered—he who had ecstatically voted for Mr. Windrip.

On a day in late October, suddenly striking in every city and village and back-hill hide-out, the Corpos ended all crime in America forever, so titanic a feat that it was mentioned in the London *Times.* Seventy thousand selected Minute Men, working in combination with town and state police officers, all under the chiefs of the government secret service, arrested every known or faintly suspected criminal in the country. They were tried under court-martial procedure; one in ten was shot immediately, four in ten were given prison sentences, three in ten released as innocent . . . and two in ten taken in the M.M.'s as inspectors.

There were protests that at least six in ten had been innocent, but this was adequately answered by Windrip's courageous statement: "The way to stop crime is to stop it!"

The next day, Medary Cole crowed at Doremus, "Sometimes I've felt like criticizing certain features of Corpo policy, but did you see what the Chief did to the gangsters and racketeers? Wonderful! I've told you right along what this country's needed is a firm hand like Windrip's. No shilly-shallying about that fellow! He saw that the way to stop crime was to just go out and stop it!"

Then was revealed the New American Education, which, as Sarason so justly said, was to be ever so much newer than the New Educations of Germany, Italy, Poland, or even Turkey.

The authorities abruptly closed some scores of the smaller, more independent colleges such as Williams, Bowdoin, Oberlin, Georgetown, Antioch, Carleton, Lewis Institute, Commonwealth, Princeton, Swarthmore, Kenyon, all vastly different one from another but alike in not yet having entirely become machines. Few of the state universities were closed; they were merely to be absorbed by central Corpo universities, one in each of the eight provinces. But the government began with only two. In the Metropolitan District, Windrip University took over the Rockefeller Center and Empire State buildings, with most of Central Park for playground (excluding the general public from it entirely, for the rest was an M.M. drill ground). The second was Macgoblin University, in Chicago and vicinity, using the buildings of Chicago and Northwestern universities, and Jackson Park. President Hutchins of Chicago was rather unpleasant about the whole thing and declined to stay on as an assistant professor, so the authorities had politely to exile him.

Tattle-mongers suggested that the naming of the Chicago plant after Macgoblin instead of Sarason suggested a beginning coolness between Sarason and Windrip, but the two leaders were able to quash such canards by appearing together at the great reception given to Bishop Cannon by the Woman's Christian Temperance Union and being photographed shaking hands.

Each of the two pioneer universities started with an enrollment of fifty thousand, making ridiculous the pre-Corpo schools, none of which, in 1935, had had more than thirty thousand students. The enrollment was probably helped by the fact that anyone could enter upon presenting a certificate showing that he had completed two years in a high school or business college, and a recommendation from a Corpo commissioner.

Dr. Macgoblin pointed out that this founding of entirely new universities showed the enormous cultural superiority of the Corpo state to the Nazis, Bolsheviks, and Fascists. Where these amateurs in re-civilization had merely kicked out all treacherous so-called "intellectual" teachers who mulishly declined to teach physics, cookery, and geography according to the principles and facts laid down by the political bureaus, and the Nazis had merely added the sound measure of discharging Jews who dared attempt to teach medicine, the Americans were the first to start new and completely orthodox institutions, free from the very first of any taint of "intellectualism."

All Corpo universities were to have the same curriculum, entirely practical and modern, free of all snobbish tradition.

Entirely omitted were Greek, Latin, Sanskrit, Hebrew, Biblical study, archaeology, philology; all history before 1500—except for one course which showed that, through the centuries, the key to civilization had been the defense of Anglo-Saxon purity against barbarians. Philosophy and its history, psychology, economics, anthropology were retained, but, to avoid the superstitious errors in ordinary textbooks, they were to be conned only in new books prepared by able young scholars under the direction of Dr. Macgoblin.

Students were encouraged to read, speak, and try to write modern languages, but they were not to waste their time on the so-called "literature"; reprints from recent newspapers were used instead of antiquated fiction and sentimental poetry. As regards English, some study of literature was permitted, to supply quotations for political speeches, but the chief choruses were in advertising, party journalism, and business correspondence, and no authors before 1800 might be mentioned, except Shakespeare and Milton.

In the realm of so-called "pure science," it was realized that only too much and too confusing research had already been done, but no pre-Corpo university had ever shown such a wealth of courses in mining engineering, lakeshore-cottage architecture, modern foremanship and production methods, exhibition gymnastics, the higher accountancy, therapeutics of athlete's foot, canning and fruit dehydration, kindergarten training, organization of chess, checkers, and bridge tournaments, cultivation of will power, band music for mass meetings, schnauzer-breeding, stainless-steel formulæ, cement-road construction, and all other really useful subjects for the formation of the new-world mind and character. And no scholastic institution, even West Point, had ever so richly recognized sport as not a subsidiary but a primary department of scholarship. All the more familiar games were earnestly taught, and to them were added the most absorbing speed contests in infantry drill, aviation, bombing, and operation of tanks, armored cars, and machine guns. All of these carried academic credits, though students were urged not to elect sports for more than one third of their credits.

What really showed the difference from old-fogy inefficiency was that with the educational speed-up of the Corpo universities, any bright lad could graduate in two years.

As he read the prospectuses for these Olympian, these Ringling-Barnum and Bailey universities, Doremus remembered that Victor Loveland, who a year ago had taught Greek in a little college called Isaiah, was now grinding out reading and arithmetic in a Corpo labor camp in Maine. Oh well, Isaiah itself had been closed, and its former president, Dr. Owen J. Peaseley, District Director of Education, was to be right-hand man to Professor Almeric Trout when they founded the University of the Northeastern Province, which was to supplant Harvard, Radcliffe, Boston University, and Brown. He was already working on the university yell, and for that "project" had sent out letters to 167 of the more prominent poets in America, asking for suggestions.

21

IT WAS NOT ONLY the November sleet, setting up a forbidding curtain before the mountains, turning the roadways into slipperiness on which a car would swing around and crash into poles, that kept Doremus stubbornly at home that morning, sitting on his shoulder blades before the fireplace. It was the feeling that there was no point in going to the office; no chance even of a picturesque fight. But he was not contented before the fire. He could find no authentic news even in the papers from Boston or New York, in both of which the morning papers had been combined by the government into one sheet, rich in comic strips, in syndicated gossip from Hollywood, and, indeed, lacking only any news.

He cursed, threw down the New York *Daily Corporate,* and tried to read a new novel about a lady whose husband was indelicate in bed and who was too absorbed by the novels he wrote about lady novelists whose husbands were too absorbed by the novels they wrote about lady novelists to appreciate the fine sensibilities of lady novelists who wrote about gentleman novelists—— Anyway, he chucked the book after the newspaper. The lady's woes didn't seem very important now, in a burning world.

He could hear Emma in the kitchen discussing with Mrs. Candy the best way of making a chicken pie. They talked without relief; really, they were not so much talking as thinking aloud. Doremus admitted that the nice making of a chicken pie was a thing of consequence, but the blur of voices irritated him. Then Sissy slammed into the room, and Sissy should an hour ago have been at high school, where she was a senior—to graduate next year and possibly go to some new and horrible provincial university.

"What ho! What are you doing home? Why aren't you in school?"

"Oh. *That.*" She squatted on the padded fender seat, chin in hands, looking up at him, not seeing him. "I don't know's I'll ever go there any more. You have to repeat a new oath every morning: 'I pledge myself to serve the Corporate State, the Chief, all Commissioners, the Mystic Wheel, and the troops of the Republic in every thought and deed.' Now I ask you! Is *that* tripe!"

"How you going to get into the university?"

"Huh! Smile at Prof Staubmeyer—if it doesn't gag me!"

"Oh, well—— Well——" He could not think of anything meatier to say.

The doorbell, a shuffling in the hall as of snowy feet, and Julian Falck came sheepishly in.

Sissy snapped, "Well, I'll be—— What are you doing home? Why aren't you in Amherst?"

"Oh. *That.*" He squatted beside her. He absently held her hand, and she did not seem to notice it, either. "Amherst's got hers. Corpos closing it today. I got tipped off last Saturday and beat it. (They have a cute way of rounding up the students when they close a college and arresting a few of 'em just to cheer up the profs.)" To Doremus: "Well, sir, I think you'll have to find a place for me on the *Informer,* wiping presses. Could you?"

"Afraid not, boy. Give anything if I could. But I'm a prisoner there. God! Just having to say that makes me appreciate what a rotten position I have!"

"Oh, I'm sorry, sir. I understand, of course. Well, I don't just know what I am going to do. Remember back in '33 and '34 and '35 how many good eggs there were—and some of them medics and law graduates and trained engineers and so on—that simply couldn't get a job? Well, it's worse now. I looked over Amherst, and had a try at Springfield, and I've been here in town two days—I'd hoped to have something before I saw you, Sis—why, I even asked Mrs. Pike if she didn't need somebody to wash dishes at the Tavern, but so far there isn't a thing. 'Young gentleman, two years in college, ninety-nine-point-three pure and thorough knowledge Thirty-nine Articles, able drive car, teach tennis and contract, amiable disposition, desires position—digging ditches.' "

"You *will* get something! I'll see you do, my poppet!" insisted Sissy. She was less modernistic and cold with Julian now than Doremus had thought her.

"Thanks, Sis, but honest to God—I hope I'm not whining, but looks like I'd either have to enlist in the lousy M.M.'s, or go to a labor camp. I can't stay home and sponge on Granddad. The poor old Reverend hasn't got enough to keep a pussycat in face powder."

"Lookit! Lookit!" Sissy clinched with Julian and bussed him, unabashed. "I've got an idea—a new stunt. You know, one of these 'New Careers for Youth' things. Listen! Last summer there was a friend of Lindy Pike's staying with her and she was an interior decorator from Buffalo, and she said they have a hell of a——"

("Siss-sy!")

"—time getting real, genuine, old hand-hewn beams that everybody wants so much now in these phony-Old-English suburban living rooms. Well, look! Round here there's ten million old barns with hand-adzed beams just falling down—farmers probably be glad to have you haul 'em off. I kind of thought about it for myself—being an architect, you know—and John Pollikop said he'd sell me a swell, dirty-looking old five-ton truck for four hundred bucks—in pre-inflation *real* money, I mean—and on time. Let's you and me try a load of assorted fancy beams."

"Swell!" said Julian.

"Well——" said Doremus.

"Come on!" Sissy leaped up. "Let's go ask Lindy what she thinks. She's the only one in this family that's got any business sense."

"I don't seem to hanker much after going out there in this weather—nasty roads," Doremus puffed.

"Nonsense, Doremus! With Julian driving? He's a poor speller and his back-hand is fierce, but as a driver, he's better than I am! Why, it's a pleasure to skid with him! Come on! Hey, Mother! We'll be back in an hour or two."

If Emma ever got beyond her distant, "Why, I thought you were in school, already," none of the three musketeers heard it. They were bundling up and crawling out into the sleet.

Lorinda Pike was in the Tavern kitchen, in a calico print with rolled sleeves, dipping doughnuts into deep fat—a picture right out of the romantic days (which Buzz Windrip was trying to restore) when a female who had brought up eleven children and been midwife to dozens of cows was regarded as too fragile to vote. She was ruddy-faced from the stove, but she cocked a lively eye at them, and her greeting was "Have a doughnut? Good!" She led them from the kitchen with its attendant and eavesdropping horde of a Canuck kitchenmaid and two cats, and they sat in the beautiful butler's-pantry, with its shelved rows of Italian majolica plates and cups and saucers—entirely unsuitable to Vermont, attesting a certain artiness in Lorinda, yet by their cleanness and order revealing her as a sound worker. Sissy sketched her plan—behind the statistics there was an agreeable picture of herself and Julian, gipsies in khaki, on the seat of a gipsy truck, peddling silvery old pine rafters.

"Nope. Not a chance," said Lorinda regretfully. "The expensive suburban-villa business—oh, it isn't gone: there's a surprising number of middlemen and professional men who are doing quite well out of having their wealth taken away and distributed to the masses. But all the building is in the hands of contractors who are in politics—good old Windrip is so consistently American that he's kept up all our traditional graft, even if he has thrown out all our traditional independence. They wouldn't leave you one cent profit."

"She's probably right," said Doremus.

"Be the first time I ever was, then!" sniffed Lorinda. "Why, I was so simple that I thought women voters knew men too well to fall for noble words on the radio!"

They sat in the sedan, outside the Tavern; Julian and Sissy in front, Doremus in the back seat, dignified and miserable in mummy swathings.

"That's that," said Sissy. "Swell period for young

dreamers the Dictator's brought in. You can march to military bands—or you can sit home—or you can go to prison. *Primavera di Bellezza!*"

"Yes. . . . Well, I'll find something to do. . . . Sissy, are you going to marry me—soon as I get a job?"

(It was incredible, thought Doremus, how these latter-day unsentimental sentimentalists could ignore him. . . . Like animals.)

"Before, if you want to. Though marriage seems to me absolute rot now, Julian. They can't go and let us see that every doggone one of our old institutions is a rotten fake, the way Church and State and everything has laid down to the Corpos, and still expect us to think they're so hot! But for unformed minds like your grandfather and Doremus, I suppose we'll have to pretend to believe that the preachers who stand for Big Chief Windrip are still so sanctified that they can sell God's license to love!"

("Sis-sy!")

"(Oh. I forgot you were there, Dad!) But anyway, we're not going to have any kids. Oh, I like children! I'd like to have a dozen of the little devils around. But if people have gone so soft and turned the world over to stuffed shirts and dictators, they needn't expect any decent woman to bring children into such an insane asylum! Why, the more you really *do* love children, the more you'll want 'em not to be born, now!"

Julian boasted, in a manner quite as lover-like and naïve as that of any suitor a hundred years ago, "Yes. But just the same, we'll be having children."

"Hell! I suppose so!" said the golden girl.

It was the unconsidered Doremus who found a job for Julian.

Old Dr. Marcus Olmsted was trying to steel himself to carry on the work of his sometime partner, Fowler Greenhill. He was not strong enough for much winter driving, and so hotly now did he hate the murderers of his friend that he would not take on any youngster who was in the M.M.'s or who had half acknowledged their authority by going to a labor camp. So Julian was chosen to drive him, night and day, and presently to help him by giving anesthetic, bandaging hurt legs; and the Julian who had within one week "decided that he wanted to be" an aviator, a music critic, an air-conditioning engineer, an archæologist excavating in Yucatan, was dead-set on medicine and replaced for Doremus his dead doctor son-in-law. And Doremus heard Julian and Sissy boasting and squabbling and squeaking in the half-lighted parlor and from them—from them and from David and Lorinda and Buck Titus—got resolution enough to go on in the *Informer* office without choking Staubmeyer to death.

22

DECEMBER TENTH was the birthday of Berzelius Windrip, though in his earlier days as a politician, before he fruitfully realized that lies sometimes get printed and unjustly remembered against you, he had been wont to tell the world that his birthday was on December twenty-fifth, like one whom he admitted to be an even greater leader, and to shout, with real tears in his eyes, that his complete name was Berzelius Noel Weinacht Windrip.

His birthday in 1937 he commemorated by the historical "Order of Regulation," which stated that though the Corporate government had proved both its stability and its good-will, there were still certain stupid or vicious "elements" who, in their foul envy of Corpo success, wanted to destroy everything that was good. The kind-hearted government was fed-up, and the country was informed that, from this day on, any person who by word or act sought to harm or discredit the State, would be executed or interned. Inasmuch as the prisons were already too full, both for these slanderous criminals and for the persons whom the kind-hearted State had to guard by "protective arrest," there were immediately to be opened, all over the country, concentration camps.

Doremus guessed that the reason for the concentration camps was not only the provision of extra room for victims but, even more, the provision of places where the livelier young M.M.'s could amuse themselves without interference from old-time professional policemen and prison-keepers, most of whom regarded their charges not as enemies, to be tortured, but just as cattle, to be kept safely.

On the eleventh, a concentration camp was enthusiastically opened, with band music, paper flowers, and speeches by District Commissioner Reek and Shad Ledue, at Trianon, nine miles north of Fort Beulah, in what had been a modern experimental school for girls. (The girls and their teachers, no sound material for Corpoism anyway, were simply sent about their business.)

And on that day and every day afterward, Doremus got from journalist friends all over the country secret news of Corpo terrorism and of the first bloody rebellions against the Corpos.

In Arkansas, a group of ninety-six former sharecroppers, who had always bellyached about their misfortunes yet seemed not a bit happier in well-run, hygienic labor camps with free weekly band concerts, attacked the superintendent's office at one camp and killed the superintendent and five assistants. They were rounded up by an M.M. regiment from Little Rock, stood up in a winter-ragged cornfield, told to run, and shot in the back with machine guns as they comically staggered away.

In San Francisco, dock-workers tried to start an absolutely illegal strike, and their leaders, known to be Communists, were so treasonable in their speeches against the government that an M.M. commander had three of them tied up to a bale of rattan, which was soaked with oil and set afire. The Commander gave warning to all such malcontents by shooting off the criminals' fingers and ears while they were burning, and so skilled a marksman was he, so much credit to the efficient M.M. training, that he did not kill one single man while thus trimming them up. He afterward went in search of Tom Mooney (released by the Supreme Court of the United States, early in 1936), but that notorious anti-Corpo agitator had had the fear of God put into him properly, and had escaped on a schooner for Tahiti.

In Pawtucket, a man who ought to have been free from the rotten seditious notions of such so-called labor-leaders, in fact a man who was a fashionable dentist and director in a bank, absurdly, resented the attentions which half-a-dozen uniformed M.M.'s—they were all on leave, and merely full of youthful spirits, anyway—bestowed upon his wife at a café and, in the confusion, shot and killed three of them. Ordinarily, since it was none of the public's business anyway, the M.M.'s did not give out details of their disciplining of rebels, but in this case, where the fool of a dentist had shown himself to be a homicidal maniac, the local M.M. commander permitted the papers to print the fact that the dentist had been given sixty-nine lashes with a flexible steel rod, then, when he came to, left to think over his murderous idiocy in a cell in which there was two feet of water in the bottom—but, rather ironically, none to drink. Unfortunately, the fellow died before having the opportunity to seek religious consolation.

In Scranton, the Catholic pastor of a working-class church was kidnaped and beaten.

In central Kansas, a man named George W. Smith pointlessly gathered a couple of hundred farmers armed with shotguns and sporting rifles and an absurdly few automatic pistols, and led them in burning an M.M. barracks. M.M. tanks were called out, and the hick would-be rebels were not, this time, used as warnings, but were overcome with mustard gas, then disposed of with hand grenades, which was an altogether intelligent move, since there was nothing of the scoundrels left for sentimental relatives to bury and make propaganda over.

But in New York City the case was the opposite—instead of being thus surprised, the M.M.'s rounded up all suspected Communists in the former boroughs of Manhattan and the Bronx, and all persons who were reported to have been seen consorting with such Communists, and interned the lot of them in the nineteen concentration camps on Long Island. . . . Most of them wailed that they were not Communists at all.

For the first time in America, except during the Civil War and the World War, people were afraid to say whatever came to their tongues. On the streets, on trains, at theaters, men looked about to see who might be listening before they dared so much as say there was a drought in the West, for someone might suppose they were blaming the drought on the Chief! They were particularly skittish about waiters, who were supposed to listen from the ambush which every waiter carries about with him anyway, and to report to the M.M.'s. People who could not resist talking politics spoke of Windrip as

"Colonel Robinson" or "Dr. Brown" and of Sarason as "Judge Jones" or "my cousin Kaspar," and you would hear gossips hissing "Shhh!" at the seemingly innocent statement, "My cousin doesn't seem to be as keen on playing bridge with the Doctor as he used to—I'll bet sometime they'll quit playing."

Every moment everyone felt fear, nameless and omnipresent. They were as jumpy as men in a plague district. Any sudden sound, any unexplained footstep, any unfamiliar script on an envelope, made them startle; and for months they never felt secure enough to let themselves go, in complete sleep. And with the coming of fear went out their pride.

Daily—common now as weather reports—were the rumors of people who had suddenly been carried off "under protective arrest," and daily more of them were celebrities. At first the M.M.'s had, outside of the one stroke against Congress, dared to arrest only the unknown and defenseless. Now, incredulously—for these leaders had seemed invulnerable, above the ordinary law—you heard of judges, army officers, ex-state governors, bankers who had not played in with the Corpos, Jewish lawyers who had been ambassadors, being carted off to the common stink and mud of the cells.

To the journalist Doremus and his family it was not least interesting that among these imprisoned celebrities were so many journalists: Raymond Moley, Frank Simonds, Frank Kent, Heywood Broun, Mark Sullivan, Earl Browder, Franklin P. Adams, George Seldes, Frazier Hunt, Garet Garrett, Granville Hicks, Edwin James, Robert Morss Lovett—men who differed grotesquely except in their common dislike of being little disciples of Sarason and Macgoblin.

Few writers for Hearst were arrested, however.

The plague came nearer to Doremus when unrenowned editors in Lowell and Providence and Albany, who had done nothing more than fail to be enthusiastic about the Corpos, were taken away for "questioning," and not released for weeks—months.

It came much nearer at the time of the book-burning.

* * *

All over the country, books that might threaten the Pax Romana of the Corporate State were gleefully being burned by the more scholarly Minute Men. This form of safeguarding the State—so modern that it had scarce been known prior to A.D. 1300—was instituted by Secretary of Culture Macgoblin, but in each province the crusaders were allowed to have the fun of picking out their own paper-and-ink traitors. In the Northeastern Province, Judge Effingham Swan and Dr. Owen J. Peaseley were appointed censors by Commissioner Dewey Haik, and their index was lyrically praised all through the country.

For Swan saw that it was not such obvious anarchists and soreheads as Darrow, Steffens, Norman Thomas, who were the real danger; like rattlesnakes, their noisiness betrayed their venom. The real enemies were men whose sanctification by death had appallingly permitted them to sneak even into respectable school libraries—men so perverse that they had been traitors to the Corpo State years and years before there had been any Corpo State; and Swan (with Peaseley chirping agreement) barred from all sale or possession the books of Thoreau, Emerson, Whittier, Whitman, Mark Twain, Howells, and *The New Freedom*, by Woodrow Wilson, for though in later life Wilson became a sound manipulative politician, he had earlier been troubled with itching ideals.

It goes without saying that Swan denounced all such atheistic foreigners, dead or alive, as Wells, Marx, Shaw, the Mann brothers, Tolstoy, and P. G. Wodehouse with his unscrupulous propaganda against the aristocratic tradition. (Who could tell? Perhaps, some day, in a corporate empire, he might be Sir Effingham Swan, Bart.)

And in one item Swan showed blinding genius—he had the foresight to see the peril of that cynical volume, *The Collected Sayings of Will Rogers.*

Of the book-burnings in Syracuse and Schenectady and Hartford, Doremus had heard, but they seemed improbable as ghost stories.

The Jessup family were at dinner, just after seven, when on the porch they heard the tramping they had half expected, altogether dreaded. Mrs. Candy—even the icicle, Mrs. Candy, held her breast in agitation before she stalked out to open the door. Even David sat at table, spoon suspended in air.

Shad's voice, "In the name of the Chief!" Harsh feet in the hall, and Shad waddling into the dining room, cap on, hand on pistol, but grinning, and with leering geniality bawling, "H' are yuh, folks! Search for bad books. Orders of the District Commissioner. Come on, Jessup!" He looked at the fireplace to which he had once brought so many armfuls of wood, and snickered.

"If you'll just sit down in the other room—"

"I will like hell 'just sit down in the other room'! We're burning the books tonight! Snap to it, Jessup!" Shad looked at the exasperated Emma; he looked at Sissy; he winked with heavy deliberation and chuckled, "H' are you, Mis' Jessup. Hello, Sis. How's the kid?"

But at Mary Greenhill he did not look, nor she at him.

In the hall, Doremus found Shad's entourage, four sheepish M.M.'s and a more sheepish Emil Staubmeyer, who whimpered, "Just orders—you know—just orders."

Doremus safely said nothing; led them up to his study.

Now a week before he had removed every publication that any sane Corpo could consider radical: his *Das Kapital* and Veblen and all the Russian novels and even Sumner's *Folkways* and Freud's *Civilization and Its Discontents;* Thoreau and the other hoary scoundrels banned by Swan; old files of the *Nation* and *New Republic* and such copies as he had been able to get of Walt Trowbridge's *Lance for Democracy;* had removed them and hidden them inside an old horsehair sofa in the upper hall.

"I told you there was nothing," said Staubmeyer, after the search. "Let's go."

Said Shad, "Huh! I know this house, Ensign. I used to work here—had the privilege of putting up those storm windows you can see there, and of getting bawled out right here in this room. You won't remember those times, Doc—when I used to mow your lawn, too, and you used to be so snotty!" Staubmeyer blushed. "You bet. I know my way around, and there's a lot of fool books downstairs in the sittin' room."

Indeed in that apartment variously called the drawing

room, the living room, the sittin' room, the Parlor and once, even, by a spinster who thought editors were romantic, the studio, there were two or three hundred volumes, mostly in "standard sets." Shad glumly stared at them, the while he rubbed the faded Brussels carpet with his spurs. He was worried. He *had* to find something seditious!

He pointed at Doremus's dearest treasure, the thirty-four-volume extra-illustrated edition of Dickens which had been his father's, and his father's only insane extravagance. Shad demanded of Staubmeyer, "That guy Dickens—didn't he do a lot of complaining about conditions—about schools and the police and everything?"

Staubmeyer protested, "Yes, but Shad—but, Captain Ledue, that was a hundred years ago——"

"Makes no difference. Dead skunk stinks worse'n a live one."

Doremus cried, "Yes, but not for a hundred years! Besides——"

The M.M.'s, obeying Shad's gesture, were already yanking the volumes of Dickens from the shelves, dropping them on the floor, covers cracking. Doremus seized an M.M.'s arm; from the door Sissy shrieked. Shad lumbered up to him, enormous red fist at Doremus's nose, growling, "Want to get the daylights beaten out of you now . . . instead of later?"

Doremus and Sissy, side by side on a couch, watched the books thrown in a heap. He grasped her hand, muttering to her, "Hush—hush!" Oh, Sissy was a pretty girl, and young, but a pretty girl schoolteacher had been attacked, her clothes stripped off, and been left in the snow just south of town, two nights ago.

Doremus could not have stayed away from the book-burning. It was like seeing for the last time the face of a dead friend.

Kindling, excelsior, and spruce logs had been heaped on the thin snow on the Green. (Tomorrow there would be a fine patch burned in the hundred-year-old sward.) Round the pyre danced M.M.'s, schoolboys, students from the rather ratty business college on Elm Street, and unknown farm lads, seizing books from the pile guarded by the broadly cheerful Shad and skimming them into the flames. Doremus saw his *Martin Chuzzlewit* fly into air and land on the burning lid of an ancient commode. It lay there open to a Phiz drawing of Sairey Gamp, which withered instantly. As a small boy he had always laughed over that drawing.

He saw the old rector, Mr. Falck, squeezing his hands together. When Doremus touched his shoulder, Mr. Falck mourned, "They took away my *Urn Burial,* my *Imitatio Christ.* I don't know why, I don't know why! And they're burning them there!"

Who owned them, Doremus did not know, nor why they had been seized, but he saw *Alice in Wonderland* and *Omar Khayyám* and Shelley and *The Man Who Was Thursday* and *A Farewell to Arms* all burning together, to the greater glory of the Dictator and the greater enlightenment of his people.

The fire was almost over when Karl Pascal pushed up to Shad Ledue and shouted, "I hear you stinkers—I've been out driving a guy, and I hear you raided my room and took off my books while I was away!"

"You bet we did, Comrade!"

"And you're burning them—burning my——"

"Oh no, Comrade! Not burning 'em. Worth too blame much, Comrade." Shad laughed very much. "They're at the police station. We've just been waiting for you. It was awful nice to find all your little Communist books. Here! *Take him along!*"

So Karl Pascal was the first prisoner to go from Fort Beulah to the Trianon Concentration Camp—no; that's wrong; the second. The first, so inconspicuous that one almost forgets him, was an ordinary fellow, an electrician who had never so much as spoken of politics. Brayden, his name was. A Minute Man who stood well with Shad and Staubmeyer wanted Brayden's job. Brayden went to concentration camp. Brayden was flogged when he declared, under Shad's questioning, that he knew nothing about any plots against the Chief. Brayden died, alone in a dark cell, before January.

An English globe-trotter who gave up two weeks of December to a thorough study of "conditions" in

America, wrote to his London paper, and later said on the wireless for the B.B.C.: "After a thorough glance at America I find that, far from there being any discontent with the Corpo administration among the people, they have never been so happy and so resolutely set on making a Brave New World. I asked a very prominent Hebrew banker about the assertions that his people were being oppressed, and he assured me, 'When we hear about such silly rumors, we are highly amused.' "

23

DOREMUS WAS NERVOUS. The Minute Men had come, not with Shad but with Emil and a strange battalion-leader from Hanover, to examine the private letters in his study. They were polite enough, but alarmingly thorough. Then he knew, from the disorder in his desk at the *Informer,* that someone had gone over his papers there. Emil avoided him at the office. Doremus was called to Shad's office and gruffly questioned about correspondence which some denouncer had reported his having with the agents of Walt Trowbridge.

So Doremus was nervous. So Doremus was certain that his time for going to concentration camp was coming. He glanced back at every stranger who seemed to be following him on the street. The fruitman, Tony Mogliani, flowery advocate of Windrip, of Mussolini, and of tobacco quid as a cure for cuts and burns, asked him too many questions about his plans for the time when he should "get through on the paper"; and once a tramp tried to quiz Mrs. Candy, meantime peering at the pantry shelves, perhaps to see if there was any sign of their being understocked, as if for closing the house and fleeing. . . . But perhaps the tramp really was a tramp.

In the office, in mid-afternoon, Doremus had a telephone call from that scholar-farmer, Buck Titus:

"Going to be home this evening, about nine? Good! Got to see you. Important! Say, see if you can have all your family and Linda Pike and young Falck there, too, will you? Got an idea. Important!"

As important ideas, just now, usually concerned being imprisoned, Doremus and his women waited jumpily. Lorinda came in twittering, for the sight of Emma always did make her twitter a little, and in Lorinda there was no relief. Julian came in shyly, and there was no relief in Julian. Mrs. Candy brought in unsolicited tea with a dash of rum, and in her was some relief, but it was all a dullness of fidgety waiting till Buck slammed in, ten minutes late and very snowy.

"Sorkeepwaiting but I've been telephoning. Here's some news you won't have even in the office yet, Dormouse. The forest fire's getting nearer. This afternoon they arrested the editor of the Rutland *Herald*—no charge laid against him yet—no publicity—I got it from a commission merchant I deal with in Rutland. You're next, Doremus. I reckon they've just been laying off you till Staubmeyer picked your brains. Or maybe Ledue has some nice idea about torturing you by keeping you waiting. Anyway, you've got to get out. And tomorrow! To Canada! To stay! By automobile. No can do by plane any more—Canadian government's stopped that. You and Emma and Mary and Dave and Sis and the whole damn shooting-match—and maybe Foolish and Mrs. Candy and the canary!"

"Couldn't possibly! Take me weeks to realize on what investments I've got. Guess I could raise twenty thousand, but it'd take weeks."

"Sign 'em over to me, if you trust me—and you better! I can cash in everything better than you can—stand in with the Corpos better—been selling 'em horses and they think I'm the kind of loud-mouthed walking gent that will join 'em! I've got fifteen hundred Canadian dollars for you right here in my pocket, for a starter."

"We'd never get across the border. The M.M.'s are watching every inch, just looking for suspects like me."

"I've got a Canadian driver's license, and Canadian registration plates ready to put on my car—we'll take mine—less suspicious. I can look like a real farmer—that's because I am one, I guess—I'm going to drive you all, by the way. I got the plates smuggled in underneath the bottles in a case of ale! So we're all set, and we'll start tomorrow night, if the weather isn't too clear—hope there'll be snow."

"But Buck! Good Lord! I'm not going to flee. I'm not guilty of anything. I haven't anything to flee for!"

"Just your life, my boy, just your life!"

"I'm not afraid of 'em."

"Oh yes you are!"

"Oh—well—if you look at it that way, probably I am! But I'm not going to let a bunch of lunatics and gunmen drive me out of the country that I and my ancestors made!"

Emma choked with the effort to think of something convincing; Mary seemed without tears to be weeping; Sissy squeaked; Julian and Lorinda started to speak and interrupted each other; and it was the uninvited Mrs. Candy who, from the doorway, led off: "Now isn't that like a man! Stubborn as mules. All of 'em. Every one. And show-offs, the whole lot of 'em. Course you just wouldn't stop and think how your womenfolks will feel if you get took off and shot! You just stand in front of the locomotive and claim that because you were on the section gang that built the track, you got more right there than the engine has, and then when it's gone over you and gone away, you expect us all to think what a hero you were! Well, maybe *some* call it being a hero but——"

"Well, confound it all all of you picking on me and trying to get me all mixed up and not carry out my duty to the State as I see it——"

"You're over sixty, Doremus. Maybe a lot of us can do our duty better now from Canada than we can here—like Walt Trowbridge," besought Lorinda. Emma looked at her friend Lorinda with no particular affection.

"But to let the Corpos steal the country and nobody protest! No!"

"That's the kind of argument that sent a few million out to die, to make the world safe for democracy and a cinch for Fascism!" scoffed Buck.

"Dad! Come with us. Because we can't go without you. And I'm getting scared here." Sissy sounded scared, too; Sissy the unconquerable. "This afternoon Shad stopped me on the street and wanted me to go out with him. He tickled my chin, the little darling! But honestly, the way he smirked, as if he was so sure of me—I got scared!"

"I'll get a shotgun and______"
"Why, I'll kill the dirty______"
"Wait'll I get my hands on______"
cried Doremus, Julian, and Buck, all together, and glared at one another, then looked sheepish as Foolish barked at the racket, and Mrs. Candy, leaning like a frozen codfish against the door jamb, snorted, "Some more locomotive-batters!"

Doremus laughed. For one only time in his life he showed genius, for he consented: "All right. We'll go. But just imagine that I'm a man of strong will power and I'm taking all night to be convinced. We'll start tomorrow night."

What he did not say was that he planned, the moment he had his family safe in Canada, with money in the bank and perhaps a job to amuse Sissy, to run away from them and come back to his proper fight. He would at least kill Shad before he got killed himself.

It was only a week before Christmas, a holiday always greeted with good cheer and quantities of colored ribbons in the Jessup household; and that wild day of preparing for flight had a queer Christmas joyfulness. To dodge suspicion, Doremus spent most of the time at the office, and a hundred times it seemed that Staubmeyer was glancing at him with just the ruler—threatening hidden ire he had used on whisperers and like young criminals in school. But he took off two hours at lunch time, and he went home early in the afternoon, and his long depression was gone in the prospect of Canada and freedom, in an excited inspection of clothes that was like preparation for a fishing trip. They worked upstairs, behind drawn blinds, feeling like spies in an E. Phillips Oppenheim story, beleagured in the dark and stone-floored ducal bedroom of an ancient inn just beyond Grasse. Downstairs, Mrs. Candy was pretentiously busy looking normal—after their flight, she and the canary were to remain and she was to be surprised when the M.M.'s reported that the Jessups seemed to have escaped.

Doremus had drawn five hundred from each of the

local banks, late that afternoon, telling them that he was thinking of taking an option on an apple orchard. He was too well-trained a domestic animal to be raucously amused, but he could not help observing that while he himself was taking on the flight to Egypt only all the money he could get hold of, plus cigarettes, six handkerchiefs, two extra pairs of socks, a comb, a toothbrush, and the first volume of Spengler's *Decline of the West*—decidedly it was not his favorite book, but one he had been trying to make himself read for years, on train journeys—while, in fact, he took nothing that he could not stuff into his overcoat pockets, Sissy apparently had need of all her newest lingerie and of a large framed picture of Julian, Emma of a Kodak album showing the three children from the ages of one to twenty, David of his new model aëroplane, and Mary of her still, dark hatred that was heavier to carry than many chests.

Julian and Lorinda were there to help them; Julian off in corners with Sissy.

With Lorinda, Doremus had but one free moment . . . in the old-fashioned guest-bathroom.

"Linda. Oh, Lord!"

"We'll come through! In Canada you'll have time to catch your breath. Join Trowbridge!"

"Yes, but to leave you—— I'd hoped somehow, by some miracle, you and I could have maybe a month together, say in Monterey or Venice or the Yellowstone. I hate it when life doesn't seem to stick together and get somewhere and have some plan and meaning."

"It's had meaning! No dictator can completely smother us now! Come!"

"Good-bye, my Linda!"

Not even now did he alarm her by confessing that he planned to come back, into danger.

Embracing beside an aged tin-lined bathtub with woodwork painted a dreary brown, in a room which smelled slightly of gas from an old hot-water heater—embracing in sunset-colored mist upon a mountain top.

Darkness, edged wind, wickedly deliberate snow, and in it Buck Titus boisterously cheerful in his veteran

Nash, looking as farmer-like as he could, in sealskin cap with rubbed bare patches and an atrocious dogskin overcoat. Doremus thought of him again as a Captain Charles King cavalryman chasing the Sioux across blizzard-blinded prairies.

They packed alarmingly into the car; Mary beside Buck, the driver; in the back, Doremus between Emma and Sissy; on the floor, David and Foolish and the toy aëroplane indistinguishably curled up together beneath a robe. Trunk rack and front fenders were heaped with tarpaulin-covered suitcases.

"Lord, I wish I were going!" moaned Julian. "Look! Sis! Grand spy-story idea! But I mean seriously: Send souvenir postcards to my granddad—views of churches and so on—just sign 'em 'Jane'—and whatever you say about the church, I'll know you really mean it about you and—— Oh, damn all mystery! I want *you,* Sissy!"

Mrs. Candy whisked a bundle in among the already intolerable mess of baggage which promised to descend on Doremus's knees and David's head, and she snapped, "Well, if you folks *must* go flyin' around the country—— It's a cocoanut layer cake." Savagely: "Soon's you get around the corner, throw the fool thing in the ditch if you want to!" She fled sobbing into the kitchen, where Lorinda stood in the lighted doorway, silent, her trembling hands out to them.

The car was already lurching in the snow before they had sneaked through Fort Beulah by shadowy back-streets and started streaking northward.

Sissy sang out cheerily, "Well, Christmas in Canada! Skittles and beer and lots of holly!"

"Oh, do they have Santa Claus in Canada?" came David's voice, wondering, childish, slightly muffled by lap robe and the furry ears of Foolish.

"Of *course* they do, dearie!" Emma reassured him and, to the grown-ups, "Now wasn't that the cutest thing!"

To Doremus, Sissy whispered, "Darn well ought to be cute. Took me ten minutes to teach him to say it, this afternoon! Hold my hand. I hope Buck knows how to drive!"

* * *

Buck Titus knew every back-road from Fort Beulah to the border, preferably in filthy weather, like tonight. Beyond Trianon he pulled the car up deep-rutted roads, on which you would have to back if you were to pass anyone. Up grades on which the car knocked and panted, into lonely hills, by a zigzag of roads, they jerked toward Canada. Wet snow sheathed the windshield, then froze, and Buck had to drive with his head thrust out through the open window, and the blast came in and circled round their stiff necks.

Doremus could see nothing save the back of Buck's twisted, taut neck, and the icy windshield, most of the time. Just now and then a light far below the level of the road indicated that they were sliding along a shelf road, and if they skidded off, they would keep going a hundred feet, two hundred feet, downward—probably turning over and over. Once they did skid, and while they panted in an eternity of four seconds, Buck yanked the car up a bank beside the road, down to the left again, and finally straight—speeding on as if nothing had happened, while Doremus felt feeble in the knees.

For a long while he kept going rigid with fear, but he sank into misery, too cold and deaf to feel anything except a slow desire to vomit as the car lurched. Probably he slept—at least, he awakened, and awakened to a sensation of pushing the car anxiously up hill, as she bucked and stuttered in the effort to make a slippery rise. Suppose the engine died—suppose the brakes would not hold and they slid back downhill, reeling, bursting off the road and down—— A great many suppositions tortured him, hour by hour.

Then he tried being awake and bright and helpful. He noticed that the ice-lined windshield, illuminated from the light on the snow ahead, was a sheet of diamonds. He noticed it, but he couldn't get himself to think much of diamonds, even in sheets.

He tried conversation.

"Cheer up. Breakfast at dawn—across the border!" he tried on Sissy.

"Breakfast!" she said bitterly.

And they crunched on, in that moving coffin with only the sheet of diamonds and Buck's silhouette alive in the world.

After unnumbered hours the car reared and tumbled and reared again. The motor raced; its sound rose to an intolerable roaring; yet the car seemed not to be moving. The motor stopped abruptly. Buck cursed, popped his head back into the car like a turtle, and the starter ground long and whiningly. The motor again roared, again stopped. They could hear stiff branches rattling, hear Foolish moaning in sleep. The car was a storm-menaced cabin in the wilderness. The silence seemed waiting, as they were waiting.

"Strouble?" said Doremus.

"Stuck. No traction. Hit a drift of wet snow—drainage from a busted culvert, I sh' think. Hell! Have to get out and take a look."

Outside the car, as Doremus crept down from the slippery running-board, it was cold in a vicious wind. He was so stiff he could scarcely stand.

As people do, feeling important and advisory, Doremus looked at the drift with an electric torch, and Sissy looked at the drift with the torch, and Buck impatiently took the torch away from them and looked twice.

"Get some——" and "Brush would help," said Sissy and Buck together, while Doremus rubbed his chilly ears.

They three trotted back and forth with fragments of brush, laying it in front of the wheels, while Mary politely asked from within, "Can I help?" and no one seemed particularly to have answered her.

The headlights picked out an abandoned shack beside the road; an unpainted gray pine cabin with broken window glass and no door. Emma, sighing her way out of the car and stepping through the lumpy snow as delicately as a pacer at a horse show, said humbly, "That little house there—maybe I could go in and make some hot coffee on the alcohol stove—didn't have room for a thermos. Hot coffee, Dormouse?"

To Doremus she sounded, just now, not at all like a wife, but as sensible as Mrs. Candy.

When the car did kick its way up on the pathway of twigs and stand panting safely beyond the drift, they had, in the sheltered shack, coffee with slabs of Mrs. Candy's voluptuous cocoanut cake. Doremus pondered, "This is a nice place. I like this place. It doesn't bounce or skid. I don't want to leave this place."

He did. The secure immobility of the shack was behind them, dark miles behind, and they were again pitching and rolling and being sick and inescapably chilly. David was alternately crying and going back to sleep. Foolish woke up to cough inquiringly and returned to his dream of rabbiting. And Doremus was sleeping, his head swaying like a masthead in long rollers, his shoulder against Emma's, his hand warm about Sissy's, and his soul in nameless bliss.

He roused to a half-dawn filmy with snow. The car was standing in what seemed to be a crossroads hamlet, and Buck was examining a map by the light of the electric torch.

"Got anywhere yet?" Doremus whispered.

"Just a few miles to the border."

"Anybody stopped us?"

"Nope. Oh, we'll make it, all right, o' man."

Out of East Berkshire, Buck took not the main road to the border but an old wood lane so little used that the ruts were twin snakes. Though Doremus said nothing, the others felt his intensity, his anxiety that was like listening for an enemy in the dark. David sat up, the blue motor robe about him. Foolish started, snorted, looked offended but, catching the spirit of the moment, comfortingly laid a paw on Doremus's knee and insisted on shaking hands, over and over, as gravely as a Venetian senator or an undertaker.

They dropped into the dimness of a tree-walled hollow. A searchlight darted, and rested hotly on them, so dazzling them that Buck almost ran off the road.

"Confound it," he said gently. No one else said anything.

He crawled up to the light, which was mounted on a platform in front of a small shelter hut. Two Minute Men stood out in the road, dripping with radiance from the car. They were young and rural, but they had efficient repeating rifles.

"Where you headed for?" demanded the elder, good-naturedly enough.

"Montreal, where we live." Buck showed his Canadian license. . . . Gasoline motor and electric light, yet Doremus saw the frontier guard as a sentry in 1864, studying a pass by lantern light, beside a farm wagon in which hid General Joe Johnston's spies disguised as plantation hands.

"I guess it's all right. Seems in order. But we've had some trouble with refugees. You'll have to wait till the Battalion-Leader comes—maybe 'long about noon."

"But good Lord, Inspector, we can't do that! My mother's awful sick, in Montreal."

"Yuh, I've heard that one before! And maybe it's true, this time. But afraid you'll have to wait for the Bat. You folks can come in and set by the fire, if you want to."

"But we've got to——"

"You heard what I said!" The M.M.'s were fingering their rifles.

"All right. But tell you what we'll do. We'll go back to East Berkshire and get some breakfast and a wash and come back here. Noon, you said?"

"Okay! And say, Brother, it does seem kind of funny, your taking this back road, when there's a first-rate highway. S'long. Be good. . . . Just don't try it again! The Bat might be here next time—and he ain't a farmer like you or me!"

The refugees, as they drove away, had an uncomfortable feeling that the guards were laughing at them.

Three border posts they tried, and at three posts they were turned back.

"Well?" said Buck.

"Yes. I guess so. Back home. My turn to drive," said Doremus wearily.

The humiliation of retreat was the worse in that none of the guards had troubled to do more than laugh at them. They were trapped too tightly for the trappers to worry. Doremus's only clear emotion as, tails between their legs, they back-tracked to Shad Ledue's sneer and to Mrs. Candy's "Well, I *never*!" was regret that he had not shot one guard, at least, and he raged:

"Now I know why men like John Brown became crazy killers!"

24

HE COULD NOT DECIDE whether Emil Staubmeyer, and through him Shad Ledue, knew that he had tried to escape. Did Staubmeyer really look more knowing, or did he just imagine it? What the deuce had Emil meant when he said, "I hear the roads aren't so good up north—not so good!" Whether they knew or not, it was grinding that he should have to shiver lest an illiterate roustabout like Shad Ledue find out that he desired to go to Canada, while a rule-slapper like Staubmeyer, a Squeers with certificates in "pedagogy," should now be able to cuff grown men instead of urchins and should be editor of the *Informer!* Doremus's *Informer*! Staubmeyer! *That* human blackboard!

Daily Doremus found it more cramping, more instantly stirring to fury, to write anything mentioning Windrip. His private office—the cheerfully rattling linotype room—the shouting pressroom with its smell of ink that to him hitherto had been like the smell of grease paint to an actor—they were hateful now, and choking. Not even Lorinda's faith, not even Sissy's jibes and Buck's stories, could rouse him to hope.

He rejoiced the more, therefore, when his son Philip telephoned him from Worcester: "Be home Sunday? Merilla's in New York, gadding, and I'm all alone here. Thought I'd just drive up for the day and see how things are in your neck of the woods."

"Come on! Splendid! So long since we've seen you. I'll have your mother start a pot of beans right away!"

Doremus was happy. Not for some time did his cursed two-way-mindedness come to weaken his joy, as he wondered whether it wasn't just a myth held over from boyhood that Philip really cared so much for Emma's beans and brown bread; and wondered just why it was that Up-to-Date Americans like Philip always used the long-distance telephone rather than undergo the dreadful toil of dictating a letter a day or two earlier. It didn't really seem so efficient, the old-fashioned village editor reflected, to spend seventy-five cents on a telephone call in order to save five cents' worth of time.

"Oh hush! Anyway, I'll be delighted to see the boy! I'll bet there isn't a smarter young lawyer in Worcester. There's one member of the family that's a real success!"

He was a little shocked when Philip came, like a one-man procession, into the living room, late on Saturday afternoon. He had been forgetting how bald his upstanding young advocate was growing even at thirty-four. And it seemed to him that Philip was a little heavy and senatorial in speech and a bit too cordial.

"By Jove, Dad, you don't know how good it is to be back in the old digs. Mother and the girls upstairs? By Jove, sir, that was a horrible business, the killing of poor Fowler. Horrible! I was simply horrified. There must have been a mistake somewhere, because Judge Swan has a wonderful reputation for scrupulousness."

"There was no mistake. Swan is a fiend. Literally!" Doremus sounded less paternal than when he had first bounded up to shake hands with the beloved prodigal.

"Really? We must talk it over. I'll see if there can't be a stricter investigation. Swan? Really! We'll certainly go into the whole business. But first I must just skip upstairs and give Mammy a good smack, and Mary and Little Sis."

And that was the last time that Philip mentioned Effingham Swan or any "stricter investigation" of the acts thereof. All afternoon he was relentlessly filial and fraternal, and he smiled like an automobile salesman when Sissy griped at him, "What's the idea of all the tender hand-dusting, Philco?"

Doremus and he were not alone till nearly midnight. They sat upstairs in the sacred study. Philip lighted one of Doremus's excellent cigars as though he were a cinema actor playing the role of a man lighting an excellent cigar, and breathed amiably:

"Well, sir, this is an excellent cigar! It certainly is excellent!"

"Why not?"

"Oh, I just mean—I was just appreciating it——"

"What is it, Phil? There's something on your mind. Shoot! Not rowing with Merilla, are you?"

"Certainly not! Most certainly not! Oh, I don't approve of everything Merry does—she's a little extravagant—but she's got a heart of gold, and let me tell you, Pater, there isn't a young society woman in Worcester that makes a nicer impression on everybody, especially at nice dinner parties."

"Well then? Let's have it, Phil. Something serious?"

"Ye-es, I'm afraid there is. Look, Dad. . . . Oh, do sit down and be comfortable! . . . I've been awfully perturbed to hear that you've, uh, that you're in slightly bad odor with some of the authorities."

"You mean the Corpos?"

"Naturally! Who else?"

"Maybe I don't recognize 'em as authorities."

"Oh, listen, Pater, please don't joke tonight! I'm serious. As a matter fact, I hear you're more than just 'slightly' in wrong with them."

"And who may your informant be?"

"Oh, just letters—old school friends. Now you *aren't* really pro-Corpo, *are* you?"

"How did you ever guess?"

"Well, I've been—— I didn't vote for Windrip, personally, but I begin to see where I was wrong. I can see now that he has not only great personal magnetism, but real constructive power—real sure-enough statesmanship. Some say it's Lee Sarason's doing, but don't you believe it for a minute. Look at all Buzz did back in his home state, before he ever teamed up with Sarason! And some say Windrip is crude. Well, so were Lincoln and Jackson. Now what I think of Windrip——"

"The only thing you ought to think of Windrip is that his gangsters murdered your fine brother-in-law! And plenty of other men just as good. Do you condone such murders?"

"No! Certainly not! How can you suggest such a thing, Dad! No one abhors violence more than I do. Still, you can't make an omelet without breaking eggs——"

"Hell and damnation!"

"Why, Pater!"

"Don't call me 'Pater'! If I ever hear that 'can't make an omelet' phrase again, I'll start doing a little murder myself! It's used to justify every atrocity under every despotism, Fascist or Nazi or Communist or American labor war. Omelet! Eggs! By God, sir, men's souls and blood are not eggshells for tyrants to break!"

"Oh, sorry, sir. I guess maybe the phrase is a little shopworn! I just mean to say—I'm just trying to figure this situation out realistically!"

" 'Realistically'! That's another buttered bun to excuse murder!"

"But honestly, you know—horrible things do happen, thanks to the imperfection of human nature, but you can forgive the means if the end is a rejuvenated nation that——"

"I can do nothing of the kind! I can never forgive evil and lying and cruel means, and still less can I forgive fanatics that use that for an excuse! If I may imitate Romain Rolland, a country that tolerates evil means—evil manners, standards of ethics—for a generation, will be so poisoned that it never will have any good end. I'm just curious, but do you know how perfectly you're quoting every Bolshevik apologist that sneers at decency and kindness and truthfulness in daily dealings as 'bourgeois morality'? I hadn't understood that you'd gone quite so Marxo-materialistic!"

"I! Marxian! Good God!" Doremus was pleased to see that he had stirred his son out of his if-your-honor-please smugness. "Why, one of the things I most admire about the Corpos is that, as I know, absolutely—I have reliable information from Washington—they have saved us from a simply ghastly invasion by red agents of Moscow—Communists pretending to be decent labor-leaders!"

"Not really!" (Had the fool forgotten that his father was a newspaperman and not likely to be impressed by "reliable information from Washington"?)

"Really! And to be realistic—sorry, sir, if you don't like the word, but to be—to be——"

"In fact, to be realistic!"

"Well, yes, then!"

(Doremus recalled such tempers in Philip from years ago. Had he been wise, after all, to restrain himself from the domestic pleasure of licking the brat?)

"The whole point is that Windrip, or anyway the Corpos, are here to *stay,* Pater, and we've got to base our future actions not on some desired Utopia but on what we really and truly have. And think of what they've actually done! Just, for example, how they've removed the advertising billboards from the highways, and ended unemployment, and their simply stupendous feat in getting rid of all crime!"

"Good God!"

"Pardon me—what y' say, Dad?"

"Nothing! Nothing! Go on!"

"But I begin to see now that the Corpo gains haven't been just material but spiritual."

"Eh?"

"Really! They've revitalized the whole country. Formerly we had gotten pretty sordid, just thinking about material possessions and comforts—about electric refrigeration and television and air-conditioning. Kind of lost the sturdiness that characterized our pioneer ancestors. Why, ever so many young men were refusing to take military drill, and the discipline and will power and good-fellowship that you only get from military training—— Oh, pardon me! I forgot you were a pacifist."

Doremus grimly muttered, "Not any more!"

"Of course there must be any number of things we can't agree on, Dad. But after all, as a publicist you ought to listen to the Voice of Youth."

"You? Youth? You're not youth. You're two thousand years old, mentally. You date just about 100 B.C. in your fine new imperialistic theories!"

"No, but you must listen, Dad! Why do you suppose I came clear up here from Worcester just to see you?"

"God only knows!"

"I want to make myself clear. Before Windrip, we'd been lying down in America, while Europe was throwing off all her bonds—both monarchy and this antiquated parliamentary-democratic-liberal system that really means rule by professional politicians and by egotistic 'intellectuals.' We've got to catch up to Europe again—got to expand—it's the rule of life. A nation, like a man, has to go ahead or go backward. Always!"

"I know, Phil. I used to write that same thing in those same words, back before 1914!"

"Did you? Well, anyway—— Got to expand! Why, what we ought to do is to grab all of Mexico, and maybe Central America, and a good big slice of China. Why, just on their *own* behalf we ought to do it, misgoverned the way they are! Maybe I'm wrong but——"

"Impossible!"

"—Windrip and Sarason and Dewey Haik and Macgoblin, all those fellows, they're *big*—they're making me stop and think! And now to come down to my errand here——"

"You think I ought to run the *Informer* according to Corpo theology!"

"Why—why yes! That was approximately what I was going to say. (I just don't see why you haven't been more reasonable about this whole thing—you with your quick mind!) After all, the time for selfish individualism is gone. We've got to have mass action. One for all and all for one——"

"Philip, would you mind telling me what the deuce you're *really* heading toward? Cut the cackle!"

"Well, since you insist—to 'cut the cackle,' as you call it—not very politely, seems to me, seeing I've taken the trouble to come clear up from Worcester!—I have reliable information that you're going to get into mighty serious trouble if you don't stop opposing—or at least markedly failing to support—the government."

"All right. What of it? It's *my* serious trouble!"

"That's just the point! It isn't! I do think that just for once in your life you might think of Mother and the girls, instead of always of your own selfish 'ideas' that you're so proud of! In a crisis like this, it just isn't funny any longer to pose as a quaint 'liberal.' "

Doremus's voice was like a firecracker. "Cut the

cackle, I told you! What you after? What's the Corpo gang to you?"

"I have been approached in regard to the very high honor of an assistant military judgeship, but your attitude, as my father——"

"Philip, I think, I rather think, that I give you my parental curse not so much because you are a traitor as because you have become a stuffed shirt! Good-night."

25

HOLIDAYS WERE INVENTED by the devil, to coax people into the heresy that happiness can be won by taking thought. What was planned as a rackety day for David's first Christmas with his grandparents was, they saw too well, perhaps David's last Christmas with them. Mary had hidden her weeping, but the day before Christmas, when Shad Ledue tramped in to demand of Doremus whether Karl Pascal had ever spoken to him of Communism, Mary came on Shad in the hall, stared at him, raised her hand like a boxing cat, and said with dreadful quietness, "You murderer! I shall kill you and kill Swan!"

For once Shad did not look amused.

To make the holiday as good an imitation of mirth as possible, they were very noisy, but their holly, their tinsel stars on a tall pine tree, their family devotion in a serene old house in a little town, was no different at heart from despairing drunkenness in the city night. Doremus reflected that it might have been just as well for all of them to get drunk and let themselves go, elbows on slopped café tables, as to toil at this pretense of domestic bliss. He now had another thing for which to hate the Corpos—for stealing the secure affection of Christmas.

For noon dinner, Louis Rotenstern was invited, because he was a lorn bachelor and, still more, because he was a Jew, now insecure and snubbed and threatened in an insane dictatorship. (There is no greater compliment to the Jews than the fact that the degree of their unpopularity is always the scientific measure of the cruelty and silliness of the régime under which they live, so that even a commercial-minded money-fondling heavily humorous

Jew burgher like Rotenstern is still a sensitive meter of barbarism.) After dinner came Buck Titus, David's most favorite person, bearing staggering amounts of Woolworth tractors and fire engines and a real bow-and-arrow, and he was raucously insisting that Mrs. Candy dance with him what he not very precisely called "the light fantastic," when the hammering sounded at the door.

Aras Dilley tramped in with four men.

"Lookin' for Rotenstern. Oh, that you, Louie? Git your coat and come on—orders."

"What's the idea? What d'you want of him? What's the charge?" demanded Buck, still standing with his arm about Mrs. Candy's embarrassed waist.

"Dunno's there be any charges. Just ordered to headquarters for questioning. District Commissioner Reek in town. Just astin' few people a few questions. Come on, *you!*"

The hilarious celebrants did not, as they had planned, go out to Lorinda's tavern for skiing. Next day they heard that Rotenstern had been taken to the concentration camp at Trianon, along with that crabbed old Tory, Raymond Pridewell, the hardware dealer.

Both imprisonments were incredible. Rotenstern had been too meek. And if Pridewell had not ever been meek, if he had constantly and testily and loudly proclaimed that he had not cared for Ledue as a hired man and now cared even less for him as a local governor, yet—why, Pridewell was a sacred institution. As well think of dragging the brownstone Baptist Church to prison.

Later, a friend of Shad Ledue took over Rotenstern's shop. It *can* happen here, meditated Doremus. It could happen to him. How soon? Before he should be arrested, he must make amends to his conscience by quitting the *Informer.*

Professor Victor Loveland, once a classicist of Isaiah College, having been fired from a labor camp for incompetence in teaching arithmetic to lumberjacks, was in town, with wife and babies, on his way to a job clerking in his uncle's slate quarry near Fair Haven. He called on Doremus and was hysterically cheerful. He called on Clarence Little—"dropped in to visit with him," Clarence would have said. Now that twitchy, intense jeweler, Clarence, who had been born on a Vermont farm and had supported his mother till she died when he was thirty, had longed to go to college and, especially, to study Greek. Though Loveland was his own age, in the mid-thirties, he looked on him as a combination of Keats and Liddell. His greatest moment had been hearing Loveland read Homer.

Loveland was leaning on the counter. "Gone ahead with your Latin grammar, Clarence?"

"Golly, Professor, it just doesn't seem worth while any more. I guess I'm kind of a weak sister, anyway, but I find that these days it's about all I can do to keep going."

"Me too! And don't call me 'Professor.' I'm a timekeeper in a slate quarry. What a life!"

They had not noticed the clumsy-looking man in plain clothes who had just come in. Presumably he was a customer. But he grumbled, "So you two pansies don't like the way things go nowadays! Don't suppose you like the Corpos! Don't think much of the Chief!" He jabbed his thumb into Loveland's ribs so painfully that Loveland yelped, "I don't think about him at all!"

"Oh, you don't, eh? Well, you two fairies can come along to the courthouse with me!"

"And who may you be?"

"Oh, just an ensign in the M.M.'s, that's all!"

He had an automatic pistol.

Loveland was not beaten much, because he managed to keep his mouth shut. But Little was so hysterical that they laid him on a kitchen table and decorated his naked back with forty slashes of a steel ramrod. They had found that Clarence wore yellow silk underwear, and the M.M.'s from factory and plowland laughed—particularly one broad young inspector who was rumored to have a passionate friendship with a battalion-leader from Nashua who was fat, eyeglassed, and high-pitched of voice.

Little had to be helped into the truck that took Loveland and him to the Trianon concentration camp. One eye was closed and so surrounded with bruised flesh that the M.M. driver said it looked like a Spanish omelet.

The truck had an open body, but they could not escape, because the three prisoners on this trip were chained hand to hand. They lay on the floor of the truck. It was snowing.

The third prisoner was not much like Loveland or Little. His name was Ben Tripper. He had been a mill hand for Medary Cole. He cared no more about the Greek language than did a baboon, but he did care for his six children. He had been arrested for trying to strike Cole and for cursing the Corpo régime when Cole had reduced his wages from nine dollars a week (in pre-Corpo currency) to seven-fifty.

As to Loveland's wife and babies, Lorinda took them in till she could pass the hat and collect enough to send them back to Mrs. Loveland's family on a rocky farm in Missouri. But then things went better. Mrs. Loveland was favored by the Greek proprietor of a lunch-room and got work washing dishes and otherwise pleasing the proprietor, who brilliantined his mustache.

The county administration, in a proclamation signed by Emil Staubmeyer, announced that they were going to regulate the agriculture on the submarginal land high up on Mount Terror. As a starter, half-a-dozen of the poorer families were moved into the large, square, quiet, old house of that large, square, quiet, old farmer, Henry Veeder, cousin of Doremus Jessup. These poorer families had many children, a great many, so that there were four or five persons bedded on the floor in every room of the home where Henry and his wife had placidly lived alone since their own children had grown. Henry did not like it, and said so, not very tactfully, to the M.M.'s herding the refugees. What was worse, the dispossessed did not like it any better. " 'Tain't much, but we got a house of our own. Dunno why we should git shoved in on Henry," said one. "Don't expect other folks to bother me, and don't expect to bother other folks. Never did like that fool kind of yellow color Henry painted his barn, but guess that's his business."

So Henry and two of the regulated agriculturists were taken to the Trianon concentration camp, and the rest remained in Henry's house, doing nothing but finish up Henry's large larder and wait for orders.

"And before I'm sent to join Henry and Karl and Loveland, I'm going to clear my skirts," Doremus vowed, along in late January.

He marched in to see County Commissioner Ledue.

"I want to quit the *Informer.* Staubmeyer has learned all I can teach him."

"Staubmeyer? Oh! You mean Assistant Commissioner Staubmeyer!"

"Chuck it, will you? We're not on parade, and we're not playing soldiers. Mind if I sit down?"

"Don't look like you cared a hell of a lot whether I mind or not! But I can tell you, right here and now, Jessup, without any monkey business about it, you're not going to leave your job. I guess I could find enough grounds for sending you to Trianon for about a million years, with ninety lashes, but—you've always been so stuck on yourself as such an all-fired honest editor, it kind of tickles me to watch you kissing the Chief's foot—and mine!"

"I'll do no more of it! That's certain! And I admit that I deserve your scorn for ever having done it!"

"Well, isn't that elegant! But you'll do just what I tell you to, and like it! Jessup, I suppose you think I had a swell time when I was your hired man! Watching you and your old woman and the girls go off on a picnic while I—oh, I was just your hired man, with dirt in my ears, your dirt! I could stay home and clean up the basement!"

"Maybe we didn't want you along, Shad! Good-morning!"

Shad laughed. There was a sound of the gates of Trianon concentration camp in that laughter.

It was really Sissy who gave Doremus his lead.

He drove to Hanover to see Shad's superior, District Commissioner John Sullivan Reek, that erstwhile jovial and red-faced politician. He was admitted after only half an hour's waiting. He was shocked to see how pale and hesitant and frightened Reek had become. But the Commissioner tried to be authoritative.

"Well, Jessup, what can I do for you?"

"May I be frank?"

"What? What? Why, certainly! Frankness has always been my middle name!"

"I hope so. Governor, I find I'm of no use on the *Informer,* at Fort Beulah. As you probably know, I've been breaking in Emil Staubmeyer as my successor. Well, he's quite competent to take hold now, and I want to quit. I'm really just in his way."

"Why don't you stick around and see what you can still do to help him? There'll be little jobs cropping up from time to time."

"Because it's got on my nerves to take orders where I used to give 'em for so many years. You can appreciate that, can't you?"

"My God, can I appreciate it? And how! Well, I'll think it over. You wouldn't mind writing little pieces for my own little sheet, at home? I own part of a paper there."

"No! Sure! Delighted!"

("Does this mean that Reek believes the Corpo tyranny is going to blow up, in a revolution, so that he's beginning to trim? Or just that he's fighting to keep from being thrown out?")

"Yes, I can see how you might feel, Brother Jessup."

"Thanks! Would you mind giving me a note to County Commissioner Ledue, telling him to let me out, without prejudice?—making it pretty strong?"

"No. Not a bit. Just wait a minute, ole fellow; I'll write it right now."

Doremus made as little ceremony as possible of leaving the *Informer,* which had been his throne for thirty-seven years. Staubmeyer was patronizing, Doc Itchitt looked quizzical, but the chapel, headed by Dan Wilgus, shook hands profusely. And so, at sixty-two, stronger and more eager than he had been in all his life, Doremus had nothing to do more important than eating breakfast and telling his grandson stories about the elephant.

But that lasted less than a week. Avoiding suspicion from Emma and Sissy and even from Buck and Lorinda, he took Julian aside:

"Look here, boy. I think it's time now for me to begin doing a little high treason. (Heaven's sake keep all of this under your hat—don't even tip off Sissy!) I guess you know, the Communists are too theocratic for my tastes. But looks to me as though they have more courage and devotion and smart strategy than anybody since the Early Christian Martyrs—whom they also resemble in hairiness and a fondness for catacombs. I want to get in touch with 'em and see if there's any dirty work at the crossroads I can do for 'em—say distributing a few Early Christian tracts by St. Lenin. But of course, theoretically, the Communists have all been imprisoned. Could you get to Karl Pascal, in Trianon, and find out whom I could see?"

Said Julian, "I think I could. Dr. Olmsted gets called in there sometimes on cases—they hate him, because he hates them, but still, their camp doctor is a drunken bum, and they have to have a real doc in when one of their warders busts his wrist beating up some prisoner. I'll try sir."

Two days afterward Julian returned.

"My God, what a sewer that Trianon place is! I'd waited for Olmsted before, in the car, but I never had the nerve to butt inside. The buildings—they were nice buildings, quite pretty, when the girls' school had them. Now the fittings are all torn out, and they've put up wallboard partitions for cells, and the whole place stinks of carbolic acid and excrement, and the air—there isn't any—you feel as if you were nailed up in a box—I don't know how anybody lives in one of those cells for an hour—and yet there's six men bunked in a cell twelve feet by ten, with a ceiling only seven feet high, and no light except a twenty-five watt, I guess it is, bulb in the ceiling—you couldn't read by it. But they get out for exercise two hours a day—walk around and around the courtyard—they're all so stooped, and they all look so ashamed, as if they'd had the defiance just licked out of 'em—even Karl a little, and you remember how proud and sort of sardonic he was. Well, I got to see him, and he says to get in touch with this man—here, I wrote it down—and for God's sake, burn it up soon as you've memorized it!"

"Was he—had they——?"

"Oh, yes, they've beaten him, all right. He wouldn't talk about it. But there was a scar right across his cheek, from his temple right down to his chin. And I had just a glimpse of Henry Veeder. Remember how he looked—like an oak tree? Now he twitches all the time, and jumps and gasps when he hears a sudden sound. He didn't know me. I don't think he'd know anybody."

Doremus announced to his family and told it loudly in Gath that he was still looking for an option on an apple orchard to which they might retire, and he journeyed southward, with pajamas and a toothbrush and the first volume of Spengler's *Decline of the West* in a briefcase.

The address given by Karl Pascal was that of a most gentlemanly dealer in altar cloths and priestly robes, who had his shop and office over a tea room in Hartford, Connecticut. He talked about the cembalo and the spinetta di serenata and the music of Palestrina for an hour before he sent Doremus on to a busy engineer constructing a dam in New Hampshire, who sent him to a tailor in a side-street shop in Lynn, who at last sent him to northern Connecticut and to the Eastern headquarters of what was left of the Communists in America.

Still carrying his little briefcase he walked up a greasy hill, impassable to any motorcar, and knocked at the faded green door of a squat New England farm cottage masked in wintry old lilac bushes and spiræa shrubs. A stringy farm wife opened and looked hostile.

"I'd like to speak to Mr. Ailey, Mr. Bailey, or Mr. Cailey."

"None of 'em home. You'll have to come again."

"Then I'll wait. What else should one do, these days?"

"All right. Cmin."

"Thanks. Give them this letter."

(The tailor had warned him, "It vill all sount very

foolish, the passvorts und everyt'ing, but if any of the central committee gets caught——" He made a squirting sound and drew his scissors across his throat.)

Doremus sat now in a tiny hall off a flight of stairs steep as the side of a roof; a hall with sprigged wall paper and Currier & Ives prints, and black-painted wooden rocking chairs with calico cushions. There was nothing to read but a Methodist hymnal and a desk dictionary. He knew the former by heart, and anyway, he always loved reading dictionaries—often had one seduced him from editorial-writing. Happily he sat conning:

> Phenyl, *n., Chem.* The univalent radical $C_6 H_5$, regarded as the basis of numerous benzene derivatives; as, phenyl hydroxid $C_6 H_5 OH$.
>
> Pherecratean, *n.* A choriambic trimeter catalectic, or catalectic glyconic; composed of a spondee, a choriambus, and a catalectic syllable.

"Well! I never knew any of *that* before! I wonder if I do now?" thought Doremus contentedly, before he realized that glowering from a very narrow doorway was a very broad man with wild gray hair and a patch over one eye. Doremus recognized him from pictures. He was Bill Atterbury, miner, longshoreman, veteran I.W.W. leader, old A. F. of L. strike-leader, five years in San Quentin and five honored years in Moscow, and reputed now to be the secretary of the illegal Communist Party.

"I'm Mr. Ailey. What can I do for you?" Bill demanded.

He led Doremus into a musty back room where, at a table which was probably mahogany underneath the scars and the clots of dirt, sat a squat man with kinky tow-colored hair and with deep wrinkles in the thick pale skin of his face, and a slender young elegant who suggested Park Avenue.

"Howryuh?" said Mr. Bailey, in a Russian-Jewish accent. Of him Doremus knew nothing save that he was not named Bailey.

"Morning," snapped Mr. Cailey—whose name was Elphrey, if Doremus guessed rightly, and who was the son of a millionaire private banker, the brother of one explorer, one bishop's wife, and one countess, and himself a former teacher of economics in the University of California.

Doremus tried to explain himself to these hard-eyed, quick-glancing plotters of ruin.

"Are you willing to become a Party member, in the extremely improbable case that they accept you, and to take orders, any orders, without question?" asked Elphrey, so suavely.

"Do you mean, Am I willing to kill and steal?"

"You've been reading detective stories about the 'Reds'! No. What you'd have to do would be much more difficult than the amusement of using a tommy-gun. Would you be willing to forget you ever were a respectable newspaper editor, giving orders, and walk through the snow, dressed like a bum, to distribute seditious pamphlets—even if, personally, you should believe the pamphlets were of no slightest damn good to the Cause?"

"Why, I—I don't know. Seems to me that as a newspaperman of quite a little training——"

"Hell! Our only trouble is keeping *out* the 'trained newspapermen'! What we need is trained bill-posters that like the smell of flour paste and hate sleeping. And—but you're a little old for this—crazy fanatics that go out and start strikes, knowing they'll get beaten up and thrown in the bull pen."

"No, I guess I—— Look here. I'm sure Walt Trowbridge will be joining up with the Socialists and some of the left-wing radical ex-Senators and the Farmer-Laborites and so on——"

Bill Atterbury guffawed. It was a tremendous, somehow terrifying blast. "Yes, I'm sure they'll join up—*all* the dirty, sneaking, half-headed, reformist Social Fascists like Trowbridge, that are doing the work of the capitalists and working for war against Soviet Russia without even having sense enough to know they're doing it and to collect good pay for their crookedness!"

"I admire Trowbridge!" snarled Doremus.

"You would!"

Elphrey rose, almost cordial, and dismissed Doremus

with, "Mr. Jessup, I was brought up in a sound bourgeois household myself, unlike these two roughnecks, and I appreciate what you're trying to do, even if they don't. I imagine that your rejection of us is even firmer than our rejection of you!"

"Dot's right, Comrade Elphrey. Both you and dis fellow got ants in your bourjui pants, like your Hugh Johnson vould say!" chuckled the Russian Mr. Bailey.

"But I just wonder if Walt Trowbridge won't be chasing out Buzz Windrip while you boys are still arguing about whether Comrade Trotzky was once guilty of saying mass facing the north? Good-day!" said Doremus.

When he recounted it to Julian, two days later, and Julian puzzled, "I wonder whether you won or they did?" Doremus asserted, "I don't think anybody won—except the ants! Anyway, now I know that man is not to be saved by black bread alone but by everything that proceedeth out of the mouth of the Lord our God. . . . Communists, intense and narrow; Yankees, tolerant and shallow; no wonder a Dictator can keep us separate and all working for him!"

Even in the 1930's, when it was radiantly believed that movies and the motorcar and glossy magazines had ended the provinciality of all the larger American villages, in such communities as Fort Beulah all the retired business men who could not afford to go to Europe or Florida or California, such as Doremus, were as aimless as an old dog on Sunday afternoon with the family away. They poked uptown to the shops, the hotel lobbies, the railway station, and at the barber shop were pleased rather than irritated when they had to wait a quarter-hour for the tri-weekly shave. There were no cafés as there would have been in Continental Europe, and no club save the country club, and that was chiefly a sanctuary for the younger people in the evening and late afternoons.

The superior Doremus Jessup, the bookman, was almost as dreary in retirement as Banker Crowley would have been.

He did pretend to play golf, but he could not see any particular point in stopping a good walk to wallop small balls and, worse, the links were now bright with M.M. uniforms. And he hadn't enough brass, as no doubt Medary Cole would have, to feel welcome hour on hour in the Hotel Wessex lobby.

He stayed in his third-story study and read as long as his eyes would endure it. But he irritably felt Emma's irritation and Mrs. Candy's ire at having a man around the house all day. Yes! He'd get what he could for the house and for what small share in *Informer* stock the government had left him when they had taken it over, and go—well, just go—the Rockies or anywhere that was new.

But he realized that Emma did not at all wish to go new places; and realized that the Emma to whose billowy warmth it had been comforting to come home after the office, bored him and was bored by him when he was always there. The only difference was that she did not seem capable of admitting that one might, without actual fiendishness or any signs of hot-footing it for Reno, be bored by one's faithful spouse.

"Why don't you drive out and see Buck or Lorinda?" she suggested.

"Don't you ever get a little jealous of my girl, Linda?" he said, very lightly—because he very heavily wanted to know.

She laughed. "You? At your age? As if anybody thought *you* could be a lover!"

Well, Lorinda thought so, he raged, and promptly he did "drive out and see her," a little easier in mind about his divided loyalties.

Only once did he go back to the *Informer* office.

Staubmeyer was not in sight, and it was evident that the real editor was that sly bumpkin, Doc Itchitt, who didn't even rise at Doremus's entrance nor listen when Doremus gave his opinion of the new make-up of the rural-correspondence pages.

That was an apostasy harder to endure than Shad Ledue's, for Shad had always been rustically certain that Doremus was a fool, almost as bad as real "city folks," while Doc Itchitt had once appreciated the tight joints and smooth surfaces and sturdy bases of Doremus's craftsmanship.

Day on day he waited. So much of a revolution for so many people is nothing but waiting. That is one reason why tourists rarely see anything but contentment in a crushed population. Waiting, and its brother death, seem so contented.

For several days now, in late February, Doremus had noticed the insurance man. He said he was a Mr. Dimick; a Mr. Dimick of Albany. He was a gray and tasteless man, in gray and dusty and wrinkled clothes, and his pop-eyes stared with meaningless fervor. All over town you met him, at the four drugstores, at the shoe-shine parlor, and he was always droning, "My name is Dimick—Mr. Dimick of Albany—Albany, New York. I wonder if I can interest you in a wonnerful new form of life-insurance policy. Wonnerful!" But he didn't sound as though he himself thought it was very wonnerful.

He was a pest.

He was always dragging himself into some unwelcoming shop, and yet he seemed to sell few policies, if any.

Not for two days did Doremus perceive that Mr. Dimick of Albany managed to meet him an astonishing number of times a day. As he came out of the Wessex, he saw Mr. Dimick leaning against a lamppost, ostentatiously not looking his way, yet three minutes later and two blocks away, Mr. Dimick trailed after him into the Vert Mont Pool & Tobacco Headquarters, and listened to Doremus's conversation with Tom Aiken about fish hatcheries.

Doremus was suddenly cold. He made it a point to sneak uptown that evening and saw Mr. Dimick talking to the driver of a Beulah-Montpelier bus with an intensity that wasn't in the least gray. Doremus glared. Mr. Dimick looked at him with watery eyes, croaked, "Devenin', Mr. D'remus; like t' talk t' you about insurance some time when you got the time," and shuffled away.

Later, Doremus took out and cleaned his revolver, said, "Oh, rats!" and put it away. He heard a ring as he did so, and went downstairs to find Mr. Dimick sitting on the oak hat rack in the hall, rubbing his hat.

"I'd like to talk to you, if y'ain't too busy," whined Mr. Dimick.

"All right. Go in there. Sit down."

"Anybody hear us?"

"No! What of it?"

Mr. Dimick's grayness and lassitude fell away. His voice was sharp:

"I think your local Corpos are on to me. Got to hustle. I'm from Walt Trowbridge. You probably guessed—I've been watching you all week, asking about you. You've got to be Trowbridge's and our representative here. Secret war against the Corpos. The 'N.U.,' the 'New Underground,' we call it—like secret Underground that got the slaves into Canada before the Civil War. Four divisions: printing propaganda, distributing it, collecting and exchanging information about Corpo outrages, smuggling suspects into Canada or Mexico. Of course you don't know one thing about me. I may be a Corpo spy. But look over these credentials and telephone your friend Mr. Samson of the Burlington Paper Company. God's sake be careful! Wire may be tapped. Ask him about me on the grounds you're interested in insurance. He's one of us. You're going to be one of us! Now *phone*!"

Doremus telephoned to Samson: "Say, Ed, is a fellow named Dimick, kind of weedy-looking, pop-eyed fellow, all right? Shall I take his advice on insurance?"

"Yes. Works for Walbridge. Sure. You can ride along with him."

"I'm riding!"

26

THE *Informer* composing room closed down at eleven in the evening, for the paper had to be distributed to villages forty miles away and did not issue a later city edition. Dan Wilgus, the foreman, remained after the others had gone, setting a Minute Man poster which announced that there would be a grand parade on March ninth, and incidentally that President Windrip was defying the world.

Dan stopped, looked sharply about, and tramped into the storeroom. In the light from a dusty electric bulb the place was like a tomb of dead news, with ancient red-and-black posters of Scotland county fairs and proofs of indecent limericks pasted on the walls. From a case of eight-point, once used for the setting of pamphlets but superseded by a monotype machine, Dan picked out bits of type from each of several compartments, wrapped them in scraps of print paper, and stored them in the pocket of his jacket. The raped type boxes looked only half filled, and to make up for it he did something that should have shocked any decent printer even if he were on strike. He filled them up with type not from another eight-point case, but with old ten-point.

Daniel, the large and hairy, thriftily pinching the tiny types, was absurd as an elephant playing at being a hen.

He turned out the lights on the third floor and clumped downstairs. He glanced in at the editorial rooms. No one was there save Doc Itchitt, in a small circle of light that through the visor of his eye shade cast a green tint on his unwholesome face. He was correcting an article by the titular editor, Ensign Emil Staubmeyer, and he snickered as he carved it with a large black pencil. He raised his head, startled.

"Hello, Doc."

"Hello, Dan. Staying late?"

"Yuh. Just finished some job work. G'night."

"Say, Dan, do you ever see old Jessup, these days?"

"Don't know when I've seen him, Doc. Oh yes, I ran into him at the Rexall store, couple days ago."

"Still as sour as ever about the régime?"

"Oh, he didn't say anything. Darned old fool! Even if he don't like all the brave boys in uniform, he ought to see the Chief is here for keeps, by golly!"

"Certainly ought to! And it's a swell régime. Fellow can get ahead in newspaper work now, and not be held back by a bunch of snobs that think they're so doggone educated just because they went to college!"

"That's right. Well, hell with Jessup and all the old stiffs. G'night, Doc!"

Dan and Brother Itchitt unsmilingly gave the M.M. salute, arms held out. Dan thumped down to the street and homeward. He stopped in front of Billy's Bar, in the middle of a block, and put his foot up on the hub of a dirty old Ford, to tie his shoelace. As he tied it—after having untied it—he looked up and down the street, emptied the bundles in his pockets into a battered sap bucket on the front seat of the car, and majestically moved on.

Out of the bar came Pete Vutong, a French-Canadian farmer who lived up on Mount Terror. Pete was obviously drunk. He was singing the pre-historic ditty "Hi lee, hi low" in what he conceived to be German, viz.: "By unz gays immer, yuh longer yuh slimmer." He was staggering so that he had to pull himself into the car, and he steered in fancy patterns till he had turned the corner. Then he was amazingly and suddenly sober; and amazing was the speed with which the Ford clattered out of town.

Pete Vutong wasn't a very good Secret Agent. He was a little obvious. But then, Pete had been a spy for only one week.

In that week Dan Wilgus had four times dropped heavy packages into a sap bucket in the Ford.

Pete passed the gate to Buck Titus's domain, slowed down, dropped the sap bucket into a ditch, and sped home.

Just at dawn, Buck Titus, out for a walk with his three Irish wolfhounds, kicked up the sap bucket and transferred the bundles to his own pocket.

And next afternoon Dan Wilgus, in the basement of Buck's house, was setting up, in eight-point, a pamphlet entitled "How Many People Have the Corpos Murdered?" It was signed "Spartan," and Spartan was one of several pen names of Mr. Doremus Jessup.

They were all—all the ringleaders of the local chapter of the New Underground—rather glad when once, on his way to Buck's, Dan was searched by M.M.'s unfamiliar to him, and on him was found no printing-material, nor any documents more incriminating than cigarette papers.

The Corpos had made a regulation licensing all dealers in printing machinery and paper and compelling them to keep lists of purchasers, so that except by bootlegging it was impossible to get supplies for the issuance of treasonable literature. Dan Wilgus stole the type; Dan and Doremus and Julian and Buck together had stolen an entire old hand printing-press from the *Informer* basement; and the paper was smuggled from Canada by that veteran bootlegger, John Pollikop, who rejoiced at being back in the good old occupation of which repeal had robbed him.

It is doubtful whether Dan Wilgus would ever have joined anything so divorced as this from the time clock and the office cuspidors out of abstract indignation at Windrip or County Commissioner Ledue. He was moved to sedition partly by fondness for Doremus and partly by indignation at Doc Itchitt, who publicly rejoiced because all the printers' unions had been sunk in the governmental confederations. Or perhaps because Doc jeered at him personally on the few occasions—not more than once or twice a week—when there was tobacco juice on his shirt front.

Dan grunted to Doremus, "All right, boss, I guess maybe I'll come in with you. And say, when we get this man's revolution going, let me drive the tumbril with Doc in it. Say, remember *Tale of Two Cities*? Good book. Say, how about getting out a humorous life of Windrip? You'd just have to tell the facts!"

Buck Titus, pleased as a boy invited to go camping, offered his secluded house and, in especial, its huge basement for the headquarters of the New Underground, and Buck, Dan, and Doremus made their most poisonous plots with the assistance of hot rum punches at Buck's fireplace.

The Fort Beulah cell of the N.U., as it was composed in mid-March, a couple of weeks after Doremus had founded it, consisted of himself, his daughters, Buck, Dan, Lorinda, Julian Falck, Dr. Olmsted, John Pollikop, Father Perefixe (and he argued with the agnostic Dan, the atheist Pollikop, more than ever he had with Buck), Mrs. Henry Veeder, whose farmer husband was in Trianon Concentration Camp, Harry Kindermann, the dispossessed Jew, Mungo Kitterick, that most un-Jewish and un-Socialistic lawyer, Pete Vutong and Daniel Babcock, farmers, and some dozen others. The Reverend Mr. Falck, Emma Jessup, and Mrs. Candy were more or less unconscious tools of the N.U. But whoever they were, of whatever faith or station, Doremus found in all of them the religious passion he had missed in the churches; and if altars, if windows of many-colored glass, had never been peculiarly holy objects to him, he understood them now as he gloated over such sacred trash as scarred type and a creaking hand press.

Once it was Mr. Dimick of Albany again; once, another insurance agent—who guffawed at the accidental luck of insuring Shad Ledue's new Lincoln; once it was an Armenian peddling rugs; once, Mr. Samson of Burlington, looking for pine-slashing for paper pulp; but whoever it was, Doremus heard from the New Underground every week. He was busy as he had never been in newspaper days, and happy as on youth's adventure in Boston.

Humming and most cheerful, he ran the small press, with the hearty bump-bump-bump of the foot treadle, admiring his own skill as he fed in the sheets. Lorinda learned from Dan Wilgus to set type, with more fervor than accuracy about *ei* and *ie.* Emma and Sissy and Mary folded news sheets and sewed up pamphlets by hand, all of them working in the high old brick-walled basement that smelled of sawdust and lime and decaying apples.

Aside from pamphlets by Spartan, and by Anthony B. Susan—who was Lorinda, except on Fridays—their chief illicit publication was *Vermont Vigilance,* a four-page weekly which usually had only two pages and, such was Doremus's unfettered liveliness, came out about three times a week. It was filled with reports smuggled to them from other N.U. cells, and with reprints from Walt Trowbridge's *Lance for Democracy* and from Canadian, British, Swedish, and French papers, whose correspondents in America got out, by long-distance telephone, news which Secretary of Education Macgoblin, head of the government press department, spent a good part of his time denying. An English correspondent sent news of the murder of the president of the University of Southern Illinois, a man of seventy-two who was shot in the back "while trying to escape," out of the country by long-distance telephone to Mexico City, from which the story was relayed to London.

Doremus discovered that neither he nor any other small citizen had been hearing one hundredth of what was going on in America. Windrip & Co. had, like Hitler and Mussolini, discovered that a modern state can, by the triple process of controlling every item in the press, breaking up at the start any association which might become dangerous, and keeping all the machine guns, artillery, armored automobiles, and aëroplanes in the hands of the government, dominate the complex contemporary population better than had ever been done in medieval days, when rebellious peasantry were armed only with pitchforks and good-will, but the State was not armed much better.

Dreadful, incredible information came in to Doremus, until he saw that his own life, and Sissy's and Lorinda's and Buck's, were unimportant accidents.

In North Dakota, two would-be leaders of the farmers were made to run in front of an M.M. automobile, through February drifts, till they dropped breathless, were beaten with a tire pump till they staggered on, fell again, then were shot in the head, their blood smearing the prairie snow.

President Windrip, who was apparently becoming considerably more jumpy than in his old, brazen days, saw two of his personal bodyguard snickering together in the anteroom of his office and, shrieking, snatching an automatic pistol from his desk, started shooting at them. He was a bad marksman. The suspects had to be finished off by the pistols of their fellow guards.

A crowd of young men, not wearing any sort of uniforms, tore the clothes from a nun on the station plaza in Kansas City and chased her, smacking her with bare hands. The police stopped them after a while. There were no arrests.

In Utah a non-Mormon County Commissioner staked out a Mormon elder on a bare rock where, since the altitude was high, the elder at once shivered and felt the glare rather bothersome to his eyes—since the Commissioner had thoughtfully cut off his eyelids first. The government press releases made much of the fact that the torturer was rebuked by the District Commissioner and removed from his post. It did not mention that he was reappointed in a county in Florida.

The heads of the reorganized Steel Cartel, a good many of whom had been officers of steel companies in the days before Windrip, entertained Secretary of Education Macgoblin and Secretary of War Luthorne with an aquatic festival in Pittsburgh. The dining room of a large hotel was turned into a tank of rose-scented water, and the celebrants floated in a gilded Roman barge. The waitresses were naked girls, who amusingly swam to the barge holding up trays and, more often, wine buckets.

Secretary of State Lee Sarason was arrested in the basement of a handsome boys' club in Washington on unspecified charges by a policeman who apologized as soon as he recognized Sarason, and released him, and who that night was shot in his bed by a mysterious burglar.

Albert Einstein, who had been exiled from Germany for his guilty devotion to mathematics, world peace, and the violin, was now exiled from America for the same crimes.

Mrs. Leonard Nimmet, wife of a Congregational pastor in Lincoln, Nebraska, whose husband had been sent to concentration camp for a pacifist sermon, was shot through the door and killed when she refused to open to an M.M. raiding section looking for seditious literature.

In Rhode Island, the door of a small orthodox synagogue in a basement was locked from the outside after thin glass containers of carbon monoxide had been thrown in. The windows had been nailed shut, and anyway, the nineteen men in the congregation did not smell the gas until too late. They were all found slumped to the floor, beards sticking up. They were all over sixty.

Tom Krell—but his was a really nasty case, because he was actually caught with a copy of *Lance for Democracy* and credentials proving that he was a New Underground messenger—strange thing, too, because everybody had respected him as a good, decent, unimaginative baggageman at a village railroad depot in New Hampshire—was dropped down a well with five feet of water in it, a smooth-sided cement well, and just left there.

Ex-Supreme Court Justice Hoblin of Montana was yanked out of bed late at night and examined for sixty hours straight on a charge that he was in correspondence with Trowbridge. It was said that the chief examiner was a man whom, years before, Judge Hoblin had sentenced for robbery with assault.

In one day Doremus received reports that four several literary or dramatic societies—Finnish, Chinese, Iowan, and one belonging to a mixed group of miners on the Mesaba Range, Minnesota—had been broken up, their officers beaten, their clubrooms smashed up and their old pianos wrecked, on the charge that they possessed illegal arms, which, in each case, the members declared to be antiquated pistols used in theatricals. And in that week three people were arrested—in Alabama, Oklahoma, and New Jersey—for the possession of the following subversive books: *The Murder of Roger Ackroyd,* by Agatha Christie (and fair enough too, because the sister-in-law of a county commissioner in Oklahoma was named Ackroyd); *Waiting for Lefty,* by Clifford Odets; and *February Hill,* by Victoria Lincoln.

* * *

"But plenty things like this happened before Buzz Windrip ever came in, Doremus," insisted John Pollikop. (Never till they had met in the delightfully illegal basement had he called Doremus anything save "Mr. Jessup.") "You never thought about them, because they was just routine news, to stick in your paper. Things like the sharecroppers and the Scottsboro boys and the plots of the California wholesalers against the agricultural union and dictatorship in Cuba and the way phony deputies in Kentucky shot striking miners. And believe me, Doremus, the same reactionary crowd that put over those crimes are just the big boys that are chummy with Windrip. And what scares me is that if Walt Trowbridge ever does raise a kinda uprising and kick Buzz out, the same vultures will get awful patriotic and democratic and parliamentarian along with Walt, and sit in on the spoils just the same."

"So Karl Pascal did convert you to Communism before he got sent to Trianon," jeered Doremus.

John Pollikop jumped four straight feet up in the air, or so it looked, and came down screaming, "Communism! Never get 'em to make a United Front! W'y, that fellow Pascal—he was just a propagandist, and I tell you—I tell you——"

Doremus's hardest job was the translation of items from the press in Germany, which was most favorable to the Corpos. Sweating, even in the March coolness in Buck's high basement, Doremus leaned over a kitchen table, ruffling through a German-English lexicon, grunting, tapping his teeth with a pencil, scratching the top of his head, looking like a schoolboy with a little false gray beard, and wailing to Lorinda, "Now how in the heck would you translate 'Er erhält noch immer eine zweideutige Stellung den Juden gegenüber'?" She answered, "Why, darling, the only German I know is the phrase that Buck taught me for 'God bless you'—'Verfluchter Schweinehund.' "

He translated word for word, from the *Völkischer Beobachter,* and later turned into comprehensible English, this gratifying tribute to his Chief and Inspirer:

> America has a brilliant beginning begun. No one congratulates President Windrip with greater sincerity than

> we Germans. The tendency points as goal to the founding of a Folkish state. Unfortunately is the President not yet prepared with the liberal tradition to break. He holds still ever a two-meaning attitude the Jews visavis. We can but presume that logically this attitude change must as the movement forced is the complete consequences of its philosophy to draw. Ahasaver the Wandering Jew will always the enemy of a free self-conscious people be, and America will also learn that one even so much with Jewry compromise can as with the Bubonic plague.

From the *New Masses,* still published surreptitiously by the Communists, at the risk of their lives, Doremus got many items about miners and factory workers who were near starvation and who were imprisoned if they so much as criticized a straw boss. . . . But most of the *New Masses,* with a pious smugness unshaken by anything that had happened since 1935, was given over to the latest news about Marx, and to vilifying all agents of the New Underground, including those who had been clubbed and jailed and killed, as "reactionary stool pigeons for Fascism," and it was all nicely decorated with a Gropper cartoon showing Walt Trowbridge, in M.M. uniform, kissing the foot of Windrip.

The news bulletins came to Doremus in a dozen insane ways—carried by messengers on the thinnest of flimsy tissue paper; mailed to Mrs. Henry Veeder and to Daniel Babcock between the pages of catalogues, by an N.U. operative who was a clerk in the mail-order house of Middlebury & Roe; shipped in cartons of toothpaste and cigarettes to Earl Tyson's drugstore—one clerk there was an N.U. agent; dropped near Buck's mansion by a tough-looking and therefore innocent-looking driver of an interstate furniture-moving truck. Come by so precariously, the news had none of the obviousness of his days in the office when, in one batch of A.P. flimsies, were tidings of so many millions dead of starvation in China, so many statesmen assassinated in central Europe, so many new churches built by kind-hearted Mr. Andrew Mellon, that it was all routine. Now, he was like an eighteenth-century missionary in northern Canada, waiting for the news that would take all spring to travel from Bristol and down Hudson Bay, wondering every instant whether France had declared war, whether Her Majesty had safely given birth.

Doremus realized that he was hearing, all at once, of the battle of Waterloo, the Diaspora, the invention of the telegraph, the discovery of bacilli, and the Crusades, and if it took him ten days to get the news, it would take historians ten decades to appraise it. Would they not envy him, and consider that he had lived in the very crisis of history? Or would they just smile at the flag-waving children of the 1930's playing at being national heroes? For he believed that these historians would be neither Communists nor Fascists nor bellicose American or English Nationalists but just the sort of smiling Liberals that the warring fanatics of today most cursed as weak waverers.

In all this secret tumult Doremus's most arduous task was to avoid suspicions that might land him in concentration camp, and to give appearance of being just the harmless old loafer he veritably had been, three weeks ago. Befogged with sleep because he had worked all night at headquarters, he yawned all afternoon in the lobby of the Hotel Wessex and discussed fishing—the picture of a man too discouraged to be a menace.

He dropped now and then, on evenings when there was nothing to do at Buck's and he could loaf in his study at home and shamefully let himself be quiet and civilized, into renewed longing for the Ivory Tower. Often, not because it was a great poem but because it was the first that, when he had been a boy, had definitely startled him by evoking beauty, he reread Tennyson's "Arabian Nights":

A realm of pleasance, many a mound
And many a shadow-chequered lawn
Full of the city's stilly sound,
And deep myrrh-thickets blowing round
And stately cedar, tamarisks,
Thick rosaries of scented thorn,

Tall orient shrubs, and obelisks
Graven with emblems of the time,
In honor of the golden prime
Of good Haroun Alraschid.

Awhile then he could wander with Romeo and Jurgen, with Ivanhoe and Lord Peter Wimsey; the *Piazza* San Marco he saw, and immemorial towers of Bagdad that never were; with Don John of Austria he was going forth to war, and he took the golden road to Samarcand without a visa.

"But Dan Wilgus setting type on proclamations of rebellion, and Buck Titus distributing them at night on a motorcycle, may be as romantic as Xanadu . . . living in a blooming epic, right now, but no Homer come up from the city room yet to write it down!"

Whit Bibby was an ancient and wordless fishmonger, and as ancient appeared his horse, though it was by no means silent, but given to a variety of embarrassing noises. For twenty years his familiar wagon, like the smallest of cabooses, had conveyed mackerel and cod and lake trout and tinned oysters to all the farmsteads in the Beulah Valley. To have suspected Whit Bibby of seditious practices would have been as absurd as to have suspected the horse. Older men remembered that he had once been proud of his father, a captain in the Civil War—and afterward a very drunken failure at farming—but the young fry had forgotten that there ever had been a Civil War.

Unconcealed in the sunshine of the late-March afternoon that touched the worn and ashen snow, Whit jogged up to the farmhouse of Truman Webb. He had left ten orders of fish, just fish, at farms along the way, but at Webb's he also left, not speaking of it, a bundle of pamphlets wrapped in very fishy newspaper.

By next morning these pamphlets had all been left in the post boxes of farmers beyond Keezmet, a dozen miles away.

Late the next night, Julian Falck drove Dr. Olmsted to the same Truman Webb's. Now Mr. Webb had an ailing aunt. Up to a fortnight ago she had not needed the doctor often, but as all the countryside could, and decidedly did, learn from listening in on the rural party telephone line, the doctor had to come every three or four days now.

"Well, Truman, how's the old lady?" Dr. Olmsted called cheerily.

From the front stoop Webb answered softly, "Safe! Shoot! I've kept a good lookout."

Julian rapidly slid out, opened the rumble seat of the doctor's car, and there was the astonishing appearance from the rumble of a tall man in urban morning coat and striped trousers, a broad felt hat under his arm, rising, rubbing himself, groaning with the pain of stretching his cramped body. The doctor said:

"Truman, we've got a pretty important Eliza, with the bloodhounds right after him, tonight! Congressman Ingram—Comrade Webb."

"Huh! Never thought I'd live to be called one of these 'Comrades.' But mighty pleased to see you, Congressman. We'll put you across the border in Canada in two days—we've got some paths right through the woods along the border—and there's some good hot beans waiting for you right now."

The attic in which Mr. Ingram slept that night, an attic approached by a ladder concealed behind a pile of trunks, was the "underground station" which, in the 1850's, when Truman's grandfather was agent, had sheltered seventy-two various black slaves escaping to Canada, and on the wall above Ingram's weary threatened head was still to be seen, written in charcoal long ago, "Thou preparest a table for me in the presence of mine enemies."

It was a little after six in the evening, near Tasbrough & Scarlett's quarries. John Pollikop, with his wrecker car, was towing Buck Titus, in his automobile. They stopped now and then, and John looked at the motor in Buck's car very ostentatiously, in the sight of M.M. patrols, who ignored so obvious a companionship. They stopped once at the edge of Tasbrough's deepest pit. Buck strolled about, yawning, while John did some more tinkering. "Right!" snapped Buck. Both of them leaped at the over-large toolbox in the back of John's car, lifted out each an armful of copies of *Vermont Vigilance* and hurled them over the edge of the quarry. They scattered in the wind.

Many of them were gathered up and destroyed by Tasbrough's foremen, next morning, but at least a hundred, in the pockets of quarrymen, were started on their journey through the world of Fort Beulah workmen.

Sissy came into the Jessup dining room wearily rubbing her forehead. "I've got the story, Dad. Sister Candy helped me. Now we'll have something good to send on to other agents. Listen! I've been quite chummy with Shad. No! Don't blow up! I know just how to yank his gun out of his holster if I should ever need to. And he got to boasting, and he told me Frank Tasbrough and Shad and Commissioner Reek were all in together on the racket, selling granite for public buildings, and he told me—you see, he was sort of boasting about how chummy he and Mr. Tasbrough have become—how Mr. Tasbrough keeps all the figures on the graft in a little red notebook in his desk—of course old Franky would never expect anybody to search the house of as loyal a Corpo as him! Well, you know Mrs. Candy's cousin is working for the Tasbroughs for a while, and damn if——"

("Sis-sy!")

"—these two old gals didn't pinch the lil red notebook this afternoon, and I photographed every page and had 'em stick it back! And the only comment our Candy makes is, 'That stove t' the Tasbroughs' don't draw well. Couldn't bake a decent cake in a stove like *that*!' "

27

Mary Greenhill, revenging the murdered Fowler, was the only one of the conspirators who seemed moved more by homicidal hate than by a certain incredulous feeling that it was all a good but slightly absurd game. But to her, hate and the determination to kill were tonic. She soared up from the shadowed pit of grief, and her eyes lighted, her voice had a trembling gayety. She threw away her weeds and came out in defiant colors—oh, they had to economize, these days, to put every available penny into the missionary fund of the New Underground, but Mary had become so fine-drawn that she could wear Sissy's giddiest old frocks.

She had more daring than Julian, or even Buck—indeed led Buck into his riskiest expeditions.

In mid-afternoon, Buck and Mary, looking very matrimonial, domestically accompanied by David and the rather doubtful Foolish, ambled through the center of Burlington, where none of them were known—though a number of dogs, city slickers and probably con-dogs, insisted to the rustic and embarrassed Foolish that they had met him somewhere.

It was Buck who muttered "Right!" from time to time, when they were free from being observed, but it was Mary who calmly, a yard or two from M.M.'s or policemen, distributed crumpled-up copies of:

A Little Sunday-school Life of

JOHN SULLIVAN REEK

Second-class Political Crook, &
Certain Entertaining Pictures
of Col. Dewey Haik, Torturer.

These crumpled pamphlets she took from a specially made inside pocket of her mink coat; one reaching from shoulder to waist. It had been recommended by John Pollikop, whose helpful lady had aforetime used just such a pocket for illicit booze. The crumpling had been done carefully. Seen from two yards away, the pamphlets looked like any waste paper, but each was systematically so wadded up that the words, printed in bold red type, "Haik himself kicked an old man to death" caught the eye. And, lying in corner trash baskets, in innocent toy wagons before hardware stores, among oranges in a fruit store where they had gone to buy David a bar of chocolate, they caught some hundreds of eyes in Burlington that day.

On their way home, with David sitting in front beside Buck and Mary in the back, she cried, "That will stir 'em up! But oh, when Daddy has finished his booklet on Swan—— God!"

David peeped back at her. She sat with eyes closed, with hands clenched.

He whispered to Buck, "I wish Mother wouldn't get so excited."

"She's the finest woman living, Dave."

"I know it, but—— She scares me so!"

One scheme Mary devised and carried out by herself. From the magazine counter in Tyson's drugstore, she stole a dozen copies of the *Reader's Digest* and a dozen larger magazines. When she returned them, they looked untouched, but each of the larger magazines contained a leaflet, "Get Ready to Join Walt Trowbridge," and each *Digest* had become the cover for a pamphlet: "Lies of the Corpo Press."

To serve as center of their plot, to be able to answer the telephone and receive fugitives and put off suspicious snoopers twenty-four hours a day, when Buck and the rest might be gone, Lorinda chucked her small remaining interest in the Beulah Valley Tavern and became Buck's housekeeper, living in the place. There was scandal. But in a day when it was increasingly hard to get enough bread and meat, the town folk had little time to suck scandal like lollipops, and anyway, who could much suspect this nagging uplifter who so obviously preferred tuberculin tests to toying with Corydon in the glade? And as Doremus was always about, as sometimes he stayed overnight, for the first time these timid lovers had space for passion.

It had never been their loyalty to the good Emma—since she was too contented to be pitied, too sure of her necessary position in life to be jealous—so much as hatred of a shabby hole-and-corner intrigue which had made their love cautious and grudging. Neither of them was so simple as to suppose that, even with quite decent people, love is always as monogamic as bread and butter, yet neither of them liked sneaking.

Her room at Buck's, large and square and light, with old landscape paper showing an endlessness of little mandarins daintily stepping out of sedan chairs beside pools laced with willows, with a four-poster, a colonial highboy, and a crazy-colored rag carpet, became in two days, so fast did one live now in time of revolution, the best-loved home Doremus had ever known. As eagerly as a young bridegroom he popped into and out of her room, and he was not overly particular about the state of her toilet. And Buck knew all about it and just laughed.

Released now, Doremus saw her as physically more alluring. With parochial superiority, he had noted, during vacations on Cape Cod, how often the fluffy women of fashion when they stripped to bathing suits were skinny, to him unwomanly, with thin shoulder blades and with backbones as apparent as though they were chains fastened down their backs. They seemed passionate to him and a little devilish, with their thin restless legs and avid lips, but he chuckled as he considered that the Lorinda whose prim gray suits and blouses seemed so much more virginal than the gay, flaunting summer cottons of the Bright Young Things was softer of skin to the touch, much richer in the curve from shoulder to breast.

He rejoiced to know that she was always there in the house, that he could interrupt the high seriousness of a tract on bond issues to dash out to the kitchen and brazenly let his arm slide round her waist.

She, the theoretically independent feminist, became flatteringly demanding about every attention. Why hadn't he brought her some candy from town? Would he mind awfully calling up Julian for her? Why hadn't he remembered to bring her the book he had promised—well, would have promised if she had only remembered to ask him for it? He trotted on her errands, idiotically happy. Long ago Emma had reached the limit of her imagination in regard to demands. He was discovering that in love it is really more blessed to give than to receive, a proverb about which, as an employer and as a steady fellow whom forgotten classmates regularly tried to touch for loans, he had been very suspicious.

He lay beside her, in the wide four-poster, at dawn, March dawn with the elm branches outside the window ugly and writhing in the wind, but with the last coals still snapping in the fireplace, and he was utterly content. He glanced at Lorinda, who had on her sleeping face a frown that made her look not older but schoolgirlish, a schoolgirl who was frowning comically over some small woe, and who defiantly clutched her old-fashioned lace-bordered pillow. He laughed. They were going to be so adventurous together! This little printing of pamphlets was only the beginning of their revolutionary activities. They would penetrate into press circles in Washington and get secret information (he was drowsily vague about what information they were going to get and how they would ever get it) which would explode the Corpo state. And with the revolution over, they would go to Bermuda, to Martinique—lovers on purple peaks, by a purple sea—everything purple and grand. Or (and he sighed and became heroic as he exquisitely stretched and yawned in the wide warm bed) if they were defeated, if they were arrested and condemned by the M.M.'s, they would die together, sneering at the firing-squad, refusing to have their eyes bandaged, and their fame, like that of Servetus and Matteotti and Professor Ferrer and the Haymarket martyrs, would roll on forever, acclaimed by children waving little flags——

"Gimme a cigarette, darling!"

Lorinda was regarding him with a beady and skeptical eye.

"You oughtn't to smoke so much!"

"You oughtn't to boss so much! Oh, my darling!" She sat up, kissed his eyes and temples, and sturdily climbed out of bed, seeking her own cigarette.

"Doremus! It's been marvelous to have this companionship with you. But——" She looked a little timid, sitting cross-legged on the rattan-topped stool before the old mahogany dressing table—no silver or lace or crystal was there, but only plain wooden hairbrush and scant luxury of small drugstore bottles. "But darling, this cause—oh, curse that word 'cause'—can't I ever get free of it?—but anyway, this New Underground business seems to me so important, and I know you feel that way too, but I've noticed that since we've settled down together, two awful sentimentalists, you aren't so excited about writing your nice venomous attacks, and I'm getting more cautious about going out distributing tracts. I have a foolish idea I have to save my life, for your sake. And I ought to be only thinking about saving my life for the revolution. Don't you feel that way? Don't you? Don't you?"

Doremus swung his legs out of bed, also lighted an unhygienic cigarette, and said grumpily, "Oh, I suppose so! But—tracts! Your attitude is simply a hold-over of your religious training. That you have a *duty* toward the dull human race—which probably enjoys being bullied by Windrip and getting bread and circuses—except for the bread!"

"Of course it's religious, a revolutionary loyalty! Why not? It's one of the few real religious feelings. A rational, unsentimental Stalin is still kind of a priest. No wonder most preachers hate the Reds and preach against 'em! They're jealous of their religious power. But—— Oh, we can't unfold the world, this morning, even over breakfast coffee, Doremus! When Mr. Dimick came back here yesterday, he ordered me to Beecher Falls—you know, on the Canadian border—to take charge of the N.U. cell there—ostensibly to open up a tea room for this summer. So, hang it, I've got to leave you, and leave Buck and Sis, and go. Hang it!"

"Linda!"

She would not look at him. She made much, too much, of grinding out her cigarette.

"Linda!"

"Yes?"

"You suggested this to Dimick! He never gave any orders till you suggested it!"

"Well——"

"Linda! Linda! Do you want to get away from me so much? You—my life!"

She came slowly to the bed, slowly sat down beside him. "Yes. Get away from you and get away from myself. The world's in chains, and I can't be free to love till I help tear them off."

"It will never be out of chains!"

"Then I shall never be free to love! Oh, if we could only have run away together for one sweet year, when I was eighteen! Then I would have lived two whole lives. Well, nobody seems to be very lucky at turning the clock back—almost twenty-five years back, too. I'm afraid Now is a fact you can't dodge. And I've been getting so—just this last two weeks, with April coming in—that I can't think of anything but you. Kiss me. I'm going. Today."

28

As usually happens in secret service, no one detail that Sissy ferreted out of Shad Ledue was drastically important to the N.U., but, like necessary bits of a picture puzzle, when added to other details picked up by Doremus and Buck and Mary and Father Perefixe, that trained extractor of confessions, they showed up the rather simple schemes of this gang of Corpo racketeers who were so touchingly accepted by the People as patriotic shepherds.

Sissy lounged with Julian on the porch, on a deceptively mild April day.

"Golly, like to take you off camping, couple months from now, Sis. Just the two of us. Canoe and sleep in a pup tent. Oh, Sis, do you *have* to have supper with Ledue and Staubmeyer tonight? I hate it. God, how I hate it! I warn you, I'll kill Shad! I mean it!"

"Yes, I do have to, dear. I think I've got Shad crazy enough about me so that tonight, when he chases good old Emil, and whatever foul female Emil may bring, out of the place, I'll get him to tell me something about who they're planning to pinch next. I'm not scared of Shad, my Julian of jewelians."

He did not smile. He said, with a gravity that had been unknown to the lively college youth, "Do you realize, with your kidding yourself about being able to handle Comrade Shad so well, that he's husky as a gorilla and just about as primitive? One of these nights—God! think of it! maybe tonight!—he'll go right off the deep end and grab you and—bing!"

She was as grave. "Julian, just what do you think could happen to me? The worst that could happen would be that I'd get raped."

"Good Lord——"

"Do you honestly suppose that since the New Civilization began, say in 1914, anyone believes that kind of thing is more serious than busting an ankle? 'A fate worse than death'! What nasty old side-whiskered deacon ever invented that phrase? And how he must have rolled it on his chapped old lips! I can think of plenty worse fates—say, years of running an elevator. No—wait! I'm not really flippant. I haven't any desire, beyond maybe a slight curiosity, to be raped—at least, not by Shad; he's a little too strong on the Bodily Odor when he gets excited. (Oh God, darling, what a nasty swine that man is! I hate him fifty times as much as you do. Ugh!) But I'd be willing to have even that happen if I could save one decent person from his bloody blackjack. I'm not the playgirl of Pleasant Hill any more; I'm a frightened woman from Mount Terror!"

It seemed, the whole thing, rather unreal to Sissy; a burlesqued version of the old melodramas in which the City Villain tries to ruin Our Nell, apropos of a bottle of Champagne Wine. Shad, even in a belted tweed jacket, a kaleidoscopic Scotch sweater (from Minnesota), and white linen plus-fours, hadn't the absent-minded seductiveness that becomes a City Slicker.

Ensign Emil Staubmeyer had showed up at Shad's new private suite at the Star Hotel with a grass widow who betrayed her gold teeth and who had tried to repair the erosions in the fair field of her neck with overmuch top-soil of brick-tinted powder. She was pretty dreadful. She was harder to tolerate than the rumbling Shad—a man for whom the chaplain might even have been a little sorry, after he was safely hanged. The synthetic widow was always nudging herself at Emil and when, rather wearily, he obliged by poking her shoulder, she giggled, "Now you *sssstop*!"

Shad's suite was clean, and had some air. Beyond that there was nothing much to say. The "parlor" was firmly furnished in oak chairs and settee with leather upholstery, and four pictures of marquises not doing anything interesting. The freshness of the linen spread on the brass bedstead in the other room fascinated Sissy uncomfortably.

Shad served them rye highballs with ginger ale from a quart bottle that had first been opened at least a day ago, sandwiches with chicken and ham that tasted of niter, and ice cream with six colors but only two flavors—both strawberry. Then he waited, not too patiently, looking as much like General Göring as possible, for Emil and his woman to get the devil out of here, and for Sissy to acknowledge his virile charms. He only grunted at Emil's pedagogic little jokes, and the man of culture abruptly got up and removed his lady, whinnying in farewell, "Now, Captain, don't you and your girlfriend do anything Papa wouldn't do!"

"Come on now, baby—come over here and give us a kiss," Shad roared, as he flopped into the corner of the leather settee.

"Now I don't know whether I *will* or not!" It nauseated her a good deal, but she made herself as pertly provocative as she could. She minced to the settee, and sat just far enough from his hulking side for him to reach over and draw her toward him. She observed him cynically, recalling her experience with most of the Boys . . . though not with Julian . . . well, not so much with Julian. They always, all of them, went through the same procedure, heavily pretending that there was no system in their manual proposals; and to a girl of spirit, the chief diversion in the whole business was watching their smirking pride in their technique. The only variation, ever, was whether they started in at the top or the bottom.

Yes. She thought so. Shad, not being so delicately fanciful as, say, Malcolm Tasbrough, started with an apparently careless hand on her knee.

She shivered. His sinewy paw was to her like the slime and writhing of an eel. She moved away with a maidenly alarm which mocked the rôle of Mata Hari she had felt herself to be gracing.

"Like me?" he demanded.

"Oh—well—sort of."

"Oh, shucks! You think I'm still just a hired man! Even though I am a County Commissioner now! and a Battalion-Leader! and prob'ly pretty soon I'll be a Commander!" He spoke the sacred names with awe. It was the twentieth time he had made the same plaint to her in the same words. "And you still think I ain't good for anything except lugging in kindling!"

"Oh, Shad dear! Why, I always think of you as being just about my oldest playmate! The way I used to tag after you and ask you could I run the lawnmower! My! I always remember that!"

"Do you, honest?" He yearned at her like a lumpish farm dog.

"Of course! And honest, it makes me tired, your acting as if you were ashamed of having worked for us! Why, don't you know that, when he was a boy, Daddy used to work as a farm hand, and split wood and tend lawn for the neighbors and all that, and he was awful glad to get the money?" She reflected that this thumping and entirely impromptu lie was beautiful. . . . That it happened not to be a lie, she did not know.

"That a fact? Well! Honest? Well! So the old man used to hustle the rake too! Never knew that! You know, he ain't such a bad old coot—just awful stubborn."

"You *do* like him, *don't* you, Shad! Nobody knows how sweet he is—I mean, in these sort of complicated days, we've got to protect him against people that might not understand him, against outsiders, don't you think so, Shad? You *will* protect him!"

"Well, I'll do what I can," said the Battalion-Leader with such fat complacency that Sissy almost slapped him. "That is, as long as he behaves himself, baby, and don't get mixed up with any of these Red rebels . . . and as long as you feel like being nice to a fella!" He pulled her toward him as though he were hauling a bag of grain out of a wagon.

"Oh! Shad! You frighten me! Oh, you must be gentle! A big, strong man like you can afford to be gentle. It's only the sissies that have to get rough. And you're so strong!"

"Well, I guess I can still feed myself! Say, talking

about sissies, what do you see in a light-waisted molly-coddle like Julian? You don't really like him, do you?"

"Oh, you know how it is," she said, trying without too much obviousness to ease her head away from his shoulder. "We've always been playmates, since we were kids."

"Well, you just said I was, too!"

"Yes, that's so."

Now in her effort to give all the famous pleasures of seduction without taking any of the risk, the amateur secret-service operative, Sissy, had a slightly confused aim. She was going to get from Shad information valuable to the N.U. Rapidly rehearsing it in her imagination, the while she was supposed to be weakened by the charm of leaning against Shad's meaty shoulder, she heard herself teasing him into giving her the name of some citizen whom the M.M.'s were about to arrest, slickly freeing herself from him, dashing out to find Julian—oh, hang it, why hadn't she made an engagement with Julian for that night?—well, he'd either be at home or out driving Dr. Olmsted—Julian's melodramatically dashing to the home of the destined victim and starting him for the Canadian border before dawn. . . . And it might be a good idea for the refugee to tack on his door a note dated two days ago, saying that he was off on a trip, so that Shad would never suspect her. . . . All this in a second of hectic story-telling, neatly illustrated in color by her fancy, while she pretended that she had to blow her nose and thus had an excuse to sit straight. Edging another inch or two away, she purred, "But of course it isn't just physical strength, Shad. You have so much power politically. My! I imagine you could send almost anybody in Fort Beulah off to concentration camp, if you wanted to."

"Well, I could put a few of 'em away, if they got funny!"

"I'll bet you could—and will, too! Who you going to arrest next, Shad?"

"Huh?"

"Oh come on! Don't be so tightwad with all your secrets!"

"What are you trying to do, baby? Pump me?"

"Why no, of course not, I just——"

"Sure! You'd like to get the poor old fathead going, and find out everything he knows—and that's plenty, you can bet your sweet life on that! Nothing doing, baby."

"Shad, I'd just—I'd just love to see an M.M. squad arresting somebody once. It must be dreadfully exciting!"

"Oh, it's exciting enough, all right, all right! When the poor chumps try to resist, and you throw their radio out of the window! Or when the fellow's wife gets fresh and shoots off her mouth too much, and so you just teach her a little lesson by letting her look on while you trip him up on the floor and beat him up—maybe that sounds a little rough, but you see, in the long run it's the best thing you can do for these beggars, because it teaches 'em to not get ugly."

"But—you won't think I'm horrid and unwomanly, will you?—but I would like to see you hauling out one of those people, just once. Come on, tell a fellow! Who are you going to arrest next?"

"Naughty, naughty! Mustn't try to kid papa! No, the womanly thing for you to do is a little love-making! Aw come on, let's have some fun, baby! You know you're crazy about me!" Now he really seized her, his hand across her breasts. She struggled, thoroughly frightened, no longer cynical and sophisticated. She shrieked, "Oh don't—don't!" She wept, real tears, more from anger than from modesty. He loosened his grip a little, and she had the inspiration to sob, "Oh, Shad, if you really want me to love you, you must give me time! You wouldn't want me to be a hussy that you could do anything you wanted to with—you, in your position? Oh, no, Shad, you couldn't do that!"

"Well, maybe," said he, with the smugness of a carp.

She had sprung up, dabbling at her eyes—and through the doorway, in the bedroom, on a flat-topped desk, she saw a bunch of two or three Yale keys. Keys to his office, to secret cupboards and drawers with Corpo plans! Undoubtedly! Her imagination in one second pictured her making a rubbing of the keys, getting John Pollikop, that omnifarious mechanic, to file substitute keys, herself and Julian somehow or other sneaking into Corpo headquarters at night, perilously creeping past the guards, rifling Shad's every dread file——

She stammered, "Do you mind if I go in and wash my face? All teary—so silly! You don't happen to have any face powder in your bathroom?"

"Say, what d'you think I am? A hick, or a monk, maybe? You bet your life I've got some face powder—right in the medicine cabinet—two kinds—how's that for service? Ladies taken care of by the day or hour!"

It hurt, but she managed something like a giggle before she went in and shut the bedroom door, and locked it.

She tore across to the keys. She snatched up a pad of yellow scratch-paper and a pencil, and tried to make a rubbing of a key as once she had made rubbings of coins, for use in the small grocery shop of C. JESSUp & J. falck groSHERS.

The pencil blur showed only the general outline of the key; the tiny notches which were the trick would not come clear. In panic, she experimented with a sheet of carbon paper, then toilet paper, dry and wet. She could not get a mold. She pressed the key into a prop hotel candle in a china stick by Shad's bed. The candle was too hard. So was the bathroom soap. And Shad was now trying the knob of the door, remarking "Damn!" then bellowing, "Whayuh doin' in there? Gone to sleep?"

"Be right out!" She replaced the keys, threw the yellow paper and the carbon paper out of the window, replaced the candle and soap, slapped her face with a dry towel, dashed on powder as though she were working against time at plastering a wall, and sauntered back into the parlor. Shad looked hopeful. In panic she saw that now, before he comfortably sat down to it and became passionate again, was her one time to escape. She snatched up hat and coat, said wistfully, "Another night, Shad—you must let me go now, dear!" and fled before he could open his red muzzle.

Round the corner in the hotel corridor she found Julian.

He was standing taut, trying to look like a watchdog, his right hand in his coat pocket as though it was holding a revolver.

She hurled herself against his bosom and howled.

"Good God! What did he do to you? I'll go in and kill him!"

"Oh, I didn't get seduced. It isn't things like that that I'm bawling about! It's because I'm such a simply terribly awful spy!"

But one thing came out of it.

Her courage nerved Julian to something he had longed for and feared: to join the M.M.'s, put on uniform, "work from within," and supply Doremus with information.

"I can get Leo Quinn—you know?—Dad's a conductor on the railroad?—used to play basketball in high school?—I can get him to drive Dr. Olmsted for me, and generally run errands for the N.U. He's got grit, and he hates the Corpos. But look, Sissy—look, Mr. Jessup—in order to get the M.M.'s to trust me, I've got to pretend to have a fierce bust-up with you and all our friends. Look! Sissy and I will walk up Elm Street tomorrow evening, giving an imitation of estranged lovers. How 'bout it, Sis?"

"Fine!" glowed that incorrigible actress.

She was to be, every evening at eleven, in a birch grove just up Pleasant Hill from the Jessups', where they had played house as children. Because the road curved, the rendezvous could be entered from four or five directions. There he was to hand on to her his reports of M.M. plans.

But when he first crept into the grove at night and she nervously turned her pocket torch on him, she shrieked at seeing him in M.M. uniform, as an inspector. That blue tunic and slanting forage cap which, in the cinema and history books, had meant youth and hope, meant only death now. . . . She wondered if in 1864 it had not meant death more than moonlight and magnolias to most women. She sprang to him, holding him as if to protect him against his own uniform, and in the peril and uncertainty now of their love, Sissy began to grow up.

29

THE PROPAGANDA throughout the country was not all to the New Underground; not even most of it; and though the pamphleteers for the N.U., at home and exiled abroad, included hundreds of the most capable professional journalists of America, they were cramped by a certain respect for facts which never enfeebled the press-agents for Corpoism. And the Corpos had a notable staff. It included college presidents, some of the most renowned among the radio announcers who aforetime had crooned their affection for mouth washes and noninsomniac coffee, famous ex-war-correspondents, ex-governors, former vice-presidents of the American Federation of Labor, and no less an artist than the public relations counsel of a princely corporation of electrical-goods manufacturers.

The newspapers everywhere might no longer be so wishily-washily liberal as to print the opinions of non-Corpos; they might give but little news from those old-fashioned and democratic countries, Great Britain, France, and the Scandinavian states; might indeed print almost no foreign news, except as regards the triumphs of Italy in giving Ethiopia good roads, trains on time, freedom from beggars and from men of honor, and all the other spiritual benefactions of Roman civilization. But, on the other hand, never had newspapers shown so many comic strips—the most popular was a very funny one about a preposterous New Underground crank, who wore mortuary black with a high hat decorated with crêpe and who was always being comically beaten up by M.M.'s. Never had there been, even in the days when Mr. Hearst was freeing Cuba, so many large red headlines. Never so many dramatic drawings of murders—the murderers were always notorious anti-Corpos. Never such a wealth of literature, worthy its twenty-four-hour immortality, as the articles proving, and proving by figures, that American wages were universally higher, commodities universally lower-priced, war budgets smaller but the army and its equipment much larger, than ever in history. Never such righteous polemics as the proofs that all non-Corpos were Communists.

Almost daily, Windrip, Sarason, Dr. Macgoblin, Secretary of War Luthorne, or Vice-President Perley Beecroft humbly addressed their Masters, the great General Public, on the radio, and congratulated them on making a new world by their example of American solidarity—marching shoulder to shoulder under the Grand Old Flag, comrades in the blessings of peace and comrades in the joys of war to come.

Much-heralded movies, subsidized by the government (and could there be any better proof of the attention paid by Dr. Macgoblin and the other Nazi leaders to the arts than the fact that movie actors who before the days of the Chief were receiving only fifteen hundred gold dollars a week were now getting five thousand?), showed the M.M.'s driving armored motors at eighty miles an hour, piloting a fleet of one thousand planes, and being very tender to a little girl with a kitten.

Everyone, including Doremus Jessup, had said in 1935, "If there ever is a Fascist dictatorship here, American humor and pioneer independence are so marked that it will be absolutely different from anything in Europe."

For almost a year after Windrip came in, this seemed true. The Chief was photographed playing poker, in shirtsleeves and with a derby on the back of his head, with a newspaperman, a chauffeur, and a pair of rugged steel-workers. Dr. Macgoblin in person led an Elks' brass band and dived in competition with the Atlantic City bathing-beauties. It was reputably reported that M.M.'s apologized to political prisoners for having to arrest them, and that the prisoners joked amiably with the guards . . . at first.

All that was gone, within a year after the inauguration, and surprised scientists discovered that whips and handcuffs hurt just as sorely in the clear American air as in the miasmic fogs of Prussia.

Doremus, reading the authors he had concealed in the horsehair sofa—the gallant Communist, Karl Billinger, the gallant anti-Communist, Tchernavin, and the gallant neutral, Lorant—began to see something like a biology of dictatorships, all dictatorships. The universal apprehension, the timorous denials of faith, the same methods of arrest—sudden pounding on the door late at night, the squad of police pushing in, the blows, the search, the obscene oaths at the frightened women, the third degree by young snipe of officials, the accompanying blows and then the formal beatings, when the prisoner is forced to count the strokes until he faints, the leprous beds and the sour stew, guards jokingly shooting round and round a prisoner who believes he is being executed, the waiting in solitude to know what will happen, till men go mad and hang themselves——

Thus had things gone in Germany, exactly thus in Soviet Russia, in Italy and Hungary and Poland, Spain and Cuba and Japan and China. Not very different had it been under the blessings of liberty and fraternity in the French Revolution. All dictators followed the same routine of torture, as if they had all read the same manual of sadistic etiquette. And now, in the humorous, friendly, happy-go-lucky land of Mark Twain, Doremus saw the homicidal maniacs having just as good a time as they had had in central Europe.

America followed, too, the same ingenious finances as Europe. Windrip had promised to make everybody richer, and had contrived to make everybody, except for a few hundred bankers and industrialists and soldiers, much poorer. He needed no higher mathematicians to produce his financial statements: any ordinary press agent could do them. To show a 100 per cent economy in military expenditures, while increasing the establishment 700 per cent, it had been necessary only to charge up all expenditures for the Minute Men to non-military departments, so that their training in the art of bayonet-sticking was debited to the Department of Education. To show an increase in average wages one did tricks with "categories of labor" and "required minimum wages," and forgot to state how many workers ever did become entitled to the "minimum," and how much was charged as wages, on the books, for food and shelter for the millions in the labor camps.

It all made dazzling reading. There had never been more elegant and romantic fiction.

Even loyal Corpos began to wonder why the armed forces, army and M.M.'s together, were being so increased. Was a frightened Windrip getting ready to defend himself against a rising of the whole nation? Did he plan to attack all of North and South America and make himself an emperor? Or both? In any case, the forces were so swollen that even with its despotic power of taxation, the Corpo government never had enough. They began to force exports, to practice the "dumping" of wheat, corn, timber, copper, oil, machinery. They increased production, forced it by fines and threats, then stripped the farmer of all he had, for export at depreciated prices. But at home the prices were not depreciated but increased, so that the more we exported, the less the industrial worker in America had to eat. And really zealous County Commissioners took from the farmer (after the patriotic manner of many Mid-Western counties in 1918) even his seed grain, so that he could grow no more, and on the very acres where once he had raised superfluous wheat he now starved for bread. And while he was starving, the Commissioners continued to try to make him pay for the Corpo bonds which he had been made to buy on the installment plan.

But still, when he did finally starve to death, none of these things worried him.

There were bread lines now in Fort Beulah, once or twice a week.

The hardest phenomenon of dictatorship for a Doremus to understand, even when he saw it daily in his own street, was the steady diminution of gayety among the people.

America, like England and Scotland, had never really been a gay nation. Rather it had been heavily and noisily jocular, with a substratum of worry and insecurity, in the image of its patron saint, Lincoln of the rollicking stories and the tragic heart. But at least there had been hearty greetings, man to man; there had been clamorous jazz for dancing, and the lively, slangy catcalls of young people, and the nervous blatting of tremendous traffic.

All that false cheerfulness lessened now, day by day.

The Corpos found nothing more convenient to milk than public pleasures. After the bread had molded, the circuses were closed. There were taxes or increased taxes on motorcars, movies, theaters, dances, and ice-cream sodas. There was a tax on playing a phonograph or radio in any restaurant. Lee Sarason, himself a bachelor, conceived of super-taxing bachelors and spinsters, and contrariwise of taxing all weddings at which more than five persons were present.

Even the most reckless youngsters went less and less to public entertainments, because no one not ostentatiously in uniform cared to be noticed, these days. It was impossible to sit in a public place without wondering which spies were watching you. So all the world stayed home—and jumped anxiously at every passing footstep, every telephone ring, every tap of an ivy sprig on the window.

The score of people definitely pledged to the New Underground were the only persons to whom Doremus dared talk about anything more incriminating than whether it was likely to rain, though he had been the friendliest gossip in town. Always it had taken ten minutes longer than was humanly possible for him to walk to the *Informer* office, because he stopped on every corner to ask after someone's sick wife, politics, potato crop, opinions about Deism, or luck at fishing.

As he read of rebels against the régime who worked in Rome, in Berlin, he envied them. They had thousands of government agents, unknown by sight and thus the more dangerous, to watch them; but also they had thousands of comrades from whom to seek encouragement, exciting personal tattle, shop talk, and the assurance that they were not altogether idiotic to risk their lives for a mistress so ungrateful as Revolution. Those secret flats in great cities—perhaps some of them really were filled with the rosy glow they had in fiction. But the Fort Beulahs, anywhere in the world, were so isolated, the conspirators so uninspiringly familiar one to another, that only by inexplicable faith could one go on.

Now that Lorinda was gone, there certainly was nothing very diverting in sneaking round corners, trying to look like somebody else, merely to meet Buck and Dan Wilgus and that good woman, Sissy!

Buck and he and the rest—they were such amateurs. They needed the guidance of veteran agitators like Mr. Ailey and Mr. Bailey and Mr. Cailey.

Their feeble pamphlets, their smearily printed newspaper, seemed futile against the enormous blare of Corpo propaganda. It seemed worse than futile, it seemed insane, to risk martyrdom in a world where Fascists persecuted Communists, Communists persecuted Social-Democrats, Social-Democrats persecuted everybody who would stand for it; where "Aryans" who looked like Jews persecuted Jews who looked like Aryans and Jews persecuted their debtors; where every statesman and clergyman praised Peace and brightly asserted that the only way to get Peace was to get ready for War.

What conceivable reason could one have for seeking after righteousness in a world which so hated righteousness? Why do anything except eat and read and make love and provide for sleep that should be secure against disturbance by armed policemen?

He never did find any particularly good reason. He simply went on.

In June, when the Fort Beulah cell of the New Underground had been carrying on for some three months, Mr. Francis Tasbrough, the golden quarryman, called on his neighbor, Doremus.

"How are you, Frank?"

"Fine, Remus. How's the old carping critic?"

"Fine, Frank. Still carping. Fine carping weather, at that. Have a cigar?"

"Thanks. Got a match? Thanks. Saw Sissy yesterday. She looks fine."

"Yes, she's fine. I saw Malcolm driving by yesterday. How did he like it in the Provincial University, at New York?"

"Oh, fine—fine. He says the athletics are grand. They're getting Primo Carnera over to coach in tennis next year—I think it's Carnera—I think it's tennis—but anyway, the athletics are fine there, Malcolm says. Say, uh, Remus, there's something I been meaning to ask you. I, uh—— The fact is—— I want you to be sure and not repeat this to anybody. I know you can be trusted with a secret, even if you are a newspaperman—or used to be, I mean, but—— The fact is (and this is inside stuff; official), there's going to be some governmental promotions all along the line—this is confidential, and it comes to me straight from the Provincial Commissioner, Colonel Haik. Luthorne is finished as Secretary of War—he's a nice fellow, but he hasn't got as much publicity for the Corpos out of his office as the Chief expected him to. Haik is to have his job, and also take over the position of High Marshal of the Minute Men from Lee Sarason—I suppose Sarason has too much to do. Well then, John Sullivan Reek is slated to be Provincial Commissioner; that leaves the office of District Commissioner for Vermont-New Hampshire empty, and I'm one of the people being seriously considered. I've done a lot of speaking for the Corpos, and I know Dewey Haik very well—I was able to advise him about erecting public buildings. Of course there's none of the County Commissioners around here that measure up to a district commissionership—not even Dr. Staubmeyer—certainly not Shad Ledue. Now if you could see your way clear to throw in with me, your influence would help——"

"Good heavens, Frank, the worst thing you could have happen, if you want the job, is to have me favor you! The Corpos don't like me. Oh, of course they know I'm loyal, not one of these dirty, sneaking anti-Corpos, but I never made enough noise in the paper to please 'em."

"That's just it, Remus! I've got a really striking idea. Even if they don't like you, the Corpos respect you, and they know how long you've been important in the State. We'd all be greatly pleased if you came out and joined us. Now just suppose you did so and let people know that it was my influence that converted you to Corpoism. That might give me quite a leg-up. And between old friends like us, Remus, I can tell you that this job of District Commissioner would be useful to me in the quarry business, aside from the social advantages. And if I got the position, I can promise you that I'd either get the *Informer* taken away from Staubmeyer and that dirty little stinker, Itchitt, and given back to you to run absolutely as you pleased—providing, of course, you had the sense to keep from criticizing the Chief and the State. Or, if you'd rather, I think I could probably wangle a job for you as military judge (they don't necessarily have to be lawyers) or maybe President Peaseley's job as District Director of Education—you'd have a lot of fun out of that!—awfully amusing the way all the teachers kiss the Director's foot! Come on, old man! Think of all the fun we used to have in the old days! Come to your senses and face the inevitable and join us and fix up some good publicity for me. How about it—huh, huh?"

Doremus reflected that the worst trial of a revolutionary propagandist was not risking his life, but having to be civil to people like Future-Commissioner Tasbrough.

He supposed that his voice was polite as he muttered, "Afraid I'm too old to try it, Frank," but apparently Tasbrough was offended. He sprang up and tramped away grumbling, "Oh, very well then!"

"And I didn't give him a chance to say anything about being realistic or breaking eggs to make an omelet," regretted Doremus.

The next day Malcolm Tasbrough, meeting Sissy on the street, made his beefy most of cutting her. At the time the Jessups thought that was very amusing. They thought the occasion less amusing when Malcolm chased little David out of the Tasbrough apple orchard, which he had been wont to use as the Great Western Forest where at any time one was rather more than likely to meet Kit Carson, Robin Hood, and Colonel Lindbergh hunting together.

Having only Frank's word for it, Doremus could do no more than hint in *Vermont Vigilance* that Colonel Dewey Haik was to be made Secretary of War, and give Haik's actual military record, which included the facts that as a first lieutenant in France in 1918, he had been under fire for less than fifteen minutes, and that his one real triumph had been commanding state militia during a strike in Oregon, when eleven strikers had been shot down, five of them in the back.

Then Doremus forgot Tasbrough completely and happily.

30

BUT WORSE than having to be civil to the fatuous Mr. Tasbrough was keeping his mouth shut when, toward the end of June, a newspaperman at Battington, Vermont, was suddenly arrested as editor of *Vermont Vigilance* and author of all the pamphlets by Doremus and Lorinda. He went to concentration camp. Buck and Dan Wilgus and Sissy prevented Doremus from confessing, and from even going to call on the victim, and when, with Lorinda no longer there as confidante, Doremus tried to explain it all to Emma, she said, Wasn't it lucky that the government had blamed somebody else!

Emma had worked out the theory that the N.U. activity was some sort of a naughty game which kept her boy, Doremus, busy after his retirement. He was mildly nagging the Corpos. She wasn't sure that it was really nice to nag the legal authorities, but still, for a little fellow, her Doremus had always been surprisingly spunky—just like (she often confided to Sissy) a spunky little Scotch terrier she had owned when she was a girl—Mr. McNabbit its name had been, a little Scotch terrier, but my! so spunky he acted like he was a regular lion!

She was rather glad that Lorinda was gone, though she liked Lorinda and worried about how well she might do with a tea room in a new town, a town where she had never lived. But she just couldn't help feeling (she confided not only to Sissy but to Mary and Buck) that Lorinda, with all her wild crazy ideas about women's rights, and workmen being just as good as their employers, had a bad influence on Doremus's tendency to show off and shock people. (She mildly wondered why Buck and Sissy snorted so. She hadn't meant to say anything particularly funny!)

For too many years she had been used to Doremus's irregular routine to have her sleep disturbed by his returning from Buck's at the improper time to which she referred as "all hours," but she did wish he would be "more on time for his meals," and she gave up the question of why, these days, he seemed to like to associate with Ordinary People like John Pollikop, Dan Wilgus, Daniel Babcock, and Pete Vutong—my! some people said Pete couldn't even read and write, and Doremus so educated and all! Why didn't he see more of lovely people like Frank Tasbrough and Professor Staubmeyer and Mr. R. C. Crowley and this new friend of his, the Hon. John Sullivan Reek?

Why couldn't he keep out of politics? She'd always *said* they were no occupation for a gentleman!

Like David, now ten years old (and like twenty or thirty million other Americans, from one to a hundred, but all of the same mental age), Emma thought the marching M.M.'s were a very fine show indeed, so much like movies of the Civil War, really quite educational; and while of course if Doremus didn't care for President Windrip, she was opposed to him also, yet didn't Mr. Windrip speak beautifully about pure language, church attendance, low taxation, and the American flag?

The realists, the makers of omelets, did climb, as Tasbrough had predicted. Colonel Dewey Haik, Commissioner of the Northeastern Province, became Secretary of War and High Marshal of M.M.'s, while the former secretary, Colonel Luthorne, retired to Kansas and the real-estate business and was well spoken of by all business men for being thus willing to give up the grandeur of Washington for duty toward practical affairs and his family, who were throughout the press depicted as having frequently missed him. It was rumored in N.U. cells that Haik might go higher even than Secretary of War; that Windrip was worried by the forced growth of a certain effeminacy in Lee Sarason under the arc light of glory.

Francis Tasbrough was elevated to District Commissionership at Hanover. But Mr. Sullivan Reek did not in series go on to be Provincial Commissioner. It was said that he had too many friends among just the old-line politicians whose jobs the Corpos were so enthusiastically taking. No, the new Provincial Commissioner, viceroy and general, was Military Judge Effingham Swan, the one man whom Mary Jessup Greenhill hated more than she did Shad Ledue.

Swan was a splendid commissioner. Within three days after taking office, he had John Sullivan Reek and seven assistant district commissioners arrested, tried, and imprisoned, all within twenty-four hours, and an eighty-year-old woman, mother of a New Underground agent but not otherwise accused of wickedness, penned in a concentration camp for the more desperate traitors. It was in a disused quarry which was always a foot deep in water. After he had sentenced her, Swan was said to have bowed to her most courteously.

The New Underground sent out warning, from headquarters in Montreal, for a general tightening up of precautions against being caught distributing propaganda. Agents were disappearing rather alarmingly.

Buck scoffed, but Doremus was nervous. He noticed that the same strange man, ostensibly a drummer, a large man with unpleasant eyes, had twice got into conversation with him in the Hotel Wessex lobby, and too obviously hinted that he was anti-Corpo and would love to have Doremus say something nasty about the Chief and the M.M.'s.

Doremus became cautious about going out to Buck's. He parked his car in half-a-dozen different wood-roads and crept afoot to the secret basement.

On the evening of the twenty-eighth of June, 1938, he had a notion that he was being followed, so closely did a car with red-tinted headlights, anxiously watched in his rear-view mirror, stick behind him as he took the Keezmet highway down to Buck's. He turned up a side road, down another. The spy car followed. He stopped, in a driveway on the left-hand side of the road, and angrily stepped out, in time to see the other car pass, with a man who looked like Shad Ledue driving. He swung round then and, without concealment, bolted for Buck's.

In the basement, Buck was contentedly typing up bundles of the *Vigilance,* while Father Perefixe, in his shirt-sleeves, vest open and black dickey swinging beneath his reversed collar, sat at a plain pine table, writing a warning to New England Catholics that though the Corpos had, unlike the Nazis in Germany, been shrewd enough to flatter prelates, they had lowered the wages of French-Canadian Catholic mill hands and imprisoned their leaders just as severely as in the case of the avowedly wicked Protestants.

Perefixe smiled up at Doremus, stretched, lighted a pipe, and chuckled, "As a great ecclesiast, Doremus, is it your opinion that I shall be committing a venial or a mortal sin by publishing this little masterpiece—the work of my favorite author—without the Bishop's imprimatur?"

"Stephen! Buck! I think they're on to us! Maybe we've got to fold up already and get the press and type out of here!" He told of being shadowed. He telephoned to Julian, at M.M. headquarters, and (since there were too many French-Canadian inspectors about for him to dare to use his brand of French) he telephoned in the fine new German he had been learning by translation:

"Denks du ihr Freunds dere haben a Idee die letzt Tag von vot ve mach here?"

And the college-bred Julian had so much international culture as to be able to answer: "Ja, Ich mein ihr vos sachen morning free. Look owid!"

How could they move? Where?

Dan Wilgus arrived, in panic, an hour after.

"Say! They're watching us!" Doremus, Buck, and the priest gathered round the black viking of a man. "Just now when I came in I thought I heard something in the bushes, here in the yard, near the house, and before I thought, I flashed my torch on him, and by golly if it wasn't Aras Dilley, and not in uniform—and you know how Aras loves his God—excuse me, Father—how he loves his uniform. He was disguised! Sure! In overalls! Looked like a jackass that's gone under a clothes-line! Well, he'd been rubbering at the house. Course these curtains are drawn, but I don't know what he saw and——"

The three large men looked to Doremus for orders.

"We got to get all this stuff out of here! Quick! Take it and hide it in Truman Webb's attic. Stephen: get John Pollikop and Mungo Kitterick and Pete Vutong on the phone—get 'em here, quick—tell John to stop by and tell Julian to come as soon as he can. Dan: start dismantling the press. Buck: bundle up all the literature." As he spoke, Doremus was wrapping type in scraps of newspaper. And at three next morning, before light, Pollikop was driving toward Truman Webb's farmhouse the entire equipment of the New Underground printing establishment, in Buck's old farm truck, from which blatted, for the benefit of all ears that might be concerned, two frightened calves.

Next day Julian ventured to invite his superior officers, Shad Ledue and Emil Staubmeyer, to a poker session at Buck's. They came, with alacrity. They found Buck, Doremus, Mungo Kitterick, and Doc Itchitt—the last an entirely innocent participant in certain deceptions.

They played in Buck's parlor. But during the evening Buck announced that anyone wanting beer instead of whisky would find it in a tub of ice in the basement, and that anyone wishing to wash his hands would find two bathrooms upstairs.

Shad hastily went for beer. Doc Itchitt even more hastily went to wash his hands. Both of them were gone much longer than one would have expected.

When the party broke up and Buck and Doremus were alone, Buck shrieked with bucolic mirth: "I could scarcely keep a straight face when I heard good old Shad opening the cupboards and taking a fine long look-see for pamphlets down in the basement. Well, Cap'n Jessup, that about ends their suspicion of this place as a den of traitors, I guess! God, but isn't Shad dumb!"

This was at perhaps 3 A.M. on the morning of June thirtieth.

Doremus stayed home, writing sedition, all the afternoon and evening of the thirtieth, hiding the sheets under pages of newspaper in the Franklin stove in his study, so that he could touch them off with a match in case of a raid—a trick he had learned from Karl Billinger's anti-Nazi *Fatherland.*

This new opus was devoted to murders ordered by Commissioner Effingham Swan.

On the first and second of July, when he sauntered uptown, he was rather noticeably encountered by the same weighty drummer who had picked him up in the Hotel Wessex lobby before, and who now insisted on their having a drink together. Doremus escaped, and was conscious that he was being followed by an unknown young man, flamboyant in an apricot-colored polo shirt and gray bags, whom he recognized as having worn M.M. uniform at a parade in June. On July third, rather panicky, Doremus drove to Truman Webb's, taking an hour of zigzagging to do it, and warned Truman not to permit any more printing till he should have a release.

When Doremus went home, Sissy lightly informed him that Shad had insisted she go out to an M.M. picnic with him on the next afternoon, the Fourth, and that, information or no, she had refused. She was afraid of him, surrounded by his ready playmates.

The night of the third Doremus slept only in sick spasms. He was reasonlessly convinced that he would be arrested before dawn. The night was overcast and electric and uneasy. The crickets sounded as though they were piping under compulsion, in a rhythm of terror. He lay throbbing to their sound. He wanted to flee—but how and where, and how could he leave his threatened family? For the first time in years he wished that he were sleeping beside the unperturbable Emma, beside her small earthy hillock of body. He laughed at himself. What could Emma do to protect him against Minute Men? Just scream! And what then? But he, who always slept with his door shut, to protect his sacred alone-ness, popped out of bed to open the door, that he might have the comfort of hearing her breathe, and the fiercer Mary stir in slumber, and Sissy's occasional young whimper.

He was awakened before dawn by early firecrackers. He heard the tramping of feet. He lay taut. Then he awoke again, at seven-thirty, and was slightly angry that nothing happened.

* * *

The M.M.'s brought out their burnished helmets and all the rideable horses in the neighborhood—some of them known as most superior plow-horses—for the great celebration of the New Freedom on the morning of Fourth of July. There was no post of the American Legion in the jaunty parade. That organization had been completely suppressed, and a number of American Legion leaders had been shot. Others had tactfully taken posts in the M.M. itself.

The troops, in hollow square, with the ordinary citizenry humbly jammed in behind them and the Jessup family rather hoity-toity on the outskirts, were addressed by Ex-Governor Isham Hubbard, a fine ruddy old rooster who could say "Cock-a-doodle-do" with more profundity than any fowl since Æsop. He announced that the Chief had extraordinary resemblances to Washington, Jefferson, and William B. McKinley, and to Napoleon on his better days.

The trumpets blew, the M.M.'s gallantly marched off nowhere in particular, and Doremus went home, feeling much better after his laugh. Following noon dinner, since it was raining, he proposed a game of contract to Emma, Mary, and Sissy—with Mrs. Candy as volunteer umpire.

But the thunder of the hill country disquieted him. Whenever he was dummy, he ambled to a window. The rain ceased; the sun came out for a false, hesitating moment, and the wet grass looked unreal. Clouds with torn bottoms, like the hem of a ragged skirt, were driven down the valley, cutting off the bulk of Mount Faithful; the sun went out as in a mammoth catastrophe; and instantly the world was in unholy darkness, which poured into the room.

"Why, it's quite dark, isn't it! Sissy, turn on the lights," said Emma.

The rain attacked again, in a crash, and to Doremus, looking out, the whole knowable world seemed washed out. Through the deluge he saw a huge car flash, the great wheels throwing up fountains. "Wonder what make of car that is? Must be a sixteen-cylinder Cadillac, I guess," reflected Doremus. The car swerved into his own gateway, almost knocking down a gatepost, and stopped with a jar at his porch. From it leaped five Minute Men, black water-proof capes over their uniforms. Before he could quite get through the reflection that he recognized none of them, they were there in the room. The leader, an ensign (and most certainly Doremus did not recognize *him*) marched up to Doremus, looked at him casually, and struck him full in the face.

Except for the one light pink of the bayonet when he had been arrested before, except for an occasional toothache or headache, or a smart when he had banged a fingernail, Doremus Jessup had not for thirty years known authentic pain. It was as incredible as it was horrifying, this torture in his eyes and nose and crushed mouth. He stood bent, gasping, and the Ensign again smashed his face, and observed, "You are under arrest."

Mary had launched herself on the Ensign, was hitting at him with a china ash tray. Two M.M.'s dragged her off, threw her on the couch, and one of them pinned her there. The other two guards were bulking over the paralyzed Emma, the galvanized Sissy.

Doremus vomited suddenly and collapsed, as though he were dead drunk.

He was conscious that the five M.M.'s were yanking the books from the shelves and hurling them on the floor, so that the covers split, and with their pistol butts smashing vases and lamp shades and small occasional tables. One of them tattooed a rough M M on the white paneling above the fireplace with shots from his automatic.

The Ensign said only, "Careful, Jim," and kissed the hysterical Sissy.

Doremus struggled to get up. An M.M. kicked him in the elbow. It felt like death itself, and Doremus writhed on the floor. He heard them tramping upstairs. He remembered then that his manuscript about the murders by Provincial Commissioner Effingham Swan was hidden in the Franklin stove in his study.

The sound of their smashing of furniture in the bedrooms on the second floor was like that of a dozen wood-choppers gone mad.

In all his agony, Doremus struggled to get up—to set fire to the papers in the stove before they should be found. He tried to look at his women. He could make out Mary, tied to the couch. (When had that ever happened?) But his vision was too blurred, his mind too bruised, to see anything clearly. Staggering, sometimes creeping on his hands and knees, he did actually get past the men in the bedrooms and up the stairs to the third floor and his study.

He was in time to see the Ensign throwing his best-beloved books and his letter files, accumulated these twenty years, out of the study window, to see him search the papers in the Franklin stove, look up with cheerful triumph and cackle, "Nice piece you've written here. I guess, Jessup. Commissioner Swan will love to see it!"

"I demand—see—Commissioner Ledue—Dist' Commissioner Tasbrough—friends of mine," stammered Doremus.

"Don't know a thing about them. I'm running this show," the Ensign chuckled, and slapped Doremus, not very painfully, merely with a shamefulness as great as Doremus's when he realized that he had been so cowardly as to appeal to Shad and Francis. He did not open his mouth again, did not whimper nor even amuse the troopers by vainly appealing on behalf of the women, as he was hustled down two flights of stairs—they threw him down the lower flight and he landed on his raw shoulder—and out to the big car.

The M.M. driver, who had been waiting behind the wheel, already had the engine running. The car whined away, threatening every instant to skid. But the Doremus who had been queasy about skidding did not notice. What could he do about it, anyway? He was helpless between two troopers in the back seat, and his powerlessness to make the driver slow up seemed part of all his powerlessness before the dictator's power . . . he who had always so taken it for granted that in his dignity and social security he was just slightly superior to laws and judges and policemen, to all the risks and pain of ordinary workers.

He was unloaded, like a balky mule, at the jail entrance of the courthouse. He resolved that when he was led before Shad he would so rebuke the scoundrel that he would not forget it. But Doremus was not taken into the courthouse. He was kicked toward a large, black-painted, unlettered truck by the entrance—literally kicked, while even in his bewildered anguish he speculated, "I wonder which is worse?—the physical pain of being kicked, or the mental humiliation of being turned into a slave? Hell! Don't be sophistical! It's the pain in the behind that hurts most!"

He was hiked up a stepladder into the back of the truck.

From the unlighted interior a moan, "My God, not you too, Dormouse!" It was the voice of Buck Titus, and with him as prisoners were Truman Webb and Dan Wilgus. Dan was in handcuffs, because he had fought so.

The four men were too sore to talk much as they felt the truck lurch away and they were thrown against one another. Once Doremus spoke truthfully, "I don't know how to tell you how ghastly sorry I am to have got you into this!" and once he lied, when Buck groaned, "Did those —— —— hurt the girls?"

They must have ridden for three hours. Doremus was in such a coma of suffering that even though his back winced as it bounced against the rough floor and his face was all one neuralgia, he drowsed and woke to terror, drowsed and woke, drowsed and woke to his own helpless wailing.

The truck stopped. The doors were opened on lights thick among white brick buildings. He hazily saw that they were on the one-time Dartmouth campus—headquarters now of the Corpo District Commissioner.

That commissioner was his old acquaintance Francis Tasbrough! He would be released! They would be freed, all four!

The incredulity of his humiliation cleared away. He came out of his sick fear like a shipwrecked man sighting an approaching boat.

But he did not see Tasbrough. The M.M.'s, silent save for mechanical cursing, drove him into a hallway, into a cell which had once been part of a sedate classroom, left him with a final clout on the head. He dropped on a wooden pallet with a straw pillow and was instantly asleep. He was too dazed—he who usually looked recordingly at places—to note then or afterward what his cell was like, except that it appeared to be filled with sulphuric fumes from a locomotive engine.

When he came to, his face seemed frozen stiff. His coat was torn, and foul with the smell of vomit. He felt degraded, as though he had done something shameful.

His door was violently opened, a dirt-clotted bowl of feeble coffee, with a crust of bread faintly smeared with oleomargarine, was thrust at him, and after he had given them up, nauseated, he was marched out into the corridor, by two guards, just as he wanted to go to the toilet. Even that he could forget in the paralysis of fear. One guard seized him by the trim small beard and yanked it, laughing very much. "Always did want to see whether a billygoat whisker would pull out or not!" snickered the guard. While he was thus tormented, Doremus received a crack behind his ear from the other man, and a scolding command, "Come on, goat! Want us to milk you? You dirty little so-and-so! What you in for? You look like a little Kike tailor, you little——"

"Him?" the other scoffed. "Naw! He's some kind of a half-eared hick newspaper editor—they'll sure shoot him—sedition—but I hope they'll beat hell out of him first for being such a bum editor."

"Him? An editor? Say! Listen! I got a swell idea. Hey! Fellas!" Four or five other M.M.'s, half dressed, looked out from a room down the hall. "This-here is a writing-fellow! I'm going to make him show us how he writes! Lookit!"

The guard dashed down the corridor to a door with the sign "Gents" hung out in front of it, came back with paper, not clean, threw it in front of Doremus, and yammered, "Come on, boss. Show us how you write your pieces! Come on, write us a piece—with your nose!" He was iron-strong. He pressed Doremus's nose down against the filthy paper and held it there, while his mates giggled. They were interrupted by an officer, commanding, though leniently, "Come on, boys, cut out the monkeyshines and take this —— to the bull pen. Trial this morning."

Doremus was led to a dirty room in which half-a-dozen prisoners were waiting. One of them was Buck

Titus. Over one eye Buck had a slatternly bandage which had so loosened as to show that his forehead was cut to the bone. Buck managed to wink jovially. Doremus tried, vainly, to keep from sobbing.

He waited an hour, standing, arms tight at his side, at the demands of an ugly-faced guard, snapping a dog whip with which he twice slashed Doremus when his hands fell lax.

Buck was led into the trial room just before him. The door was closed. Doremus heard Buck cry out terribly, as though he had been wounded to death. The cry faded into a choked gasping. When Buck was led out of the inner room, his face was as dirty and as pale as his bandage, over which blood was now creeping. The man at the door of the inner room jerked his thumb sharply at Doremus, and snarled, "You're *next*!"

Now he would face Tasbrough!

But in the small room into which he had been taken—and he was confused, because somehow he had expected a large courtroom—there was only the Ensign who had arrested him yesterday, sitting at a table, running through papers, while a stolid M.M. stood on either side of him, rigid, hand on pistol holster.

The Ensign kept him waiting, then snapped with disheartening suddenness, "Your name!"

"You know it!"

The two guards beside Doremus each hit him.

"Your name?"

"Doremus Jessup."

"You're a Communist!"

"No I'm not!"

"Twenty-five lashes—and the oil."

Not believing, not understanding, Doremus was rushed across the room, into a cellar beyond. A long wooden table there was dark with dry blood, stank with dry blood. The guards seized Doremus, sharply jerked his head back, pried open his jaws, and poured in a quart of castor oil. They tore off his garments above the belt, flung them on the sticky floor. They threw him face downward on the long table and began to lash him with a one-piece steel fishing rod. Each stroke cut into the flesh of his back, and they beat him slowly, relishing it, to keep him from fainting too quickly. But he was unconscious when, to the guards' great diversion, the castor oil took effect. Indeed he did not know it till he found himself limp on a messy piece of gunnysacking on the floor of his cell.

They awakened him twice during the night to demand, "You're a Communist, heh? You better admit it! We're going to beat the living tar out of you till you do!"

Though he was sicker than he had ever been in his life, yet he was also angrier; too angry to admit anything whatever, even to save his wrecked life. He simply snarled "No." But on the third beating he savagely wondered if "No" was now a truthful answer. After each questioning he was pounded again with fists, but not lashed with the steel rod, because the headquarters doctor had forbidden it.

He was a sporty-looking young doctor in plus-fours. He yawned at the guards, in the blood-reeking cellar, "Better cut out the lashes or this —— will pass out on you."

Doremus raised his head from the table to gasp, "You call yourself a doctor, and you associate with these murderers?"

"Oh, shut up, you little ——! Dirty traitors like you deserve to be beaten to death—and maybe you will be, but I think the boys ought to save you for the trial!" The doctor showed his scientific mettle by twisting Doremus's ear till it felt as though it were torn off, chuckled, "Go to it, boys," and ambled away, ostentatiously humming.

For three nights he was questioned and lashed—once, late at night, by guards who complained of the inhuman callousness of their officers in making them work so late. They amused themselves by using an old harness strap, with a buckle on it, to beat him.

He almost broke down when the examining Ensign declared that Buck Titus had confessed their illegal propaganda, and narrated so many details of the work that Doremus could almost have believed in the confession. He did not listen. He told himself, "No! Buck would die before he'd confess anything. It's all Aras Dilley's spying."

The Ensign cooed, "Now if you'll just have the sense

to copy your friend Titus, and tell us who's in the conspiracy besides him and you and Wilgus and Webb, we'll let you go. We know, all right—oh, we know the whole plot!—but we just want to find out whether you've finally come to your senses and been converted, my little friend. Now who else was there? Just give us their names. We'll let you go. Or would you like the castor oil and the whip again?"

Doremus did not answer.

"Ten lashes," said the Ensign.

He was chased out for half an hour's walk on the campus every afternoon—probably because he would have preferred lying on his hard cot, trying to keep still enough so that his heart would stop its deathly hammering. Half a hundred prisoners marched there, round and round senselessly. He passed Buck Titus. To salute him would have meant a blow from the guards. They greeted each other with quick eyelids, and when he saw those untroubled spaniel eyes, Doremus knew that Buck had not squealed.

And in the exercise yard he saw Dan Wilgus, but Dan was not walking free; he was led out from the torture rooms by guards, and with his crushed nose, his flattened ear, he looked as though he had been pounded by a prizefighter. He seemed partly paralyzed. Doremus tried to get information about Dan from a guard in his cell corridor. The guard—a handsome, clear-cheeked young man, noted in a valley of the White Mountains as a local beau, and very kind to his mother—laughed, "Oh, your friend Wilgus? That chump thinks he can lick his weight in wildcats. I hear he always tries to soak the guards. They'll take that out of him, all right!"

Doremus thought, that night—he could not be sure, but he thought he heard Dan wailing, half the night. Next morning he was told that Dan, who had always been so disgusted when he had had to set up the news of a weakling's suicide, had hanged himself in his cell.

Then, unexpectedly, Doremus was taken into a room, this time reasonably large, a former English classroom turned into a court, for his trial.

But it was not District Commissioner Francis Tasbrough who was on the bench, nor any Military Judge, but no less a Protector of the People than the great new Provincial Commissioner, Effingham Swan.

Swan was looking at Doremus's article about him as Doremus was led up to stand before the bench. He spoke—and this harsh, tired-looking man was no longer the airy Rhodes Scholar who had sported with Doremus once like a boy pulling the wings off flies.

"Jessup, do you plead guilty to seditious activities?"

"Why——" Doremus looked helplessly about for something in the way of legal counsel.

"Commissioner Tasbrough!" called Swan.

So at last Doremus did see his boyhood playmate.

Tasbrough did nothing so commendable as to avoid Doremus's eyes. Indeed he looked at Doremus directly, and most affably, as he spoke his piece:

"Your Excellency, it gives me great pain to have to expose this man, Jessup, whom I have known all my life, and tried to help, but he always was a smart-aleck—he was a laughing-stock in Fort Beulah for the way he tried to show off as a great political leader!—and when the Chief was elected, he was angry because he didn't get any political office, and he went about everywhere trying to disaffect people—I have heard him do so myself."

"That's enough. Thanks. County Commissioner Ledue . . . Captain Ledue, is it or is it not true that the man Jessup tried to persuade you to join a violent plot against my person?"

But Shad did not look at Doremus as he mumbled, "It's true."

Swan crackled, "Gentlemen, I think that that, plus the evidence contained in the prisoner's own manuscript, which I hold here, is sufficient testimony. Prisoner, if it weren't for your age and your damn silly senile weakness, I'd sentence you to a hundred lashes, as I do all the other Communists like you that threaten the Corporate State. As it is, I sentence you to be held in concentration camp, at the will of the Court, but with a minimum sentence of seventeen years." Doremus calculated rapidly. He was sixty-two now. He would be seventy-nine *then.* He never would see freedom again.

"And, in the power of issuing emergency decrees, conferred upon me as Provincial Commissioner, I also sentence you to death by shooting, but I suspend that sentence—though only until such time as you may be caught trying to escape! And I hope you'll have just lots and lots of time in prison, Jessup, to think about how clever you were in this entrancing article you wrote about me! And to remember that any nasty cold morning they may take you out in the rain and shoot you." He ended with a mild suggestion to the guards: "And twenty lashes!"

Two minutes later they had forced castor oil down him; he lay trying to bite at the stained wood of the whipping-table; and he could hear the whish of the steel fishing rod as a guard playfully tried it out in the air before bringing it down across the crisscross wounds of his raw back.

31

As the open prison van approached the concentration camp at Trianon, the last light of afternoon caressed the thick birch and maples and poplars up the pyramid of Mount Faithful. But the grayness swiftly climbed the slope, and all the valley was left in cold shadow. In his seat the sick Doremus drooped again in listlessness.

The prim Georgian buildings of the girls' school which had been turned into a concentration camp at Trianon, nine miles north of Fort Beulah, had been worse used than Dartmouth, where whole buildings were reserved for the luxuries of the Corpos and their female cousins, all very snotty and parvenu. The Trianon school seemed to have been gouged by a flood. Marble doorsteps had been taken away. (One of them now graced the residence of the wife of the Superintendent, Mrs. Cowlick, a woman fat, irate, jeweled, religious, and given to announcing that all opponents of the Chief were Communists and ought to be shot offhand.) Windows were smashed. "Hurrah for the Chief" had been chalked on brick walls and other chalked words, each of four letters, had been rubbed out, not very thoroughly. The lawns and hollyhock beds were a mess of weeds.

The buildings stood on three sides of a square; the fourth side and the gaps between buildings were closed with unpainted pine fences topped with strands of barbed wire.

Every room except the office of Captain Cowlick, the Superintendent (he was as near nothing at all as any man can be who has attained to such honors as being a captain in the Quartermaster Corps and the head of a prison), was smeared with filth. His office was merely dreary, and scented with whisky, not, like the other rooms, with ammonia.

Cowlick was not too ill-natured. He wished that the camp guards, all M.M.'s, would not treat the prisoners viciously, except when they tried to escape. But he was a mild man; much too mild to hurt the feelings of the M.M.'s and perhaps set up inhibitions in their psyches by interfering with their methods of discipline. The poor fellows probably meant well when they lashed noisy inmates for insisting they had committed no crime. And the good Cowlick saved Doremus's life for a while; let him lie for a month in the stuffy hospital and have actual beef in his daily beef stew. The prison doctor, a decayed old drunkard who had had his medical training in the late 'eighties and who had been somewhat close to trouble in civil life for having performed too many abortions, was also good-natured enough, when sober, and at last he permitted Doremus to have Dr. Marcus Olmsted in from Fort Beulah, and for the first time in four weeks Doremus had news, any news whatsoever, of the world beyond prison.

Where in normal life it would have been agony to wait for one hour to know what might be happening to his friends, his family, now for one month he had not known whether they were alive or dead.

Dr. Olmsted—as guilty as Doremus himself of what the Corpos called treason—dared speak to him only a moment, because the prison doctor stayed in the hospital ward all the while, drooling over whip-scarred patients and daubing iodine more or less near their wounds. Olmsted sat on the edge of his cot, with its foul blankets, unwashed for months, and muttered rapidly:

"Quick! Listen! Don't talk! Mrs. Jessup and your two girls are all right—they're scared, but no signs of their being arrested. Hear Lorinda Pike is all right. Your grandson, David, looks fine—though I'm afraid he'll grow up a Corpo, like all the youngsters. Buck Titus is alive—at another concentration camp—the one near Woodstock. Our N.U. cell at Fort Beulah is doing what it can—no publishing, but we forward information—get a lot from Julian Falck—great joke: he's been promoted, M.M. Squad-Leader now! Mary and Sissy and Father

Perefixe keep distributing pamphlets from Boston; they help the Quinn boy (my driver) and me to forward refugees to Canada. . . . Yes, we carry on. . . . About like an oxygen tent for a patient that's dying of pneumonia! . . . It hurts to see you looking like a ghost, Doremus. But you'll pull through. You've got pretty good nerves for a little cuss! That aged-in-the-keg prison doctor is looking this way. Bye!"

He was not permitted to see Dr. Olmsted again, but it was probably Olmsted's influence that got him, when he was dismissed from the hospital, still shaky but well enough to stumble about, a vastly desirable job as sweeper of cells and corridors, cleaner of lavatories and scrubber of toilets, instead of working in the woods gang, up Mount Faithful, where old men who sank under the weight of logs were said to be hammered to death by guards under the sadistic Ensign Stoyt, when Captain Cowlick wasn't looking. It was better, too, than the undesirable idleness of being disciplined in the "doghouse" where you lay naked, in darkness, and where "bad cases" were reformed by being kept awake for forty-eight or even ninety-six hours. Doremus was a conscientious toilet-cleaner. He didn't like the work very much, but he had pride in being able to scrub as skillfully as any professional pearl-diver in a Greek lunch room, and satisfaction in lessening a little the wretchedness of his imprisoned comrades by giving them clean floors.

For, he told himself, they were his comrades. He saw that he, who had thought of himself as a capitalist because he could hire and fire, and because theoretically he "owned his business," had been as helpless as the most itinerant janitor, once it seemed worth while to the Big Business which Corpoism represented to get rid of him. Yet he still told himself stoutly that he did not believe in a dictatorship of the proletariat any more than he believed in a dictatorship of the bankers and utility-owners; he still insisted that any doctor or preacher, though economically he might be as insecure as the humblest of his flock, who did not feel that he was a little better than they, and privileged to enjoy working a little harder, was a rotten doctor or a preacher without grace.

He felt that he himself had been a better and more honorable reporter than Doc Itchitt, and a thundering sight better student of politics than most of his shopkeeper and farmer and factory-worker readers.

Yet bourgeois pride was so gone out of him that he was flattered, a little thrilled, when he was universally called "Doremus" and not "Mr. Jessup" by farmer and workman and truck-driver and plain hobo; when they thought enough of his courage under beating and his good-temper under being crowded with others in a narrow cell to regard him as almost as good as their own virile selves.

Karl Pascal mocked him. "I told you so, Doremus! You'll be a Communist yet!"

"Yes, maybe I will, Karl—after you Communists kick out all your false prophets and bellyachers and power drunkards, and all your press-agents for the Moscow subway."

"Well, all right, why don't you join Max Eastman? I hear he's escaped to Mexico and has a whole big pure Trotzkyite Communist party of seventeen members there!"

"Seventeen? Too many. What I want is mass action by just one member, alone on a hilltop. I'm a great optimist, Karl. I still hope America may some day rise to the standards of Kit Carson!"

As sweeper and scrubber, Doremus had unusual chances for gossip with other prisoners. He chuckled when he thought of how many of his fellow criminals were acquaintances: Karl Pascal, Henry Veeder, his own cousin, Louis Rotenstern, who looked now like a corpse, unforgettingly wounded in his old pride of having become a "real American," Clarence Little, the jeweler, who was dying of consumption, Ben Tripper, who had been the jolliest workman in Medary Cole's gristmill, Professor Victor Loveland, of the defunct Isaiah College, and Raymond Pridewell, that old Tory who was still so contemptuous of flattery, so clean amid dirt, so hawk-eyed, that the guards were uncomfortable when they beat him. . . . Pascal, the Communist, Pridewell, the squirearchy Republican, and Henry Veeder, who had never cared a hang about politics, and who had recovered from the first shocks of imprisonment, these three had become intimates, because they had more arrogance of utter courage than anyone else in the prison.

For home Doremus shared with five other men a cell twelve feet by ten and eight feet high, which a finishing-school girl had once considered outrageously confined for one lone young woman. Here they slept, in two tiers of three bunks each; here they ate, washed, played cards, read, and enjoyed the leisurely contemplation which, as Captain Cowlick preached to them every Sunday morning, was to reform their black souls and turn them into loyal Corpos.

None of them, certainly not Doremus, complained much. They got used to sleeping in a jelly of tobacco smoke and human stench, to eating stews that always left them nervously hungry, to having no more dignity or freedom than monkeys in a cage, as a man gets used to the indignity of having to endure cancer. Only it left in them a murderous hatred of their oppressors so that they, men of peace all of them, would gladly have hanged every Corpo, mild or vicious. Doremus understood John Brown much better.

His cell mates were Karl Pascal, Henry Veeder, and three men whom he had not known: a Boston architect, a farm hand, and a dope fiend who had once kept questionable restaurants. They had good talk—especially from the dope fiend, who placidly defended crime in a world where the only real crime had been poverty.

The worst torture to Doremus, aside from the agony of actual floggings, was the waiting.

The Waiting. It became a distinct, tangible thing, as individual and real as Bread or Water. How long would he be in? How long would he be in? Night and day, asleep and waking, he worried it, and by his bunk saw waiting the figure of Waiting, a gray, foul ghost.

It was like waiting in a filthy station for a late train, not for hours but for months.

Would Swan amuse himself by having Doremus taken out and shot? He could not care much, now; he could not picture it, any more than he could picture kissing Lorinda, walking through the woods with Buck, playing with David and Foolish, or anything less sensual than the ever derisive visions of roast beef with gravy, of a hot bath, last and richest of luxuries where their only way of washing, except for a fortnightly shower, was with a dirty shirt dipped in the one basin of cold water for six men.

Besides Waiting, one other ghost hung about them—the notion of Escaping. It was of that (far more than of the beastliness and idiocy of the Corpos) that they whispered in the cell at night. When to escape. How to escape. To sneak off through the bushes when they were out with the woods gang? By some magic to cut through the bars on their cell window and drop out and blessedly not be seen by the patrols? To manage to hang on underneath one of the prison trucks and be driven away? (A childish fantasy!) They longed for escape as hysterically and as often as a politician longs for votes. But they had to discuss it cautiously, for there were stool pigeons all over the prison.

This was hard for Doremus to believe. He could not understand a man's betraying his companions, and he did not believe it till, two months after Doremus had gone to concentration camp, Clarence Little betrayed to the guards Henry Veeder's plan to escape in a hay wagon. Henry was properly dealt with. Little was released. And Doremus, it may be, suffered over it nearly as much as either of them, sturdily though he tried to argue that Little had tuberculosis and that the often beatings had bled out his soul.

Each prisoner was permitted one visitor a fortnight and, in sequence, Doremus saw Emma, Mary, Sissy, David. But always an M.M. was standing two feet away, listening, and Doremus had from them nothing more than a fluttering, "We're all fine—we hear Buck is all right—we hear Lorinda is doing fine in her new tea room—Philip writes he is all right." And once came Philip himself, his pompous son, more pompous than ever now as a Corpo judge, and very hurt about his father's insane radicalism—considerably more hurt when

Doremus tartly observed that he would much rather have had the dog Foolish for visitor.

And there were letters—all censored—worse than useless to a man who had been so glad to hear the living voices of his friends.

In the long run, these frustrate visits, these empty letters, made his waiting the more dismal, because they suggested that perhaps he was wrong in his nightly visions; perhaps the world outside was not so loving and eager and adventurous as he remembered it, but only dreary as his cell.

He had little known Karl Pascal, yet now the argumentative Marxian was his nearest friend, his one amusing consolation. Karl could and did prove that the trouble with leaky valves, sour cow pastures, the teaching of calculus, and all novels was their failure to be guided by the writings of Lenin.

In his new friendship, Doremus was old-maidishly agitated lest Karl be taken out and shot, the recognition usually given to Communists. He discovered that he need not worry. Karl had been in jail before. He was the trained agitator for whom Doremus had longed in New Underground days. He had ferreted out so many scandals about the financial and sexual shenanigans of every one of the guards that they were afraid that even while he was being shot, he might tattle to the firing-squad. They were much more anxious for his good opinion than for that of Captain Cowlick, and they timidly brought him little presents of chewing tobacco and Canadian newspapers, as though they were schoolchildren honeying up to teacher.

When Aras Dilley was transferred from night patrols in Fort Beulah to the position of guard at Trianon—a reward for having given to Shad Ledue certain information about R. C. Crowley which cost that banker hundreds of dollars—Aras, that slinker, that able snooper, jumped at the sight of Karl and began to look pious and kind. He had known Karl before!

Despite the presence of Stoyt, Ensign of guards, an ex-cashier who had once enjoyed shooting dogs and who now, in the blessed escape of Corpoism, enjoyed lashing human beings, the camp at Trianon was not so cruel as the district prison at Hanover. But from the dirty window of his cell Doremus saw horrors enough.

One mid-morning, a radiant September morning with the air already savoring the peace of autumn, he saw the firing-squad marching out his cousin, Henry Veeder, who had recently tried to escape. Henry had been a granite monolith of a man. He had walked like a soldier. He had, in his cell, been proud of shaving every morning, as once he had done, with a tin basin of water heated on the stove, in the kitchen of his old white house up on Mount Terror. Now he stooped, and toward death he walked with dragging feet. His face of a Roman senator was smeared from the cow dung into which they had flung him for his last slumber.

As they tramped out through the quadrangle gate, Ensign Stoyt, commanding the squad, halted Henry, laughed at him, and calmly kicked him in the groin.

They lifted him up. Three minutes later Doremus heard a ripple of shots. Three minutes after that the squad came back bearing on an old door a twisted clay figure with vacant open eyes. Then Doremus cried aloud. As the bearers slanted the stretcher, the figure rolled to the ground.

But one thing worse he was to see through the accursed window. The guards drove in, as new prisoners, Julian Falck, in torn uniform, and Julian's grandfather, so fragile, so silvery, so bewildered and terrified in his muddied clericals.

He saw them kicked across the quadrangle into a building once devoted to instruction in dancing and the more delicate airs for the piano; devoted now to the torture room and the solitary cells.

Not for two weeks, two weeks of waiting that was like ceaseless ache, did he have a chance, at exercise hour, to speak for a moment to Julian, who muttered, "They caught me writing some inside dope about M.M. graft. It was to have gone to Sissy. Thank God, nothing on it to show who it was for!" Julian had passed on. But Doremus had had time to see that his eyes were hopeless, and that his neat, smallish, clerical face was blue-black with bruises.

The administration (or so Doremus guessed) decided that Julian, the first spy among the M.M.'s who had been caught in the Fort Beulah region, was too good a subject of sport to be wastefully shot at once. He should be kept for an example. Often Doremus saw the guards kick him across the quadrangle to the whipping room and imagined that he could hear Julian's shrieks afterward. He wasn't even kept in a punishment cell, but in an open barred den on an ordinary corridor, so that passing inmates could peep in and see him, welts across his naked back, huddled on the floor, whimpering like a beaten dog.

And Doremus had sight of Julian's grandfather sneaking across the quadrangle, stealing a soggy hunk of bread from a garbage can, and fiercely chewing at it.

All through September Doremus worried lest Sissy, with Julian now gone from Fort Beulah, be raped by Shad Ledue. . . . Shad would leer the while, and gloat over his ascent from hired man to irresistible master.

Despite his anguish over the Falcks and Henry Veeder and every uncouthest comrade in prison, Doremus was almost recovered from his beatings by late September. He began delightedly to believe that he would live for another ten years; was slightly ashamed of his delight, in the presence of so much agony, but he felt like a young man and—— And straightway Ensign Stoyt was there (two or three o'clock at night it must have been), yanking Doremus out of his bunk, pulling him to his feet, knocking him down again with so violent a crack in his mouth that Doremus instantly sank again into all his trembling fear, all his inhuman groveling.

He was dragged into Captain Cowlick's office.

The Captain was courtly:

"Mr. Jessup, we have information that you were connected with Squad-Leader Julian Falck's treachery. He has, uh, well, to be frank, he's broken down and confessed. Now you yourself are in no danger, no danger whatever, of further punishment, if you will just help us. But we really must make a warning of young Mr. Falck, and so if you will tell us all you know about the boy's shocking infidelity to the colors, we shall hold it in your favor. How would you like to have a nice bedroom to sleep in, all by yourself?"

A quarter hour later Doremus was still swearing that he knew nothing whatever of any "subversive activities" on the part of Julian.

Captain Cowlick said, rather testily, "Well, since you refuse to respond to our generosity, I must leave you to Ensign Stoyt, I'm afraid. . . . Be gentle with him, Ensign."

"Yessr," said the Ensign.

The Captain wearily trotted out of the room and Stoyt did indeed speak with gentleness, which was a surprise to Doremus, because in the room were two of the guards to whom Stoyt liked to show off:

"Jessup, you're a man of intelligence. No use your trying to protect this boy, Falck, because we've got enough on him to execute him anyway. So it won't be hurting him any if you give us a few more details about his treason. And you'll be doing yourself a good turn."

Doremus said nothing.

"Going to talk?"

Doremus shook his head.

"All right, then . . . Tillett!"

"Bring in the guy that squealed on Jessup!"

Doremus expected the guard to fetch Julian, but it was Julian's grandfather who wavered into the room. In the camp quadrangle Doremus had often seen him trying to preserve the dignity of his frock coat by rubbing at the spots with a wet rag, but in the cells there were no hooks for clothes, and the priestly garment—Mr. Falck was a poor man and it had not been very expensive at best—was grotesquely wrinkled now. He was blinking with sleepiness, and his silver hair was a hurrah's nest.

Stoyt (he was thirty or so) said cheerfully to the two elders, "Well, now, you boys better stop being naughty and try to get some sense into your mildewed old brains, and then we can all have some decent sleep. Why don't you two try to be honest, now that you've each confessed that the other was a traitor?"

"What?" marveled Doremus.

"Sure! Old Falck here says you carried his grandson's

pieces to the *Vermont Vigilance.* Come on, now, if you'll tell us who published that rag——"

"I have confessed nothing. I have nothing to confess," said Mr. Falck.

Stoyt screamed, "Will you shut up? You old hypocrite!" Stoyt knocked him to the floor, and as Mr. Falck weaved dizzily on hands and knees, kicked him in the side with a heavy boot. The other two guards were holding back the sputtering Doremus. Stoyt jeered at Mr. Falck, "Well, you old bastard, you're on your knees, so let's hear you pray!"

"I shall!"

In agony Mr. Falck raised his head, dust-smeared from the floor, straightened his shoulders, held up trembling hands, and with such sweetness in his voice as Doremus had once heard in it when men were human, he cried, "Father, Thou hast forgiven so long! Forgive them not but curse them, for they know what they do!" He tumbled forward, and Doremus knew that he would never hear that voice again.

In *La Voix littéraire* of Paris, the celebrated and genial professor of belles-lettres, Guillaume Semit, wrote with his accustomed sympathy:

> I do not pretend to any knowledge of politics, and probably what I saw on my fourth journey to the States United this summer of 1938 was mostly on the surface and cannot be considered a profound analysis of the effects of Corpoism, but I assure you that I have never before seen that nation so great, our young and gigantic cousin in the West, in such bounding health and good spirits. I leave it to my economic confrères to explain such dull phenomena as wage-scales, and tell only what I saw, which is that the innumerable parades and vast athletic conferences of the Minute Men and the lads and lassies of the Corpo Youth Movement exhibited such rosy, contented faces, such undeviating enthusiasm for their hero, the Chief, M. Windrip, that involuntarily I exclaimed, "Here is a whole nation dipped in the River of Youth."
>
> Everywhere in the country was such feverish re-

building of public edifices and apartment houses for the poor as has never hitherto been known. In Washington, my old colleague, M. le Secretary Macgoblin, was so good as to cry, in that virile yet cultivated manner of his which is so well known, "Our enemies maintain that our labor camps are virtual slavery. Come, my old one! You shall see for yourself." He conducted me by one of the marvelously speedy American automobiles to such a camp, near Washington, and having the workers assembled, he put to them frankly: "Are you low in the heart?" As one man they chorused, "No," with a spirit like our own brave soldiers on the ramparts of Verdun.

During the full hour we spent there, I was permitted to roam at will, asking such questions as I cared to, through the offices of the interpreter kindly furnished by His Excellency, M. le Dr. Macgoblin, and every worker whom I thus approached assured me that never has he been so well fed, so tenderly treated, and so assisted to find an almost poetic interest in his chosen work as in this labor camp—this scientific coöperation for the well-being of all.

With a certain temerity I ventured to demand of M. Macgoblin what truth was there in the reports so shamefully circulated (especially, alas, in our beloved France) that in the concentration camps the opponents of Corpoism are ill fed and harshly treated. M. Macgoblin explained to me that there are no such things as "concentration camps," if that term is to carry any penological significance. They are, actually, schools, in which adults who have unfortunately been misled by the glib prophets of that milk-and-water religion, "Liberalism," are reconditioned to comprehend the new day of authoritative economic control. In such camps, he assured me, there are actually no guards, but only patient teachers, and men who were once utterly uncomprehending of Corpoism, and therefore opposed to it, are now daily going forth as the most enthusiastic disciples of the Chief.

Alas that France and Great Britain should still be thrashing about in the slough of Parliamentarianism and so-called Democracy, daily sinking deeper into

> debt and paralysis of industry, because of the cowardice and traditionalism of our Liberal leaders, feeble and outmoded men who are afraid to plump for either Fascism or Communism; who dare not—or who are too power hungry—to cast off outmoded techniques, like the Germans, Americans, Italians, Turks, and other really courageous peoples, and place the sane and scientific control of the all-powerful Totalitarian State in the hands of Men of Resolution!

In October, John Pollikop, arrested on suspicion of having just possibly helped a refugee to escape, arrived in the Trianon camp, and the first words between him and his friend Karl Pascal were no inquiries about health, but a derisive interchange, as though they were continuing a conversation broken only half an hour before:

"Well, you old Bolshevik, I told you so! If you Communists had joined with me and Norman Thomas to back Frank Roosevelt, we wouldn't be here now!"

"Rats! Why, it's Thomas and Roosevelt that started Fascism! I ask you! Now shut up, John, and listen: What was the New Deal but pure Fascism? Whadthey do to the worker? Look here! No, wait now, listen——"

Doremus felt at home again, and comforted—though he did also feel that Foolish probably had more constructive economic wisdom than John Pollikop, Karl Pascal, Herbert Hoover, Buzz Windrip, Lee Sarason, and himself put together; or if not, Foolish had the sense to conceal his lack of wisdom by pretending that he could not speak English.

Shad Ledue, back in his hotel suite, reflected that he was getting a dirty deal. He had been responsible for sending more traitors to concentration camps than any other county commissioner in the province, yet he had not been promoted.

It was late; he was just back from a dinner given by Francis Tasbrough in honor of Provincial Commissioner Swan and a board consisting of Judge Philip Jessup, Director of Education Owen J. Peaseley, and Brigadier

Kippersly, who were investigating the ability of Vermont to pay more taxes.

Shad felt discontented. All those damned snobs trying to show off! Talking at dinner about this bum show in New York—this first Corpo revue, *Callin' Stalin,* written by Lee Sarason and Hector Macgoblin. How those nuts had put on the agony about "Corpo art," and "drama freed from Jewish suggestiveness" and "the pure line of Anglo-Saxon sculpture" and even, by God, about "Corporate physics"! Simply trying to show off! And they had paid no attention to Shad when he had told his funny story about the stuck-up preacher in Fort Beulah, one Falck, who had been so jealous because the M.M.'s drilled on Sunday morning instead of going to his gospel shop that he had tried to get his grandson to make up lies about the M.M.'s, and whom Shad had amusingly arrested right in his own church! Not paid one bit of attention to him, even though he had carefully read all through the Chief's *Zero Hour* so he could quote it, and though he had been careful to be refined in his table manners and to stick out his little finger when he drank from a glass.

He was lonely.

The fellows he had once best known, in pool room and barber shop, seemed frightened of him, now, and the dirty snobs like Tasbrough still ignored him.

He was lonely for Sissy Jessup.

Since her dad had been sent to Trianon, Shad didn't seem able to get her to come around to his rooms, even though he was the County Commissioner and she was nothing now but the busted daughter of a criminal.

And he was crazy about her. Why, he'd be almost willing to marry her, if he couldn't get her any other way! But when he had hinted as much—or almost as much—she had just laughed at him, the dirty little snob!

He had thought, when he was a hired man, that there was a lot more fun in being rich and famous. He didn't feel one bit different than he had then! Funny!

32

DR. LIONEL ADAMS, B.A. of Yale, Ph.D. of Chicago, Negro, had been a journalist, American consul in Africa and, at the time of Berzelius Windrip's election, professor of anthropology in Howard University. As with all his colleagues, his professorship was taken over by a most worthy and needy white man, whose training in anthropology had been as photographer on one expedition to Yucatan. In the dissension between the Booker Washington school of Negroes who counseled patience in the new subjection of the Negroes to slavery, and the radicals who demanded that they join the Communists and struggle for the economic freedom of all, white or black, Professor Adams took the mild, Fabian former position.

He went over the country preaching to his people that they must be "realistic," and make what future they could; not in some Utopian fantasy but on the inescapable basis of the ban against them.

Near Burlington, Vermont, there is a small colony of Negroes, truck farmers, gardeners, houseworkers, mostly descended from slaves who, before the Civil War, escaped to Canada by the "Underground Railway" conducted by such zealots as Truman Webb's grandfather, but who sufficiently loved the land of their forcible adoption to return to America after the war. From the colony had gone to the great cities young colored people who (before the Corpo emancipation) had been nurses, doctors, merchants, officials.

This colony Professor Adams addressed, bidding the young colored rebels to seek improvement within their own souls rather than in mere social superiority.

As he was in person unknown to this Burlington colony, Captain Oscar Ledue, nicknamed "Shad," was summoned to censor the lecture. He sat hulked down in a chair at the back of the hall. Aside from addresses by M.M. officers, and moral inspiration by his teachers in grammar school, it was the first lecture he had ever heard in his life, and he didn't think much of it. He was irritated that this stuck-up nigger didn't spiel like the characters of Octavus Roy Cohen, one of Shad's favorite authors, but had the nerve to try to sling English just as good as Shad himself. It was more irritating that the loud-mouthed pup should look so much like a bronze statue, and finally, it was simply more than a guy could stand that the big bum should be wearing a Tuxedo!

So when Adams, as he called himself, claimed that there were good poets and teachers and even doctors and engineers among the niggers, which was plainly an effort to incite folks to rebellion against the government, Shad signaled his squad and arrested Adams in the midst of his lecture, addressing him, "You God-damn dirty, ignorant, stinking nigger! I'm going to shut your big mouth for you, for keeps!"

Dr. Adams was taken to the Trianon concentration camp. Ensign Stoyt thought it would be a good joke on those fresh beggars (almost Communists, you might say) Jessup and Pascal to lodge the nigger right in the same cell with them. But they actually seemed to like Adams; talked to him as though he were white and educated! So Stoyt placed him in a solitary cell, where he could think over his crime in having bitten the hand that had fed him.

The greatest single shock that ever came to the Trianon camp was in November, 1938, when there appeared among them, as the newest prisoner, Shad Ledue.

It was he who was responsible for nearly half of them being there.

The prisoners whispered that he had been arrested on charges by Francis Tasbrough; officially, for having grafted on shopkeepers; unofficially, for having failed to share enough of the graft with Tasbrough. But such cloudy causes were less discussed than the question of how they would murder Shad now they had him safe.

* * *

All Minute Men who were under discipline, except only such Reds as Julian Falck, were privileged prisoners in the concentration camps; they were safeguarded against the common, i.e., criminal, i.e., political inmates; and most of them, once reformed, were returned to the M.M. ranks, with a greatly improved knowledge of how to flog malcontents. Shad was housed by himself in a single cell like a not-too-bad hall-bedroom, and every evening he was permitted to spend two hours in the officers' mess room. The scum could not get at him, because his exercise hour was at a time different from theirs.

Doremus begged the plotters against Shad to restrain themselves.

"Good Lord, Doremus, do you mean that after the sure-enough battles we've gone through you're still a bourgeois pacifist—that you still believe in the sanctity of a lump of hog meat like Ledue?" demanded Karl Pascal.

"Well, yes, I do—a little. I know that Shad came from a family of twelve underfed brats up on Mount Terror. Not much chance. But more important than that, I don't believe in individual assassination as an effective means of fighting despotism. The blood of the tyrants is the seed of the massacre and——"

"Are you taking a cue from me and quoting sound doctrine when it's the time for a little liquidation?" said Karl. "This one tyrant's going to lose a lot of blood!"

The Pascal whom Doremus had considered as, at his most violent, only a gas bag, looked at him with a stare in which all friendliness was frozen. Karl demanded of his cell mates, a different set now than at Doremus's arrival, "Shall we get rid of this typhus germ, Ledue?"

John Pollikop, Truman Webb, the surgeon, the carpenter, each of them nodded, slowly, without feeling.

At exercise hour, the discipline of the men marching out to the quadrangle was broken when one prisoner stumbled, with a cry, knocked over another man, and loudly apologized—just at the barred entrance of Shad Ledue's cell. The accident made a knot collect before the cell. Doremus, on the edge of it, saw Shad looking out, his wide face blank with fear.

Someone, somehow, had lighted and thrown into Shad's cell a large wad of waste, soaked with gasoline. It caught the thin wall board which divided Shad's cell from the next. The whole room looked presently like the fire box of a furnace. Shad was screaming, as he beat at his sleeves, his shoulders. Doremus remembered the scream of a horse clawed by wolves in the Far North.

When they got Shad out, he was dead. He had no face at all.

Captain Cowlick was deposed as superintendent of the camp, and vanished to the insignificance whence he had come. He was succeeded by Shad's friend, the belligerent Snake Tizra, now a battalion-leader. His first executive act was to have all the two hundred inmates drawn up in the quadrangle and to announce, "I'm not going to tell you guys anything about how I'm going to feed you or sleep you till I've finished putting the fear of God into every one of you murderers!"

There were offers of complete pardon for anyone who would betray the man who had thrown the burning waste into Shad's cell. It was followed by enthusiastic private offers from the prisoners that anyone who did thus tattle would not live to get out. So, as Doremus had guessed, they all suffered more than Shad's death had been worth—and to him, thinking of Sissy, thinking of Shad's testimony at Hanover, it had been worth a great deal; it had been very precious and lovely.

A court of special inquiry was convened, with Provincial Commissioner Effingham Swan himself presiding (he was very busy with all bad works; he used aëroplanes to be about them). Ten prisoners, one out of every twenty in the camp, were chosen by lot and shot summarily. Among them was Professor Victor Loveland, who, for all his rags and scars, was neatly academic to the last, with his eyeglasses and his slick tow-colored hair parted in the middle as he looked at the firing-squad.

Suspects like Julian Falck were beaten more often, kept longer in those cells in which one could not stand, sit, nor lie.

Then, for two weeks in December, all visitors and all letters were forbidden, and newly arrived prisoners were shut off by themselves; and the cell mates, like boys in a dormitory, would sit up till midnight in whispered discussion as to whether this was more vengeance by Snake Tizra, or whether something was happening in the World Outside that was too disturbing for the prisoners to know.

33

When the Falcks and John Pollikop had been arrested and had joined her father in prison, when such more timid rebels as Mungo Kitterick and Harry Kindermann had been scared away from New Underground activities, Mary Greenhill had to take over the control of the Fort Beulah cell, with only Sissy, Father Perefixe, Dr. Olmsted and his driver, and half-a-dozen other agents left, and control it she did, with angry devotion and not too much sense. All she could do was to help in the escape of refugees and to forward such minor anti-Corpo news items as she could discover, with Julian gone.

The demon that had grown within her ever since her husband had been executed now became a great tumor, and Mary was furious at inaction. Quite gravely she talked about assassinations—and long before the day of Mary Greenhill, daughter of Doremus, gold-armored tyrants in towers had trembled at the menace of young widows in villages among the dark hills.

She wanted, first, to kill Shad Ledue who (she did not know, but guessed) had probably done the actual shooting of her husband. But in this small place it might hurt her family even more than they had been hurt. She humorlessly suggested, before Shad was arrested and murdered, that it would be a pretty piece of espionage for Sissy to go and live with him. The once flippant Sissy, so thin and quiet ever since her Julian had been taken away, was certain that Mary had gone mad, and at night was terrified. . . . She remembered how Mary, in the days when she had been a crystal-hard, crystal-bright sportswoman, had with her riding-crop beaten a farmer who had tortured a dog.

Mary was fed-up with the cautiousness of Dr. Olmsted

and Father Perefixe, men who rather liked a vague state called Freedom but did not overmuch care for being lynched. She stormed at them. Call themselves men? Why didn't they go out and *do* something?

At home, she was irritated by her mother, who lamented hardly more about Doremus's jailing than she did about the beloved little tables that had been smashed during his arrest.

It was equally the blasts about the greatness of the new Provincial Commissioner, Effingham Swan, in the Corpo press and memoranda in the secret N.U. reports about his quick death verdicts against prisoners that made her decide to kill this dignitary. Even more than Shad (who had not yet been sent to Trianon), she blamed him for Fowler's fate. She thought it out quite calmly. That was the sort of thinking that the Corpos were encouraging among decent home-body women by their program for revitalizing national American pride.

Except with babies accompanying mothers, two visitors together were forbidden in the concentration camps. So, when Mary saw Doremus and, in another camp, Buck Titus, in early October, she could only murmur, in almost the same words to each of them, "Listen! When I leave you I'll hold up David—but, heavens, what a husky lump he's become!—at the gate, so you can see him. If anything should ever happen to me, if I should get sick or something, when you get out you'll take care of David—won't you, *won't* you?"

She was trying to be matter-of-fact, that they might not worry. She was not succeeding very well.

So she drew out, from the small fund which her father had established for her after Fowler's death, enough money for a couple of months, executed a power of attorney by which either her mother or her sister could draw the rest, casually kissed David and Emma and Sissy good-bye, and—chatty and gay as she took the train—went off to Albany, capital of the Northeastern Province. The story was that she needed a change and was going to stay near Albany with Fowler's married sister.

She did actually stay with her sister-in-law—long enough to get her bearings. Two days after her arrival, she went to the new Albany training-field of the Corpo Women's Flying Corps and enlisted for lessons in aviation and bombing.

When the inevitable war should come, when the government should decide whether it was Canada, Mexico, Russia, Cuba, Japan, or perhaps Staten Island that was "menacing her borders," and proceed to defend itself outwards, then the best women flyers of the Corps were to have Commissions in an official army auxiliary. The old-fashioned "rights" granted to women by the Liberals might (for their own sakes) be taken from them, but never had they had more right to die in battle.

While she was learning, she wrote to her family reassuringly—mostly postcards to David, bidding him mind whatever his grandmother said.

She lived in a lively boarding-house, filled with M.M. officers who knew all about and talked a little about the frequent inspection trips of Commissioner Swan, by aëroplane. She was complimented by quite a number of insulting proposals there.

She had driven a car ever since she had been fifteen; in Boston traffic, across the Quebec plains, on rocky hill roads in a blizzard; she had made repairs at midnight; and she had an accurate eye, nerves trained outdoors, and the resolute steadiness of a madman evading notice while he plots of death. After ten hours of instruction, by an M.M. aviator who thought the air was as good a place as any to make love in and who could never understand why Mary laughed at him, she made her first solo flight, with an admirable landing. The instructor said (among other things less apropos) that she had no fear; that the one thing she needed for mastery was a little fear.

Meantime she was an obedient student in classes in bombing, a branch of culture daily more propagated by the Corpos.

She was particularly interested in the Mills hand grenade. You pulled out the safety pin, holding the lever against the grenade with your fingers, and tossed. Five seconds after the lever was thus loosened, the grenade exploded and killed a lot of people. It had never been used from planes, but it might be worth trying, thought

Mary. M.M. officers told her that Swan, when a mob of steel-workers had been kicked out of a plant and started rioting, had taken command of the peace officers, and himself (they chuckled with admiration of his readiness) hurled such a grenade. It had killed two women and a baby.

Mary took her sixth solo flight on a November morning gray and quiet under snow clouds. She had never been very talkative with the ground crew but this morning she said it excited her to think she could leave the ground "like a reg'lar angel" and shoot up and hang around that unknown wilderness of clouds. She patted a strut of her machine, a high-wing Leonard monoplane with open cockpit, a new and very fast military machine, meant for both pursuit and quick jobs of bombing . . . quick jobs of slaughtering a few hundred troops in close formation.

At the field, as she had been informed he would, District Commissioner Effingham Swan was boarding his big official cabin plane for a flight presumably into New England. He was tall; a distingushed, military-looking, polo-suggesting dignitary in masterfully simple blue serge with just a light flying-helmet. A dozen yes-men buzzed about him—secretaries, bodyguards, a chauffeur, a couple of county commissioners, educational directors, labor directors—their hats in their hands, their smiles on their faces, their souls wriggling with gratitude to him for permitting them to exist. He snapped at them a good deal and bustled. As he mounted the steps to the cabin (Mary thought of "Casey Jones" and smiled), a messenger on a tremendous motorcycle blared up with the last telegrams. There seemed to be half a hundred of the yellow envelopes, Mary marveled. He tossed them to the secretary who was humbly creeping after him. The door of the viceregal coach closed on the Commissioner, the secretary, and two bodyguards lumpy with guns.

It was said that in his plane Swan had a desk that had belonged to Hitler, and before him to Marat.

To Mary, who had just lifted herself up into the cockpit, a mechanic cried, admiringly pointing after Swan's plane as it lurched forward, "Gee, what a grand guy that is—Boss Swan. I hear where he's flying down to Washington to chin with the Chief this morning—gee, think of it, with the Chief!"

"Wouldn't if be awful if somebody took a shot at Mr. Swan and the Chief? Might change all history," Mary shouted down.

"No chance of that! See those guards of his? Say, they could stand off a whole regiment—they could lick Walt Trowbridge and all the other Communists put together!"

"I guess that's so. Nothing but God shooting down from heaven could reach Mr. Swan."

"Ha, ha! That's good! But couple days ago I heard where a fellow was saying he figured out God had gone to sleep."

"Maybe it's time for Him to wake up!" said Mary, and raised her hand.

Her plane had a top of two hundred and eighty-five miles an hour—Swan's golden chariot had but two hundred and thirty. She was presently flying above and a little behind him. His cabin plane, which had seemed huge as the *Queen Mary* when she had looked up at its wing-spread on the ground, now seemed small as a white dove, wavering above the patchy linoleum that was the ground.

She drew from the pockets of her flying-jacket the three Mills hand grenades she had managed to steal from the school yesterday afternoon. She had not been able to get away with any heavier bomb. As she looked at them, for the first time she shuddered; she became a thing of warmer blood than a mere attachment to the plane, mechanical as the engine.

"Better get it over before I go ladylike," she sighed, and dived at the cabin plane.

No doubt her coming was unwelcome. Neither Death nor Mary Greenhill had made a formal engagement with Effingham Swan that morning; neither had telephoned, nor bargained with irritable secretaries, nor been neatly typed down on the great lord's schedule for his last day of life. In his dozen offices, in his marble home, in council hall and royal reviewing-stand, his most precious excellence was guarded with steel. He could not be approached by vulgarians like Mary Greenhill—save in the air, where emperor and vulgarian alike are upheld only by toy wings and by the grace of God.

Three times Mary maneuvered above his plane and dropped a grenade. Each time it missed. The cabin plane was descending, to land, and the guards were shooting up at her.

"Oh well!" she said, and dived bluntly at a bright metal wing.

In her last ten seconds she thought how much the wing looked like the zinc washboard which, as a girl, she had seen used by Mrs. Candy's predecessor—now what was her name?—Mamie or something. And she wished she had spent more time with David the last few months. And she noticed that the cabin plane seemed rather rushing up at her than she down at it.

The crash was appalling. It came just as she was patting her parachute and rising to leap out—too late. All she saw was an insane whirligig of smashed wings and huge engines that seemed to have been hurled up into her face.

34

Speaking of Julian before he was arrested, probably the New Underground headquarters in Montreal found no unusual value in his reports on M.M. grafting and cruelty and plans for apprehending N.U. agitators. Still, he had been able to warn four or five suspects to escape to Canada. He had had to assist in several floggings. He trembled so that the others laughed at him; and he made his blows suspiciously light.

He was set on being promoted to M.M. district headquarters in Hanover, and for it he studied typing and shorthand in his free time. He had a beautiful plan of going to that old family friend, Commissioner Francis Tasbrough, declaring that he wanted by his own noble qualities to make up to the divine government for his father's disloyalty, and of getting himself made Tasbrough's secretary. If he could just peep at Tasbrough's private files! Then there would be something juicy for Montreal!

Sissy and he discussed it exultantly in their leafy rendezvous. For a whole half hour she was able to forget her father and Buck in prison, and what seemed to her something like madness in Mary's increasing restlessness.

Just at the end of September she saw Julian suddenly arrested.

She was watching a review of M.M.'s on the Green. She might theoretically detest the blue M.M. uniform as being all that Walt Trowbridge (frequently) called it, "The old-time emblem of heroism and the battle for freedom, sacrilegiously turned by Windrip and his gang into a symbol of everything that is cruel, tyrannical, and false," but it did not dampen her pride in Julian to see him trim and shiny, and officially set apart as a squad-leader commanding his minor army of ten.

While the company stood at rest, County Commissioner Shad Ledue dashed up in a large car, sprang up, strode to Julian, bellowed, "This guy—this man is a traitor!" tore the M.M. steering-wheel from Julian's collar, struck him in the face, and turned him over to his private gunmen, while Julian's mates groaned, guffawed, hissed, and yelped.

She was not allowed to see Julian at Trianon. She could learn nothing save that he had not yet been executed.

When Mary was killed, and buried as a military heroine, Philip came bumbling up from his Massachusetts judicial circuit. He shook his head a great deal and pursed his lips.

"I swear," he said to Emma and Sissy—though actually he did nothing so wholesome and natural as to swear—"I swear I'm almost tempted to think, sometimes, that both Father and Mary have, or shall I say had, a touch of madness in them. There must be, terrible though it is to say it, but we must face facts in these troublous days, but I honestly think, sometimes, there must be a strain of madness somewhere in our family. Thank God I have escaped it!—if I have no other virtues, at least I am certainly sane! even if that may have caused the Pater to think I was nothing but mediocre! And of course you are entirely free from it, Mater. It's you that must watch yourself, Cecilia." (Sissy jumped slightly; not at anything so grateful as being called crazy by Philip, but at being called "Cecilia." After all, she admitted, that probably was her name.) "I hate to say it, Cecilia, but I've often thought you had a dangerous tendency to be thoughtless and selfish. Now Mater: as you know, I'm a very busy man, and I simply can't take a lot of time arguing and discussing, but it seems best to me, and I think I can almost say that it seems wise to Merilla, also, that, now that Mary has passed on, you should just close up this big house, or much better, try to rent it, as long as the poor Pater is—uh—as long as he's away. I don't pretend to have as big a place as this, but it's ever so much more modern, with gas furnace and up-to-date plumbing and all, and I have one of the first television sets in Rose Lane. I hope it won't hurt your feelings, and as you know, whatever people may say about me, certainly I'm one of the first to believe in keeping up the old traditions, just as poor, dear old Eff Swan was, but at the same time, it seems to me that the old home here is a little on the dreary and old-fashioned side—of course I never *could* persuade the Pater to bring it up to date, but—— Anyway, I want Davy and you to come live with us in Worcester, immediately. As for you, Sissy, you will of course understand that you are entirely welcome, but perhaps you would prefer to do something livelier, such as joining the Women's Corpo Auxiliary——"

He was, Sissy raged, so damned *kind* to everybody! She couldn't even stir herself to insult him much. She earnestly desired to, when she found that he had brought David an M.M. uniform, and when David put it on and paraded about shouting, like most of the boys he played with, "Hail Windrip!"

She telephoned to Lorinda Pike at Beecher Falls and was able to tell Philip that she was going to help Lorinda in the tea room. Emma and David went off to Worcester—at the last moment, at the station, Emma decided to be pretty teary about it, though David begged her to remember that they had Uncle Philip's word for it that Worcester was just the same as Boston, London, Hollywood, and a Wild West Ranch put together. Sissy stayed to get the house rented. Mrs. Candy, who was going to open her bakery now and who never did inform the impractical Sissy whether or no she was being paid for these last weeks, made for Sissy all the foreign dishes that only Sissy and Doremus cared for, and they not uncheerfully dined together, in the kitchen.

So it was Shad's time to swoop.

He came blusteringly calling on her, in November. Never had she hated him quite so much, yet never so much feared him, because of what he might do to her father and Julian and Buck and the others in concentration camps.

He grunted, "Well, your boy-friend Jule, that thought

he was so cute, the poor heel, we got all the dope on his double-crossing us, all right! *He'll* never bother you again!"

"He's not so bad. Let's forget him. . . . Shall I play you something on the piano?"

"Sure. Shoot. I always did like high-class music," said the refined Commissioner, lolling on a couch, putting his heels up on a damask chair, in the room where once he had cleaned the fireplace. If it was his serious purpose to discourage Sissy in regard to that anti-Corpo institution, the Dictatorship of the Proletariat, he was succeeding even better than Judge Philip Jessup. Sir William Gilbert would have said of Shad that he was so very, very prolet-ari-an.

She had played for but five minutes when he forgot that he was now refined, and bawled, "Oh, cut out the highbrow stuff and come on and sit down!"

She stayed on the piano stool. Just what would she do if Shad became violent? There was no Julian to appear melodramatically at the nickoftime and rescue her. Then she remembered Mrs. Candy, in the kitchen, and was content.

"What the heck you snickerin' at?" said Shad.

"Oh—oh I was just thinking about that story you told me about how Mr. Falck bleated when you arrested him!"

"Yeh, that was comical. Old Reverend certainly blatted like a goat!"

(Could she kill him? Would it be wise to kill him? Had Mary meant to kill Swan? Would They be harder on Julian and her father if she killed Shad? Incidentally, did it hurt much to get hanged?)

He was yawning, "Well, Sis, ole kid, how about you and me taking a little trip to New York in a couple weeks? See some high life. I'll get you the best soot in the best hotel in town, and we'll take in some shows—I hear this *Callin' Stalin* is a hot number—real Corpo art—and I'll buy you some honest-to-God champagne wine! And then if we find we like each other enough, I'm willing for us, if you are, to get hitched!"

"But, Shad! We could never live on your salary. I

mean—I mean of course the Corpos ought to pay you better—mean, even better than they do."

"Listen, baby! I ain't going to have to get along on any miserable county commissioner's salary the rest of my life! Believe me, I'm going to be a millionaire before very long!"

Then he told her: told her precisely the sort of discreditable secret for which she had so long fished in vain. Perhaps it was because he was sober. Shad, when drunk, reversed all the rules and became more peasant-like and cautious with each drink.

He had a plan. That plan was as brutal and as infeasible as any plan of Shad Ledue for making large money would be. Its essence was that he should avoid manual labor and should make as many persons miserable as possible. It was like his plan, when he was still a hired man, to become wealthy by breeding dogs—first stealing the dogs and, preferably, the kennels.

As County Commissioner he had not merely, as was the Corpo custom, been bribed by the shopkeepers and professional men for protection against the M.M.'s. He had actually gone into partnership with them, promising them larger M.M. orders, and, he boasted, he had secret contracts with these merchants all written down and signed and tucked away in his office safe.

Sissy got rid of him that evening by being difficult, while letting him assume that the conquest of her would not take more than three or four more days. She cried furiously after he had gone—in the comforting presence of Mrs. Candy, who first put away a butcher knife with which, Sissy suspected, she had been standing ready all evening.

Next morning Sissy drove to Hanover and shamelessly tattled to Francis Tasbrough about the interesting documents Shad had in his safe. She did not ever see Shad Ledue again.

She was very sick about his being killed. She was very sick about all killing. She found no heroism but only barbaric bestiality in having to kill so that one might so far live as to be halfway honest and kind and secure. But she knew that she would be willing to do it again.

The Jessup house was magniloquently rented by that noble Roman, that political belch, Ex-Governor Isham Hubbard, who, being tired of again trying to make a living by peddling real estate and criminal law, was pleased to accept the appointment as successor to Shad Ledue.

Sissy hastened to Beecher Falls and to Lorinda Pike.

Father Perefixe took charge of the N.U. cell, merely saying, as he had said daily since Buzz Windrip had been inaugurated, that he was fed-up with the whole business and was immediately going back to Canada. In fact, on his desk he had a Canadian time-table.

It was now two years old.

Sissy was in too snappish a state to stand being mothered, being fattened and sobbed over and brightly sent to bed. Mrs. Candy had done only too much of that. And Philip had given her all the parental advice she could endure for a while. It was a relief when Lorinda received her as an adult, as one too sensible to insult by pity—received her, in fact, with as much respect as if she were an enemy and not a friend.

After dinner, in Lorinda's new tea room, in an aged house which was now empty of guests for the winter except for the constant infestation of whimpering refugees, Lorinda, knitting, made her first mention of the dead Mary.

"I suppose your sister did intend to kill Swan, eh?"

"I don't know. The Corpos didn't seem to think so. They gave her a big military funeral."

"Well, of course, they don't much care to have assassinations talked about and maybe sort of become a general habit. I agree with your father. I think that, in many cases, assassinations are really rather unfortunate—a mistake in tactics. No. Not good. Oh, by the way, Sissy, I think I'm going to get your father out of concentration camp."

"What?"

Lorinda had none of the matrimonial moans of Emma; she was as business-like as ordering eggs.

"Yes. I tried everything. I went to see Tasbrough, and that educational fellow, Peaseley. Nothing doing. They want to keep Doremus in. But that rat, Aras Dilley, is at Trianon as guard now. I'm bribing him to help your father escape. We'll have the man here for Christmas, only kind of late, and sneak him into Canada."

"Oh!" said Sissy.

A few days afterward, reading a coded New Underground telegram which apparently dealt with the delivery of furniture, Lorinda shrieked, "Sissy! All you-know-what has busted loose! In Washington! Lee Sarason has deposed Buzz Windrip and grabbed the dictatorship!"

"Oh!" said Sissy.

35

In his two years of dictatorship, Berzelius Windrip daily became more a miser of power. He continued to tell himself that his main ambition was to make all citizens healthy, in purse and mind, and that if he was brutal it was only toward fools and reactionaries who wanted the old clumsy systems. But after eighteen months of Presidency he was angry that Mexico and Canada and South America (obviously his own property, by manifest destiny) should curtly answer his curt diplomatic notes and show no helpfulness about becoming part of his inevitable empire.

And daily he wanted louder, more convincing Yeses from everybody about him. How could he carry on his heart-breaking labor if nobody ever encouraged him? he demanded. Anyone, from Sarason to inter-office messenger, who did not play valet to his ego he suspected of plotting against him. He constantly increased his bodyguard, and as constantly distrusted all his guards and discharged them, and once took a shot at a couple of them, so that in all the world he had no companion save his old aide Lee Sarason, and perhaps Hector Macgoblin, to whom he could talk easily.

He felt lonely in the hours when he wanted to shuck off the duties of despotism along with his shoes and his fine new coat. He no longer went out racketing. His cabinet begged him not to clown in barrooms and lodge entertainments; it was not dignified, and it was dangerous to be too near to strangers.

So he played poker with his bodyguard, late at night, and at such times drank too much, and he cursed them and glared with bulging eyes whenever he lost, which, for all the good-will of his guards about letting him win, had to be often, because he pinched their salaries badly and locked up the spoons. He had become as unbouncing and unbuzzing a Buzz as might be, and he did not know it.

All the while he loved the People just as much as he feared and detested Persons, and he planned to do something historic. Certainly! He would give each family that five thousand dollars a year just as soon now as he could arrange it.

And Lee Sarason, forever making his careful lists, as patient at his desk as he was pleasure-hungry on the couch at midnight parties, was beguiling officials to consider him their real lord and the master of Corpoism. He kept his promises to them, while Windrip always forgot. His office door became the door of ambition. In Washington, the reporters privily spoke of this assistant secretary and that general as "Sarason men." His clique was not a government within a government; it was the government itself, minus the megaphones. He had the Secretary of Corporations (a former vice-president of the American Federation of Labor) coming to him secretly every evening, to report on labor politics and in especial on such proletarian leaders as were dissatisfied with Windrip as Chief—i.e., with their own share in the swag. He had from the Secretary of the Treasury (though this functionary, one Webster Skittle, was not a lieutenant of Sarason but merely friendly) confidential reports on the affairs of those large employers who, since under Corpoism it was usually possible for a millionaire to persuade the judges in the labor-arbitration courts to look at things reasonably, rejoiced that with strikes outlawed and employers regarded as state officials, they would now be in secure power forever.

Sarason knew the quiet ways in which these reinforced industrial barons used arrests by the M.M.'s to get rid of "trouble-makers," particularly of Jewish radicals—a Jewish radical being a Jew with nobody working for him. (Some of the barons were themselves Jews; it is not to be expected that race-loyalty should be carried so insanely far as to weaken the pocketbook.)

The allegiance of all such Negroes as had the sense to

be content with safety and good pay instead of ridiculous yearnings for personal integrity Sarason got by being photographed shaking hands with the celebrated Negro Fundamentalist clergyman, the Reverend Dr. Alexander Nibbs, and through the highly publicized Sarason Prizes for the Negroes with the largest families, the fastest time in floor-scrubbing, and the longest periods of work without taking a vacation.

"No danger of our good friends, the Negroes, turning Red when they're encouraged like that," Sarason announced to the newspapers.

It was a satisfaction to Sarason that in Germany, all military bands were now playing his national song, "Buzz and Buzz" along with the Horst Wessel hymn, for, though he had not exactly written the music as well as the words, the music was now being attributed to him abroad.

As a bank clerk might, quite rationally, worry equally over the whereabouts of a hundred million dollars' worth of the bank's bonds, and of ten cents of his own lunch money, so Buzz Windrip worried equally over the welfare—that is, the obedience to himself—of a hundred and thirty-odd million American citizens and the small matter of the moods of Lee Sarason, whose approval of him was the one real fame. (His wife Windrip did not see oftener than once a week, and anyway, what that rustic wench thought was unimportant.)

The diabolic Hector Macgoblin frightened him; Secretary of War Luthorne and Vice-President Perley Beecroft he liked well enough, but they bored him; they smacked too much of his own small-town boyhood, to escape which he was willing to take the responsibilities of a nation. It was the incalculable Lee Sarason on whom he depended, and the Lee with whom he had gone fishing and boozing and once, even, murdering, who had seemed his own self made more sure and articulate, had thoughts now which he could not penetrate. Lee's smile was a veil, not a revelation.

It was to discipline Lee, with the hope of bringing him back, that when Buzz replaced the amiable but clumsy Colonel Luthorne as Secretary of War by Colonel

Dewey Haik, Commissioner of the Northeastern Province (Buzz's characteristic comment was that Luthorne was not "pulling his weight"), he also gave to Haik the position of High Marshal of the M.M.'s, which Lee had held along with a dozen other offices. From Lee he expected an explosion, then repentance and a new friendship. But Lee only said, "Very well, if you wish," and said it coldly.

Just how *could* he get Lee to be a good boy and come play with him again? wistfully wondered the man who now and then planned to be emperor of the world.

He gave Lee a thousand-dollar television set. Even more coldly did Lee thank him, and never spoke afterward of how well he might be receiving the still shaky television broadcasts on his beautiful new set.

As Dewey Haik took hold, doubling efficiency in both the regular army and the Minute Men (he was a demon for all-night practice marches in heavy order, and the files could not complain, because he set the example), Buzz began to wonder whether Haik might not be his new confidant. . . . He really would hate to throw Lee into prison, but still, Lee was so thoughtless about hurting his feelings, when he'd gone and done so much for him and all!

Buzz was confused. He was the more confused when Perley Beecroft came in and briefly said that he was sick of all this bloodshed and was going home to the farm, and as for his lofty Vice-Presidential office, Buzz knew what he could do with it.

Were these vast national dissensions no different from squabbles in his father's drugstore? fretted Buzz. He couldn't very well have Beecroft shot: it might cause criticism. But it was indecent, it was sacrilegious to annoy an emperor, and in his irritation he had an ex-Senator and twelve workmen who were in concentration camps taken out and shot on the charge that they had told irreverent stories about him.

Secretary of State Sarason was saying good-night to President Windrip in the hotel suite where Windrip really lived.

No newspaper had dared mention it, but Buzz was

both bothered by the stateliness of the White House and frightened by the number of Reds and cranks and anti-Corpos who, with the most commendable patience and ingenuity, tried to sneak into that historic mansion and murder him. Buzz merely left his wife there, for show, and, except at great receptions, never entered any part of the White House save the office annex.

He liked this hotel suite; he was a sensible man, who preferred straight bourbon, codfish cakes, and deep leather chairs to Burgundy, trout *bleu,* and Louis Quinze. In this twelve-room apartment, occupying the entire tenth floor of a small unnotorious hotel, he had for himself only a plain bedroom, a huge living room which looked like a combination of office and hotel lobby, a large liquor closet, another closet with thirty-seven suits of clothes, and a bathroom with jars and jars of the pine-flavored bath salts which were his only cosmetic luxury. Buzz might come home in a suit dazzling as a horse blanket, one considered in Alfalfa Center a triumph of London tailoring, but, once safe, he liked to put on his red morocco slippers that were down at the heel and display his red suspenders and baby-blue sleeve garters. To feel correct in those decorations, he preferred the hotel atmosphere that, for so many years before he had ever seen the White House, had been as familiar to him as his ancestral corn cribs and Main Streets.

The other ten rooms of the suite, entirely shutting his own off from the corridors and elevators, were filled night and day with guards. To get through to Buzz in this intimate place of his own was very much like visiting a police station for the purpose of seeing a homicidal prisoner.

"Haik seems to me to be doing a fine job in the War Department, Lee," said the President. "Of course you know if you ever want the job of High Marshal back——"

"I'm quite satisfied," said the great Secretary of State. "What do you think of having Colonel Luthorne back to help Haik out? He's pretty good on fool details."

Sarason looked as nearly embarrassed as the self-satisfied Lee Sarason ever could look.

"Why, uh—I supposed you knew it. Luthorne was liquidated in the purge ten days ago."

"Good God! Luthorne killed? Why didn't I know it?"

"It was thought better to keep it quiet. He was a pretty popular man. But dangerous. Always talking about Abraham Lincoln!"

"So I just never know anything about what's going on! Why, even the newspaper clippings are predigested, by God, before I see 'em!"

"It's thought better not to bother you with minor details, boss. You know that! Of course, if you feel I haven't organized your staff correctly——"

"Aw now, don't fly off the handle, Lee! I just meant—— Of course I know how hard you've tried to protect me so I could give all my brains to the higher problems of State. But Luthorne—— I kind of liked him. He always had quite a funny line when we played poker." Buzz Windrip felt lonely, as once a certain Shad Ledue had felt, in a hotel suite that differed from Buzz's only in being smaller. To forget it he bawled, very brightly, "Lee, do you ever wonder what'll happen in the future?"

"Why, I think you and I may have mentioned it."

"But golly, just think of what might happen in the future, Lee! Think of it! Why, we may be able to pull off a North American kingdom!" Buzz half meant it seriously—or perhaps quarter meant it. "How'd you like to be Duke of Georgia—or Grand Duke, or whatever they call a Grand Exalted Ruler of the Elks in this peerage business? And then how about an Empire of North and South America after that? I might make you a king under me, then—say something like King of Mexico. How-juh like that?"

"Be very amusing," said Lee mechanically—as Lee always did say the same thing mechanically whenever Buzz repeated this same nonsense.

"But you got to stick by me and not forget all I've done for you, Lee, don't forget that."

"I never forget anything! . . . By the way, we ought

to liquidate, or at least imprison, Perley Beecroft, too. He's still technically Vice-President of the United States, and if the lousy traitor managed some skullduggery so as to get you killed or deposed, he might be regarded by some narrow-minded literalists as President!"

"No, no, no! He's my friend, no matter what he says about me . . . the dirty dog!" wailed Buzz.

"All right. You're the boss. G'night," said Lee, and returned from this plumber's dream of paradise to his own gold-and-black and apricot-silk bower in Georgetown, which he shared with several handsome young M.M. officers. They were savage soldiers, yet apt at music and at poetry. With them, he was not in the least passionless, as he seemed now to Buzz Windrip. He was either angry with his young friends, and then he whipped them, or he was in a paroxysm of apology to them, and caressed their wounds. Newspapermen who had once seemed to be his friends said that he had traded the green eyeshade for a wreath of violets.

At cabinet meeting, late in 1938, Secretary of State Sarason revealed to the heads of the government disturbing news. Vice-President Beecroft—and had he not told them the man should have been shot?—had fled to Canada, renounced Corpoism, and joined Walt Trowbridge in plotting. There were bubbles from an almost boiling rebellion in the Middle West and Northwest, especially in Minnesota and the Dakotas, where agitators, some of them formerly of political influence, were demanding that their states secede from the Corpo Union and form a coöperative (indeed almost Socialistic) commonwealth of their own.

"Rats! Just a lot of irresponsible wind bags!" jeered President Windrip. "Why! I thought you were supposed to be the camera-eyed gink that kept up on everything that goes on, Lee! You forget that I myself, personally, made a special radio address to that particular section of the country last week! And I got a wonderful reaction. The Middle Westerners are absolutely loyal to me. They appreciate what I've been trying to do!"

Not answering him at all, Sarason demanded that, in

order to bring and hold all elements in the country together by that useful Patriotism which always appears upon threat of an outside attack, the government immediately arrange to be insulted and menaced in a well-planned series of deplorable "incidents" on the Mexican border, and declare war on Mexico as soon as America showed that it was getting hot and patriotic enough.

Secretary of the Treasury Skittle and Attorney General Porkwood shook their heads, but Secretary of War Haik and Secretary of Education Macgoblin agreed with Sarason high-mindedly. Once, pointed out the learned Macgoblin, governments had merely let themselves slide into a war, thanking Providence for having provided a conflict as a febrifuge against internal discontent, but of course, in this age of deliberate, planned propaganda, a really modern government like theirs must figure out what brand of war they had to sell and plan the selling-campaign consciously. Now, as for him, he would be willing to leave the whole set-up to the advertising genius of Brother Sarason.

"No, no, no!" cried Windrip. "We're not ready for a war! Of course, we'll take Mexico some day. It's our destiny to control it and Christianize it. But I'm scared that your darn scheme might work just opposite to what you say. You put arms into the hands of too many irresponsible folks, and they might use 'em and turn against you and start a revolution and throw the whole dern gang of us out! No, no! I've often wondered if the whole Minute Men business, with their arms and training, may not be a mistake. That was your idea, Lee, not mine!"

Sarason spoke evenly: "My dear Buzz, one day you thank me for originating that 'great crusade of citizen soldiers defending their homes'—as you love to call it on the radio—and the next day you almost ruin your clothes, you're so scared of them. Make up your mind one way or the other!"

Sarason walked out of the room, not bowing.

Windrip complained, "I'm not going to stand for Lee's talking to me like that! Why, the dirty double-crosser, I made him! One of these days, he'll find a new secretary of state around this joint! I s'pose he thinks jobs like that grow on every tree! Maybe he'd like to be a bank president or something—I mean, maybe he'd like to be Emperor of England!"

President Windrip, in his hotel bedroom, was awakened late at night by the voice of a guard in the outer room: "Yuh, sure, let him pass—he's the Secretary of State." Nervously the President clicked on his bedside lamp. . . . He had needed it lately, to read himself to sleep.

In that limited glow he saw Lee Sarason, Dewey Haik, and Dr. Hector Macgoblin march to the side of his bed. Lee's thin sharp face was like flour. His deep-buried eyes were those of a sleepwalker. His skinny right hand held a bowie knife which, as his hand deliberately rose, was lost in the dimness. Windrip swiftly thought: Sure would be hard to know where to buy a dagger, in Washington; and Windrip thought: All this is the doggonedest foolishness—just like a movie or one of these old history books when you were a kid; and Windrip thought, all in that same flash: Good God, I'm going to be killed!

He cried out, "Lee! You couldn't do *that* to me!"

Lee grunted, like one who has detected a bad smell.

Then the Berzelius Windrip who could, incredibly, become President really awoke: "Lee! Do you remember the time when your old mother was so sick, and I gave you my last cent and loaned you my flivver so you could go see her, and I hitch-hiked to my next meeting? Lee!"

"Hell. I suppose so. General."

"Yes?" answered Dewey Haik, not very pleasantly.

"I think we'll stick him on a destroyer or something and let him sneak off to France or England. . . . The lousy coward seems afraid to die. . . . Of course, we'll kill him if he ever does dare to come back to the States. Take him out and phone the Secretary of the Navy for a boat and get him on it, will you?"

"Very well, sir," said Haik, even less pleasantly.

It had been easy. The troops, who obeyed Haik, as Secretary of War, had occupied all of Washington.

Ten days later Buzz Windrip was landed in Havre and went sighingly to Paris. It was his first view of Europe except for one twenty-one-day Cook's Tour. He was profoundly homesick for Chesterfield cigarettes, flapjacks, Moon Mullins, and the sound of some real human being saying "Yuh, what's bitin' you?" instead of this perpetual sappy "oui?"

In Paris he remained, though he became the sort of minor hero of tragedy, like the ex-King of Greece, Kerensky, the Russian Grand Dukes, Jimmy Walker, and a few ex-presidents from South America and Cuba, who is delighted to accept invitations to drawing rooms where the champagne is good enough and one may have a chance of finding people, now and then, who will listen to one's story and say "sir."

At that, though, Buzz chuckled, he had kinda put it over on those crooks, for during his two sweet years of despotism he had sent four million dollars abroad, to secret, safe accounts. And so Buzz Windrip passed into wabbly paragraphs in recollections by ex-diplomatic gentlemen with monocles. In what remained of Ex-President Windrip's life, everything was *ex.* He was even so far forgotten that only four or five American students tried to shoot him.

The more dulcetly they had once advised and flattered Buzz, the more ardently did most of his former followers, Macgoblin and Senator Porkwood and Dr. Almeric Trout and the rest, turn in loud allegiance to the new President, the Hon. Lee Sarason.

He issued a proclamation that he had discovered that Windrip had been embezzling the people's money and plotting with Mexico to avoid war with that guilty country; and that he, Sarason, in quite alarming grief and reluctance, since he more than anyone else had been deceived by his supposed friend, Windrip, had yielded to the urging of the Cabinet and taken over the Presidency, instead of Vice-President Beecroft, the exiled traitor.

President Sarason immediately began appointing the fancier of his young officer friends to the most responsible offices in State and army. It amused him, seemingly, to shock people by making a pink-cheeked, moist-eyed boy of twenty-five Commissioner of the Federal District, which included Washington and Maryland. Was he not supreme, was he not semi-divine, like a Roman emperor? Could he not defy all the muddy mob that he (once a Socialist) had, for its weak shiftlessness, come to despise?

"Would that the American people had just one neck!" he plagiarized, among his laughing boys.

In the decorous White House of Coolidge and Harrison and Rutherford Birchard Hayes he had orgies (an old name for "parties") with weaving limbs and garlands and wine in pretty fair imitations of Roman beakers.

It was hard for imprisoned men like Doremus Jessup to believe it, but there were some tens of thousands of Corpos, in the M.M.'s, in civil service, in the army, and just in private ways, to whom Sarason's flippant régime was tragic.

They were the Idealists of Corpoism, and there were plenty of them, along with the bullies and swindlers; they were the men and women who, in 1935 and 1936, had turned to Windrip & Co., not as perfect, but as the most probable saviors of the country from, on one hand, domination by Moscow and, on the other hand, the slack indolence, the lack of decent pride of half the American youth, whose world (these idealists asserted) was composed of shiftless distaste for work and refusal to learn anything thoroughly, of blatting dance music on the radio, maniac automobiles, slobbering sexuality, the humor and art of comic strips—of a slave psychology which was making America a land for sterner men to loot.

General Emmanuel Coon was one of the Corpo Idealists.

Such men did not condone the murders under the Corpo régime. But they insisted, "This is a revolution, and after all, when in all history has there been a revolution with so little bloodshed?"

They were aroused by the pageantry of Corpoism: enormous demonstrations, with the red-and-black flags a flaunting magnificence like storm clouds. They were proud of new Corpo roads, hospitals, television stations, aëroplane lines; they were touched by processions of the Corpo Youth, whose faces were exalted with pride in the myths of Corpo heroism and clean Spartan strength and the semi-divinity of the all-protecting Father, President Windrip. They believed, they made themselves believe, that in Windrip had come alive again the virtues of Andy Jackson and Farragut and Jeb Stuart, in place of the mob cheapness of the professional athletes who had been the only heroes of 1935.

They planned, these idealists, to correct, as quickly as might be, the errors of brutality and crookedness among officials. They saw arising a Corpo art, a Corpo learning, profound and real, divested of the traditional snobbishness of the old-time universities, valiant with youth, and only the more beautiful in that it was "useful." They were convinced that Corpoism was Communism cleansed of foreign domination and the violence and indignity of mob dictatorship; Monarchism with the chosen hero of the people for monarch; Fascism without grasping and selfish leaders; freedom with order and discipline; Traditional America without its waste and provincial cockiness.

Like all religious zealots, they had blessed capacity for blindness, and they were presently convinced that (since the only newspapers they ever read certainly said nothing about it) there were no more of blood-smeared cruelties in court and concentration camp; no restrictions of speech or thought. They believed that they never criticized the Corpo régime not because they were censored, but because "that sort of thing was, like obscenity, such awfully bad form."

And these idealists were as shocked and bewildered by Sarason's coup d'état against Windrip as was Mr. Berzelius Windrip himself.

The grim Secretary of War, Haik, scolded at President Sarason for his influence on the nation, particularly on the troops. Lee laughed at him, but once he was sufficiently flattered by Haik's tribute to his artistic powers to write a poem for him. It was a poem which was later to be sung by millions; it was, in fact, the most popular of the soldiers' ballads which were to spring automatically from anonymous soldier bards during the war between the United States and Mexico. Only, being as pious a believer in Modern Advertising as Sarason himself, the efficient Haik wanted to encourage the spontaneous generation of these patriotic folk ballads by providing the automatic springing and the anonymous bard. He had as much foresight, as much "prophetic engineering," as a motorcar manufacturer.

Sarason was as eager for war with Mexico (or Ethiopia or Siam or Greenland or any other country that would provide his pet young painters with a chance to portray Sarason being heroic amid curious vegetation) as Haik; not only to give malcontents something outside the country to be cross about, but also to give himself a chance to be picturesque. He answered Haik's request by writing a rollicking military chorus at a time while the country was still theoretically entirely friendly with Mexico. It went to the tune of "Mademoiselle from Armentières"—or "Armenteers." If the Spanish in it was a little shaky, still, millions were later to understand that "Habla oo?" stood for "Habla usted?" signifying "Parlez-vous?" It ran thus, as it came from Sarason's purple but smoking typewriter:

Señorita from Guadalupe,
Qui usted?
Señorita go roll your hoop,
Or come to bed!
Señorita from Guadalupe
If Padre sees us we're in the soup,
Hinky, dinky, habla oo?

Señorita from Monterey,
Savvy Yank?
Señorita what's that you say?
You're Swede, Ay tank!
But Señorita from Monterey,
You won't hablár when we hit the hay,
Hinky, dinky, habla oo?

Señorita from Mazatlan,
Once we've met,
You'll smile all over your khaki pan,
You won't forget!
For days you'll holler, "Oh, what a man!"

And you'll never marry a Mexican.
Hinky, dinky, habla oo?

If at times President Sarason seemed flippant, he was not at all so during his part in the scientific preparation for war which consisted in rehearsing M.M. choruses in trolling out this ditty with well-trained spontaneity.

His friend Hector Macgoblin, now Secretary of State, told Sarason that this manly chorus was one of his greatest creations. Macgoblin, though personally he did not join in Sarason's somewhat unusual midnight diversions, was amused by them, and he often told Sarason that he was the only original creative genius among this whole bunch of stuffed shirts, including Haik.

"You want to watch that cuss Haik, Lee," said Macgoblin. "He's ambitious, he's a gorilla, and he's a pious Puritan, and that's a triple combination I'm scared of. The troops like him."

"Rats! He has no attraction for them. He's just an accurate military bookkeeper," said Sarason.

That night he had a party at which, for a novelty, rather shocking to his intimates, he actually had girls present, performing certain curious dances. The next morning Haik rebuked him, and—Sarason had a hangover—was stormed at. That night, just a month after Sarason had usurped the Presidency, Haik struck.

There was no melodramatic dagger-and-uplifted-arm business about it, this time—though Haik did traditionally come late, for all Fascists, like all drunkards, seem to function most vigorously at night. Haik marched into the White House with his picked storm troops, found President Sarason in violet silk pajamas among his friends, shot Sarason and most of his companions dead, and proclaimed himself President.

Hector Macgoblin fled by aëroplane to Cuba, then on. When last seen, he was living high up in the mountains of Haiti, wearing only a singlet, dirty white-drill trousers, grass sandals, and a long tan beard; very healthy and happy, occupying a one-room hut with a lovely native girl, practicing modern medicine and studying ancient voodoo.

* * *

When Dewey Haik became President, then America really did begin to suffer a little, and to long for the good old democratic, liberal days of Windrip.

Windrip and Sarason had not minded mirth and dancing in the street so long as they could be suitably taxed. Haik disliked such things on principle. Except, perhaps, that he was an atheist in theology, he was a strict orthodox Christian. He was the first to tell the populace that they were not going to get any five thousand dollars a year but, instead, "reap the profits of Discipline and of the Scientific Totalitarian State not in mere paper figures but in vast dividends of Pride, Patriotism, and Power." He kicked out of the army all officers who could not endure marching and going thirsty; and out of the civil branch all commissioners—including one Francis Tasbrough—who had garnered riches too easily and too obviously.

He treated the entire nation like a well-run plantation, on which the slaves were better fed than formerly, less often cheated by their overseers, and kept so busy that they had time only for work and for sleep, and thus fell rarely into the debilitating vices of laughter, song (except war songs against Mexico), complaint, or thinking. Under Haik there were less floggings in M.M. posts and in concentration camps, for by his direction officers were not to waste time in the sport of beating persons, men, women, or children, who asserted that they didn't care to be slaves on even the best plantation, but just to shoot them out of hand.

Haik made such use of the clergy—Protestant, Catholic, Jewish, and Liberal-Agnostic—as Windrip and Sarason never had. While there were plenty of ministers who, like Mr. Falck and Father Stephen Perefixe, like Cardinal Faulhaber and Pastor Niemoeller in Germany, considered it some part of Christian duty to resent the enslavement and torture of their appointed flocks, there were also plenty of reverend celebrities, particularly large-city pastors whose sermons were reported in the newspapers every Monday morning, to whom Corpoism had given a chance to be noisily and lucratively patriotic. These were the chaplains-at-heart, who, if there was no war in which they could humbly help to purify and comfort the poor brave boys who were fighting, were glad to help provide such a war.

These more practical shepherds, since like doctors and lawyers they were able to steal secrets out of the heart, became valued spies during the difficult months after February, 1939, when Haik was working up war with Mexico. (Canada? Japan? Russia? They would come later.) For even with an army of slaves, it was necessary to persuade them that they were freemen and fighters for the principle of freedom, or otherwise the scoundrels might cross over and join the enemy!

So reigned the good king Haik, and if there was anyone in all the land who was discontented, you never heard him speak—not twice.

And in the White House, where under Sarason shameless youths had danced, under the new reign of righteousness and the blackjack, Mrs. Haik, a lady with eyeglasses and a smile of resolute cordiality, gave to the W.C.T.U., the Y.W.C.A., and the Ladies' League against Red Radicalism, and their inherently incidental husbands, a magnified and hand-colored Washington version of just such parties as she had once given in the Haik bungalow in Eglantine, Oregon.

36

THE BAN ON INFORMATION at the Trianon camp had been raised; Mrs. Candy had come calling on Doremus—complete with cocoanut layer cake—and he had heard of Mary's death, the departure of Emma and Sissy, the end of Windrip and Sarason. And none of it seemed in the least real—not half so real and, except for the fact that he would never see Mary again, not half so important as the increasing number of lice and rats in their cell.

During the ban, they had celebrated Christmas by laughing, not very cheerfully, at the Christmas tree Karl Pascal had contrived out of a spruce bough and tinfoil from cigarette packages. They had hummed "Stille Nacht" softly in the darkness, and Doremus had thought of all their comrades in political prisons in America, Europe, Japan, India.

But Karl, apparently, thought of comrades only if they were saved, baptized Communists. And, forced together as they were in a cell, the growing bitterness and orthodox piety of Karl became one of Doremus's most hateful woes; a tragedy to be blamed upon the Corpos, or upon the principle of dictatorship in general, as savagely as the deaths of Mary and Dan Wilgus and Henry Veeder. Under persecution, Karl lost no ounce of his courage and his ingenuity in bamboozling the M.M. guards, but day by day he did steadily lose all his humor, his patience, his tolerance, his easy companionship, and everything else that made life endurable to men packed in a cell. The Communism that had always been his King Charles's Head, sometimes amusing, became a religious bigotry as hateful to Doremus as the old bigotries of the Inquisition or the Fundamentalist Protestants; that attitude of slaughtering to save men's souls from which the Jessup family had escaped during these last three generations.

It was impossible to get away from Karl's increasing zeal. He chattered on at night for an hour after all the other five had growled, "Oh, shut up! I want to sleep! You'll be making a Corpo out of me!"

Sometimes, in his proselytizing, he conquered. When his cell mates had long enough cursed the camp guards, Karl would rebuke them: "You're a lot too simple when you explain everything by saying that the Corpos, especially the M.M.'s, are all fiends. Plenty of 'em are. But even the worst of 'em, even the professional gunmen in the M.M. ranks, don't get as much satisfaction out of punishing us heretics as the honest, dumb Corpos who've been misled by their leaders' mouthing about Freedom, Order, Security, Discipline, Strength! All those swell words that even before Windrip came in the speculators started using to protect their profits! Especially how they used the word 'Liberty'! Liberty to steal the didies off the babies! I tell you, an honest man gets sick when he hears the word 'Liberty' today, after what the Republicans did to it! And I tell you that a lot of the M.M. guards right here at Trianon are just as unfortunate as we are—lot of 'em are just poor devils that couldn't get decent work, back in the Golden Age of Frank Roosevelt—bookkeepers that had to dig ditches, auto agents that couldn't sell cars and went sour, ex-looeys in the Great War that came back to find their jobs pinched off 'em and that followed Windrip, quite honestly, because they thought, the saps, that when he said Security he meant *Security*! They'll learn!"

And having admirably discoursed for another hour on the perils of self-righteousness among the Corpos, Comrade Pascal would change the subject and discourse upon the glory of self-righteousness among the Communists—particularly upon those sanctified examples of Communism who lived in bliss in the Holy City of Moscow, where, Doremus judged, the streets were paved with undepreciable roubles.

The Holy City of Moscow! Karl looked upon it with exactly such uncritical and slightly hysterical adoration as other sectarians had in their day devoted to Jerusalem, Mecca, Rome, Canterbury, and Benares. Fine, all right, thought Doremus. Let 'em worship their sacred fonts—it was as good a game as any for the mentally retarded. Only, why then should they object to his considering as sacred Fort Beulah, or New York, or Oklahoma City?

Karl once fell into a froth because Doremus wondered if the iron deposits in Russia were all they might be. Why certainly! Russia, being Holy Russia, must, as a useful part of its holiness, have sufficient iron, and Karl needed no mineralogists' reports but only the blissful eye of faith to know it.

He did not mind Karl's worshiping Holy Russia. But Karl did, using the word "naïve," which is the favorite word and just possibly the only word known to Communist journalists, derisively mind when Doremus had a mild notion of worshiping Holy America. Karl spoke often of photographs in the Moscow *News* of nearly naked girls on Russian bathing-beaches as proving the triumph and joy of the workers under Bolshevism, but he regarded precisely the same sort of photographs of nearly naked girls on Long Island bathing-beaches as proving the degeneration of the workers under Capitalism.

As a newspaper man, Doremus remembered that the only reporters who misrepresented and concealed facts more unscrupulously than the Capitalists were the Communists.

He was afraid that the world struggle today was not of Communism against Fascism, but of tolerance against the bigotry that was preached equally by Communism and Fascism. But he saw too that in America the struggle was befogged by the fact that the worst Fascists were they who disowned the word "Fascism" and preached enslavement to Capitalism under the style of Constitutional and Traditional Native American Liberty. For they were thieves not only of wages but of honor. To their purpose they could quote not only Scripture but Jefferson.

That Karl Pascal should be turning into a zealot, like most of his chiefs in the Communist party, was grievous to Doremus because he had once simple-heartedly hoped that in the mass strength of Communism there might be an escape from cynical dictatorship. But he saw now that he must remain alone, a "Liberal," scorned by all the noisier prophets for refusing to be a willing cat for the busy monkeys of either side. But at worst, the Liberals, the Tolerant, might in the long run preserve some of the arts of civilization, no matter which brand of tyranny should finally dominate the world.

"More and more, as I think about history," he pondered, "I am convinced that everything that is worth while in the world has been accomplished by the free, inquiring, critical spirit, and that the preservation of this spirit is more important than any social system whatsoever. But the men of ritual and the men of barbarism are capable of shutting up the men of science and of silencing them forever."

Yes, this was the worst thing the enemies of honor, the pirate industrialists and then their suitable successors, the Corpos with their blackjacks, had done: it had turned the brave, the generous, the passionate and half-literate Karl Pascals into dangerous fanatics. And how well they had done it! Doremus was uncomfortable with Karl; he felt that his next turn in jail might be under the warden-ship of none other than Karl himself, as he remembered how the Bolsheviks, once in power, had most smugly imprisoned and persecuted those great women, Spiridinova and Breshkovskaya and Ismailovitch, who, by their conspiracies against the Czar, their willingness to endure Siberian torture on behalf of "freedom for the masses," had most brought on the revolution by which the Bolsheviks were able to take control—and not only again forbid freedom to the masses, but this time inform them that, anyway, freedom was just a damn silly bourgeois superstition.

So Doremus, sleeping two-and-a-half feet above his old companion, felt himself in a cell within a cell. Henry Veeder and Clarence Little and Victor Loveland and Mr. Falck were gone now, and to Julian, penned in solitary, he could not speak once a month.

He yearned for escape with a desire that was near to

insanity; awake and asleep it was his obsession; and he thought his heart had stopped when Squad-Leader Aras Dilley muttered to him, as Doremus was scrubbing a lavatory floor, "Say! Listen, Mr. Jessup! Mis' Pike is fixin' it up and I'm going to help you escape jus' soon as things is right!"

It was a question of the guards on sentry-go outside the quadrangle. As sweeper, Doremus was reasonably free to leave his cell, and Aras had loosened the boards and barbed wire at the end of one of the alleys leading from the quadrangle between buildings. But outside, he was likely to be shot by a guard on sight.

For a week Aras watched. He knew that one of the night guards had a habit of getting drunk, which was forgiven him because of his excellence in flogging troublemakers but which was regarded by the more judicious as rather regrettable. And for that week Aras fed the guard's habit on Lorinda's expense money, and was indeed so devoted to his duties that he was himself twice carried to bed. Snake Tizra grew interested—but Snake also, after the first couple of drinks, liked to be democratic with his men and to sing "The Old Spinning Wheel."

Aras confided to Doremus: "Mis' Pike—she don't dast send you a note, less somebody get hold of it, but she says to me to tell you not to tell anybody you're going to take a sneak, or it'll get out."

So on the evening when Aras jerked a head at him from the corridor, then rasped, surly-seeming, "Here you, Jessup—you left one of the cans all dirty!" Doremus looked mildly at the cell that had been his home and study and tabernacle for six months, glanced at Karl Pascal reading in his bunk—slowly waving a shoeless foot in a sock with the end of it gone, at Truman Webb darning the seat of his pants, noted the gray smoke in filmy tilting layers about the small electric bulb in the ceiling, and silently stepped out into the corridor.

The late-January night was foggy.

Aras handed him a worn M.M. overcoat, whispered, "Third alley on right; moving-van on corner opposite the church," and was gone.

On hands and knees Doremus briskly crawled under the loosened barbed wire at the end of the small alley and carelessly stepped out, along the road. The only guard in sight was at a distance, and he was wavering in his gait. A block away, a furniture van was jacked up while the driver and his helper painfully prepared to change one of the tremendous tires. In the light of a corner arc, Doremus saw that the driver was that same hard-faced long-distance cruiser who had carried bundles of tracts for the New Underground.

The driver grunted, "Get in—hustle!" Doremus crouched between a bureau and a wing chair inside.

Instantly he felt the tilted body of the van dropping, as the driver pulled out the jack, and from the seat he heard, "All right! We're off. Crawl up behind me here and listen, Mr. Jessup. . . . Can you hear me? . . . The M.M.'s don't take so much trouble to prevent you gents and respectable fellows from escaping. They figure that most of you are too scary to try out anything, once you're away from your offices and front porches and sedans. But I guess you may be different, some ways, Mr. Jessup. Besides, they figure that if you do escape, they can pick you up easy afterwards, because you ain't onto hiding out, like a regular fellow that's been out of work sometimes and maybe gone on the bum. But don't worry. We'll get you through. I tell you, there's nobody got friends like a revolutionist. . . . *And* enemies!"

Then first did it come to Doremus that, by sentence of the late lamented Effingham Swan, he was subject to the death penalty for escaping. But "Oh, what the hell!" he grunted, like Karl Pascal, and he stretched in the luxury of mobility, in that galloping furniture truck.

He was free! He saw the lights of villages going by!

Once, he was hidden beneath hay in a barn; again, in a spruce grove high on a hill; and once he slept overnight on top of a coffin in the establishment of an undertaker. He walked secret paths; he rode in the back of an itinerant medicine-peddler's car and, concealed in fur cap and high-collared fur coat, in the sidecar of an Underground worker serving as an M.M. squad-leader. From this he dismounted, at the driver's command, in front of an obviously untenanted farmhouse on a snaky back-road between Monadnock Mountain and the Averill lakes—a very slattern of an old unpainted farmhouse, with sinking roof and snow up to the frowsy windows.

It seemed a mistake.

Doremus knocked, as the motorcycle snarled away, and the door opened on Lorinda Pike and Sissy, crying together, "Oh, my dear!"

He could only mutter, "Well!"

When they had made him strip off his fur coat in the farmhouse living room, a room with peeling wall paper, and altogether bare except for a cot, two chairs, a table, the two moaning women saw a small man, his face dirty, pasty, and sunken as by tuberculosis, his once fussily trimmed beard and mustache ragged as wisps of hay, his overlong hair a rustic jag at the back, his clothes ripped and filthy—an old, sick, discouraged tramp. He dropped on a straight chair and stared at them. Maybe they were genuine—maybe they really were there—maybe he was, as it seemed, in heaven, looking at the two principal angels, but he had been so often fooled so cruelly in his visions these dreary months! He sobbed, and they comforted him with softly stroking hands and not too confoundedly much babble.

"I've got a hot bath for you! And I'll scrub your back! And then some hot chicken soup and ice cream!"

As though one should say: The Lord God awaits you on His throne and all whom you bless shall be blessed, and all your enemies brought to their knees!

Those sainted women had actually had a long tin tub fetched to the kitchen of the old house, filled it with water heated in kettle and dishpan on the stove, and provided brushes, soap, a vast sponge, and such a long caressing bath towel as Doremus had forgotten existed. And somehow, from Fort Beulah, Sissy had brought plenty of his own shoes and shirts and three suits that now seemed to him fit for royalty.

He who had not had a hot bath for six months, and for three had worn the same underclothes, and for two (in clammy winter) no socks whatever!

If the presence of Lorinda and Sissy was token of heaven, to slide inch by slow ecstatic inch into the tub was its proof, and he lay soaking in glory.

When he was half dressed, the two came in, and there was about as much thought of modesty, or need for it, as though he were the two-year-old babe he somewhat resembled. They were laughing at him, but laughter became sharp whimpers of horror when they saw the gridironed meat of his back. But nothing more demanding than "Oh, my dear!" did Lorinda say, even then.

Though Sissy had once been glad that Lorinda spared her any mothering, Doremus rejoiced in it. Snake Tizra and the Trianon concentration camp had been singularly devoid of any mothering. Lorinda salved his back and powdered it. She cut his hair, not too unskillfully. She cooked for him all the heavy, earthy dishes of which he had dreamed, hungry in a cell: hamburg steak with onions, corn pudding, buckwheat cakes with sausages, apple dumplings with hard and soft sauce, and cream of mushroom soup!

It had not been safe to take him to the comforts of her tea room at Beecher Falls; already M.M.'s had been there, snooping after him. But Sissy and she had, for such refugees as they might be forwarding for the New Underground, provided this dingy farmhouse with half-a-dozen cots, and rich stores of canned goods and beautiful bottles (Doremus considered them) of honey and marmalade and bar-le-duc. The actual final crossing of the border into Canada was easier than it had been when Buck Titus had tried to smuggle the Jessup family over. It had become a system, as in the piratical days of bootlegging; with new forest paths, bribery of frontier guards, and forged passports. He was safe. Yet just to make safety safer, Lorinda and Sissy, rubbing their chins as they looked Doremus over, still discussing him as brazenly as though he were a baby who could not understand them, decided to turn him into a young man.

"Dye his hair and mustache black and shave the beard, I think. I wish we had time to give him a nice Florida tan with an Alpine lamp, too," considered Lorinda.

"Yes, I think he'll look sweet that way," said Sissy.

"I will not have my beard off!" he protested. "How do I know what kind of a chin I'll have when it's naked?"

"Why, the man still thinks he's a newspaper proprietor and one of Fort Beulah's social favorites!" marveled Sissy as they ruthlessly set to work.

"Only real reason for these damn wars and revolutions anyway is that the womenfolks get a chance—ouch! be careful!—to be dear little Amateur Mothers to every male they can get in their clutches. *Hair dye!*" said Doremus bitterly.

But he was shamelessly proud of his youthful face when it was denuded, and he discovered that he had a quite tolerably stubborn chin, and Sissy was sent back to Beecher Falls to keep the tea room alive, and for three days Lorinda and he gobbled steaks and ale, and played pinochle, and lay talking infinitely of all they had thought about each other in the six desert months that might have been sixty years. He was to remember the sloping farmhouse bedroom and a shred of rag carpet and a couple of rickety chairs and Lorinda snuggled under the old red comforter on the cot, not as winter poverty but as youth and adventurous love.

Then, in a forest clearing, with snow along the spruce boughs, a few feet across into Canada, he was peering into the eyes of his two women, curtly saying good-bye, and trudging off into the new prison of exile from the America to which, already, he was looking back with the long pain of nostalgia.

37

His beard had grown again—he and his beard had been friends for many years, and he had missed it of late. His hair and mustache had again assumed a respectable gray in place of the purple dye that under electric lights had looked so bogus. He was no longer impassioned at the sight of a lamb chop or a cake of soap. But he had not yet got over the pleasure and slight amazement at being able to talk as freely as he would, as emphatically as might please him, and in public.

He sat with his two closest friends in Montreal, two fellow executives in the Department of Propaganda and Publications of the New Underground (Walt Trowbridge, General Chairman), and these two friends were the Hon. Perley Beecroft, who presumably was the President of the United States, and Joe Elphrey, an ornamental young man who, as "Mr. Cailey," had been a prize agent of the Communist Party in America till he had been kicked out of that almost imperceptible body for having made a "united front" with Socialists, Democrats, and even choir-singers when organizing an anti-Corpo revolt in Texas.

Over their ale, in this café, Beecroft and Elphrey were at it as usual: Elphrey insisting that the only "solution" of American distress was dictatorship by the livelier representatives of the toiling masses, strict and if need be violent, but (this was his new heresy) not governed by Moscow. Beecroft was gaseously asserting that "all we needed" was a return to precisely the political parties, the drumming up of votes, and the oratorical legislating by Congress, of the contented days of William B. McKinley.

But as for Doremus, he leaned back not vastly caring

what nonsense the others might talk so long as it was permitted them to talk at all without finding that the waiters were M.M. spies; and content to know that, whatever happened, Trowbridge and the other authentic leaders would never go back to satisfaction in government of the profits, by the profits, for the profits. He thought comfortably of the fact that just yesterday (he had this from the chairman's secretary), Walt Trowbridge had dismissed Wilson J. Shale, the ducal oil man, who had come, apparently with sincerity, to offer his fortune and his executive experience to Trowbridge and the cause.

"Nope. Sorry, Will. But we can't use you. Whatever happens—even if Haik marches over and slaughters all of us along with all our Canadian hosts—you and your kind of clever pirates are finished. Whatever happens, whatever details of a new system of government may be decided on, whether we call it a 'Coöperative Commonwealth' or 'State Socialism' or 'Communism' or 'Revived Traditional Democracy,' there's got to be a new feeling—that government is not a game for a few smart, resolute athletes like you, Will, but a universal partnership, in which the State must own all resources so large that they affect all members of the State, and in which the one worst crime won't be murder or kidnaping but taking advantage of the State—in which the seller of fraudulent medicine, or the liar in Congress, will be punished a whole lot worse than the fellow who takes an ax to the man who's grabbed off his girl . . . Eh? What's going to happen to magnates like you, Will? God knows! What happened to the dinosaurs?"

So was Doremus in his service well content.

Yet socially he was almost as lonely as in his cell at Trianon; almost as savagely he longed for the not exorbitant pleasure of being with Lorinda, Buck, Emma, Sissy, Steve Perefixe.

None of them save Emma could join him in Canada, and she would not. Her letters suggested fear of the un-Worcesterian wildernesses of Montreal. She wrote that Philip and she hoped they might be able to get Doremus forgiven by the Corpos! So he was left to associate only with his fellow refugees from Corpoism, and he knew a life that had been familiar, far too familiar, to political exiles ever since the first revolt in Egypt sent the rebels sneaking off into Assyria.

It was no particularly indecent egotism in Doremus that made him suppose, when he arrived in Canada, that everyone would thrill to his tale of imprisonment, torture, and escape. But he found that ten thousand spirited tellers of woe had come there before him, and that the Canadians, however attentive and generous hosts they might be, were actively sick of pumping up new sympathy. They felt that their quota of martyrs was completely filled, and as to the exiles who came in penniless, and that was a majority of them, the Canadians became distinctly weary of depriving their own families on behalf of unknown refugees, and they couldn't even keep up forever a gratification in the presence of celebrated American authors, politicians, scientists, when they became common as mosquitoes.

It was doubtful if a lecture on Deplorable Conditions in America by Herbert Hoover and General Pershing together would have attracted forty people. Ex-governors and judges were glad to get jobs washing dishes, and ex-managing-editors were hoeing turnips. And reports said that Mexico and London and France were growing alike apologetically bored.

So Doremus, meagerly living on his twenty-dollar-a-week salary from the N.U., met no one save his own fellow exiles, in just such salons of unfortunate political escapists as the White Russians, the Red Spaniards, the Blue Bulgarians, and all the other polychromatic insurrectionists frequented in Paris. They crowded together, twenty of them in a parlor twelve by twelve, very like the concentration-camp cells in area, inhabitants, and eventual smell, from 8 P.M. till midnight, and made up for lack of dinner with coffee and doughnuts and exiguous sandwiches, and talked without cessation about the Corpos. They told as "actual facts" stories about President Haik which had formerly been applied to Hitler, Stalin, and Mussolini—the one about the man who was alarmed to find he had saved Haik from drowning and begged him not to tell.

In the cafés they seized the newspapers from home. Men who had had an eye gouged out on behalf of freedom, with the rheumy remaining one peered to see who had won the Missouri Avenue Bridge Club Prize.

They were brave and romantic, tragic and distinguished, and Doremus became a little sick of them all and of the final brutality of fact that no normal man can very long endure another's tragedy, and that friendly weeping will some day turn to irritated kicking.

He was stirred when, in a hastily built American interdenominational chapel, he heard a starveling who had once been a pompous bishop read from the pine pulpit:

"By the rivers of Babylon, there we sat down, yea, we wept, when we remembered Zion. We hanged our harps upon the willows in the midst thereof. . . . How shall we sing the Lord's song in a strange land? If I forget thee, O Jerusalem, let my right hand forget her cunning. If I do not remember thee, let my tongue cleave to the roof of my mouth; if I prefer not Jerusalem above my chief joy."

Here in Canada the Americans had their Weeping Wall, and daily cried with false, gallant hope, "Next year in Jerusalem!"

Sometimes Doremus was vexed by the ceaseless demanding wails of refugees who had lost everything, sons and wives and property and self-respect, vexed that they believed they alone had seen such horrors; and sometimes he spent all his spare hours raising a dollar and a little weary friendliness for these sick souls; and sometimes he saw as fragments of Paradise every aspect of America—such oddly assorted glimpses as Meade at Gettysburg and the massed blue petunias in Emma's lost garden, the fresh shine of rails as seen from a train on an April morning, and Rockefeller Center. But whatever his mood, he refused to sit down with his harp by any foreign waters whatever and enjoy the importance of being a celebrated beggar.

He'd get back to America and chance another prison. Meantime he neatly sent packages of literary dynamite out from the N.U. offices all day long, and efficiently directed a hundred envelope-addressers who once had been professors and pastrycooks.

He had asked his superior, Perley Beecroft, for assignment in more active and more dangerous work, as secret agent in America—out West, where he was not known. But headquarters had suffered a good deal from amateur agents who babbled to strangers, or who could not be trusted to keep their mouths shut while they were being flogged to death. Things had changed since 1929. The N.U. believed that the highest honor a man could earn was not to have a million dollars but to be permitted to risk his life for truth, without pay or praise.

Doremus knew that his chiefs did not consider him young enough or strong enough, but also that they were studying him. Twice he had the honor of interviews with Trowbridge about nothing in particular—surely it must have been an honor, though it was hard to remember it, because Trowbridge was the simplest and friendliest man in the whole portentous spy machine. Cheerfully Doremus hoped for a chance to help make the poor, overworked, worried Corpo officials even more miserable than they normally were, now that war with Mexico and revolts against Corpoism were jingling side by side.

In July, 1939, when Doremus had been in Montreal a little over five months, and a year after his sentence to concentration camp, the American newspapers which arrived at N.U. headquarters were full of resentment against Mexico.

Bands of Mexicans had raided across into the United States—always, curiously enough, when our troops were off in the desert, practice-marching or perhaps gathering sea shells. They burned a town in Texas—fortunately all the women and children were away on a Sunday-school picnic, that afternoon. A Mexican Patriot (aforetime he had also worked as an Ethiopian Patriot, a Chinese Patriot, and a Haitian Patriot) came across, to the tent of an M.M. brigadier, and confessed that while it hurt him to tattle on his own beloved country, conscience compelled him to reveal that his Mexican superiors were planning to fly over and bomb Laredo, San Antonio, Bisbee, and probably Tacoma, and Bangor, Maine.

This excited the Corpo newspapers very much indeed, and in New York and Chicago they published photographs of the conscientious traitor half an hour after he had appeared at the Brigadier's tent . . . where, at that moment, forty-six reporters happened to be sitting about on neighboring cactuses.

America rose to defend her hearthstones, including all the hearthstones on Park Avenue, New York, against false and treacherous Mexico, with its appalling army of 67,000 men, with thirty-nine military aëroplanes. Women in Cedar Rapids hid under the bed; elderly gentlemen in Cattaraugus County, New York, concealed their money in elm-tree boles; and the wife of a chicken-raiser seven miles N.E. of Estelline, South Dakota, a woman widely known as a good cook and a trained observer, distinctly saw a file of ninety-two Mexican soldiers pass her cabin, starting at 3:17 A.M. on July 27, 1939.

To answer this threat, America, the one country that had never lost a war and never started an unjust one, rose as one man, as the Chicago *Daily Evening Corporate* put it. It was planned to invade Mexico as soon as it should be cool enough, or even earlier, if the refrigeration and air-conditioning could be arranged. In one month, five million men were drafted for the invasion, and started training.

Thus—perhaps too flippantly—did Joe Cailey and Doremus discuss the declaration of war against Mexico. If they found the whole crusade absurd, it may be stated in their defense that they regarded all wars always as absurd; in the baldness of the lying by both sides about the causes; in the spectacle of grown-up men engaged in the infantile diversions of dressing-up in fancy clothes and marching to primitive music. The only thing not absurd about wars, said Doremus and Cailey, was that along with their skittishness they did kill a good many millions of people. Ten thousand starving babies seemed too high a price for a Sam Browne belt for even the sweetest, touchingest young lieutenant.

Yet both Doremus and Cailey swiftly recanted their assertion that all wars were absurd and abominable; both of them made exception of the people's war against tyranny, as suddenly America's agreeable anticipation of stealing Mexico was checked by a popular rebellion against the whole Corpo régime.

The revolting section was, roughly, bounded by Sault Ste. Marie, Detroit, Cincinnati, Wichita, San Francisco, and Seattle, though in that territory large patches remained loyal to President Haik, and outside of it, other large patches joined the rebels. It was the part of America which had always been most "radical"—that indefinite word, which probably means "most critical of piracy." It was the land of the Populists, the Non-Partisan League, the Farmer-Labor Party, and the La Follettes—a family so vast as to form a considerable party in itself.

Whatever might happen, exulted Doremus, the revolt proved that belief in America and hope for America were not dead.

These rebels had most of them, before his election, believed in Buzz Windrip's fifteen points; believed that when he said he wanted to return the power pilfered by the bankers and the industrialists to the people, he more or less meant that he wanted to return the power of the bankers and industrialists to the people. As month by month they saw that they had been cheated with marked cards again, they were indignant; but they were busy with cornfield and sawmill and dairy and motor factory, and it took the impertinent idiocy of demanding that they march down into the desert and help steal a friendly country to jab them into awakening and into discovering that, while they had been asleep, they had been kidnaped by a small gang of criminals armed with high ideals, well-buttered words, and a lot of machine guns.

So profound was the revolt that the Catholic Archbishop of California and the radical Ex-Governor of Minnesota found themselves in the same faction.

At first it was a rather comic outbreak—comic as the ill-trained, un-uniformed, confusedly thinking revolutionists of Massachusetts in 1776. President General Haik publicly jeered at them as a "ridiculous rag-tag rebellion of hoboes too lazy to work." And at first they were unable to do anything more than scold like a flock of crows, throw bricks at detachments of M.M.'s and policemen, wreck troop trains, and destroy the property of such honest private citizens as owned Corpo newspapers.

It was in August that the shock came, when General Emmanuel Coon, Chief of Staff of the regulars, flew from Washington to St. Paul, took command of Fort Snelling, and declared for Walt Trowbridge as Temporary President of the United States, to hold office until there should be a new, universal, and uncontrolled presidential election.

Trowbridge proclaimed acceptance—with the proviso that he should not be a candidate for permanent President.

By no means all of the regulars joined Coon's revolutionary troops. (There are two sturdy myths among the Liberals: that the Catholic Church is less Puritanical and always more esthetic than the Protestant; and that professional soldiers hate war more than do congressmen and old maids.) But there were enough regulars who were fed up with the exactions of greedy, mouth-dripping Corpo commissioners and who threw in with General Coon so that immediately after his army of regulars and hastily trained Minnesota farmers had won the battle of Mankato, the forces at Leavenworth took control of Kansas City, and planned to march on St. Louis and Omaha; while in New York, Governor's Island and Fort Wadsworth looked on, neutral, as unmilitary-looking and mostly Jewish guerrillas seized the subways, power stations, and railway terminals.

But there the revolt halted, because in the America which had so warmly praised itself for its "widespread popular free education," there had been so very little education; widespread, popular, free, or anything else, that most people did not know what they wanted—indeed knew about so few things to want at all.

There had been plenty of schoolrooms; there had been lacking only literate teachers and eager pupils and school boards who regarded teaching as a profession worthy of as much honor and pay as insurance-selling or embalming or waiting on table. Most Americans had learned in school that God had supplanted the Jews as chosen people by the Americans, and this time done the job much better, so that we were the richest, kindest, and cleverest nation living; that depressions were but passing headaches and that labor unions must not concern themselves with anything except higher wages and shorter hours and, above all, must not set up an ugly class struggle by combining politically; that, though foreigners tried to make a bogus mystery of them, politics were really so simple that any village attorney or any clerk in the office of a metropolitan sheriff was quite adequately trained for them; and that if John D. Rockefeller or Henry Ford had set his mind to it, he could have become the most distinguished statesman, composer, physicist, or poet in the land.

Even two-and-half years of despotism had not yet taught most electors humility, nor taught them much of anything except that it was unpleasant to be arrested too often.

So, after the first gay eruption of rioting, the revolt slowed up. Neither the Corpos nor many of their opponents knew enough to formulate a clear, sure theory of self-government, or irresistibly resolve to engage in the sore labor of fitting themselves for freedom. . . . Even yet, after Windrip, most of the easy-going descendants of the wisecracking Benjamin Franklin had not learned that Patrick Henry's "Give me liberty or give me death" meant anything more than a high-school yell or a cigarette slogan.

The followers of Trowbridge and General Coon—"The American Coöperative Commonwealth" they began to call themselves—did not lose any of the territory they had seized; they held it, driving out all Corpo agents, and now and then added a county or two. But mostly their rule, and equally the Corpos' rule, was as unstable as politics in Ireland.

So the task of Walt Trowbridge, which in August had seemed finished, before October seemed merely to have begun. Doremus Jessup was called into Trowbridge's office, to hear from the chairman:

"I guess the time's come when we need Underground agents in the States with sense as well as guts. Report to General Barnes for service proselytizing in Minnesota.

Good luck, Brother Jessup! Try to persuade the orators that are still holding out for Discipline and clubs that they ain't so much stalwart as funny!"

And all that Doremus thought was, "Kind of a nice fellow, Trowbridge. Glad to be working with him," as he set off on his new task of being a spy and professional hero without even any funny passwords to make the game romantic.

38

HIS PACKING was done. It had been very simple, since his kit consisted only of toilet things, one change of clothes, and the first volume of Spengler's *Decline of the West.* He was waiting in his hotel lobby for time to take the train to Winnipeg. He was interested by the entrance of a lady more decorative than the females customarily seen in this modest inn: a hand-tooled presentation copy of a lady, in crushed levant and satin doublure; a lady with mascara'd eyelashes, a permanent wave, and a cobweb frock. She ambled through the lobby and leaned against a fake-marble pillar, wielding a long cigarette-holder and staring at Doremus. She seemed amused by him, for no clear reason.

Could she be some sort of Corpo spy?

She lounged toward him, and he realized that she was Lorinda Pike.

While he was still gasping, she chuckled, "Oh, no, darling, I'm not so realistic in my art as to carry out this role too far! It just happens to be the easiest disguise to win over the Corpo frontier guards—if you'll agree it really is a disguise!"

He kissed her with a fury which shocked the respectable hostelry.

She knew, from N.U. agents, that he was going out into a very fair risk of being flogged to death. She had come solely to say farewell and bring him what might be his last budget of news.

Buck was in concentration camp—he was more feared and more guarded than Doremus had been, and Linda had not been able to buy him out. Julian, Karl, and John Pollikop were still alive, still imprisoned. Father Perefixe was running the N.U. cell in Fort Beulah, but slightly confused because he wanted to approve of war with Mexico, a nation which he detested for its treatment of Catholic priests. Lorinda and he had, apparently, fought bloodily all one evening about Catholic rule in Latin America. As is always typical of Liberals, Lorinda managed to speak of Father Perefixe at once with virtuous loathing and the greatest affection. Emma and David were reported as well content in Worcester, though there were murmurs that Philip's wife did not too thankfully receive her mother-in-law's advice on cooking. Sissy was becoming a deft agitator who still, remembering that she was a born architect, drew plans for houses that Julian and she would some day adorn. She contrived blissfully to combine assaults on all Capitalism with an entirely capitalistic conception of the year-long honeymoons Julian and she were going to have.

Less surprising than any of this were the tidings that Francis Tasbrough, very beautiful in repentance, had been let out of the Corpo prison to which he had been sent for too much grafting and was again a district commissioner, well thought of, and that his housekeeper was now Mrs. Candy, whose daily reports on his most secret arrangements were the most neatly written and sternly grammatical documents that came into Vermont N.U. headquarters.

Then Lorinda was looking up at him as he stood in the vestibule of his Westbound train and crying, "You look so well again! Are you happy? Oh, be happy!"

Even now he did not see this defeminized radical woman crying. . . . She turned away from him and raced down the station platform too quickly. She had lost all her confident pose of flip elegance. Leaning out from the vestibule he saw her stop at the gate, diffidently raise her hand as if to wave at the long anonymity of the train windows, then shakily march away through the gates. And he realized that she hadn't even his address; that no one who loved him would have any stable address for him now any more.

Mr. William Barton Dobbs, a traveling man for harvesting machinery, an erect little man with a small gray beard and a Vermont accent, got out of bed in his hotel in a section in Minnesota which had so many Bavarian-American and Yankee-descended farmers, and so few "radical" Scandinavians, that it was still loyal to President Haik.

He went down to breakfast, cheerfully rubbing his hands. He consumed grapefruit and porridge—but without sugar: there was an embargo on sugar. He looked down and inspected himself; he sighed, "I'm getting too much of a pod, with all this outdoor work and being so hungry; I've got to cut down on the grub"; and then he consumed fried eggs, bacon, toast, coffee made of acorns, and marmalade made of carrots—Coon's troops had shut off coffee beans and oranges.

He read, meantime, the Minneapolis *Daily Corporate.* It announced a Great Victory in Mexico—in the same place, he noted, in which there had already been three Great Victories in the past two weeks. Also, a "shameful rebellion" had been put down in Andalusia, Alabama; it was reported that General Göring was coming over to be the guest of President Haik; and the pretender Trowbridge was said "by a reliable source" to have been assassinated, kidnaped, and compelled to resign.

"No news this morning," regretted Mr. William Barton Dobbs.

As he came out of the hotel, a squad of Minute Men were marching by. They were farm boys, newly recruited for service in Mexico; they looked as scared and soft and big-footed as a rout of rabbits. They tried to pipe up the newest-oldest war song, in the manner of the Civil War ditty "When Johnny Comes Marching Home Again":

When Johnny comes home from Greaser Land,
Hurray, hurraw,
His ears will be full of desert sand,
Hurray, hurraw,
But he'll speaka de Spiggoty pretty sweet
And he'll bring us a gun and a señorit',
And we'll all get stewed when
Johnny comes marching home!

Their voices wavered. They peeped at the crowd along the walk, or looked sulkily down at their dragging feet, and the crowd, which once would have been yelping "Hail Haik!" was snickering "You beggars 'll never get to Greaser Land!" and even, from the safety of a second-story window, "Hurray, hurraw for Trowbridge!"

"Poor devils!" thought Mr. William Barton Dobbs, as he watched the frightened toy soldiers . . . not too toy-like to keep them from dying.

Yet it is a fact that he could see in the crowd numerous persons whom his arguments, and those of the sixty-odd N.U. secret agents under him, had converted from fear of the M.M.'s to jeering.

In his open Ford convertible—he never started it but he thought of how he had "put it over on Sissy" by getting a Ford all his own—Doremus drove out of the village into stubble-lined prairie. The meadow larks' liquid ecstasy welcomed him from barbed-wire fences. If he missed the strong hills behind Fort Beulah, he was yet exalted by the immensity of the sky, the openness of prairie that promised he could go on forever, the gayety of small sloughs seen through their fringes of willows and cottonwoods, and once, aspiring overhead, an early flight of mallards.

He whistled boisterously as he bounced on along the section-line road.

He reached a gaunt yellow farmhouse—it was to have had a porch, but there was only an unpainted nothingness low down on the front wall to show where the porch would be. To a farmer who was oiling a tractor in the pig-littered farmyard he chirped, "Name's William Barton Dobbs—representing the Des Moines Combine and Up-to-Date Implement Company."

The farmer galloped up to shake hands, breathing, "By golly this is a great honor, Mr. J——"

"Dobbs!"

"That's right. 'Scuse me."

In an upper bedroom of the farmhouse, seven men were waiting, perched on chair and table and edges of the bed, or just squatted on the floor. Some of them were apparently farmers; some unambitious shopkeepers. As Doremus bustled in, they rose and bowed.

"Good-morning gentlemen. A little news," he said. "Coon has driven the Corpos out of Yankton and Sioux Falls. Now I wonder if you're ready with your reports?"

To the agent whose difficulty in converting farm-owners had been their dread of paying decent wages to farm hands, Doremus presented for use the argument (as formalized yet passionate as the observations of a life-insurance agent upon death by motor accident) that poverty for one was poverty for all. . . . It wasn't such a very new argument, nor so very logical, but it had been a useful carrot for many human mules.

For the agent among the Finnish-American settlers, who were insisting that Trowbridge was a Bolshevik and just as bad as the Russians, Doremus had a mimeographed quotation from the *Izvestia* of Moscow damning Trowbridge as a "social Fascist quack." For the Bavarian farmers down the other way, who were still vaguely pro-Nazi, Doremus had a German émigre paper published in Prague, proving (though without statistics or any considerable quotation from official documents) that, by agreement with Hitler, President Haik was, if he remained in power, going to ship back to the German Army all German-Americans with so much as one grandparent born in the Fatherland.

"Do we close with a cheerful hymn and the benediction, Mr. Dobbs?" demanded the youngest and most flippant—and quite the most successful—agent.

"I wouldn't mind! Maybe it wouldn't be so unsuitable as you think. But considering the loose morals and economics of most of you comrades, perhaps it would be better if I closed with a new story about Haik and Mae West that I heard, day before yesterday. . . . Bless you all! Good-bye!"

As he drove to his next meeting, Doremus fretted, "I don't believe that Prague story about Haik and Hitler is true. I think I'll quit using it. Oh, I know—I know, Mr. Dobbs; as you say, if you did tell the truth to a Nazi, it would still be a lie. But just the same I think I'll quit using it. . . . Lorinda and me, that thought we could get free of Puritanism! . . . Those cumulus clouds are better than a galleon. If they'd just move Mount Terror and Fort Beulah and Lorinda and Buck here, this would be Paradise. . . . Oh, Lord, I don't want to, but I suppose I'll have to order the attack on the M.M. post at Osakis now; they're ready for it. . . . I wonder if that shotgun charge yesterday *was* intended for me? . . . Didn't really like Lorinda's hair fixed up in that New York style at all!"

He slept that night in a cottage on the shore of a sandy-bottomed lake ringed with bright birches. His host and his host's wife, worshipers of Trowbridge, had insisted on giving him their own room, with the patchwork quilt and the hand-painted pitcher and bowl.

He dreamed—as he still did dream, once or twice a week—that he was back in his cell at Trianon. He knew again the stink, the cramped and warty bunk, the never relaxed fear that he might be dragged out and flogged.

He heard magic trumpets. A soldier opened the door and invited out all the prisoners. There, in the quadrangle, General Emmanuel Coon (who, to Doremus's dreaming fancy, looked exactly like Sherman) addressed them:

"Gentlemen, the Commonwealth army has conquered! Haik has been captured! You are free!"

So they marched out, the prisoners, the bent and scarred and crippled, the vacant-eyed and slobbering, who had come into this place as erect and daring men: Doremus, Dan Wilgus, Buck, Julian, Mr. Falck, Henry Veeder, Karl Pascal, John Pollikop, Truman Webb. They crept out of the quadrangle gates, through a double line of soldiers standing rigidly at Present Arms yet weeping as they watched the broken prisoners crawling past.

And beyond the soldiers, Doremus saw the women and children. They were waiting for him—the kind arms of Lorinda and Emma and Sissy and Mary, with David behind them, clinging to his father's hand, and Father Perefixe. And Foolish was there, his tail a proud plume, and from the dream-blurred crowd came Mrs. Candy, holding out to him a cocoanut cake.

Then all of them were fleeing, frightened by Shad Ledue——

His host was slapping Doremus's shoulder, muttering, "Just had a phone call. Corpo posse out after you."

So Doremus rode out, saluted by the meadow larks, and onward all day, to a hidden cabin in the Northern Woods where quiet men awaited news of freedom.

And still Doremus goes on in the red sunrise, for a Doremus Jessup can never die.

Afterword

As titles go, *It Can't Happen Here* is as ironic as *The Red Badge of Courage*, the title of Stephen Crane's novel about a soldier afraid of war. Sinclair Lewis began to write his cautionary tale about the rise of American fascism in May 1935, finished a draft on August 12, and completed final revisions on September 28.[1] When it appeared on October 21, 1935, near the nadir of the Great Depression, the novel struck a nerve. (The grim national joke of 1933: What's the capital of the United States? Half of what it was last year.) The economic crisis had sparked extremist political movements in industrialized nations around the world. That is, the American political climate was raucous when Lewis's novel was issued, the winds gusting with crackpot solutions to the problems of poverty and unemployment or what Lewis describes in the novel as programs "that promised prosperity without anyone's having to work."

Many of them were floated by demogogues with ambition and an agenda, and their schemes often included the nationalization of key industries, the abolition of independent labor unions, the centralization of economic decision making, and income redistribution. The poet Ezra Pound, for example, was attracted to both Benito Mussolini's fascist politics and C. H. Douglas's financial theories, which Douglas conceded were incompatible with traditional democracy. Father Charles Coughlin, whose radio broadcasts in the 1930s attracted an estimated thirty million listeners each week, mixed a heavy dose of anti-Semitism with an appeal for a brand of "social justice" based on confiscating wealth. Coughlin became the model for Bishop Prang in Lewis's novel. But the best-known alternative to Franklin Roosevelt's New Deal came from one of the primary targets of Lewis's satire, former governor and U.S. senator

Huey Long of Louisiana. The slogan of Long's "Share Our Wealth" movement was "Every Man a King (But No One Wears a Crown)." Lewis revised the slogan in *It Can't Happen Here*: "Every man is a king so long as he has someone to look down on." Like Senator Berzelius ("Buzz") Windrip in *It Can't Happen Here*, Long proposed to limit individual fortunes and inheritances through taxation, to double the amount of money in circulation to facilitate credit, and to provide each family with a guaranteed annual income of upward of four thousand dollars. In February 1935, according to Axel Knoenagel, "there were supposedly more than 27,000 [Share the Wealth] clubs with a total of more than 7 million members" in the U.S.[2] When he died, the "Kingfish," as he was nicknamed, was building a political machine to supplant the Democrats and elect him President in 1940. In none of these economic plans, however, do the figures make sense. All of them depended upon smoke and mirrors to disguise their impracticality.

Sinclair Lewis was no wild-eyed leftist. While he had toyed with Fabian socialism as an undergraduate at Yale and worked briefly in 1906–7 as a janitor at Helicon Hall, Upton Sinclair's utopian community in New Jersey, he was hardly a firebrand. In the mid-1930s, he was a Liberal, a supporter of the New Deal. His friend Ramon Guthrie insisted that "it would be a mistake to attribute to Sinclair Lewis any kind of sustained political conviction,"[3] and his wife, the journalist Dorothy Thompson, later described him as "basically apolitical, but insofar as his social ideas were articulate and consistent, he was an old-fashioned populist."[4] His political opinions were a bit like those of Rick Blaine in the movie *Casablanca*. When asked his allegiances by a Gestapo major, Blaine replies, "I'm an alcoholic," to which the nonaligned prefect of police adds, "That makes Rick a citizen of the world."

Still, Lewis was alarmed by the threat of despotism and homegrown fascism. As he explained in an interview with the *New York Post* in May 1936: "I have a vague, general fear that if somebody like Coughlin gets in, there'll be hell to pay. Either this group could put over a real dictatorship or they could have it taken away from them by a hard-boiled group of reactionaries who to save themselves and their families would overthrow the whole government and substitute their own brand of Fascism."[5]

The moment seemed ripe for right-wing extremism. In 1922, the first American local of the German Nazi Party was founded in New York, and by 1935, the German-American Bund claimed a total membership of about ten thousand members. In 1933, William Dudley Pelley founded the anti-Semitic organization Silver Legion, which soon spread across the country and whose members wore silver shirts in imitation of the Brown Shirts in Germany and Black Shirts in Italy. In February 1933, Franklin Roosevelt (or Rosenfeldt, according to some of his anti-Semitic critics) was the target of a would-be assassin; a disgruntled Italian immigrant killed the mayor of Chicago, who had been sitting next to the President-elect, by mistake. Then in November 1934, Major General Smedley D. Butler, the most decorated U.S. Marine in history to that date, testified before Congress about a military coup planned and sponsored by some anti–New Deal corporate leaders. In other words, "if Long had not been assassinated" in September 1935, as the contemporary scholar Andrew C. Yerkes has argued, "we might be reading [*It Can't Happen Here*] as prophecy rather than speculation."[6] Nor was it the first American novel that envisioned a fascist future wrapped in the American flag published during the Depression. It was, in fact, the third, after Nathanael West's *A Cool Million* (1934) and Edward Dahlberg's *Those Who Perish* (1934).

Lewis's interest in the subject was no doubt piqued by Dorothy Thompson, who had interviewed Hitler in 1931 and who, in August 1934, became the first American journalist to be expelled from Nazi Germany. Lewis's biographer Mark Schorer bluntly asserts that "*It Can't Happen Here* would never have been written if Sinclair Lewis had not been married to Dorothy Thompson."[7] George Seldes, a freelance investigative reporter and, in 1935, Lewis's Vermont neighbor, similarly claims that Lewis owed "several books to Dorothy, most notably *It Can't Happen Here. . . .* She inspired the book" and "gave him the story of Nazi-fascist dictatorships in Europe as she had experienced them." Thompson also owned a copy of Raymond Gram Swing's *Forerunners of American Fascism* (1935), on which Lewis modeled some of the incidents in the novel. Seldes had covered the rise of fascism in Italy in the 1920s and written an exposé of Mussolini entitled *Sawdust Caesar* (1935). Lewis had developed the "habit of pumping everyone for information" about the European political scene and, as Seldes remembered, "he especially pumped me on this subject. I had to relate every meeting with Mussolini, every glimpse of him, every day I could remember of the year and more in Rome under Fascism. He pumped day and night, lunch and dinner, cocktail hour and auto trips."[8] To acknowledge Seldes and other reporters who had helped him with the novel, Lewis listed them among the journalists imprisoned by Windrip. *It Can't Happen Here* is doubtlessly also indebted to Jack London's dystopian novel *The Iron Heel* (1913), which depicts the rise of a ruthless oligarchy in the U.S. As a young writer early in the century, Lewis not only befriended London but sold him story ideas.

In 1930, Lewis became the first American to be awarded the Nobel Prize for Literature for his five major novels of the 1920s: *Main Street*, *Babbitt*, *Elmer Gantry*, *Arrowsmith*, and *Dodsworth*. In them, he was a provoceteur par excellence, stirring the water rather than calming it. Similarly, he had conceded from the first that *It Can't Happen Here* was pure propaganda, though he added that "it is propaganda for only one thing: American democracy."[9] As he once asked his friend Frazier Hunt, "Don't you understand that it's my mission in life to be the despised critic, the eternal fault-finder? I must carp and scold until everyone despises me. That's what I was put here for."[10] As late as 1949, in his last press interview, Lewis reiterated that he was "a diagnostician, not a reformer."[11]

Certainly nothing in *It Can't Happen Here* is liable to comfort a reader familiar with world events in the mid-1930s. As early as the first chapter, according to the scholar Robert McLaughlin, "it becomes clear that the installation of a fascist government will not be a revolution or coup d'état; rather, the groundwork for fascism has already been constructed in the ideological worldviews of the majority of Americans. The riposte to the claim that 'It can't happen here' is 'It already has.'"[12] The centerpiece of Windrip's campaign is his "Fifteen Points of Victory for the Forgotten Man," a hodgepodge of contradictory ideas, many gleaned from Long's "Share-the-Wealth" platform—which in addition proposes to disenfranchise blacks and atheists and imprison communists, socialists, and anarchists. As Lewis's hero Doremus Jessup remarks, "Windrip never *mentioned* free speech and the freedom of the press in his articles of faith." The final rally of Windrip's campaign takes place in Madison Square Garden two days before the election, an affair sometimes compared to the mass demonstrations at the Berlin Sportpalast organized by Joseph Goebbels on Hitler's behalf—but Lewis was also prescient. On October 3, 1937, nearly two years after publication of his novel, more than a thousand Storm Troopers rallied at Madison Square Garden in New York, and to mark Washington's Birthday in February 1939, some twenty thousand members of the German-American Bund and other fascists met in Madison Square Garden to hear a speech by Fritz Kuhn, the so-called "American Führer."

Much as Hitler and the Nationalist Socialists assumed power in Germany in 1933 through democratic means, then abolished democracy, Windrip ("the Chief") is elected to office fairly, and then establishes martial law in the U.S. He redistricts the country to facilitate his form of governing and seizes control of the press and universities. Some of his changes (e.g., the neutering of Congress and the abolition of the Supreme Court) are immediate and public (wind-rip) and others (e.g., the erection of concentration camps, the torture and murder of political rivals) so gradual and secretive, they go virtually unnoticed (win-drip). As if to prove Samuel Johnson's adage that "patriotism is the last refuge of scoundrels," all of these violations of the Constitution occur under the blanket pretense that they are emergency measures necessary to preserve the American Way of Life.

The parallels between historical figures and events in Germany and characters and events in Lewis's novel do not end here. Like Hitler's *Mein Kampf* (or, for that matter, Long's *Every Man a King*), Windrip's *Zero Hour* is regarded as a "Bible" by his followers. The German Storm Troopers, or SA, were the model for the Minute Men or MM, the Nazi Resistance for the New Underground. Dr. Joseph Goebbels and Werner von Blomberg were the originals of Dr. Hector Macgoblin and Dewey Haik. Hermann Göring and Ernst Röhm suggested Lee Sarason, who dies as Röhm died during the Night of the Long Knives in early July 1934. In Germany all political parties except the National Socialists were abolished in March 1933, much as in the novel all parties except the Corpos are abolished in August 1937. The book burnings in Germany in May 1933 are replicated in the book burnings by Shad Ladue and his underlings, including the torching of Doremus's "dearest treasure, the thirty-four-volume extra-illustrated edition of Dickens." (For the record, soon after finishing the novel, Lewis acquired just such an edition of Dickens's complete works.[13]) Lewis even imagines an American equivalent of the Horst Wessel song, "Bring Out the Old-Time Musket" composed by Mrs. Adelaide Tarr Gimmitch, modeled on the right-wing writer Elizabeth (Mrs. Albert W.) Dilling. Lewis's novel was also prescient in anticipating the colonial and imperial designs of fascist states. It describes in its final pages the start of a U.S. war with Mexico months before Italy invaded Ethiopia and years before Germany annexed the Sudetenland and Austria and invaded Poland.

As Lewis depicts the future, given a choice between freedom and security in the election of 1936, Americans opt for security. Ironically, the Corpos and their candidate Windrip, a "ringmaster-revolutionist," promise bread and circuses but deliver only the circus, such as by founding "Ringling-Barnum and Bailey universities." The small-town editor Doremus (door-mouse) jokes after the election that Windrip "had taken to riding down Pennsylvania Avenue on an elephant." But he cannot remain complacent after his son-in-law is shot. He soon realizes that

> "The tyranny of this dictatorship isn't primarily the fault of Big Business, nor of the demagogues who do their dirty work. It's the fault of Doremus Jessup! Of all the conscientious, respectable, lazy-minded Doremus Jessups, who have let the demogogues wriggle in, without fierce enough protest."[14]

He blamed "the *lumpen*," the flag-waving conformists or "the American Legion type," for their apathy in the face of the fascist threat. H. G. Wells later complained to Lewis that he "didn't show enough the role" of the industrial lobby in right-wing American politics and insisted "that it would be the Babbitts who would be the leaders of fascism in America—backed by the Ku Klux Klan, the American

Legion, and the N[ational] A[ssociation of] M[anufacturers]." Other critics wondered why Lewis had portrayed the leader of the anti-fascists, Walt Trowbridge, the candidate Windrip defeats in 1936, as a Republican. Lewis had a ready answer: "The Republican represents the old school of honesty and integrity. It takes that kind of leadership to defeat fascism." He was probably thinking of Senator Arthur H. Vandenberg of Michigan. "I think Arthur Vandenberg would be a good Presidential candidate," he told an interviewer later. "I like Arthur. I think he is an honest man."[15]

Certainly Lewis failed—or refused—to sketch a solution to the threat of fascism. He was a social satirist, not a systematic political thinker or theorist. Worth noting, however, is that while Windrip's platform consigns women to the home and domestic duties (like the Nazis' *Kinder, Küche, Kirche*), all of the significant female characters in Lewis's novel, except Doremus's wife, Emma, are active in the Resistance. To be sure, the novel closes with the founding of the vaguely Social Democratic "American Coöperative Commonwealth" by opponents of the Corpo regime. But as a liberal humanist, Lewis's response to those critics who thought he should have provided a map out of the quagmire may be found in a single sentence in the novel: "I am convinced that everything that is worth while in the world has been accomplished by the free, inquiring, critical spirit, and that the preservation of this spirit is more important than any social system whatsoever."

In any case, most of the reviewers commended Lewis for his audacity, if not his artistry. His friend Clifton Fadiman lauded *It Can't Happen Here* extravagantly in the *New Yorker*: "one of the most important books ever produced in this country. . . . It is so crucial, so passionate, so honest, so vital that only dogmatists, schismatics, and reactionaries will care to pick flaws in it." Fanny Butcher declared in the *Chicago Tribune* that it exhibited "the passion of *Uncle Tom's Cabin*," a chorus joined by E. H. Walton in the *Forum* ("an important piece of political pamphleteering") and R. P. Blackmur in the *Nation* ("a weapon of the intellect"). Malcolm Cowley considered it "a vigorous antifascist tract" even if it was "not much of a novel" and J. Donald Adams echoed the point in the *New York Times Book Review*: "exciting reading, even if it does nothing to advance Mr. Lewis's art as a novelist." Robert Morss Lovett agreed in the *New Republic* that the novel "carries freight in abundance, of large importance, under high steam power of righteous indignation and generous good will." Lewis Gannett was paradoxical in his praise in the *New York Herald Tribune*: "It is his worst book since *Elmer Gantry*; I think it is also, and more truly, his best book since *Arrowsmith*." Though in the novel Lewis is critical of communists and fascists alike for their intolerance and bigotry, Granville Hicks asserted in the Marxist magazine *New Masses* that Lewis had "written a courageous and tremendously useful book."[16] It was an even greater commercial than critical success. It became the bestselling novel of Lewis's career to date, with total sales of some 320,000 copies.[17] With a circulation of more than sixty thousand, the *New York Post* serialized it without abridgment in the summer of 1936.

Long before it became a bestseller, Hollywood had taken notice. Lewis sold movie rights to MGM while the novel was still in manuscript. The studio commissioned a shooting script by the playwright Sidney Howard, a Pulitzer Prize recipient for drama in 1925 who had adapted Lewis's *Dodsworth* the year before; cast the venerable Lionel Barrymore, recipient of the Academy Award for Best Actor in 1931, in the lead role as Doremus; built the sets; and then *canceled* the film in mid-February 1936. Exactly what happened depends on who tells the story. Lewis insisted that the Production Code Administration, popularly known as the Hays Office, in "a fantastic exhibition of folly and cowardice" had effectively banned the film for fear of "international complications." That is, the Office had interfered to avoid offending the German and Italian governments.

Because he had sold film rights for a flat sum, Lewis had no financial interest in the movie, but he was outraged nevertheless. "Are we . . . to be delivered over to a film industry whose every step must be governed by whether or not the film will please or displease some foreign power?" he asked. "Democracy is certainly on the defensive when two European dictators, without opening their mouths or knowing anything about the issue, can shut down an American film."[18] The Council of the Authors' League of America, at a meeting on February 26, 1936, condemned the Hays Office for its action while the German film association announced that it was "very friendly of America to halt such a film" and described Lewis as a "full-blooded Communist." (Thompson quipped, "I'm glad they don't make [him] an anemic one."[19]) For his part, Howard claimed that he had seen a memo from Joseph Breen, Will Hays's successor as director of the Production Code Administration, claiming that the script contained "dangerous material" and urging a major revision of it, perhaps casting communists rather than fascists as the villains. According to Howard, Breen did not "ban" the film: "He just talked the producers out of making it."[20] Meanwhile, Louis B. Mayer, head of studio operations for MGM, played dumb. He announced that the project had been postponed because it was too expensive, though the studio had already invested around $200,000 in it.[21] Finally, Schorer offers an explanation that seems too clever by half: "the motive for stopping the film was probably less political than economic. Not only would this film have been banned in Germany and Italy and other foreign markets, but probably all Metro films would henceforth have been kept out of Germany and Italy."[22] But the reason for the ban would have been the political content of the film, so on what basis does Schorer speculate that Mayer's motive for canceling production was "less political than economic"? In this instance, the economic is the political.

While not adapted to the screen in 1936, the novel was adapted to the stage in 1937 under the auspices of the Federal Theater Project, a part of the Works Progress Administration. Lewis collaborated on the script with Jack Moffitt, an experienced playwright and screenwriter, though not happily. Hallie Flanagan, director of the Federal Theater Project, reminisced later that Lewis and Moffitt feuded all the while they were working on the play in separate suites of the Essex House in New York. Or as Flanagan put it, "The play was produced by polygenesis. It was partly created by Mr. Moffitt, who paced up and down in his apartment at the Essex House and threatened, if Mr. Lewis did not omit certain scenes and include others, various unusual reprisals; it was simultaneously springing almost visibly from the brain of Sinclair Lewis, who, in another apartment of the Essex House, composed and acted every part differently every day." Still, the play was a smash hit. Twenty-one different productions opened simultaneously in eighteen different cities on October 27, 1937—with four productions in the New York area, the main one at the Adelphi Theater and another in Yiddish, as well as a Spanish production in Tampa and an African-American production in Seattle. The play "seemed to have practically unlimited audience appeal," according to Flanagan. The Adelphi production was performed ninety-five times over the next few weeks to audiences totaling 110,518 people; the Yiddish version was played eighty-six times to 25,160 people. "In an amazing variety of methods, in English, Yiddish, and Spanish, in cities, towns and villages, before audiences of every conceivable type, *It Can't Happen Here* played, under Federal Theatre, 260 weeks, or the equivalent of five years."[23] In 1938, Lewis published a revised version of the script, and on August 22 of that year, he debuted in the role of Doremus in a summer stock production in Cohasset, Massachusetts. Fay Wray, best known as the damsel in distress in the original *King Kong* (1933), met him in Hollywood as he was preparing to act in the play. "He was unattractive in appearance—tall, gangly, and skeletal, his narrow face pockmarked, his teeth and fingers yellow from smoking," she remembered. But "he had fallen in love with the theater and saw it as a fresh life experience."[24]

Lewis abandoned literature for the next few years to work almost exclusively as an actor, director, and theatrical producer. But he remained the provocateur onstage that he had always been in his best writing, especially in *It Can't Happen Here*. As the final curtain falls in the revised theatrical version of the play, Doremus waits to die in an assault by armed fascists—but confident of the eventual triumph of "the free inquiring, critical spirit" incarnate in his grandson. As recently as 2011, the play was performed at twenty theaters across the U.S. to mark the seventy-fifth anniversary of its premier in 1936. Lewis's message—his protest of middle-class complacency and intellectual regimentation, what we today call "political correctness" on both the left and the right—remains as relevant and timely as ever.

—Gary Scharnhorst
University of New Mexico

Notes

[1]Mark Schorer, *Sinclair Lewis: An American Life* (New York: McGraw-Hill, 1961), p. 609; Frederick Betz and Jörg Thunecke, "Sinclair Lewis's Cautionary Tale *It Can't Happen Here*," *Orbis Litterarum*, 52 (1997), 36.

[2]Knoenagel, "The Historical Context of Sinclair Lewis' *It Can't Happen Here*," *Southern Humanities Review*, 29 (Summer 1995), 225

[3]Guthrie, "Sinclair Lewis and the 'Labor Novel,'" *Proceedings of the American Academy of Arts and Letters*, ns 2 (1952), 72–73; rpt. in *Sinclair Lewis Remembered*, ed. Gary Scharnhorst and Matthew Hofer (Tuscaloosa: University of Alabama Press, 2012), p. 172.

[4]Thompson, "The Boy and Man from Sauk Centre," *Atlantic Monthly*, 206 (November 1960), 42.

[5]Quoted in Betz, "'Here Is the Story the Movies Dared Not Make': The Contemporary Context and Reception Strategies of the *New York Post*'s Serialization of *It Can't Happen Here*," *Midwestern Miscellany*, 29 (Fall 2001), 35.

[6]Andrew Corey Yerkes, "'A Biology of Dictatorships': Liberalism and Modern Realism in Sinclair Lewis's *It Can't Happen Here*," *Studies in the Novel*, 42 (Fall 2010), 292.

[7]Schorer, p. 608.

[8]Seldes, *Witness to a Century* (New York: Ballantine, 1987), pp. 293–94; rpt. in *Sinclair Lewis Remembered*, pp. 262–63; Betz and Thunecke, p. 49.

[9]"Lewis Says Hays Bans Film of Book," *New York Times*, 16 February 1936, pp. 1, 35

[10]Hunt, *One American and His Attempt at Education* (New York: Simon and Schuster, 1938), pp. 253–54; rpt. in *Sinclair Lewis Remembered*, pp. 97–98.

[11]Joseph A. Barry, "Sinclair Lewis, 65 and Far from Main Street," *New York Times*, 5 February 1950, p. 153.

[12]McLaughlin, "Mark Schorer, Dialogic Discourse, and *It Can't Happen Here*," in *Sinclair Lewis: New Essays in Criticism*, ed. James M. Hutchisson (Troy, NY: Whiston, 1997), pp. 21–37.

[13]Allen Austin, "An Interview with Sinclair Lewis," *University of Kansas City Review*, 24 (1958), 206; rpt. in *Sinclair Lewis Remembered*, p. 327.

[14]Lewis, Sinclair. *It Can't Happen Here*. New York: Signet Classics, 2005. 186.

[15]Austin, pp. 205–6; rpt. in *Sinclair Lewis Remembered*, p. 326.

[16]Fadiman, "Books: Red Lewis," *New Yorker*, 29 October 1935, p. 99; Butcher, "Sinclair Lewis Uses Dictator for New Satire," *Chicago Tribune* 19 October 1935, p. 16; Walton, *Forum* 94 (December 1935), p. vi; Blackmur, *Nation*, 30 October 1935, p. 516; Cowley, *The Dream of the Golden Mountains* (New York: Viking, 1980), pp. 296–97; Adams, "America Under the Iron Heel," *New York Times Book Review*, 20 October 1935, p. 1; Lovett, "Mr. Lewis Says It Can," *New Republic*, 6 November 1935, pp. 366–67; Gannett, *New York Herald Tribune*, 21 October 1935, p. 13; Knoenagel, p. 232.

[17]Schorer, p. 610.

[18]"Lewis Says Hays Bans Film of Book," p. 35.

[19]"Lewis Book Ban Pleases Italian, German Chiefs," *Washington Post*, 17 February 1936, p. 3.

[20]Schorer, p. 616; "Sidney Howard Backs Lewis in Film Row," *New York Times*, 23 February 1936, p. 3.

[21]"Studio Chief Denies Ban," *New York Times*, 16 February 1936, p. 35.

[22]Schorer, p. 616.

[23]Flanagan, *Arena* (New York: Duell, Sloan and Pearce, 1940); rpt. in *Sinclair Lewis Remembered*, pp. 254–56.

[24]Wray, *On the Other Hand: A Life Story* (New York: St. Martin's, 1989); rpt. in *Sinclair Lewis Remembered*, p. 265.

Selected Bibliography

Works by Sinclair Lewis

Hike and the Aeroplane (1912, writing as Tom Graham)
Our Mr. Wrenn (1914)
The Trail of the Hawk (1916)
The Job (1917)
The Innocents (1917)
Free Air (1919)
Main Street (1920)
Babbitt (1922)
Arrowsmith (1925)
Mantrap (1926)
Elmer Gantry (1927)
The Man Who Knew Coolidge (1928)
Dodsworth (1929)
Ann Vickers (1933)
Work of Art (1934)
It Can't Happen Here (1935)
The Prodigal Parents (1938)
Bethel Merriday (1940)
Gideon Planish (1943)
Cass Timberlane (1945)
Kingsblood Royal (1947)
The God-Seeker (1949)
World So Wide (1951, posthumously)

Bibography and Criticism

Anderson, Carl L. *The Swedish Acceptances of American Literature.* Philadelphia: University of Pennsylvania Press, 1957.
Chalupova, Eva. "The Thirties and the Artistry of Lewis,

Farrell, Dos Passos and Steinbeck." *Brno Studies in English* 14 (1981): 107–15.

Coard, Robert L. "Jack London's Influence on Sinclair Lewis." *Sinclair Lewis at 100: Papers Presented at a Centennial Conference.* Ed. Michael Connaughton. St. Cloud, MN: St. Cloud State University, 1985, pp. 157–70.

Hapke, Laura. *Tales of the Working Girl: Wage-Earning Women in American Literature, 1890–1925.* Boston: Twayne-Macmillan, 1992.

Hutchisson, James M. *The Rise of Sinclair Lewis, 1920–1930.* University Park: Pennsylvania State University Press, 1996.

Jones, James T. "A Middle-Class Utopia: Lewis's *It Can't Happen Here." Sinclair Lewis at 100: Papers Presented at a Centennial Conference.* Ed. Michael Connaughton. St. Cloud, MN: St. Cloud State University, 1985, pp. 213–25.

Karfeldt, Erik Axel. "Why Sinclair Lewis Got the Nobel Prize." *Why Sinclair Lewis Got the Nobel Prize and Address by Sinclair Lewis Before the Swedish Academy.* Trans. Naboth Hedin. New York: Harcourt Brace, 1930. Rpt. in *Twentieth Century Interpretations of* Arrowsmith: *A Collection of Critical Essays.* Ed. Robert J. Griffin. Englewood Cliffs, NJ: Prentice Hall, 1968, pp. 77–82.

Knoenagel, Axel. "The Historical Context of Sinclair Lewis' *It Can't Happen Here." Southern Humanities Review* 29 (1995): 221–36.

Lingeman, Richard. *Sinclair Lewis: Rebel from Main Street.* New York: Random House, 2002.

Love, Glen A. *Babbitt: An American Life.* New York: Twayne, 1993.

McLaughlin, Robert L. "Mark Schorer, Dialogic Discourse, and *It Can't Happen Here." Sinclair Lewis: New Essays in Criticism.* Ed. James M. Hutchisson. Troy, New York: Whitston, 1997, pp. 21–37.

Parry, Sally E. "The Changing Fictional Faces of Sinclair Lewis' Wives." *Studies in American Fiction* 17.1 (1989): 65–79.

Perham, Judy F. "Reading *It Can't Happen Here* with College Freshmen." *Sinclair Lewis at 100: Papers Presented at a Centennial Conference.* Ed. Michael Connaughton. St. Cloud, MN: St. Cloud State University, 1985, pp. 235–44.

Schorer, Mark. *Sinclair Lewis: An American Life.* New York: McGraw-Hill, 1961.

Tanner, Stephen L. "Sinclair Lewis and Fascism." *Studies in the Novel* 22 (1990): 57–66.

Updike, John. "Exile on Main Street," *New Yorker* (17 May 1993): 91–97.

Vidal, Gore. "The Romance of Sinclair Lewis." *New York Review of Books* 39 (8 October 1992): 14, 16–20.

Watts, Emily Stipes. *The Businessman in American Literature.* Athens: University of Georgia Press, 1982.